the HOPE FACTORY

Also by Lavanya Sankaran

The Red Carpet

the HOPE FACTORY

LAVANYA SANKARAN

TINDER
PRESS

Published by arrangement with The Bantam Dell Publishing Group,
a division of Random House, Inc.

First published in Great Britain in 2013 by Tinder Press
An imprint of HEADLINE PUBLISHING GROUP

1

Cataloguing in Publication Data is available from the British Library

ISBN (HB)   978 0 7553 2787 4
ISBN (TPB) 978 0 7553 2788 1

HEADLINE PUBLISHING GROUP
An Hachette UK Company
338 Euston Road
London NW1 3BH

www.tinderpress.co.uk
www.headline.co.uk
www.hachette.co.uk

To Aarya, my love

an ancient line for modern times . . .

sarveshaam mangalam bhavatu

may all prosper

One

Anand K. Murthy had two windows in his office. The first, narrow and with a stiff latch that he struggled to open, provided a glimpse of the factory campus. The second, his favorite, was a soundproofed scenic window that overlooked a production bay. Anand was long past the stage where he needed to supervise the workings of the factory floor in minute daily detail, but it was a sight that gave him an unfailing sense of satisfaction.

He stood there now, the weight of the approaching day settling about him. He was not prone to nervousness, no, certainly not, but today he was unquestionably experiencing a phantom version of it: dry mouth, quickened breathing, a pulse that danced uncontrollably up and down his spine. He reached for a glass of water set on a plastic coaster that had the words CAUVERY AUTO embossed in orange letters upon an indigo blue background.

A knock on the open door; he put down the water glass and smiled in welcome.

'Come in, come in, good morning.' The sight of Mr Ananthamurthy did something to soothe him.

The operations manager had worked with Anand since the early years of the company. Fifteen years previously, Ananthamurthy had been an older man whose quiet manner belied years of operational experience; now Anand realized, with a sudden shock, that he was looking at someone approaching retirement. Physically, the years had not changed Ananthamurthy beyond turning the few long hairs combed over the bald surface of his head a little grayer and lining the outsides of his eyes. Otherwise, he was still the same: lean, upright, with that quality of absolute reliability, like an old Swiss watch, forever accurate and unfailing.

'Good morning, sir. You have eaten?' For fifteen years, Ananthamurthy had started their workday with this ritual query.

'Yes, yes,' said Anand, though that was rarely true. He was never hungry in the mornings. Later, he might have a glucose biscuit with his coffee. 'And you?'

'Yes, sir, thank you.' Ananthamurthy did not, as was his wont, turn briskly to the work ahead. Instead, with a shy diffidence that overlay his usual gravity, he ceremoniously placed a plastic box on Anand's table.

'My wife and daughters insisted, sir,' he said. 'Such an important day for the factory, we visited the temple in the morning and they have sent this prasadam for you. Please take, sir.'

Anand obediently placed a tiny morsel of the sanctified sweet halwa in his mouth, feeling the sugar and wheat dissolve across his tongue. 'Please thank your wife for me.'

'I will, sir. She has plans to continue prayers through the day.'

Ananthamurthy would not say so, but Anand saw in his eyes a reflection of the same eager hope that burnt within him.

Anand pressed a button on his phone to speak to his secretary. In a fantasy world, this would be a young woman, perhaps from Goa, who answered to a name like Miss Rita and sported daring short skirts and blouses that clung to her bosom. Reality, however, was Mr Kamath, bald and so frighteningly efficient, he was one of the

bulwarks of Anand's professional life, never to be voluntarily sacrificed. 'Kamath? Where is everybody? And later, I want to see that
computer fellow.'

His words served as an automatic trigger to Ananthamurthy.

'That fellow,' he said, referring to the newly hired computer
service engineer, 'is not able to take direction.' Anand listened
patiently, knowing that Ananthamurthy's complaints were not really
against the person but about the process. The increased automation
in the factory premises was spreading with virus-like pervasiveness,
to the great perturbation of Ananthamurthy, who, with aging
consternation, was still unsuccessfully grappling with the notion of
email, tapping out his correspondence letter by letter, glancing
feverishly between screen and fingers with every stroke. Anand
often thought it was time to organize a mandatory course on word
processing for all his employees.

Two more people entered his office, and Anand assessed them
with new eyes, as though seeing them for the first time.

Mrs Padmavati of the accounts department was the first to arrive.
She walked in as she usually did, with a brisk air and a quick step.
Her efficiency was legendary – as was her quick temper at the
careless mistakes of others. Her appearance, like her work style, was
excessively tidy: her cotton saree neatly folded and pinned at the
shoulder, her long hair severely quieted with coconut oil and tied
into a braid that lay in a thick line from her neck to the base of
her spine. Her decorative accessories were few and not beyond the
obligatory: small gold earrings at her lobes, a thin gold chain with
her marriage mangalsutra at the end. No rings, no bangles, all her
accessorial energies seemed to revolve around the enormous
handbag that accompanied her to every meeting, a bag so capa-
cious that awed male colleagues had witnessed the emergence of
infinite objects from within, from wallets to a laptop, magazines, a
present for a colleague, and, improbably, a tiny videogame console

that Mrs Padmavati claimed belonged to her nine-year-old son but in fact was spotted feverishly attacking on the commute home on the factory bus. She had worked with the company for five years, gaining seniority, and this was the first time Anand had invited her to a senior-level management meeting.

If he was honest, it hadn't been very often that he had had a management meeting. Until recently, 'senior management' had consisted of just himself and Ananthamurthy, each of them undertaking a variety of tasks.

But it was time to change all that. He had broached the idea with Ananthamurthy a few weeks previously, and Ananthamurthy, who had recently been gifted a management book by his son-in-law and was reading it in his spare time, had agreed with him: 'We must professionalize, sir. That is the key.'

Accordingly, Anand, who had kept the company finances under his strict control, was now toying with the idea of making Mrs Padmavati his CFO. She was pleased to be included in the meeting and, Anand could tell, was both nervous and eager to prove herself. She placed her handbag on the floor and sat erect, holding a notepad, a pen, and a calculator at the ready. In addition, they had hired a new HR person, who trailed into the meeting after her.

'Okay then,' said Anand, after they had liberally partaken of Ananthamurthy's box of sweet prasadam. 'Let's review our preparations, so we know exactly where we stand.' He hesitated, pushed his glasses up his nose, and then stated what everybody in the room already knew. 'Tomorrow can be the most important day for our company, I think.'

The sheet moldings and pressings made by Cauvery Auto were sold to automotive companies that assembled passenger cars and other vehicles out of them for the Indian market. They had built the business painstakingly over the years, chasing after orders, waiting for hours, sometimes days, for meetings with purchasing managers, godlike beings in sanctified inner offices who were seemingly unaware of Anand in the waiting room, his 9:00 A.M. appointment ticking past lunch and through the afternoon until he was asked, sweaty, hungry, angry, but still patient, to come back the next day. Yes, so sorry, sir is very busy, hopefully he will be able to see you tomorrow.

But now, finally, they were on the cusp of a different phase. The following morning, their largest customers would arrive, bringing with them representatives of the Japanese parent company. They would tour the facilities, scrutinize, inspect, and have endless discussions on production capabilities and future scope. If the day went well, Cauvery Auto could end up supplying the international market as well. The thought of that was unbelievably heady. Anand could not fool himself; this was a rare prize; there would be plenty of other companies competing for it, many of them (he feared) better positioned than Cauvery Auto.

If they won the order, it would transform all their lives. It would spell stability, growth, profits, not just for the company but for all of them – him, Ananthamurthy, Mrs Padmavati, everyone – easing the financial struggles of their lives and allowing very different futures to bloom for their families.

In the late morning, Anand went on a tour of inspection. The production floor was always kept in good working condition, but some of the workers' uniforms had been replaced, and the accounts department had used the occasion to purchase new ergonomic chairs in a bright orange for their workstations. Anand did not mind; these things contributed to workplace efficiency, ease, and bonhomie, and he had overridden Ananthamurthy's muttered objections to the expense. 'After all,' the operations manager had said, 'we are not one of those American-style call centers, is it not?' His own daughter worked in one such call center in the

city, and Mr Ananthamurthy had visited her workplace one day
and come away slightly scandalized. 'Too much waste,' he said.
'And all for what? For answering a few phone calls. Where is the
skill in that?'

Neat flower beds lined the outside walls of the factory buildings; the gardeners were scouring them for weeds. Anand felt the
knot in his back ease, an involuntary welling of pleasure within,
a shy disbelief that his efforts had yielded this campus, this precision, this grace.

He paused outside one of the warehouses, whose freshly painted
sign said: GOWDON 2.

'That is a wrong spelling, no?' he said. 'That is not how you
spell godown.'

'I'll check, sir,' said the painting supervisor and made a note.

The watchmen saluted as he walked past. Their uniforms were
in the corporate colors – orange shirts and indigo pants, chosen
in line with his mother-in-law's suggestion, in the days when her
opinion mattered. 'So pretty, these colors,' she had said. 'Like bird-
of-paradise, my favorite flower.' Anand had blindly agreed – and
was aghast to learn that in her youth she had once been referred
to as a bird-of-paradise herself, a compliment never forgotten. She
now spent her time telling acquaintances of her son-in-law's delicate tribute. He in turn ignored her arch references to the subject,
which, in his mind, made the best of an awkward situation.

The clock ran faster than Anand; he didn't pause for lunch,
satisfying his hunger with passing cups of coffee and glucose biscuits
grabbed off the plates Kamath supplied for every meeting in his
office. They were without end, everyone nervous, running plans
and presentations by him relentlessly.

After the initial faux pas with the bird-of-paradise colors, his
wife had recommended the anonymous safety of an interior designer
who could create for Anand an office as it ought to be: well

carpeted and tastefully furnished. Anand had ignored her suggestion. His office was just as he liked it: simple, uncluttered, a large
desk, some chairs to one side that could be dragged up for a
conference, and best of all, the soundproofed scenic factory window.

At 6:00 P.M., Ananthamurthy, Mrs Padmavati, the HR person,
and Kamath assembled in his office, a collective air of exhaustion
about them. They had done all that they could; tomorrow was in
the hands of the gods. Ananthamurthy, on the principle of leaving
no stone unturned, was detailing the early morning prayers he
would conduct on the morrow to ensure divine favors. For Anand,
divinity consisted of preparing meticulously and leaving nothing
to chance. He did not know quite how to articulate his next
concern; he said: 'I will be wearing a jacket, I think. And a tie.'

'You will be very hot, sir,' said Ananthamurthy, with mild surprise
at this suggested deviation from the customary dress code of polyester pants and cotton shirts.

It was Mrs Padmavati who grasped the underlying point Anand
was trying to make. '*Everyone* should wear ties, sir, is it not? Or, in
my case, a silk saree. For smart appearance.'

'Yes,' said Anand in relief. 'Yes. I think so.'

Ananthamurthy stood next to him, gazing down at the large, high-
ceilinged bay, the machinery gleaming, the room flooded with
light, so clean, so sterile; the very air seemed subdued and devoid
of the dust particles that circulated outside the factory. The others
had filed out, leaving the two of them alone.

Anand was normally the one to energize, to reassure, but now
he gave way to sudden doubt. 'We are ready, no?'

'I think we're ready, sir,' said Ananthamurthy.

'A great success if it comes through,' said Anand. 'A great success
for us, Ananthamurthy.'

'If it comes through,' said Ananthamurthy, prosaically, 'we will be in urgent need of more land, sir. At least ten acres. Without it, we will not be able to proceed. As it is . . .'

Anand sighed. 'Yes, yes.' Land outside the city for industrial development was notoriously difficult to organize. 'I'll get on to it right away, Ananthamurthy.'

On the way home, on a sudden impulse, Anand took a small, unplanned detour into a low-grade industrial area. It was just a few kilometers from his factory, but it was an entry into a different, desperate world. The roads were hasty-made, unplanned, unpaved, and ravined by the rains. There were no large, graceful factory compounds here, no high-roofed shop floors, no landscaping. These factory sheds were little more than utilitarian shop floors built in desperate confinement, cheek by jowl, not wasting space, aesthetic-free, populated by workers who wore no uniforms and belonged to no unions. Anand's low-bottomed car was out of place here; this was an area frequented by scooters and hardy transportation vans.

He parked on a muddy side slope, setting his hand brake, ignoring the few curious glances he received, and made his way to a shed in the distance. It was indistinguishable from its peers, tin-roofed, coated with grime and soot, the dark enfolded within barely alleviated with a few tube lights. He ignored the somnolent watchman who sat on a stool below a board bearing the name of the current proprietor and peeped in.

The hot-oil odor of the place, the clangorous noise of over-worked secondhand machines remained unchanged. He didn't know the present owners, whoever they were, but this shed held the history of his first years as an independent businessman. He could not afford a car then and had driven to work through mud and rain on a sky-blue scooter, license number KA O4 R 618, which, by the end of its days, had sported dents and a long rip on the backseat.

Anand had recently watched, mesmerized, a National Geographic television program about early American pioneers pressing into the hostile western regions of their country – and had thoroughly identified with them. Like those pioneers, he had survived an unimaginably hostile world. A world where everything had to be fought for, every detail planned. Things that could go wrong, would. Things that shouldn't go wrong, did. Add to that the Indian government, a strange, cavernous beast that lay hidden in grottoes and leapt out, tentacles flailing, suckers greedy for bribes. When things broke down, one kept moving, for to stop was to signal the end. To complain was to waste breath. To fuss was a luxury. And the next time around, one planned even more cautiously, as best as one could, creating backup at every level, for untrained workers that the law did not easily allow to fire, for insufficient power, for no water, for no sewerage, for telephones-on-the-blink, potholed roads, disintegrating ports, for whimsical suppliers, careless of quality, who had to be chased and cornered to deliver on their promises – yes, sir, of course, sir, I am delivering today, sir. Oh, sir, don't say that, of course I am delivering today. God promise, sir. Problem is, sir, my sister's husband's niece's wedding.

There were times, in the early years, when the battle fatigue hit Anand so hard he would almost stop, dreading the next phone call, harbinger of trouble, of something gone wrong, of chaos unanticipated. But something in him had clung on, blindly, and he had managed to pull himself out of the primordial slime and say, very simply, yes, we can do it. We can produce things of world-class quality, and we can deliver them on time. And in him lay the strength that comes from such alchemical magic, the power discovered within himself to take environmental dross and turn it into pure gold.

He walked back to his car and reversed slowly out of the area. He would mention this visit to Ananthamurthy, who had toiled in this old, greasy shed by his side. Or perhaps not. Neither of them was particularly given to romanticizing their past; Ananthamurthy would probably stare at him in surprise and wonder why Anand was telling him things he already knew.

On the drive home, Anand found himself rehearsing parts of the speech that he would be making the following day. 'Welcome,' he said, to the steering wheel. '*Wel*come.' He fell prey to his usual insecurities for a fleeting moment and wished that he had certain natural advantages: of height, a better speaking voice, the ability to size up people at a glance and the charisma to instantly win them over. 'Wel*come,*' he tried. The highway bestrode a gentle ridge, covered by the rising tide of the endless city, colored cinder-block houses topped with black plastic water tanks racing up the slope in a wave. His car nudged past stained city walls layered with cinema and political advertisements, the film actors posed with an engaging artfulness not quite mastered by the politicians: plug-ugly, with odd hair and shifty smiles like wanted crime posters gone coy and desperate to please. 'Welcome,' he said, in passing. Not. Behenchuths.

Two

The shiny little hatchback car appeared in exquisite contrast to its surroundings, the metal glossy, the padded interior cool with air-conditioned comfort. The road it traversed was composed of tar and dirt and fetid garbage and flooded with a wash of pedestrian traffic that spilled into the path of the car in careless, dusty profusion. There was little room to maneuver within the press of human habitation: shops, dwellings, tiffin rooms, all crammed together, higgledy-piggledy, dangerously one-atop-the-other, falling right off, a miracle of wishful architecture and denuded finances.

From where she stood, next to the onion seller's cart, Kamala studied the passage of the vehicle with something akin to pride. She did not own the car, it was true. She had never been inside this or any other car. But she had watched the owner grow into his current eminence from a dusty schoolboy (not too different from her own) playing cricket in the gully outside her home and being scolded by his mother, who, like her, cleaned houses for a living.

The car stopped next to a new building painted a cheerful pink. He was here to visit his parents after a break of several months; Kamala, along with the rest of the neighborhood, knew all the details. Who could have anticipated it? That he would win a scholarship, that he would study engineering, that he would find employment with a company in Pune, and flourish so well that his parents could give up their jobs cleaning houses and tending gardens and live, like royalty, in bright pink homes and have him visit, driving all the way from Pune in his bright new car.

She would pay them a visit later, Kamala decided, carrying some fruit with her. That would be perfectly acceptable. To visit, and to congratulate them on their success – and find out how such success was to be achieved.

She turned her attention back to the onion in her hand, testing the weight of it on her palm. It was still warm, trapping within itself the dregs of the day's heat and of the various human hands that had handled it. Unlike with other vegetables, there was no real art to the purchase of an onion. For tomatoes in season, for instance, one might bide one's time through the day – wait for the morning rush of customers to subside, for the remaining tomatoes to ripen further in the noonday sun, turning lush and red and plump with juice, until evening time, when the vendors were eager to get rid of them at any price; the tomatoes would not survive the damp of the night. That was the judicious time to buy. But onions were different; hardy, unromantic vegetables, their price did not change with the passage of the day but with seasonal supply. At times, a kilo of onions cost five rupees and, frugally husbanded, could last a week, but in the low season, the prices went up by so much that one usually did without.

'Sister, are you going to purchase it or not? What is so special about that one onion?'

Kamala started. 'Forgive me, brother, I'll take these,' she said and picked out two more, handing them to the onion seller for weighing.

The paper-wrapped onions joined the other vegetables inside

her woven plastic bag. In addition to onions, she had bought a quarter kilo of green beans, some potatoes, carrots, and two tomatoes. She would cook them into a rich kurma, she decided, the stew thickened with coconut and spices and oil, and serve it on steaming hot rice to her son for dinner.

She walked homeward, passing the parked car on her way, and could not resist peeping in through the glass window, touching the metal door handle for good luck.

The gully she lived in was off the main alley and narrow enough that she could span the gap between the houses by stretching out her hand. 'Stop, stop,' she called to the young boys hitting at a cricket ball. 'Rest your game a moment till I pass.' Until recently, her son would have been one of their number, playing cricket in the gully and getting scolded when the ball bounced and crashed against the walls of the houses that ran down each side, but, as he grew, he discovered new pursuits that took him farther afield. Right now, he was nowhere to be seen, but he would come home as soon as dinner was ready, as though summoned magically by the scent of fresh-cooked food.

She entered a small, narrow courtyard with several single-story dwellings clustered around it. The largest comprised four rooms and was the home of the landlord. The smallest, a single room, belonged to Kamala.

She put her bag of vegetables down and went to the bathing area to wash her hands and feet. By the time Kamala was seated on the stoop outside her door, the pile of vegetables washed, a plate and a knife laid ready on the ground, the landlord's mother had emerged from her own house, as she usually did, with some of her own dinner preparations in hand. The chopping of vegetables and the cleaning of rice gave them an opportunity to inspect each other's menus, proffer suggestions, and enjoy a gentle gossip.

'Oho!' the landlord's mother said. 'You are planning a feast of vegetables.'

'I got a little greedy, yes, amma,' said Kamala. 'It's been a time since I prepared a nice vegetable kurma for my boy.'

'Kamala-daughter, he is at the age when he could eat all the vegetables in the world and still be hungry for more,' said the landlord's mother. 'His schoolwork, it's going well?'

Kamala grimaced; a boy as clever as her son should not find it so difficult to sit quietly at his studies. 'His studies would go well,' she said, 'if he paid them a little more attention.'

'He is very smart,' the landlord's mother said placatingly. 'He is sure to do well, do not worry. He is smart and full of ambition.'

Kamala was unable to explain why it was her son's sense of ambition that made her so uneasy.

'And your good son, amma?' she asked. 'He is well, and your daughter-in-law also?' This was a delicate question, since the landlord's wife had recently quarreled with her husband and was now living at her brother's house. The courtyard had echoed with raised voices and slammed doors, an unusual occurrence for an otherwise quiet-spoken couple, but with three children fully grown, they had not planned for her current pregnancy and it seemed to throw both of them into turmoil. 'As well as can be expected. Pregnant, after all these years! What a pair of fools they are, at this age.'

Mindful of her audience, Kamala didn't give full rein to her enjoyment of such an intemperate latter-day romance, though she could not resist saying, 'Blame it on the full moon, amma. Even Radha and Krishna were not immune to it.'

The old lady regarded her with a fulminating eye. 'Radha and Krishna were not old enough to be grandparents themselves!' She laughed reluctantly. 'Well, a baby is always welcome. Such a joy, unlike us old ones, always grumbling . . .'

★   ★   ★

The peace of the evening settled about the courtyard; the sounds of cicadas and crickets mingled with the voices from the other rooms, pleasantly close, pleasantly hushed. An old kerosene lamp warmed Kamala's room and filled it with a gentle yellow light that made strange shadows upon the walls.

Her ears caught the creak of the courtyard gate as the vegetable kurma was on its last simmer. The air was redolent with spices and coconut, and her son came nosing through, sniffing like a starving puppy.

'No! No!' she said. 'Not a mouthful until you have washed yourself.'

The mug's worth of water splashed over his face and hands and feet was more a ritual of pleasing his mother than any real attempt to clean himself; Narayan flung himself on the ground next to Kamala as she heaped his plate with hot rice and ladled the vegetable stew over it. At first he was too hungry to do more than eat, mixing the rice and gravy quickly with his right hand and shoveling it into his mouth, his fingers ready with the next morsel before he had swallowed the last. His eyes, though, held the sparkle of news, and Kamala waited patiently for him to finish. There was a simple contentment in watching him eat that never went away.

The fact was, and she accepted it now, that no matter how much she fed him, his skin would never achieve the soft luxuriance that the children of the wealthy possessed, ample with flesh and free from city dust. The bread and coffee she gave him for breakfast, the three rotis she packed with pickle for his lunch, the rice and vegetables she fed him at dinner could not compete with the quantities of food available in the homes where she worked, their kitchens filled with eggs and meats and packets of chips and milk and cake. They ate so much, those children, that their plumpness frequently distended to fat, their bellies bursting forth to hang above their trousers.

Not so, her son. His body used every scrap of food ingested, much as hers did. His face was lean, his naked body thin and corded with muscle and bone. For all that, he was strong; he could lift his mother and swing her about, laughing while she shrieked. And his mind was ever alert, constantly devising new ways of getting himself into trouble. When he had been younger, she had been charmed by his inventiveness, laughing with pleasure at his antics and comparing him favorably to his peers, especially that stolid Ganesha who lived opposite, whose mud-encrusted mind was free from independent thought and always looked to his mother's face for answers. But now, that same stolid Ganesha had grown into a boy who worked at his studies in the evenings and gave his mother no trouble.

'Did they give you much homework today, in school?' she asked. Narayan's eyes met hers, so brimful of mischief that her heart immediately sank. She gazed sternly at him, trying to decipher his actions. And immediately understood. 'Bad boy!' she raged. 'How could you! Do not tell me you have missed school again! Bad child! Why do you do this!'

'Don't shout, Amma,' he said. 'It was for a very good reason. See what I have brought for you.' He emptied out his pockets and displayed, before his mother's astonished gaze, a collection of notes and coins. 'All for you! See?'

'But where did you get this? Child, what have you done!'

But Narayan, with his inborn air of a showman, was not to be hurried. He ate the last scraps of his food. He washed out his plate and placed it to dry. And when he judged his mother was ready to explode, he sat down and told her his news.

'It was that Raghavan's idea,' he said, not quieting Kamala's anxiety a bit. Raghavan was three years older than her son, and a product of the streets. His father was a drunk, his mother something worse, and he had survived doing god-knows-what. He was tough, resourceful, and in Kamala's view, not at all to be trusted. Not for Raghavan a life of decent hard work; he had about him an air of raffish dissoluteness and was always talking of ways to make money quickly.

Kamala disliked him and absolutely hated his friendship with her son. He would lead Narayan down wrongful paths, Raghavan, with his heavy-lidded eyes, and his pack of lazy, good-for-nothing friends, who thought that smoking cigarettes like their favorite movie star was sufficient to render them just like him. And if in his movie roles, the star stared with disrespectful, lustful eyes at passing girls, so must they. As he fought and defeated the corrupt lathi-stick-wielding policeman with his bare hands, so too must they mock and harass the local traffic policeman, who did nothing worse than stand tiredly at the street corner occasionally mis-directing the traffic. When his movies suggested that outspoken, defiant damsels needed acid thrown on their faces or were indeed asking to be raped, they nodded wisely. When he played a poor man who challenged the authority of the rich, he did so to the untrammeled appreciation of Raghavan and his friends, who refused to recognize that the actor lived, in his off-camera life, an existence fully as wealth-encrusted as the ones he opposed on-screen. Kamala could not accept any of it. That irritating young male braggadocio, besides being unpleasantly disrespectful, conveyed, at its base, a distinct lack of common sense. That wretched actor, instead of (in his latest comedy) portraying a young man who defied his parents and survived on his wits by resorting to robbery along with a pretty female companion, why couldn't he have played a young man who studied hard and listened to his mother and aspired to a job offer at a nice city office? Then all his besotted young male followers would follow suit, and all across the state, mothers would light lamps in thankfulness and young girls (and policemen) would sigh in relief. Or if the movie star should plead innocence and say, why, my work is just entertainment, why should I be asked to behave like a pious temple priest a-blessing the poor, then why couldn't young idiots like Raghavan, thought Kamala, coming to the nub of the matter, realize that movies were one thing and real life something quite different? Fools.

So now she prepared to listen to Narayan with a certain amount of prejudice in her mind and a dread that the money he held had been acquired through illegal, dubious means.

'Guess where I got this from, Amma,' he said. She was in no mood to play guessing games over his latest deviltry. 'Nonsense,' she said. 'Tell me immediately, how did you receive this money?'

'From the street corner,' he said.

'What do you mean, from the street corner. What nonsense have you been up to? That policeman is going to catch you and give you a beating! And perhaps that would be a good thing!'

'No, he will not, Amma. Don't worry. He knows what I was doing; he is now my friend. Don't worry so, it's nothing wrong.'

And, trying her patience no further, he told her: he had spent the day selling magazines and newspapers to vehicles that halted at the traffic lights on the main road. 'It works like this,' he said. 'The agent for the area gives us a full ten percent for selling magazines, and for some, even fifteen, twenty percent. And, Amma, I am really good at this; even the policeman said so. After just two hours I was selling as much as the senior boys who have been doing this for a long time.'

'And that useless street-rascal Raghavan also did this? He sold magazines?'

'Yes. Actually, he was the one who told us about it. But after a while, he went off to see a movie. I kept at it the entire day!' Narayan counted out the money he had made – it was almost a hundred rupees. 'Do you see?' he said, gloating. 'If I do this every day, Amma, I can earn as much as you do in a month!'

Kamala had not anticipated something like this. That her son, her little Narayan, should find out this clever way of making money and then proceed to do so very well at it – and not let himself be distracted by those louts who went off to the movie. The money he had made was not insignificant at all, not a sum she could dismiss. If what he said was true, if he could indeed sell these magazines so well – it made her mind spin giddily with the notion of suddenly having twice as much money at her disposal and the great easing of burden that would bring. But hard on the heels of such fantasy came a sobering reflection: if she let Narayan get seduced by such earnings today, then she would seal his fate; he would give up his hated studies immediately and settle into selling magazines for the rest of his life. There would be no school, no English, no office.

She paused a moment more, fighting the temptation of money. She met the brightness of her son's eye with a smile and bit back her uncertainty. 'It is a wonderful thing you have done,' she said. 'The little Lord Krishna, with all his mischief and cleverness, could not have done better!'

'Tomorrow, I am going to go extra early,' he said, 'and make still more.'

'You may do so,' she said, 'and again the day after, for it is the weekend. But on Monday, you will have to go back to school.'

'But, Mother . . .' he said, aghast at her foolishness.

'No, Narayan,' she said. 'You cannot be selling things on the roadside your whole life. Do you not want to learn to speak English nicely and then get a job where you will make much more money?'

'I can speak English,' he said indignantly, and demonstrated by saying in that language: *'I speaking English. I speaking English very good.'*

She laughed. 'See?' he said, encouraged. 'I do not have to go to that stupid school to learn that. I can speak Hindi and Tamil too;

I have even learned a few words of Telugu.' This was true; her son had, over the course of his life, magically absorbed these languages right through the pores of his skin from the very air in the city, which throbbed and thrummed with the spoken words of people from all over the world.

But she would not let his linguistic facility change her mind: Narayan must complete his schooling.

Three

The compound wall of his house stood tall, white, unadorned, and forbidding. When they had finally been able to afford the land, Anand had imagined a small, neat house with a large garden, his mind fondly resting on the old-fashioned Lakshmipuram bungalows in Mysore with their monkey-top gables and sloping roofs, but his wife had thrown her hands up in horror, oh, dear lord, no, let's have a modern aesthetic for goodness' sake, and since he knew nothing of such matters, he acquiesced and found himself with a sharp-angled house that seemed far too large for their needs. Far too large, certainly, for his: an overweight, cantilevered structure coyly trying to squeeze itself into a space several sizes too small, bursting at its plotular seams, almost spilling over onto the neighbors, leaving room for a small patch of grass in front and little else, sucking up air and space and whatever financial resources he could muster. Each month, Anand diligently paid off a segment of the bank loan that had funded the land and the construction; it would be another five years, he estimated, before the house was theirs. Longer, perhaps, for him to feel entirely at home in it.

All seemed quiet when he entered, the house settled in for the night, but this impression was deceptive. His wife erupted out of the bedroom.

'You're coming, no?' Vidya said. 'Don't ditch, now!' Her long hair spilled in sheaths down the front of her blouse, its manicured straightness a sign that she had spent the afternoon in the beauty parlor. 'Don't tell me "tomorrow is a very important day so you can't come."'

Anand took refuge in dignity. 'I do have an important day tomorrow,' he said, 'but I'm coming. Of course I'm not ditching.'

'Then come quickly,' she said. 'I've been ready for half an hour already.'

Anand could tell, by the way she was inserting large golden hoops into her ears as she walked downstairs, that this was not strictly true. 'I won't be long,' he said. 'The children are upstairs?'

'Yeah,' she said. 'Valmika has some studying to do. Ey, she got an A on her bio test. Damn good, no? . . . And, listen, I just settled Pingu down to sleep, so don't go disturbing him now.'

'I won't,' he said, running up the stairs.

He went straight to his son's bedroom. Vyasa was tucked into bed; Valmika, fourteen years old and seven years older than her brother, was seated on a rocking chair by his side, her toe balanced on the edge of the bed, swaying gently to and fro as she read aloud from a storybook. Anand paused a moment in the doorway watching their absorption in the story before they noticed him with matching smiles.

He hugged his daughter. 'An A in bio, well done, yaar!'

'Appa!' said his son, impatiently claiming his attention. 'I got hurt today. Mama shouted at me, and Akka laughed.'

Anand gave in to temptation. He flopped onto the bed next to Vyasa and arranged his arm about him. 'How did you get hurt?' he asked. 'And why did Mama shout?'

'I fell down in cricket, and I failed in maths so Mama shouted.'

'Why, what happened?'

'I was running to catch the ball and tripped. Then we had maths.

My foot was hurting, and that's why I forgot to study for the test, Appa.'

'And I laughed,' said his sister, poking at him with her big toe, 'because you're a goose . . . You should have studied for it the previous day, nut-mutt.'

Anand quieted his son's indignation and kissed him good night, fighting the urge to surrender himself to the fatigue of the day, to be lulled into a gentle doze by the ebb and flow of his daughter's voice as she resumed her storytelling. His children: a powerful joy, so simply achieved – a pleasant, straightforward act, and, nine months later, like magic, an exquisite happiness. He had expected to feel delight at the birth of his first child – for indeed, like everyone else, he had been weaned on ancient Indian tales of parental love on an epic scale: fathers who died when separated from their sons; mothers commanding respect from the strongest of men; daughters swept away by matrimony, carrying with them their fathers' broken hearts; parents cursing those who harm their children through endless birth cycles – but he had yet been startled by the intensity of emotion that swept through him when his daughter was first placed in his arms. And, once again, two miscarriages and seven years later, at the birth of his son. And startled still further when such intensity didn't fade with time; when, instead, it continued to manifest itself at odd moments, when he unexpectedly caught a glimpse of his children or heard their voices on the stairs and felt his heart tighten; when he listened to their accomplishments at school with a pleasureful, bashful pride; when he disciplined them for misbehavior and felt himself softening with tenderness even as he lectured them with stern voice.

'Appa,' his daughter hissed. 'Mama's coming.' His wife's tread sounded on the stairs and Anand ran for the shower, leaving his giggling children behind.

★　★　★

The drive to Amir and Amrita's house was a relatively short one, twenty minutes rendered unpleasant by the shriek and grind of late evening traffic. Vidya was busy with her cellphone, returning the calls and messages that ran through the social arteries of her life; Anand alternately cursed at the traffic and worried if all was ready for the following day's presentation.

The flat on Cunningham Road was plunged in darkness when they arrived. The sleeping watchman had to be roused, and Anand and Vidya followed his sluggish, waving torchlight down a path and round the back of the building. Vidya stumbled in her high heels on the pavement stones and Anand held out a hand to steady her.

'God,' she said, clutching tightly to his fingers, 'I can't believe they gave up that gorgeous Whitefield bungalow for this place. All that money from selling their software company – a deal that's in all the bloody newspapers – and they move to a building without a generator. I mean, it's all very well that they are giving all their money away to charitable causes, but at least they could live some-place decent!'

'I don't think they're giving it all away, no?' said Anand. 'Just some of it.'

'Don't always disagree with me,' she said, pulling her hand away as they reached the apartment.

'Unscheduled power cut,' their hostess laughed as she opened the door. 'Watch the step.' She ushered them through the house, her guests moving all by guess and to the sound of her voice urging them to step this way, mind that side table – through the living room and out to a little verandah.

Vidya might differ, but for Anand this verandah, facing a tiny garden, had a relaxed, comfortable charm that he missed in his own house with its studied, stylish formality. A long, low table was littered with candles and wine bottles; the surrounding divan piled with block-printed cushions. Anand sank down into the cushions next to his host, Amir, who was absentmindedly plucking chords on his guitar.

Though he had met Amir through Vidya, they had formed an instant friendship, the ease that Amir and Amrita shared with each other spilling over onto their friends and acquaintances. Anand sipped at his whiskey, lying back luxuriously and feeling the tension within him ease for the first time in hours. This was his notion of hospitality: casual, unfussy, a few good friends.

Amir was discussing road signs. '"Pederastrian Bridge,"' he said, 'my favorite of the day. And there were actually people walking through, right under that sign. Quite shamelessly. Some holding children by the hand too.'

'"Bed shits,"' Amrita called. 'Saw that yesterday outside a linen sale. And "Ladies Bottoms."' She placed a bowl of nuts and a plate of kebabs on the low table and picked up her wineglass.

'Ah, few things nicer than well-made ladies' bottoms,' her husband lazily said, putting aside his guitar and reaching for the nut bowl. 'You should have bought a few.'

'I'm gifting you with bed shits instead,' Amrita said. 'Vidya! A drink?'

Vidya flipped her phone closed. 'Sorry,' she said and sat on a cushion, slipping off her high-heeled sandals, 'these endless calls are so annoying . . . You know, so nice to have an evening like this! So relaxing.'

'Have a drink,' said Amir.

'Lovely!' Vidya sipped at her vodka-tonic but left the glass sweating on the table when her phone rang. 'Oh, it's Pingu. Yes, baby? Couldn't sleep . . . ? Yes, I'll be home soon, you just close your eyes and think of something nice . . . Akka's there, but don't disturb her, okay? She's studying hard . . .'

'Who else are you expecting?' Anand thought he knew the answer to this, but couldn't resist asking.

'Just another couple,' said Amir. 'Colleagues from our old software days . . . Nice people. And Kavika. I've barely met her since she's been back – be good to see her again.'

Anand glanced around. Vidya was busy with another call, another message. 'What is Kavika doing here? She was with the UN, wasn't she?'

'That's right! And really successful too,' said Amrita. 'But she's given that up and she's back with her baby. Well, toddler. She seems to be exploring options, but in the short term, she is going to be working with me on fund-raising for that scholarship program for under-privileged schoolchildren.' She tapped Anand on the knee and smiled. 'Thanks for your contribution, by the way. That was really generous.'

He shrugged it off, embarrassed, and asked instead: 'She's going to be here for some time?'

'I hope so,' said Amrita. 'She's brilliant. Fun. Quite unconventional, but her heart's in the right place.'

'Lord,' said Amir, smiling at old memories, 'we used to be such a neighborhood brat pack growing up; all of us: Kavika – such a rowdy, like my brother, Kabir . . . Vidya was better behaved, I remember. Kabir and Kavika stole Harry Chinappa's cigarettes once and hid them under my pillow . . . Ammi gave me such a walloping! Jesus. Who knew she had such powerful biceps?'

Amrita shook her head reprovingly, and Anand burst out laughing. Amir's mother was famously gentle and mild. Vidya joined the conversation: 'Oh, that cigarette story! So funny! All the parents were so angry!' She waved her phone at them. 'Kavika should be here in two minutes.'

He had met her once before, one evening at his father-in-law's house the previous week. She had worn a Fabindia kurta that covered her to her knees, a girl of four cuddled sleepily into her lap. Smiling and chatting on the chintz sofa, sandwiched between

Ruby Chinappa and another guest like a thin slice of meat in the soft, enfolding cheeks of a bun. Anand had said very little.

'You won't believe!' Vidya had eagerly burst out when she first heard the news, for after years of absence, a glamorous international professional existence, and a complete loss of contact with her old childhood friends, Kavika had returned home with a child – but no husband – and, more interesting, no record of a husband ever having been. 'My god, can you imagine!' Vidya had said to Anand. 'Can you just imagine! God, yaar! I can't believe her mother didn't tell us!' But Harry Chinappa, perhaps in deference to Kavika's mother, had soon deemed her acceptable and Vidya had immediately followed suit. None of it was particularly his business and Anand had paid it no attention – until he met her that first time and some comment she made in passing, something trivial, something humorous, had caught his surprised interest.

Tonight she was dressed far more casually, her tall, slender, narrow-chested frame in a white tank-top ganji and loose block-printed cotton pants that were not too different in pattern from the cushions on the verandah. Her gray-flecked hair was cut so short it framed her skull in an almost military style, adding distinction to a face that was much younger than its thirty-five years. She had knotted a thin dupatta around her neck in a manner that left her shoulders bare.

She settled cross-legged on a large cushion, her chappals kicked away in a corner. She was close enough that he could lean over and touch her. Anand was conscious of the presence of his wife and of all the other people on the verandah, the other couple who had just arrived, Amir pouring drinks before rejoining Kavika and Amrita in conversation. He schooled his face to polite indifference, and perhaps he overdid it, for eventually he heard Vidya's voice at his ear: 'Oh my god, at least *try* to appear interested!'

'Amir, I'm stunned that I was able to reach your house without paying a single bribe to anyone,' Kavika was saying. 'All week, I haven't been able to get a single thing done without somebody asking me for baksheesh! Crazy!' In the glow of the candles, her skin gleamed smooth, flushing occasionally as she laughed. As far as he could tell, she was wearing no makeup.

'It *is* crazy – and the first step to changing things,' said Amir, climbing onto one of his favorite hobbyhorses, 'is for people like us to stop paying bribes completely. Not the fifty rupees to the lineman to get the electricity line fixed. Not the few hundreds to get a copy of our marriage certificate, let alone for bigger things . . .'

'Now *that's* a novel idea,' said Kavika and dodged the peanut Amir threw at her.

'Seriously, Amir,' Anand said, 'nice in theory. But come on, you know as well as I do that sometimes there is just no other way. Those buggers won't do anything otherwise.' As soon as the words left his mouth, he rolled over onto his back and closed his eyes in regret. He was going to get Amir's 'be part of the solution, not part of the problem' lecture.

Sure enough.

'Tell me,' Anand interrupted, after listening dutifully for a while. 'Are you guys going to that music gig next week?'

'Yes! You? . . . Excellent!' Amir was diverted.

Anand's eye eventually fell to his watch, and he scrambled up. He had already informed his hosts that he would be leaving early; Vidya was to stay behind and get a lift home with Kavika.

'You don't mind?' Anand asked. 'It's out of your way . . .'

'I don't mind at all,' Kavika said, cheerfully. He smiled back awkwardly. Vidya, he was aware, was frowning after him as he left the party.

At home, he made straight for his little office on the ground floor, the room his wife referred to as 'the study' and he referred to as 'mine.' This was his territory. The one corner of the house he claimed as his own and valiantly defended against all comers, spreading his paperwork just how he liked, easing into his comfort on the long sofa, forbidding maids from dusting even the shelves which Vidya had filled with glossy leatherbound books he never looked at. They had not called in an expensive professional for the house interiors; Vidya had bought a couple of books on the subject and wanted to experiment. Her efforts were praised by their friends; she had spoken briefly of pursuing it as a career before losing interest.

At his desk, Anand flipped open his laptop, clicking on the following day's presentation. His thoughts were turbulent and ill-timed; he could not concentrate.

The study door opened. 'Aha! I *thought* I heard you come in.' Valmika peeped in.

'Hi, kutty,' he said, smiling, his preoccupation instantly banished. 'Homework done?'

'Yup.' Valmika slouched over to the sofa. 'I hate physics. And it hates me.'

'Pingu's asleep?'

'Yeah.' She noticed the files and laptop open on the desk. 'You're working right now?'

'Yeah. Some important meetings tomorrow, Valmika,' he said and, seeing her inquiring gaze, 'some people are coming over to the factory, and if all goes well, we could actually enter the export market.'

'Appa! That's wonderful! Will you know by tomorrow itself?'

'No, kutty.' He smiled at her glee. 'It will take a few months . . . And nothing is definite . . . but one has to prepare . . .' She yawned hugely. 'Tired? You should go to bed. It's late, no?'

'Yes. I suppose. If Newton had sat down under a coconut tree instead of an apple tree, we wouldn't have had his stupid laws to study because he'd have been struck dead. Which would have been a good thing. Are you staying up late?'

'Probably.'

'If tomorrow is important, Appa,' she said, parroting what he always said to her on the eve of an exam, 'you should sleep early so you will be bright and fresh for it!'

He laughed. 'Good night, laddu.'

The front door slammed at midnight; he hastily frowned at his laptop.

'I can't believe you left so early.' Vidya seemed undeterred by his apparent absorption elsewhere. She sat on the couch and pulled off her sandals. Her makeup was slightly shop-soiled, the eyeliner slipping at the edge of one eye, the lipstick eaten away until no more than a bright pink outer ring remained. 'And I can't believe you said you pay bribes . . .'

I try to avoid it, said Anand.

'I was talking to Kavika tonight . . . The things she's done! I think she is just fabulous . . . I'm going to meet her again tomorrow.'

He kept his eyes on the computer screen. Good, he said. That's good.

Her slight frown was speculative. 'Ey, I know what it is! I know why you left early. It's Kavika. Isn't it?' she said, with an uncomfortable, unexpected perspicuity.

He looked up, not daring to speak.

'You know, Anand,' his wife said. 'There's nothing wrong in being a strong, independent woman like her. You should learn to handle it.'

Four

The next morning, Narayan was ready before Kamala was. He stuffed his bread and coffee into his mouth and proudly told her not to bother with making and packing his lunch. 'I will buy something,' he said, 'with the money that I earn.'

Eat things that will give you strength, she wanted to say. Do not overtire yourself. Do not get into mischief. Be careful with your earnings; do not spend it all on some nonsense. But she said none of it, watching him run off.

She turned to lock her door and stopped, glaring. The pile of garbage was still there. Insouciantly resting against the wall by her door like a guest who has every intention of outstaying his welcome. It had been there the previous day – and there it was still. In fact, it had indisputably grown larger overnight.

She could hear them inside their room, her neighbors, in sweet newlywed tones that could change with lightning speed to sharp words and shouts that echoed around the courtyard and disturbed everyone else. She wondered whether to slap on their door. Just then, as though summoned by Kamala's angry thoughts, the new bride emerged, dressed in the most slatternly way, her face unwashed, her hair uncombed, in a thin polyester kaftan that immodestly delineated the ridges and valleys of her body.

'What am I,' Kamala said straightaway, 'your maid-servant?'

The young woman seemed surprised, as she did every time Kamala scolded her. 'Why are you shouting again, old woman?' she said, taking outrageous liberties with Kamala's age. 'Who asked you to be anything?'

'Do you expect me to clean up after you?'

'It is just a bit of dirt. I am cleaning it up. I will do it.'

'Do it now,' said Kamala, knowing it would not happen. She locked her room, placing the key at the bottom of her woven plastic bag. 'How many times am I to ask. Do it now.'

The bride yawned at Kamala, the garbage already forgotten. 'Tell your friend Thangam that I have the money ready.'

'Tell her yourself,' said Kamala, walking away crossly.

Despite the occasional irritation of infelicitous neighbors, her home was ideal for her needs. The little room was painted a lime green, and if the color had faded with time and was stained in places, it nevertheless remained cheerful. Her possessions were stacked neatly against the wall: two bedrolls, the kerosene stove, aluminum cooking utensils, a few shelves for their clothes. Years before, Kamala had covered the tiny window with a sheet of plastic; this occasionally left the room filled with cooking smoke but blocked out the discomfiting stares of passing strangers on the gully outside, which was more important for her peace of mind.

A tap in the courtyard supplied water; there was also a common bath and toilet. It worked well, as long as one coordinated one's bathroom habits with everyone else in the courtyard and with the flow of water from the tap, officially rationed to one hour in the morning and an hour in the evening, but which sometimes ran for less on governmental whimsy. Of course, it was a matter of unwritten protocol that the landlord's family got first use of the facilities, but they were good people, sensible of the silent, impatient queue that waited around the courtyard concealed imperfectly behind closed doors, and so did not linger unnecessarily.

Her place of work was little more than a short brisk walk from her home, beyond this village that existed inexplicably in the middle of the burgeoning city. A decade ago, the village had been surrounded by fields; now it lay engulfed by suburbia, small industry, and the noise of highway construction. Swallowed whole, it had changed from quiet rural hamlet to urban slum, infested by workers who serviced the houses and industries around. The end of the dirt road widened astonishingly into tarred splendor. The transition from grime to rich suburban grace was marked and sudden, divided by a gutter and little else. Here, chaos. There, her employer's neighborhood: lavish bungalows neatly planned, fronted by tiled pavements, enclosed by walls and gardens and security guards; houses so large, they reversed traditional slum proportions: instead of one room for four people, they appeared to have four rooms per inhabitant.

'Namaste, sister,' the watchman said, as she neared the gate. 'You are late this morning, are you not?'

'No, am I?' she said, worriedly. She did not possess a watch, and time was always a slippery affair, expanding and contracting, sliding this way and that, so her judgment never seemed to match reality.

'No,' said the watchman, with a passing kindness, 'perhaps not. Do not worry.'

She slipped down the narrow side path that led to the back kitchen entrance and placed her rubber chappals on the shelf provided for the purpose.

Her eyes first went to the wall clock; no, habba, she was fine.

'Ah, sister, there you are!' Thangam sat cross-legged on the mosaic kitchen floor, an ever-present accounts book open on her lap. 'Come and listen!'

'What is it?'

'Hush! Listen! That fool has gone upstairs to ask for money, with the usual results . . .'

Sure enough, the sounds of raised voices bounced down the stairs: argument, and counterargument; anger, pleading counterpoint.

Thangam seemed to relish the drama playing out abovestairs between their employer and Shanta the cook as though it were being staged for her own entertainment. 'Shanta expects success where she has failed before; she will never learn,' she said. Indeed, their employer's querulous speech had morphed from the import-ance of fiscal prudence to the ingratitude of servants who kept wanting more. 'How foolish! She will not get the money and we shall be forced to suffer Vidya-ma's bad temper for the rest of the day.'

This was precisely what Kamala feared. She herself had a request to make of Vidya-ma and she did not want it jeopardized. Thangam pulled out a small mirror from her purse, inspecting her face and wiping an infinitesimal speck of kajal from the corner of one eye.

'Are you coming upstairs?' Kamala asked.

'In a few moments,' said Thangam. 'I just want to finish these chit fund entries.'

Kamala knew it was useless to argue; Thangam's aversion to her cleaning duties was in direct proportion to her interest in matters of financial import and personal grooming. Kamala collected the brooms and bucket and mopping cloth. 'Oh, and that girl in my courtyard – impertinent thing! – said she had the money ready for you . . .'

'About time,' said Thangam. 'She is already late on her payments. I'll collect it this evening.'

'Vidya-ma will give you permission to visit?'

'Sister, don't be silly.' Thangam's attention was back on her accounts book. 'I will not be telling her.'

Shanta's heavy tread came down the stairs, her round, doughy face with its forever open mouth like an uddin-vada, hiding the harsh bite of chiles and peppercorns. She pushed past Kamala, vanishing into the servants' bathroom in the back.

'Ey!' Kamala swelled up with an annoyance that was quickly deflated by Vidya-ma's echoing voice. 'Kamala!'

'Aanh, barthini, coming, ma!' Kamala ran up, impeded by the brooms and plastic bucket slapping against her legs. Thangam might walk out when she liked, but Kamala lacked that blithe courage. She herself would ask for permission.

Vidya-ma was in her night pajamas, her hair knotted on her head, her face bearing traces of anger from her conversation with Shanta and smeared with fairness cream. 'At least you are not late. Good. I am tired of people taking advantage of my kindness. Kamala, you will do the housecleaning today, for Thangam is not free; she will help me turn out the children's clothes cupboards, they are utterly messy.'

Kamala knew that she had not picked the winning ticket in the day's work lottery. She and Thangam were responsible for cleaning the house and ideally they would be allowed to do so, working their way from top to bottom, sweeping, swabbing, dusting, and tidying. But Vidya-ma had the habit of intruding on their work with ideas of her own, of mixing them up, asking each to do this and that and something else again, so sometimes the day was half over before their regular cleaning could even begin. Occasionally, on a day like this, one was asked to do the work of two.

Kamala risked her request. 'Amma, if it is not a trouble, may I leave work for one hour before lunch? I have something to attend to.'

She saw the shadow pass over Vidya-ma's face and felt her anxiety rise. But her employer nodded reluctantly. 'Very well, but do not delay. I will not be taken advantage of.'

Kamala planned her work, quickly finishing the master bedroom and Pingu's room. She glanced at the clock on the wall; she was right on schedule. In Valmika's room, it was just as she suspected, the bed covered with piles of clothing; Thangam stood bored and idle while Vidya-ma finished some telephone call in the next room. From tiresome past experience, Kamala knew such telephone calls could lead to other plans in which Vidya-ma might decide to go out, the turning-out job either abandoned with the clothes bundled back into the cupboard in greater disorder than when they had emerged or, worse, resumed hours later, involving everybody now, all the maids, the children, the watchman, the neighbor's cat, headaches, grumbles, and dragging on well past Kamala's usual end-of-job timings into the late hours of the evening. In compensation for such extra toil Vidya-ma might say, 'Eat your dinner before you go,' but who could sit in the kitchen stuffing food into her belly when there was a child waiting hungrily at home?

Thangam's eyes widened appreciatively when she saw Kamala work hurriedly through the room, for this was cleaning in a style she understood. 'Come and help,' said Kamala, crossly, 'at least the beds.'

'Very well,' said Thangam, 'but why do you act like a pregnant woman whose water is about to break?'

'I have permission to take a leave of one hour,' said Kamala, low-voiced, 'but do not tell anybody just yet, all right?' By which she meant Shanta.

'Aiyo, no fears,' said Thangam, with immediate understanding. 'I am not speaking to her today. She is in an awful temper . . . as though I did not warn her! And besides, such a shouting she gave me last night, just because my head hurt and I could not help her wash the dishes. She is a serpent, that woman.'

But Kamala would not be distracted by such enjoyable gossip, not today. She did not even stop for her usual eleven o'clock cup of tea and slice of bread in the kitchen. In a frenzy she worked, finishing the bedrooms and the study, bearing from room to room the brooms and bucket and other tools of her trade; rolling up the carpets after sweeping them with the hard coconut broom; using the softer broom on the floor; dipping and squeezing her mop cloth in the water before squatting on her haunches like a crab and wiping the floor clean.

She went briskly to the kitchen; it was already half past eleven; she had no time to waste. Her tea had been made earlier and stood waiting in a steel tumbler upon the table, cold to the touch and wearing an ugly skin of cream on top. The bread balanced on top of the tumbler had turned a little dry. Shanta pointedly ignored her; Kamala rinsed out her tea tumbler without drinking from it and slipped out of the back door to put on her slippers.

'And where might you be going?' Shanta demanded, rendered suspicious by this untimely activity.

'Vidya-ma has given me permission,' said Kamala, a certain smugness in her voice. 'I will return in an hour.'

'Some of us,' said the cook, 'do All The Work in this house, while others seem to expect All The Service.'

'True,' said Kamala. 'And she who expects the service, sister, is not Me.'

And on this triumphant note, she went to the servants' bathroom to wash her hands, splash water on her face, smooth her hair, and adjust the folds of her saree.

At the main intersection, the air was loud with horns, the traffic barely controlled by the lights, straining at the leash as though even a moment's delay would bring the commerce of the entire great city to a halt. One ineffectual policeman reigned over the tumult. Kamala squatted at a corner with a clear view of the flow and halt of the traffic through the four junctions.

The magazine boys were a mixed jumble, barely distinguishable through the fumes and noise. At last she was able to spot him – sporting a jaunty red cap like the others, holding a stack of magazines in his hand, and moving briskly from car to scooter to jeep to minivan. He was managing to sell a few, she could see that right away.

The light turned green, the traffic began to move and along with it her heart, not settling down to an even pace until she saw him emerge on the far side of the road, unscathed. He did not pause but ran swiftly to the next intersection where the traffic was halted. Not all the other boys did so; some of them stuck to one light, resting at the times when the traffic moved. They would surely sell less than her son.

His sales technique went beyond his tirelessness. Where had he learned it? Where had he learned to approach irritable drivers with a confident, cheerful smile and engage them in a nonverbal interaction conducted with difficulty through the tinted windows of their cars, until, sooner or later, the car window slid open, a hand emerged with money and vanished with a magazine?

This astonishing being, so different, from another world surely, her son.

At the end of an hour, she stood up and walked away. Narayan had not spotted her and he hadn't stopped to rest in all the time she had watched him. She walked back to her job, a small, proud smile playing on her lips, her mind already planning his night meal.

And, she determined, she would very soon plan a visit to the bright pink apartment building where lived the engineer's parents, happy in their new prosperity. She would take some apples. They would be expensive, but a worthy exchange for invaluable advice on how to secure a child's future. She thought of her meager savings. Or would bananas possibly suffice?

Five

It seemed intrinsic to his restless nature to never be able to sleep comfortably through the night. For more aggressive cases of insomnia Anand liked to pace the study listening to a motley collection of seventies rock, a musical habit that dated from college. He had recently come across an old Doobie Brothers CD while browsing at a music store on Brigade Road, and pacing to it usually relaxed him to the point where he could pick up *The Economist*. This was a magazine he subscribed to because it seemed appropriate; he dutifully labored his way through the editorial pages and an occasional article on politics or business. He rarely bothered to read the rest of the magazine unless he found himself awake at night. Then, the arts and books section was the perfect curative: subjects he had little interest in, instantly sedating; he could get drowsy within the first paragraph. There was one in particular, on the recovery of presumed-destroyed Babylonian artwork, that was his favorite in this regard. So sleep-inducing, even the very words *Bab-y-lon-ian-art-work* repeated slowly heralded visions of happy insensibility. 'Babble,' he liked to say, 'babble-onion, art-wuk.' And such repetition had borne strange fruit one day when someone was boring on at a dinner about the importance of preserving art against the tides of time and human agency, and bang on cue,

Anand's mouth had opened, he'd said, 'Babble-onion art-wuk,' and had his wife not choked on her wine, it would undoubtedly have been a bit of a feather in his cap.

But this was a night when neither *The Economist* nor the Doobie Brothers worked. He fiddled with his presentation for the following day, finally going to bed only to fight awkwardly with his pillow, plagued by specters of success and failure and fantastical what-ifs.

His body came awake before his mind did. He felt it, a high-tension humming in his blood, an electric glow, a moment of untrammeled, endless possibility – and then his mind snapped to alertness, propelling him out of bed, instantly reengaging with plans, schemes, and to-do lists. The warm shower waters rinsed away the vestiges of the night. Vidya lay undisturbed, swathed and blanketed in the icy freeze of the air-conditioned bedroom as he stole past and ran downstairs to his car.

In the early morning cool of an awakening world, through traffic as yet muted and desultory, the small sedan maneuvered its way toward the distant city outskirts. Forty-five minutes later, he appraised the approaching factory with a stern, clinical eye: the dust and distressed road yielding to a manicured strip of green grass; the glossy factory wall, freshly repainted the previous day, the large manufacturing sheds beyond.

Right on the appointed hour, two cars pulled into the compound. Six people emerged; at quick scan, they seemed to cover all the races: two Japanese, two Europeans, a man from England of African parentage.

Anand felt the usual awkwardness well up within him. He wished he could be at ease with foreigners; they were sometimes intimidating and frequently incomprehensible; he did not have the means within him to easily cross vast cultural divides. His management team stood behind him: Mrs Padmavati's oiled hair and silk saree glistening in the morning light; the HR man wearing a startlingly strong checked jacket for the occasion; Ananthamurthy's tie looking narrow and uncomfortable, but all of them with smiles rich with expectation and nervous excitement. Anand dried his palms on a handkerchief, thankful that the gray jacket he wore covered the sweat that had soaked instantly through his shirt, and hastened forward to meet the visitors, pinning a warm smile of welcome to his face.

The day passed surprisingly smoothly. The visitors toured the factory and seemed interested and impressed. Mrs Padmavati had had the foresight to make copies of Anand's presentation; he was gratified to see the visitors scratching notes as he talked. The projector did not fail; the computer's hard drive did not die halfway through. Ananthamurthy did not bring up his antediluvian notions on caste, worship, and vegetarianism but instead led the tour through the plant with the calm competence that came from knowing the location of every nut and bolt on the manufacturing floor and answered all the questions posed to him thoughtfully and capably. The lunch had been organized from a five-star hotel; the visitors appeared to enjoy the food, though Anand was too nervous to eat.

In the late afternoon, the entire team collapsed in Anand's office. They congratulated themselves. Everything had gone well, they agreed. They could not have planned anything better. They reviewed the questions that had been asked, trying to discern in them a measure of approval. As they talked, rehashing the various conversations of the day, Anand received an email from the liaison who had set up this visit.

Alas, the excitement it generated was soon laid to rest; it was just a routine email of thanks for the visit. Any real indication on whether Cauvery Auto had passed muster would have to wait while the visitors toured other factories in the country and then returned to their own home offices and talked things through. The discussions, negotiations, and due diligence might take days, weeks to resolve.

Ananthamurthy said he would redouble his prayers. Anand smiled automatically in response, already feeling the excitements of the day recede from his being, immediately replaced by everyday operational concerns.

As though on cue, his cellphone rang.

Anand hesitated before reluctantly touching his thumb to the screen of his iPhone.

'Hello? Hello? Can you hear me? I can't hear you. Hello?' His father-in-law distrusted cellular technology and bellowed to compensate.

'Hello,' said Anand.

'It must be a bad line . . . Right. You will be glad to know. I have organized it.' At Anand's cautious silence, his father-in-law's voice grew slightly more impatient. 'Hello? Can you hear me?'

'Organized it?' said Anand.

'Yes. That is what I said . . . The land you require for your factory . . . I have set up some meetings. You come and meet me tomorrow – no, wait, I can't tomorrow – fine, you meet me next week and I will brief you,' shouted his father-in-law before ringing off.

The second window in his office faced the factory campus, and Anand frowned at the view. This two acres – bought so very proudly just four years before, two acres for which Anand had mortgaged all he owned (which admittedly had not been very much) and taken an additional bank loan – was now too small. Orders had flooded in; Anand and Ananthamurthy had built factory sheds to the very edges of the lot; there was no further room to grow unless one counted the flower beds, the watchman's room, and the realms that existed between the earth and the holes in the ozone layer.

'We are needing more land, sir,' Ananthamurthy had taken to saying on an almost daily basis, 'especially if this Japan deal comes through and even,' he would say, 'if not.'

Buying industrial land outside the city was fraught with complications, very different from the relatively straightforward process of buying property within the city through real estate agents. This, instead, was a murky business, with dubious titles and complicated family ownership histories, influenced by different mafias and forever enmeshed with inscrutable political machinery and zoning laws.

In the distance stood the neighboring property, with enormous warehouse walls, in disuse and covered with rusty metal sheets, built right up to the common compound wall, looming, entirely spoiling the vista. The factory gardener had planted an intervening hedge of bright pink bougainvillea, but this obscured only about three feet of the eyesore, which, if anything, seemed even uglier in contrast. Anand had approached his idiot neighbors, whose property stretched beyond the ugly warehouses for twenty acres, much of it in disuse and disrepair.

He had heard that they were in trouble; a pair of quarreling brothers, one prone to drink and the other to whores; they might be willing to sell. They were – and proved their reputations as business failures by quoting a price so ridiculously high and greedy, even for this city, where escalating land prices seemed a way of life, that Anand glared in disgust at the rust on their encroaching warehouse walls. May it grow, bastards, this rust, until it filters and covers all parts of your life, from your dick to your drinking glass. Behenchuths.

When Anand had bought his current two-acre site, the seller had been a friend of a friend, in financial trouble and eager to sell, with clear titles. That kind of serendipity couldn't be counted upon – and this time, his requirements were larger. There were land

brokers, of course, for this sort of purchase, but they did not advertise themselves or work without personal reference.

He had mentioned some of this, in passing, to Vidya. She had
apparently conveyed it almost immediately to her father, who,
naturally, had taken it upon himself to get involved in the matter.

His father-in-law's phone call acted as a trigger. Anand mentally
worked his way through a roster of friends and acquaintances who
might be able to help him. His friend Vinayak claimed to know
everything and everyone; he was the person to call. Anand fingered
his way through the iPhone menu, forgiving its occasional tele-
phonic inefficiency with the blind affection a parent reserves for
a wayward but much-loved child.

'Vinayak?' he said. 'Listen, buddy, I need your help.'

and, lest we forget . . .

matru devo bhava

mother is god

pitru devo bhava

father is god

athiti devo bhava

guest is god

Six

In the light of the early morning, Kamala was engaged in lecturing her son.

'So will you hurry yourself? As quickly as you can manage? Do not delay, do not engage in useless conversations with your friends, do not be distracted by anything other than the desire to please your mother and present yourself to the house in good speed.'

'I will, Mother,' said Narayan.

'And dress well! I do not want to be shamed by the rags you are so fond of wearing.'

'Mother,' said Narayan, 'I am not the one who is going to be late. Weren't you supposed to be there by now?'

Kamala glared at such impertinence and continued to scold: 'And do not forget, while you are there, to keep a civil tongue in your head, to speak respectfully, to work hard, and . . .'

'I will, Mother,' said Narayan. 'Calm yourself. I will do just as you have said.'

'Yes,' said Kamala. 'I know that. I know that.'

The day was barely birthed when she walked with quick, urgent steps to her employer's house. She had promised to be there early – for there was seven days' work to be completed in one.

'Even the gods' – Thangam seemed barely able to open her irritable, sleep-encrusted eyes – 'could not commence work on such a day without something first to eat and drink. Have you broken your fast this morning, sister?' She banged the bucket on the floor. 'And when does your son arrive?'

'He will be here very soon,' said Kamala. 'He was awake when I left and he is not one to tarry.'

Narayan appeared when they were drinking their tea. There was a crowd in the kitchen that early morning. In addition to Kamala and Thangam and Shanta, there was the driver, the driver's wife, and two watchmen, none of whom were normally encouraged to visit the kitchen, but exceptions were being made.

Kamala saw immediately and with approval that her son had followed all her instructions. His face was washed, his hair was neatly parted and combed, and he was dressed in his best shirt and pants. She had readied them for him the previous Sunday, washing them and then plucking them off the drying line when they were still warm from the sun, folding and pressing them with her hands. The result was almost wrinkle-free. She thought he looked very smart. His eyes were bright and eager, and a little shy.

'What is it, boy? What is it you want?' Shanta the cook spoke first, her voice sharp.

'Vidya-ma has summoned him here today,' said Kamala. 'To help us.'

'Oh, it's good you have arrived, young one!' said Thangam, in a mixture of friendliness and relief. 'Come in, come in, lad. Have something to eat – your insides must be as empty and parched as the wells in summer.'

Kamala was grateful for Thangam's kindness in making Narayan feel welcome. Shanta looked sulky but did not hesitate to put a tumbler of hot tea in front of him, a slice of bread placed over it like a lid, saying: 'After you are done, boy, be sure to rinse your tumbler and place it behind the sink. I have too much to do to clean up after every tousle-headed urchin who wanders through my kitchen.'

Narayan's cheeks worked quickly at his food, his eyes meeting Kamala's in a glimmer of amusement, as though he recognized in the cook's rudeness all the truth of the gossip his mother brought home each evening.

Kamala and Thangam, with Narayan's help, concentrated on cleaning the ground floor of the house well ahead of their normal schedule. They were barely done when the family upstairs awoke – and on the heels of their rising came an endless array of other chores: of carrying the tea trays up and the water jugs down, of beds to be made and breakfast to be served. None of the jobs were difficult to do, all of them were routine, but between them they engaged all the women until it was time to break for their own meal.

They collected in the kitchen, their faces sharp with hunger. The driver's wife was washing up the family's breakfast plates, Shanta was wreathed in enticing-smelling steam, and with a little bounce of pleasure, Kamala realized that this would, after all, be one of those good days.

The long central platform in the kitchen was laden with semia upma and a plate of hot dosas, with chutney and sambar on the side. Kamala helped Narayan to a plateful before getting her own, suspending the feeding of her own appetite in the enjoyment of sating his, watching his eyes close in happy disbelief and his mouth open again and again in greed and hunger. Everyone ate quickly, saving their conversation. Narayan washed his plate and tumbler out and was careful to thank Shanta: 'Please forgive my impudence in saying so, aunty,' he said, 'but your cooking is the finest I have ever tasted.'

Shanta's mouth twitched into a reluctant half smile, she said: 'Your good mother surely does not say so.'

'Indeed, she is the first to praise your cooking, always.'

'Indeed, Shanta, we all are,' said Thangam, eagerly reaching for a last dosa. But before she could lift it up and place it on her plate, a voice rang out from the dining room.

'Oh, my god! So little has been done! And there's simply no time left for anything!' Vidya-ma appeared at the kitchen door, and her face was set in scolding, panicked lines. 'Come along, everybody, do not linger. So much to be done! This is not the time for relaxing!'

Every now and then, Vidya-ma and Anand-saar liked to invite guests to their home, in intimate gatherings of ten to large crowds of a hundred, and the staff work varied accordingly. 'I thought twenty couples,' she had said to Anand-saar over breakfast one morning. 'It will give Kavika a chance to meet some people . . .'

'Great,' he had replied. 'That sounds nice.'

'Should we not finish the upstairs first, Vidya-ma?' Thangam's query was waved aside. Vidya commandeered all the staff – the maids, Narayan, the driver, the driver's wife, the watchmen, and even, briefly, the transient gardener – to roll the carpets out of the way, push the sofas to the walls, and shift the coffee tables from the center of the room to the edges. She walked about, talking aloud to herself.

'The caterers will set up there, and the bar will be here; this area should be kept free for people to stand and mingle, the tall lamps here . . .'

But it appeared that arranging the main ground-floor rooms for the evening was neither a quick nor a simple process. 'Oh yes,' Vidya-ma would say as the sofas and tables and potted plants settled in place and, two minutes later, 'No, that really doesn't work, does it?'

She did not expect agreement from them, so they kept silent as she devised anew. The telephone, never silent, seemed to ring today with a great energy and tenacity. Vidya-ma refused no telephone calls, and as she talked – 'Oh, I'm so glad. Looking forward to seeing you then,' or 'Oh, no special occasion, extremely casual evening, just throwing together some food and friends, making no effort at all, really' – she continued to direct them in their dance; waving them about, sending them staggering this way and that, and shaking her head. Occasionally, she would scold: 'Be careful!' and 'Please, do as I say! Do you not understand me?' and 'Careful, you fool!'

Kamala did not mind the scoldings, but she wondered anxiously if her son would be able to follow Vidya-ma's complicated instructions. She need not have worried: in the swirl of words – move this, shift that, no, not so much, a little more this side – Narayan seemed to grasp the end result Vidya-ma was looking for before it actually happened. And right toward the end, he spoke up.

'Shall I place it there, amma?' he asked softly, as his mother's employer contemplated an exasperating side table, which was always out of place and never at home. Kamala tensed. Vidya-ma looked cross and irritable. 'Where?' she said, her irritation undiminished. Narayan pointed to the far side of the room, and her face magically relaxed into smiles. 'Why, the very place!' she said. 'Clever boy. Yes, do so.' As Narayan scurried over to move the side table into position, Vidya-ma said to Kamala, 'Your son, no? Smart boy.' Kamala quickly controlled the untoward display of happiness on her face for fear of provoking the jealousies of the others.

She had worried so much and, it appeared, so needlessly. The night before, she had hardly slept, envisioning all the things that might go wrong: Narayan accidentally breaking the best crystal; or his choosing this day of all days to play some mischievous trick; or having his friends appear at the gate of the house in boisterous, upsetting fashion. Now, in her pleasure, she pulled at his ear gently. 'You little rascal,' she whispered, and he grinned.

But pleasure was soon offset by a growing fatigue: the day was not yet half over, there was still so much to be done, and Kamala could sense herself faltering. Finally, long after Thangam's face had turned sour and sulky, and the gardener had absconded, and the driver's wife had conquered her shyness to start a slow muttering under her breath, Vidya-ma sighed. 'Yes, I think this will do . . .' she said. 'And now you must start on the brass polishing . . . And I want someone to help me with the garden chairs . . .'

'But, amma!' said Thangam, voicing a query that was growing in Kamala's mind as well, 'is the upstairs not to be cleaned?'

It appeared that Vidya-ma had forgotten. 'Oh my god!' she said. 'The full upstairs? And now look at the time!'

'Don't worry, amma,' said Kamala hastily, 'we can do it quickly.'

'But the full upstairs!' said Vidya-ma. 'If you all go upstairs now, I will not see you again before the evening, and that will be too late! Why on earth could you not have reminded me earlier?'

Thangam opened her mouth and said, unthinkingly: 'But, Vidya-ma, I did! I did remind you!'

And as their mistress's wrath broke over Thangam, Kamala caught her eye sympathetically, but some part of her could not help thinking that there was a virtue in knowing when to speak and when to keep silent.

'Now,' said Vidya-ma, when she had calmed down. 'I'll tell you what we shall do. Kamala, you and your boy shall start on brass polishing. The driver and watchmen shall help me set up the garden. Shanta needs the driver's wife in the kitchen. And you, Thangam, shall go upstairs to clean.'

'Vidya-ma!' said Thangam. 'Am I to clean the full upstairs by myself? I cannot manage!'

'Oh,' said Vidya-ma, her irritation evident. Her eyes wandered. 'Kamala, perhaps your son can go and help her?'

'That is a good idea, Vidya-ma,' said Thangam, ingratiatingly.

Oh, never, thought Kamala. Never would she allow Narayan to work under Thangam, who would surely see that he did all the work while she stood idly by. She did not like to contradict Vidya-ma, who was looking flushed, unhappy, and cross, but she had to say something. 'Let me go help her, Vidya-ma,' she said. 'I can do it quicker.'

'But the brass? And who will do the flowers? . . . Oh,' said Vidya-ma. 'You are all so unhelpful. At a time like this, you are all so unhelpful.'

The words in Kamala's mind popped out of her mouth: 'Let the driver's wife start the polishing, Vidya-ma. My son can help her . . . Shanta is such a clever woman, she is sure to be able to manage in the kitchen by herself. After all, she is not cooking for the function.'

'Oh, a sow's teat,' Kamala said. 'A braying donkey curse this house and all those who labor in it. Even a dog's fart would smell better than this place.'

The pain had settled deep within her groin. It was right on schedule; it should not have taken her by surprise. She had known since the previous day, when her monthly cycle had started, in coy red drops that settled in the cloth between her legs and welled to a majestic flow by this morning. Her son found her squatting on the floor, one hand pressed to her belly, her head resting on her knees, eyes closed tight to prevent tears escaping, mouth moving silently in a hundred nameless curses. Her broom and bucket lay idle next to her.

'Mother? Are you not well? What ails you?' The worry in his voice roused her, but, naturally, she could not meet the concern and alarm in his eyes with the truth.

'It is a back pain, child,' she said. 'And a little bit in the stomach. But do not worry, it will soon be better. Have you finished the jobs you were given?'

'Yes, yes,' he said, 'all done, but, Mother! Can't you rest yourself awhile? Isn't there some medicine that you can take?'

She forced a smile. 'Do not worry, child. It will soon be better. I will drink some water, and it will go away.'

Her normal practice, at such times, was to speak to Vidya-ma before her pains became unbearable – all the females in the house did – and they would receive a special pain pill that Vidya-ma kept for her own use and that was not available at the neighborhood medicine shop. Like magic, within a half hour, the pulsing pain in the groin would be stemmed. But Kamala could not think of approaching Vidya-ma today. And she cursed her own foul judgment, that on a day like this, amid all her other preparations – the readying of her son's clothes, the earnest lectures to him, the this, the that – in not taking care to provide herself with a little pill of her own. As she slowly straightened, her legs trembled – in reaction to the work already done, and in anticipation of the work to come.

When the clock showed half past three, she could bear it no longer. 'I will be back,' she whispered to her son, who had loyally spent the past few minutes trying to swab the floor for her. 'You have done well. I am happy with you, Son.' His answering smile eased the pain within her a little. 'Keep at your work a few minutes more,' she said. 'I must visit the bathroom.'

From the other end of the room, Thangam stared at them both suspiciously; it had not escaped her notice that Kamala's pace of work had slowed considerably. Her frown deepened as Kamala left the room. 'Come here, boy,' she called to Narayan. 'Come and help here.'

Kamala visited the bathroom and then collapsed on the kitchen stoop that led to the small backyard. The ceaseless actions of the day had increased the flow of blood; she could feel it settling between her legs, the stickiness mingling with the sweat that ran in rivulets down her back and to the tops of her thighs. The pain in her groin had extended to her lower back, in a tight band that stretched across her tailbone, and the dullness of her soul now had an overlay of temper, an irritability so acute and so devoid of respite that even the bright blue afternoon sky made her cross.

Behind her, she could hear cooking vessels being banged about, the noise seeming to increase in volume. The sink was filled with dirty plates and dishes, and Shanta wandered between them and the pot of sambar simmering on the stove for the servants' lunch.

'It's nice to see,' Shanta addressed the kitchen stoop, 'that some people have the time to relax.' Silence, then the slamming of a cupboard door, a rising catechism of complaint.

'I hope,' she said, 'that the driver's wife is proving herself useful upstairs?

'She must be very grateful to you,' she said, 'for your suggestion, and the chance to polish brass with uplifted mortals like yourself, instead of assisting a simple soul like me.

'There is no need,' she said, 'to suppose for one moment that I am not capable of attending to my duties in the kitchen. I have fed and cleaned after this family for so many years now, I can do all this and more, sister! All this and more! But then,' said Shanta, banging stainless-steel cooking vessels down, 'hard work is something that only few of us understand! Not all of us feel free to put down our work and stretch our feet and relax while all others toil about us.'

Kamala felt her own blood heat, her temper begin to flash and sparkle. She did not look around. 'You mind your own business, sister,' she said.

'If only I could!' said Shanta. 'But it seems, even that is not allowed to me. I am forced to mind everyone else's business as well. Vidya-ma seems to be in a very generous mood, in her desire to employ people and disburse rations to all and sundry. Is it my job, then, to press food into the mouths of all the young rabble of the neighboring slum? Am I to slave myself to the bones, till my very fingers collapse with arthritis, just to feed the son of every woman too lazy to prepare food for her own family?'

'Guard your mouth, sister!' said Kamala, her control snapping at this reference to her son. 'You speak as though the weight of preparing the food for the entire party rests on your shoulders. But that is being done by others. You are here to feed us, who are working around the house till our very bones dissolve into puddles of fatigue. And if you choose not to, akka, I am very happy, I assure you, to let Vidya-ma know that on your behalf. Allow me to provide you with that small service. I am happy to oblige!'

Shanta did not reply. Kamala rested her head against the wall and wondered if a drink of hot water would help. Behind her the kitchen grew silent. The back courtyard too seemed wrapped in sympathetic quiet. It was usually a scene of constant noise and activity – clothes were washed and hung to dry, the door to the servants' bathroom always opening and closing, the whole area moist and wet – but today, all the staff were busy inside, the square granite clothes-washing stone stood idle, the drying lines were light and free of their normal burden. The only noise the soft buzz of flies that hovered ceaselessly and excitedly over the large bin that held the kitchen garbage. Vidya-ma insisted that they keep the garbage bin well covered, but Shanta never really bothered.

The cramps struck again, and Kamala doubled over, resting her head on her knees.

And it was in this position that she was discovered by Vidya-ma. 'Kamala! What is the meaning of this!

'How can one rest while others toil? On a day like this, when all have so much to do. Even I have not stopped for a second, no, not even paused for a drink of water, but you! Relaxing like a queen. I cannot believe this! Such a nerve! If you are not interested in this work, why don't you just go home now?'

Kamala stood up. She placed her teeth on her lip to control the quivering and kept her eyes lowered. Vidya-ma's ankles were covered by her jeans, but her naked foot peeked out, soft and scrubbed, with toenails painted a jewel red.

They had quickly collected a small audience, freshly arrived for their lunch: Kamala could sense the triumph in Shanta's face, the eager curiosity in Thangam's, the nervous fright in the driver's wife, and, just beyond, Narayan, his eyes worried and angry.

Vidya-ma, spleen emptied, turned her attention to Shanta. 'So, what did you want me to see?' The cook led her meekly to the table where the tablecloths and napkins lay ready for inspection. 'Yes, that one,' Vidya-ma said impatiently. 'I already told you so this morning.'

She left and the frozen tableau relaxed – Thangam and the driver's wife went to the sink to wash their hands; Shanta patted the stacks of napkins in some satisfaction; and Kamala walked out of the kitchen to squat in the courtyard, angry tears rolling down her cheeks. She felt her son's arms about her shoulders.

'So mean!' he said, in an angry whisper. 'How could she do such a thing!'

'I tell you. She is like that!' said Kamala.

'It is the height of meanness. Especially when you have been slaving all day long.'

'Yes,' said Kamala, comforted. 'It is.'

'Could she not see that you were not well? Your sickness is written upon your face.'

'She is not one to see anything that does not suit her.'

'Then why must you work here? I do not like it, Mother!'

Kamala was touched. She pushed her son's hair back off his forehead. 'There will always be someone like her, you know. In any job.'

'But you have never said anything about it! From your words, I thought she was nice!'

Kamala stared at him. 'When did I say so! I have always cursed that she-demon, Shanta.'

'Not Shanta!' said Narayan. 'Vidya-ma. She's not nice. She's mean! She does not care.'

Kamala was shocked. 'No, Son. Don't say that. It is all Shanta's fault. She is the one who brought her down here, on purpose to get me into trouble. She is a she-demon, that one.'

Narayan shut his mouth, but his face still carried doubt.

Seven

The new Human Resources man had him cornered, pinning Anand to his desk with stratagems – 'We should take, sir,' the HR man's eyes were alight with mad sociological schemes that raised his hair in little black and gray tufts behind his ears, 'the entire management to off-site. There is a place near Mysore which is having very good facilities for off-site. Rope climbing, coracle racing.' Anand regarded him doubtfully; he had hired the Human Resources manager to handle things like pay and perks and absenteeism; this man spent all his energies organizing picnics.

'Very good for bonding, sir,' said the HR man. 'For team-building.'

'I'll think about it,' said Anand.

'Oh, very good, sir.' The HR man seemed to take this for unabashed consent. 'I will organize . . . And there is a candidate here for that post of systems engineer. Mr Ananthamurthy has seen him, and he requests you also to please interview. You are able to see him?'

Anand hesitated. He had a myriad list of things to do, but the expanding factory fattened steadily on a diet of new employees, and Anand gained a quiet pleasure from the quality of people who were beginning to seek employment with them. 'Okay,' he said. 'Quickly.'

He glanced at the day's headlines. THE LOK AYUKTA ANTI-CORRUPTION RAID YIELDS TWO CRORES IN BRIBES.

STRAY DOGS ATTACK FOUR-YEAR-OLD CHILD, BUT STILL TOLERATED. 'It is not in our Hindu culture to kill animals,' said a neighboring resident.

VIJAYAN — NEW HOPE FOR INDIAN POLITICS? with a photograph of the politician in question waving from a podium.

In the frivolous party pages, there was a photograph of his friend Vinayak, looking pleased and cool and prosperous at an art auction and, on the same page, Anand's father-in-law, clutching a glass of gin and tonic with vulpine satisfaction. Harry Chinappa's hooded eyes were ringed by dark dissipation; with his artificially blackened hair and his prominent hooked nose, he resembled a dissolute bird of prey.

Anand thrust the newspaper away when the interviewee entered the room. The young applicant was slender, bespectacled, and dressed in striped shirt and tie. His hair was parted on the side and neatly combed over, possibly with Brylcreem, for he introduced no odor of coconut oil into the room. According to the notes scribbled by Ananthamurthy, he belonged to a Gujarati bania caste and, therefore, was probably vegetarian, home-loving, and good with numbers. He perched nervously in front of Anand's desk.

'Your good name?' The applicant, Anand noted, was about twenty-six years old, with the requisite four years of experience, and fluent in Kannada, as well as Hindi and Gujarati and English. 'Born where? Oh, came to Bangalore as a child, is it? Father is doing what?'

For Ananthamurthy, caste and community were important hiring considerations, but Anand tried to guard against this. He himself had married out of caste — and that, in his mind, was a sign of progress, of stepping away from the rigid brahminical mind-set of his parents. Of course, there was still a tendency to hire the familiar, that was a natural impulse; if he analyzed his employee lists, he saw that most were Kannadiga or at least South Indian, some were brahmin – but, as leavening, there were three Muslims, two Kerala Christians, and several North Indians. In fact, if one considered the new machinery consultants, there were even two foreign – Korean – faces wandering around. As a welcoming gesture, special food was brought for them from the Korean restaurant in the city, and when Mr Ananthamurthy, in a further gesture of first-day hospitality, decided to eat with them, he found the visitors unwrapping sea leaves, fish, and chicken, the unpalatable smells spreading across the table and staying the consumption of his own strictly vegetarian tiffin.

Mr Ananthamurthy was conservative in his habits, consuming a large home-cooked meal in the morning and carrying to work a small steel tiffin box packed by his wife and daughters to shield him from the perils of oversalted canteen food. But, in truth, the factory canteen food was tasty; the same dishes were served to workers and managers alike (which Anand personally insisted upon): a good everyday menu of vegetables, dal, rice-sambar-saaru, chapattis, a mixed rice such as chitranna bhath or lemon rice, curds, and a sweet. Fully vegetarian, of course, for that was the preferred way. Indian manufactories might work to upgrade their production methods to international standards, but they were still populated by old-fashioned people with old-fashioned values; one could not argue with that. As Ananthamurthy had discovered, in the call centers and software development offices in the city, things were different. There they introduced American-style ways: fast food, casual attitudes, fun games, crazy decorations. This was apparently done to create environments that no employee would dream of leaving, but of course, that did not work either. Employee turnover continued unabated, like water swirling down an unplugged sink.

It took, on average, three months for new hires to lose their bewilderment, six months to find their feet, and one year to become fully reliable. And then, just as one could put them to work in a thorough fashion and turn one's attention to other things, they came in blithely ready to quit – citing other job offers, or stress, or nonsense like that one giddy idiot who quit the accounts department to write a book. Employers, it seemed, had to make themselves attractive to potential employees in new and unprecedented ways, as though they were products stacked on supermarket shelves and seeking out buyers.

'You are married? Children?' The good employees usually were. Marriage and children forced a seriousness upon them, prevented them from scurrying from job to job, tempted by any passing incremental offer like a woman of easy virtue and no discrimination.

'Yes, sir. And with two children, sir,' said the applicant, adding considerably to his own worth. 'But I am fully willing to travel, if necessary, sir.'

Unfortunately, the thoroughness with which the young man had prepared for the interview had also made him acutely aware of his own market worth. He was asking for 20 percent more than Anand had planned to pay.

In the abstract, Anand fully approved of such a thing. This was what happened when a society slowly moved out of poverty. Better pay, better lifestyles. It still had the power to astonish him, that he should bear witness to this transformation, striking him afresh every time he wandered into a hypermarket, the rows of products from around the world that were on sale; it moved him, even as his children obliviously shopped for the things they took so much for granted – so different from the small two-type-biscuit, three-type-sweet, one-type-pen kaka shops he had grown up with.

But practically, it made him cautious and thoughtful when he hired. This systems engineer, though, appeared to be worth it. Anand signed a note to the HR man approving his hire.

That afternoon he received a call from his mother, telephoning to complain about the plumbing. The commode kept backing up, she said, and the plumber, in the nature of plumbers, was recalcitrant, inefficient, and mystifying in his proposed solutions. What did Anand think she should do? Over the years, she had taken to calling him on such things, everyday matters, bypassing his father, who seemed content to spend his days in a banian vest and dhoti, discussing philosophy and the importance of not giving in to material desires while Anand solved his plumbing problems from a distance of a hundred miles. 'Okay, Amma,' he said. 'Okay. I'll attend to it.'

Each month, without his father's knowledge, he sent money to his mother, depositing it directly into her account; his father never checked account balances.

'How is he?' he said now.

'Same,' his mother said. 'Prostate giving trouble, so maybe the doctor will advise surgery . . . Are you eating well?' she said. 'And sleeping? . . . Don't work too hard.'

'Okay, Amma,' he said, knowing that this standard maternal exhortation hid a complete ignorance of what he did for a living.

Anand's father could never comprehend or approve of his son's choice of profession, which he felt sacrificed learning for profit. Years before, visiting Anand's first factory unit, he could not hide his shock and disgust. He had never returned for a repeat visit; his son's work became a topic he refused to discuss.

Anand had never forgotten, never forgiven his father's shame. When his new factory was scheduled to open, he nevertheless dutifully called to invite him to the opening ceremony.

'You should come,' he said.

'Is it?' his father replied. 'But isn't that the week of Guruprasad's daughter's wedding in Hubli . . .' Anand did not argue with this stated conflict with a function of a distant cousin his father had always despised. Instead of pressing his parent as was expected, he said:

'Is it? Then you should go for that.'

His father had not attended the factory inauguration; the resultant distance between Mysore and Bangalore had stretched from a hundred miles to four years. Naturally Anand's mother could not visit her son's factory without being disloyal to her husband, and if the increased amounts Anand was depositing in her account indicated his growing financial stability, she made no mention of it, functioning between the two men like a secret agent, marked by guile, covert phone calls, and essays of great diplomacy.

'I'm going out for half an hour,' Anand said casually. The trick lay in making it sound uninteresting; an outing that would not register on his wife's sensitive social radar. 'With Vinayak . . .'

'Vinayak Agarwal?' she asked, looking up from her magazine. 'Will his wife be there?'

'No . . . he wants my help . . .' – he aimed for vague and boring – 'on some engineering matter.'

As he hoped, she immediately lost interest.

Unfortunately, Vinayak, like Vidya, had his own set of socializing concerns; he wanted to meet at the new pub that was the latest in latest things. It would be noisy and crowded, not conducive to the kind of discussion Anand had in mind, but he did want Vinayak's help and could not quibble.

The Latest Latest Bar was located in the ELIPT Mall – its name was supposedly an acronym for the names of the four brothers who built the mall, but a local wag had immediately expanded it to Extremely Luxurious but In Poor Taste, an opinion that Anand

found difficult to disagree with. Shiny escalators swooped upward
in a space seemingly imported from shrieking Dubai; an amazement of gilt and a fresco-covered ceiling in a mock-up of the
Sistine Chapel: Man reaching upward, milky-eyed with greed, the
Creator's hand holding out not the promise of life at the tip of a
finger but, Santa Claus–like, a gift wrapped in paper and ribbons,
the angels clustered behind him carrying the urgent promise of
more: handbags, perfume bottles, designer-labeled shopping bags.
Let there be Lights – and an explosion of spending.

Anand was the first to reach the bar, submitting to the lazy
security check and fighting his way to a corner of the bar counter.
He ordered his beer and sorrowfully contemplated the bowl of
olives that accompanied it. What, ultimately, was the magic of the
olive that allowed it to flourish at the expense of other condiments;
that took it from being a local fruit in a regional cuisine – probably
once plucked and eaten by sweat-streaked, tree-climbing schoolboys
in Italy before angry farmers could chase them away, much as he
had raided nellikayi gooseberry trees in Mysore, dipping the spoils
in salt and chili powder for a stolen after-school treat – and raised
it to the status of an internationally hallowed bar food? He ate
one: salty, squashy, cold, and green.

'Want to order some snacks, sir?' The bartender was dressed, like
the other bar employees, in a white shirt, black pants, and red
Converse shoes. SELVADURAI, his name badge said. Anand shook his
head and noticed with relief the large figure lumbering in.

Vinayak levered his bulk with effort onto the barstool next to
Anand. 'Shit! These things are damn uncomfortable.' He placed an
olive in his mouth and looked around, but all the tables were occupied. 'Whiskey please, yes, that Aberlour is fine, and some paneer
tikkas and masala nuts . . . What do you mean, no masala nuts. No
tikkas also? Let me see that menu . . . Okay, fine, bruschetta and,
yeah, grilled mushrooms. Okay with you, Anand?' Anand nodded;

he didn't actually care. Vinayak was a strict vegetarian, having apparently attained his size on ghee and dal-bhatti alone. Food and drink
ordered, Vinayak relaxed and inspected the other people in the bar.
He waved at someone at a distant table. 'See that guy? He got that
large government order apparently by providing whores to the
minister involved. What a pimp job, yaar . . .' Like his namesake,
Ganesha, Vinayak was gifted with a potbelly, a penchant for prosperity, the cunning to market a stroll around his parents into a world
odyssey, and a long, trunk-like nose perfect for poking into everyone
else's affairs. 'Are we seeing you at Chetty's party this weekend?'

'Yeah,' said Anand. 'I suppose so.'

'Lucky bastard, Chetty, he sleeps around and his wife celebrates
by throwing parties.'

'Ey, regarding that land broker you were mentioning,' said Anand,
refusing to be sidetracked by Vinayak's bits of heated gossip.

'Right,' said Vinayak, agreeably. 'So you are planning some expansion, is it?'

Anand explained briefly, glossing quickly over his expansion
ideas and just speaking of the land he required.

'So, about ten, fifteen acres, right? . . . And in that area? . . . Who
did you deal with last time? Your father-in-law?'

'No, no,' said Anand, explaining.

'Great man, your father-in-law.' Vinayak spoke in tones that were
entirely reverential. 'Met him over the weekend, at that art thing . . .
He knows everybody, no? Politicians, industrialists, everyone . . .
even in Bombay-Delhi.'

'Yes, he certainly knows everyone.' Anand saw that Vinayak was
looking at him quizzically. 'And of course, my first thought was to
talk to him, but the thing is, he deals with these high-profile types.
And someone was saying that it's better to keep these land trans-
actions low-key until everything comes through . . . What do you
think?'

'Oh, absolutely.' Vinayak was gratified to have his opinion solicited. 'Yeah, best to keep it low-key . . . And I know the perfect guy for you. I'll ask him to call you,' he said. 'He is very good. Very low-key.'

'Great,' said Anand. 'And listen, nothing too expensive, okay? We're a small company; making those damn monthly debt obligations is still a struggle . . .'

'Arrey, don't worry,' said Vinayak. 'He'll get the job done for you.'

Anand nodded and then stifled a groan when he saw who approached their table. He should have anticipated this, for where Vinayak roamed, could the rat he rode on be far behind?

'Vinayak,' he said urgently. 'Don't discuss any of this with anyone. Not my expansion, and not the land thing. Anyone.'

Vinayak's eyes gleamed with the wet pleasure of secrecy. 'Of course not, yaar,' he said. 'I don't believe in gossip. Hey, Sameer!'

'Bastard,' said the new arrival, placing a sweaty hand on Vinayak, 'what's all this ghaas-poos veg shit, yaar? Where's my chicken? Hi, Anand.'

Sameer Reddy was the dumb son of a smart father, whose growing mining empire and political contacts were sufficient cause for Vinayak – who never did things without an implicit calculation – to claim a friendship with him and act as his social sponsor. 'Cute chicks here tonight,' Sameer said. 'Damn hot babes.'

The pale granite glitter of the bar was ice-cold, yet the heat and noise rushed at Anand; he was submerged, drowning, the sound of music so loud he could feel the drum beat in his chest, crowding his heart. Faces passed flushed with a strange, pulsing fervor, the men inexplicably abandoning their calm morning demeanors for spangled shirts and gel-spiked hair and restless, roving eyes; the women in tight skirts and painful shoes and bright, exclaiming smiles. A cocktail of races, European, African, East Asian, percolated and distilled into this lounge bar by the virulent forces of inter-national mercantilism.

'Hey, buddy, how are ya?' A blond man emerged from the crowd, red-faced, an arm draped around a pretty girl.

'Hi, Brian,' Vinayak said: 'He's with Cisco . . .' he explained to Anand and Sameer. 'A good guy. From California, I think. But did you see who he was with? Dilip Bannerjee's daughter. I wonder if the parents know she's hanging out with phirangs. But they are quite liberal themselves, her parents, so they probably won't mind.'

'She's hot.' Sameer Reddy eyed the young woman's elegant legs, accentuated by her short dress and high heels.

'I have to go,' said Anand.

'No, no,' said Vinayak. 'Stay, bugger. Have another beer.'

Anand acquiesced reluctantly. Vinayak was doing him a favor; he would stay.

Sameer Reddy was nodding his head at a trio of Japanese busi-nessmen. 'They are going to kick our arses. Those guys.'

'What?' said Anand. 'Who? The Japanese?'

'The Chinese. They are going to kick our arses to Mongolia and back. There's no way we can compete with them. In manu-facturing or anything else.'

'I hope you are wrong,' said Anand.

'I am not wrong, yaar. This is what my father thinks. And do you know why they will succeed? I'll tell you. No democracy. They can do whatever they want. They don't have to worry about elections and how to win votes. If they have to defend the country, they do it. If they have to build a new road, they just do it, without running around asking each and every villager what to do before they take a single decision.'

'That's a good point,' said Vinayak. 'Though, I have to say, your father, Sameer, is an expert at getting around this system.'

'Yeah, he keeps those government guys happy. They look after

us well. And they should. I mean, we taxpayers are the true unpro-
tected minority in this country. Right, guys, right?' Sameer Reddy
laughed heavily.

Anand struggled for diplomacy and failed. 'A really privileged
minority,' he said, pushing his glasses up. 'And, secondly, of course
we can manufacture things as well as the Chinese do. And as
cheaply. We're doing it already. And we'll get better. We have no
choice. And, thirdly, bugger, if there was no democracy in India,
you know where we'd all be sitting?'

'Where?'

'At the gates of the American Embassy, squealing to get in.'

He said good night abruptly, too annoyed to stay longer.

Sameer Reddy was an idiot, an incompetent behenchuth who
couldn't fuck his own sister without assistance. Like so many people,
he tended to confuse democracy with the problems of bad governance – that endemic, virulent disease that made working in India
akin to racing a car in low gear: a sense of strain and impending
doom.

His mind went to the foreign team who had visited the
factory . . . What must they have thought? Would they confuse
the apathy of poor governance with the quality of Indian people
themselves? Or were they able to see through the noise and the
dust to the will of the people and their desire for better circum-
stance? Why did it have to be like this? Why couldn't government
be a support? To build what they build well, to maintain it, to
work hard, to think sensibly. To ask of themselves, in short, what
the citizens asked of each other. Inviting visitors to the country
was like bringing friends to a home where alcoholic parents
rampaged out of control. One could apologize once or twice for
the inconvenience rendered, but, beyond that, simply bury one's
face in one's hands in embarrassment.

★   ★   ★

The phone on his table buzzed the following day.

One landbroker, Kamath said, had arrived. Did Anand want to see him? The austerity in Kamath's voice suggested otherwise.

The Landbroker walked in, and Anand could immediately comprehend Mr Kamath's disapproval. A bright red polyester shirt molded his lean torso, gold chains rested on a hairy, partially exposed chest, sunglasses (tinted gold) sat on his hair, a luxuriant mustache above his mouth. The Landbroker was like a peacock amidst the sober plumage of the factory employees. Through the open door, Anand could see others stopped in their tracks, staring curiously after this apparition, Mrs Padmavati craning her neck for a better look.

Without even stepping outside, Anand knew that the Landbroker's car would be big and expensive and flashy.

'Namaskara,' said Anand, after a pause. 'Bani, bani.'

'Aanh,' said the Landbroker. 'Namaskara.'

He did not sit down when Anand offered him a chair. He spent a few moments wandering around the office, inspecting the furnishings, staring at the files on the table, coming to a halt before the production bay window. He leaned one hand against the glass, staring intently at the workers, at the lines of machinery, absorbed in an intense process of internal computation and evaluation, as a callused, yellow-nailed toe in a black Bata sandal scratched the back of his calf through the shiny gray material of his pant. The Landbroker radiated a restlessness that carried the scent of him over to Anand, a musk of sweat and sun and some deep, fervent desire.

Within moments, all sense of amusement had vanished from Anand.

The Landbroker looked like a first-rate thug; Anand felt annoyed at his blatant, unshadowed assessment of the factory. He should have refused to see him; he should have met him outside; he should have thought of some other alternative; Vinayak was a buggered-up idiot and Anand a bigger one for listening to him. This man was startlingly different from normal real estate agents, who inhabited nice offices and accompanied their sales of city properties with a line of upbeat, cheerful patter. The Landbroker did not spring from such a pleasant-faced, well-regulated mercantile landscape. He seemed the embodiment of a more primitive commercial force, like a tiger in the wild, rare and thrilling to encounter but admittedly not without its risks.

Anand felt like a cow left tethered in the middle of the jungle.

He cleared his throat. The Landbroker turned away from the window and eased himself into a chair. He placed an ankle on the opposite knee and then proceeded to scratch it absentmindedly with the nail of his left little finger, which, unlike his other bitten-to-the-quick nails, was long and luxuriant and painted a bright red. As he talked, the red nail moved to his ear, to explore the interiors and extricate what wax it could.

'Aanh, saar,' the Landbroker said. 'So you need land, it seems.' His Kannada bore the rough edges of street-speak.

'For the factory,' said Anand. 'We have fully expanded here.'

'Yes, I saw, I saw.' The Landbroker's assessment was now concentrated on Anand. 'So how is it you know Mr Vinayak? Joint business with him?'

'No,' said Anand, wrenching his gaze away from the long red fingernail. 'He is a friend. You have done work for him, isn't it?'

'Yes, a little,' said the Landbroker. 'Some twenty acres in Bangalore and then again some land in Hubli. I have contacts there as well. He has told you about that?'

Vinayak hadn't, but Anand nodded anyway. 'He is a good person, a good businessperson,' said the Landbroker, 'so when he mentioned about you, I knew it would be no problem. In my line of work, it is very important to work only with people who are of good quality, who will deal straight. No tricks, no games, no crooks.'

'Yes,' said Anand.

'So, how much land are you looking for, saar? And how soon?'

'About ten acres would be perfect. As close to this factory as possible. And the need is urgent.'

The Landbroker sank into brief thought. 'I will show you two plots this morning,' he said. 'Come, saar.'

They took the Landbroker's car; contrary to Anand's expectations, it was small and nondescript.

'What are the payment terms as such?' asked Anand.

'We will discuss everything, saar, the rates, the payment terms,' said the Landbroker. 'But first we will find something that you like. Then we will discuss everything else.'

He drove quickly and efficiently, speaking brusquely into his cellphone, the car juddering over ill-finished roads that led into the interiors of the land. A few minutes' drive brought them to the first plot.

It was surrounded by a high concrete wall, with power cables running into the property and a bore well sunk in one corner. 'This is about four acres. It is officially converted to industrial land – therefore more expensive.'

Anand stood at the entrance for not more than a minute; the convenience of such a plot was rendered irrelevant by its size – four acres was too small.

The second plot was larger. It was unfenced; Anand tracked the land visually from the side of the road to the distant tree and again to the hillock and back to the road.

'This is about six acres. This is farmland, so it is slightly cheaper. But you will have to pay to get government sanction to convert it to industrial land . . . It is very good soil, saar.' The Landbroker could not seem to help saying this even though he knew Anand's interests were not agricultural, 'and the water table is not too deep.'

It emerged that he was a son of the soil, this very soil, having his roots in a village of the area and, if the condition of his feet was any indication, not even one generation removed from the farmers he was now seeking to do business with.

'How large, you said?' Anand asked, 'Six acres, no?' and he turned away, shaking his head, dissatisfied. A waste of time.

In the car, the Landbroker spoke airily of other deals he had put together and the other investors he had worked with. He kept his left hand on the gear stick, his little finger extended, the long red nail almost scratching at Anand's leg, such an affront, Anand was tempted to reach over and break it off.

If Anand spent the drive back to the factory sunk in annoyance, the Landbroker seemed to spend it arriving at some conclusions of his own.

'Saar,' he said. 'Maybe I can find you a slightly larger spread . . . It will take a few days. You let me work it out.'

'Larger?' said Anand. 'How much larger?'

'About twelve acres,' said the Landbroker.

'That would also work,' said Anand. 'Is it possible?'

'Possible, saar,' said the Landbroker. 'It is little more complicated. But you leave it to me. It will happen.'

'Complicated how?' said Anand.

'You leave it to me,' said the Landbroker. He gave Anand a sudden, startling smile. 'Not to worry, sir. When I am making a promise, I am keeping it.'

Anand got out at the entrance to the factory and waited until the Landbroker bumped away in his little, nondescript car. He called Vinayak. 'Nice shirt he wears, your Landbroker.'

'Come on, yaar, what are you, the fucking fashion police? He's really good.'

'Yeah? He took me to two useless plots and then said that he would find what I required.'

'Congratulations. That means he has decided to work with you.'

Anand went silent, digesting this. 'By the way, what does he mean when he says something is "complicated"?'

'You leave it to him. He has to put together these deals. It's not like there is just one seller and one buyer. Each two-, three-acre plot of farmland will be owned by several people, usually many members of a family. He has to contact all the individual owners of each plot and convince them to sell and put the deal together. Like creating a land bank. It's not easy or straightforward.'

'He keeps talking about work he has done with that politician . . . that film actor . . . I don't want any political goondas or land-mafia types getting involved in this . . .'

'Are you crazy?' said Vinayak. 'Who does? No, bugger, don't worry. He'll steer clear of all of that. He's very good. Very discreet. Not one to talk. Very low-key.'

He then proceeded to contradict himself by describing a progression of prominent politicians and film stars and businessmen who had bought properties through this Landbroker. Sensing Anand's growing dismay, he laughed. 'Don't worry, bugger. He's very discreet. He'll do your job for you. And he's an expert at handling those corrupt bastards at the land registrar's office. He has them eating out of his hand. But don't worry, he'll see that they don't overcharge you on the bribes. He's very pragmatic.'

Anand was used to thinking of himself as pragmatic – which, for him, translated into doing what one can with what is in front of one. To Vinayak, however, being pragmatic seemed to mean living easily and comfortably in a world of official corruption, wasting no energy on the matter beyond recognizing how to survive it. Anand wondered, uncomfortably, if their respective positions were separated by nothing more than a slippery slope.

'And his prices?'

'Are reasonable . . . I would still negotiate, but if he holds firm, pay him what he asks. And he will ask for cash up front – that's okay. He will need that money to put the deal together. To make advance payments and keep everyone happy.'

'What happens if he can't?'

'Don't worry – he hasn't failed yet.'

Eight

When Shanta's loan request was repeated and again refused, she sulked for a day and then vanished, without notice, in the middle of a working morning. The first Kamala learned of this was when she was interrupted while flicking her dusting cloth over the upholstered armchairs in the drawing room. 'Has your hearing failed?' Vidya-ma's voice was sharp with annoyance. 'Did you not hear me calling for her?'

'Amma?' said Kamala, confused.

'Shanta! Where is she? Don't just stand there. Go and see where she is!'

Kamala went to the kitchen to do her mistress's bidding, and then to the backyard, to the small bathroom they all shared, and then, in mounting surprise and still clutching her dusting cloth in her hand, up the side path to the front gate. 'Anna,' she asked the watchman, 'the mistress is looking for Shanta?'

'I saw her leave,' said the watchman, 'ten minutes, thirty minutes ago. No, I have no idea where.'

'What? What nonsense!' said Vidya-ma. 'What do you mean, she has left? Where to? Why did you not tell me she was leaving? How irresponsible!'

'I did not know, amma,' said Kamala. 'She did not tell me.'

Thangam, when questioned, also denied knowledge of Shanta's whereabouts. And when minutes passed and Shanta did not return, as Vidya-ma's anger escalated, Kamala resumed her own work with a pious sense of satisfaction. After the way Shanta behaved, like some all-knowing supervisor appointed by the gods themselves to supervise lesser mortals, it was a sound moral victory to see her get into such trouble. And for dereliction of duty, no less.

Vidya-ma's displeasure, increasingly audible through muttered comments that trailed after Thangam and Kamala, frothed over like boiling rice water when the doorbell rang and, no, it was not Shanta but her own friend, come for lunch.

'Kavika!' they heard her say in English, 'I'm so sorry . . . my cook has vanished – the wretched cow – and I don't know what to do . . . I'm so sorry, everything's chaotic!'

'Hey, no problem, yaar,' Vidya-ma's friend said, 'we can order something in . . . unless you'd prefer me to leave? We can do this another day . . .'

'No, no, no, no,' said Vidya-ma, visibly decompressing like a pressure cooker relieved of steam. 'Yes, of course, it is no big deal . . . Right, we'll order in. You don't mind?'

'Of course not,' said her friend. 'And, Vidya! I can't thank you enough for the clothes you sent over. My daughter will love them, they're perfect for her.'

'Hey, no problem at all.' Vidya-ma's smile transformed her face. 'I saw them when I was shopping for Valmika and Pingu and thought they might work.'

'You're a sweetheart,' said her friend, sitting on a ledge in the kitchen, quite at her ease, her long, jean-clad legs swinging. 'Now, what should we get for lunch? How many of us are there?'

'Two of us. The children are at school, Anand's at work,' said Vidya-ma.

'And your staff,' said Vidya-ma's friend. She smiled at Kamala and asked in Kannada. 'How many are you?'

Kamala darted a nervous look at Vidya-ma and kept silent. Thangam answered: 'We are three of us, ma, including Shanta.'

'Great.' Vidya-ma's friend proceeded to order food for five people. 'Hey, do you remember how crazy we were for hariyali chicken kebabs when we were kids?'

'Especially you. You were a pig. You'd eat half the plate before the rest of us got a chance.'

'I was, wasn't I? Well, watch out at lunch!'

Kamala stared after them, her mouth already watering.

But neither Vidya-ma nor her friend ate with great appetite; the dishes placed before them were sampled but not properly eaten by any means. They plucked at their rotis, leaving them half shredded upon their plates, the friend eating the long carrot sticks that Thangam had sliced and placed upon a plate, Vidya-ma herself talking so fast, her English speeding by at incomprehensible speed; she seemed to have forgotten the main business of the table.

Thangam did not seem surprised. 'She likes to complain to this one,' she muttered.

Kamala was impressed. 'Do you understand all that they are saying?'

'Certainly,' said Thangam, with some scorn. 'Do you not? . . . She is complaining about Anand-saar.'

'That can't be,' said Kamala. 'Truly? Why?'

Anand-saar seemed to shield his wife from hardship, besides being a devoted father to his children. Did Vidya-ma not see this as a blessing? Perhaps he had some secret vice?

'No, no . . . nothing like that . . .' said Thangam, listening closely at Kamala's urging. 'He is not sympathetic to her wishes, he does not comprehend something . . .'

'Comprehend what?'

'I have no idea,' said Thangam, losing interest. 'Tell me, who can comprehend her wishes?'

Kamala peeped at Vidya-ma's friend when she went in with a hot roti, heated on the tava to a crisp, oily perfection. She was nice but surely as odd-looking as Vidya-ma was pretty: too thin, her gray hair cropped short like that of the old watchman at the front gate.

Later, over an expansive lunch of leftovers – chicken kebabs and North Indian–style curries rich with ground masalas and nut butters and cream – Kamala, seated luxuriously right where she wanted to, speculated lazily on Shanta's whereabouts. 'So strange of her to vanish like this . . .'

'She must have gone to see that husband of hers,' said Thangam.

'I did not know she is married! She has never said . . .'

Shanta had never been forthcoming on any topic, right from the start. Quite the contrary. Witness her first and only statement when Kamala, on her first day of work, paused thankfully in her labors to accept a glass of hot tea and a slice of white bread in the kitchen. Thangam settled down on the floor, and Kamala went to join her – innocent, one might say, of any wrongdoing – only to be stopped by a brusque 'Not there. Do not sit there. That is my place.'

Kamala was startled at such unceremonious ways but quick-tongued in her own defense. 'Why?' she said to Shanta. 'Does your noble father own this entire floor?'

Shanta ignored the provocative comment; Thangam pulled Kamala to another side of the floor to drink her tea and talk of other things, urging her, later, simply to ignore Shanta, adding: 'That is her nature. She is like that with everybody.'

Kamala soon discovered this to be true; Shanta extended her incivility to the world with great impartiality. When Vidya-ma entered the kitchen to make a third alteration to the dinner menu, Shanta abruptly said, 'No. I cannot do that.'

'Why not?' said Vidya-ma. 'Why do you say that?'

'Where is the time to prepare akki-rotis,' said Shanta. She turned her back on her mistress and began to wash dishes in the sink, noisily banging steel plates against vessels.

Vidya-ma's face flushed. 'Of course there is time.'

'No,' said Shanta and increased her banging.

Judging by Vidya-ma's expression, her next words, Kamala felt sure, would be 'pack up your things and instantly go.' Instead, her new mistress just glared at Shanta and left the kitchen, leaving a trail of angry words in her wake. '. . . so unhelpful. Why I put up with it, I don't know . . .'

Kamala didn't either – and had to wait until lunchtime to have that question answered. For Shanta Ruthie Ebenezer's qualities were an unfortunate stew: of a miserly temper, a sharp tongue, an unforgiving mind, a capacity for small meannesses – and an unfair, semidivine ability to cook like a dream. Her Sunday prayers at the Roman Catholic church did not serve to sweeten her soul; instead, the Goddess Mary gifted her with swiftness of hand, so she could slice her way through entire trays of vegetables, reducing them to shreds and slivers in minutes; strength of muscle, so her arms could tirelessly stir the gravies on the stove and grind the raw, soaked rice and lentils into smooth batters in the old stone grinder that was cemented into the floor; and a litany of incantations that converted the spices that lay in everyone's kitchen into magical tools of alchemy. A simple chunk of gingerroot, in Shanta's hands, tugged at the senses in ways that one could never imagine possible.

If she were in a good mood, the meal she laid before them was elaborate and generous, sometimes exceeding the food she served to the family at the dining table. This was rare. But even if her mood was so sour that she could not bring herself to feed the other servants with anything other than a large vat of rice and another of lightly spiced sambar, it was still sambar so flavorful that it gently teased the mouth before settling delightfully in the stomach.

One day, during that first week, there was a stack of parathas next to the rice. Kamala took two and stopped in amazement after the first bite. She had never eaten a paratha like this before, with magical layers of spice and flavor and tenderness that Shanta's harsh qualities could not possibly have been capable of producing. Kamala ate a second piece – and immediately thought of her son. How he would enjoy this . . . She eyed the rotis on her plate. Perhaps she could take them home with her at the end of the day? What difference did it make if she ate them now or later?

She pushed them to one side of her plate, contenting herself with rice, waiting until everyone else had finished before rolling them up. She was about to stuff them into her bag when a firm hand gripped her wrist.

'Put that back. I am not cooking for every grubby street brat whose mother is too lazy to cook for her own child.'

Kamala felt herself tremble in rage and embarrassment, her fingers dropping the rotis. The silent malevolence of Shanta's gaze made it clear that she would take great pleasure in thwarting Kamala.

They had existed in a state of uneasy quick-to-fire truculence ever since then, Kamala's passages through the kitchen marked by Shanta's comments and her own rebuttals. There was no question of a pleasant exchange of personal information.

'Yes, she is married, but naturally, as the second wife, she does not speak freely about it.' Thangam seemed to know all the details. 'It is not the sort of thing one can speak of with pride, is it? The truth of the matter is he spends most of his time with the first wife – Shanta sees him only when he requires money.'

'Has she children?'

'One, but there were two,' said Thangam. 'Both young men in their twenties. The elder died three years ago in a road accident.

He was walking home in the rains – you remember those bad floods? – and he fell into an open manhole in the road. The government promised Shanta twenty thousand rupees as reparation and gave her twelve – which her husband immediately took from her . . .'

'And the other?'

'Oh, he is in every way his father's son. He does no work; he spends his life as an alcoholic and runs after his mother, like an unweaned baby, for food, for money, for whatever she can give.'

'Poor thing,' said Kamala. 'That is trouble indeed . . .'

'Yes,' said Thangam, 'but tell me, sister, who does not have troubles? The rest of us manage to smile occasionally, do we not?'

Kamala, at her ease in the kitchen for the first time, said, 'It would be nice – would it not? – if she would stay away a few days . . . Then we could feast like this every day . . .'

'Akka, which film have you been watching?' said Thangam, with some asperity. 'We would eat like this only if Vidya-ma's friend also lived here. Such leftovers wouldn't come our way normally. They would be put into the fridge – and you would be resigned to eating whatever rubbish I make. Here,' she said, picking up a few kebabs, 'put these in a dabba . . . take them home when you leave.'

'Are you certain? Would you not like them for yourself?' Kamala said for ceremony's sake, before delightedly packing them away. Narayan would savor them with his evening meal.

Vidya-ma and her friend went out in the afternoon. Thangam vanished upstairs to clean the master bedroom, and Kamala finished washing the lunch dishes. The kitchen was still imbued with quiet and peace. The dhobi-man had returned the children's clothes freshly ironed; she carried them upstairs to place inside their respective cupboards.

When she returned, she saw a shadow in the kitchen – and

knew that Shanta was back. Urgent curiosity warred with the superior urge to slice through the cook's pretensions.

'So, sister,' Kamala called out, very much on her dignity, 'who is it, then, who goes out to enjoy herself and leaves the work to others?'

Shanta was standing over the sink, her back to Kamala. She did not turn around, and Kamala, annoyed at being ignored in her moment of triumph, went up to her, repeating: Who is it then who leaves the work to others?

Oh, sister, she said. Oh.

The side of Shanta's face was bruised; angry marks, as though drawn by a crazed lipstick, slithered down her skin to vanish behind her saree pallu and reemerge on her arm. She leaned against the sink, her arms and legs trembling. She would not look at Kamala; she would not ask for help, but Kamala was not deterred; she gently held her, bearing the weight of the beaten woman upon her own body. At Shanta's usual place against the wall, Kamala helped her sit, crooning to her, nonsense words as she might to a child. 'Sit, sister, sit,' she murmured. 'You are safe now, safe. All will be well.'

She soaked a cloth in cool water and touched it gently to Shanta's bruises, loosening her blouse and tracking the passage of the husband's hand down her body. He had held her by her hair, pulling some out in the process, slapped her, fattening her eye, and left the impress of his fingers on her skin as an enduring gift.

Kamala rooted about inside her woven plastic bag for a moment. 'Here,' she said to Shanta, pulling out a Crocin tablet, white in its blue wrapping. 'Take this, it will ease the pain.'

Shanta sipped at the hot, sweet tea from the steel tumbler that Kamala soon held to her lips, wiping tears that flowed from a swollen eye. 'He needed money,' she said. 'I gave him all I had, but that was not enough.' She swallowed the pill and closed her eyes, her head lolling against the wall. Her hand, holding tight to Kamala's, would not let go.

Thangam dropped her bucket and brooms in a noisy clatter when she saw the scene in the kitchen. 'Oh, that sinner!' she said. 'That rakshasa-spawn!'

At that moment, the front doorbell pealed. 'That must be Vidya-ma! Quick,' said Thangam. 'Hurry yourself, Kamala sister; you answer the door and I will help Shanta into the back room; Vidya-ma must not see this . . .'

Kamala pushed the brooms that Thangam had dropped to one side and hastened to the door. Vidya-ma looked displeased. 'What is the meaning of this delay?' she said. 'I wondered if my entire household had vanished along with Shanta.'

Kamala was relieved to hear Thangam's voice behind her. 'She has returned, amma.'

'Oh, is it? Well, where is she? . . . Resting? Why is that? First, she takes a holiday without permission, then . . . what, is this a dharamshala?'

'She has had an accident, ma,' said Thangam. 'On the road . . . She meant to absent herself for just ten minutes to purchase some medicine, then met with an accident. A scooter banged into her, she fainted, went to the hospital, and now she is back.'

'Let her rest, then,' said Vidya-ma. 'You will have to cook until she is better, Thangam . . . though hopefully she will be well enough to cook for the guests on Wednesday evening. But why should she go anywhere without permission?'

Thangam and Kamala maintained a prudent silence.

The harsh blue morning sky was curtained by evening with cooling gray clouds, ponderous and heavy, timing their guttered waterfall for the precise moment when Kamala was to walk home. She dithered reluctantly for a few minutes before venturing forth, a large plastic shopping bag cut open on one side and placed over her head. She would be soaked through, but after such a day she was desperate to return to her own home.

The rain embraced her as she stepped out, fat drops slapping against the plastic on her head and clinging to her saree at her hips. Kamala concentrated on where she placed her feet; the clouds had eliminated twilight, plunging the world straight into the dark of night, barely illumined by the weak light of the distant street-lamp, and she did not want to slip on the broken pavements, their jagged edges angled, waiting, treacherous.

A shadow moved next to her. There stood Narayan, holding an umbrella proudly. 'I thought you might be returning home now.' He placed a protective arm about his mother's shoulders, holding the umbrella over her head.

'Where did you get this, child?' she asked, amazed. 'To waste money on such a thing!'

'It was available cheap, Mother. At that corner shop,' he said. 'It folds up and you may carry it every day in your bag . . . Have you heard the latest news? You will never guess!'

She would have kissed him if he was but a little younger; she contented herself with listening to his chatter, relishing the warmth of the arm that held her close.

'What news? Tell me. I cannot guess. Very well then . . . Did that Ganesha trip over a stone and break his leg? . . . No? Perhaps the landlord's wife has delivered twins . . . No? Well then?'

'That Chikkagangamma who lives opposite has been captured by a ghost!' Narayan nodded at his mother. 'Do not look so dis-believing − she was seized by the ghost in the middle of the night − her own children told me so!'

'What, those two little fools? They are seven and eight years old, what do they know of ghosts?' Chikkagangamma was a shiftless woman who combined an inability to hold jobs with certain morally dubious proclivities that Kamala would not consider discussing with her son.

'In the middle of the night, the ghost entered her body; she began to scream and vomit and act very strange . . . Their uncle came in the morning and whisked her away, while you were at work. He told them that he would be taking her to a temple so that the priest could say the right prayers to drive the ghost away!'

This astonishing story was later confirmed around the neighborhood – and just when Kamala began to ponder the possibilities of the vengeful ghost, freed by prayer from Chikkagangamma's brain, searching for a new soul to possess and lighting on Kamala or her son – the landlord's mother disabused her of her notions.

'Ghost!' the old lady said. 'Nonsense! Is that the story they are spreading? That foolish woman – you know her bad habits – could not squeeze the money she wanted out of the latest fellow she is consorting with, so she attempted to drown her sorrows in an unseemly amount of alcohol. She merely had a drunken fit in the middle of the night. That is all.'

'The priest?'

'There is no priest. Her brother has taken her away to prevent her from drinking more. He has left those children in the care of the corner tiffin canteen – they are to sleep there and earn their keep by doing the washing.'

It was a sad story of neglectful motherhood, but Kamala's primary emotion was one of relief that there was no ghost wandering about, looking for an unwary home. Just to be on the safe side, she added an extra fervor to her usual evening pooja, praying for the well-being of her son and for her job and the security it provided.

If, in the interstices of a disturbed night, Kamala had harbored any notions that the relationship between her and Shanta might forever change, that Shanta might repay her concern with kindness of her own, if she had envisioned the two of them holding hands and skipping along like beloved friends in a movie, Vidya-ma's kitchen transformed in a magical instant into a field of frothy, frolicsome flowers, such notions were short-lived. When Kamala reported for work the following morning, she was startled to see the cook not resting in recovery but hard at work in the kitchen, slicing vegetables, a slight stiffness in her movements, a swollen eye the only visible manifestations of her troubles of the previous day. Rama-rama, sister, Kamala almost exclaimed. Should you not be resting? Is this wise?

Shanta looked up and frowned. 'You're late,' she said, her manner not a whit less brusque that usual. 'Vidya-ma was asking for you.'

Kamala said nothing, collecting her buckets and brooms and stalking upstairs.

Nine

'Isn't this nice? So fresh . . . Come on, yaar. Stop yawning and
stretch . . .'

At six-thirty, Cubbon Park was suffused with the fresh pink of
early morning, the red buildings and green trees glowing; the smattering of early morning exercisers looking determined. Like Anand,
Valmika was in sweatpants and T-shirt. Father and daughter set off
together on a slow trot into the depths of the park, past the walkers
and clumps of yoga-contortionists on the grass, occasionally being
overtaken by more serious runners.

It was years since Anand had been running; his wife didn't question his sudden commitment to fitness; Valmika (with a stern eye
on her slim waistline) agreed to join him, and Pingu's pre-bedtime
enthusiasm did not survive the night. 'Lazy bum,' Valmika now
huffed with the austere censoriousness of an older sibling. 'We
should have forced him to come, Appa. He's getting unfit.'

'Next time,' said Anand. His muscles, long unused, were already
aching; he was surprised at the strain; his naturally slender physique
concealed the sly weakening of the years, the slithering depreda-
tions of approaching middle age. He saw the ease with which his
daughter kept up with him and suddenly determined to do this
more often, to build up his stamina, to run ten miles with ease, to

compete in marathons, to discover, in short, the elixir of immortal youth and enchantment, right here, in Cubbon Park. Moisture coated his face, dripped down his neck into his T-shirt, a relic of a recent family holiday, soaking the image of palm trees and waves forming the word PHUKET.

'So how come Cubbon Park?' his daughter asked, when they slowed to a walk. 'We could have gone running around Sankey Tank; that's closer to home.'

'This is green and nice, no?' said Anand.

Valmika glanced slyly at him. 'You know who we might meet here? Someone who lives rather close by . . . Guess who.'

Anand focused on his breathing and wiped his forehead with the edge of his T-shirt.

'Thatha! He comes here . . . on his "morning constitutional."' Valmika did a surprisingly good imitation of Harry Chinappa's intonation, and Anand tried not to laugh. 'Hey now, don't,' he said. 'Be respectful . . . He's gone to Coorg, actually,' he said, in spite of himself.

'He's going to take us there soon,' said Valmika. 'He promised. He is planning to breed one of his dogs – and he's convinced Mama to let us have a puppy. Pingu and I get first choice. Won't that be great?'

'Yeah, great. What kind of dog?'

'Yellow Labrador. Fanta . . . Do you remember her? She must have been a puppy herself the last time you came . . .'

Anand didn't remember. Though the children loved traveling there with their maternal grandparents, his own visits to his in-laws' property in Coorg were few and far between.

'A dog should be good fun,' he said, 'we can—' Valmika interrupted him with 'Oh, look! There's Kavika-aunty.'

She waved and ran over. Kavika was walking across the grass toward them, holding on to the leash of an aging cocker spaniel.

Like them, she was in T-shirt and sweatpants. She was not alone
with her dog; she was accompanied by her little four-year-old
daughter. Anand watched her laughing and talking with Valmika,
who was kneeling and fussing over the dog. The child hung back
a little, perhaps rendered shy by this beaming teenage energy.

He walked over slowly. His heart rate had still not recovered
from his running; he could do little more than nod and smile
when she looked in his direction. The child peeped at him from
behind her mother's leg, and he found himself instantly relaxing.
The responsive twinkle in his eye drew her out; soon she was
exchanging confidences, showing him the bruise she had acquired
the day before in her grandmother's garden. Her skin was two
shades lighter than her mother's, just like her hair and eyes; these
were the only hints of her putative foreign paternity; in the rest
of her, her direct glance, the spark of her intelligence, her laughter,
it seemed he could detect the graces of her mother.

'Come, Valmika,' he said eventually. 'We should complete our
run.' His daughter pulled away reluctantly; he turned away more
slowly still, watching them walk away at the dawdling pace of
young child and aging dog.

He and Valmika completed their circle around the park, jogging
back to their car past the red High Court buildings, the stretched
residence of a short British past and vainglorious Vidhana Soudha,
full of aggrandized aspirations.

'We should do this every week, Appa,' his daughter said, her face
aglow with heat and endorphins. 'Isn't Kavika-aunty cool?' she said.
He smiled but did not answer.

His calf muscles were already tightening and painful by the time
he reached his office, but he forgot them when he looked at his
emails. There, number five from the top on a long list of incoming
messages, was the mail they had been waiting for. He read and

read again: Cauvery Auto had made the short list; the Japanese parent car company would very much like to take things further in a series of future meetings.

He immediately forwarded the email to Ananthamurthy and Mrs Padmavati; they arrived in his office minutes later, their happiness written across their faces.

'It is because of our prayers,' Ananthamurthy said, 'and also the level of preparation we put into the meeting.'

'Can it be that they are looking nowhere else?' Mrs Padmavati asked. 'That they have already decided upon us?'

'No, no,' said Anand, decidedly. 'There is a short list. We cannot count our blessings, yet.'

'They are like chickens, is it not?' said Ananthamurthy, and after a short, baffled pause, Anand agreed with him. Blessings were indeed like chickens.

'Did you read the second half of the email?' he asked them, for this is what had caught his attention. They were asked to provide clarifications of a detailed nature: in case they were selected, would Cauvery Auto be ready with the resources necessary to handle the expansion?

'Yes, sir,' said Mrs Padmavati. 'We need to make a list . . . From a financial point of view, we need to speak to the bankers to extend the loan facility.'

'We need more land, sir. From a production standpoint,' said Ananthamurthy. 'We cannot proceed otherwise. Even if bank funding comes through.'

'Right,' said Anand.

In the early years of his working life, meetings with bankers were frequently combustible affairs, where need and dignity were in opposition; Anand had to convince skeptical bankers of both his desperation and his worthiness at one go, a humiliating process with variable outcomes. But he had been meticulous about his loan repayments, and he hoped that such scruples had earned him a measure of goodwill.

He decided to take Mrs Padmavati with him to the meetings, to reinforce his organizational capability in front of the bankers; it would also be a good proving ground for her. Both of them spent the rest of the day preparing for the meeting, calculating their future requirements: for purchase of the land, for equipment, for new buildings, for new employees. Mrs Padmavati was conscientious and conservative in her estimates, which pleased Anand, for despite their steady growth, Cauvery Auto was not flush; every expense still needed to be carefully planned for. Hopefully this Japanese deal would give them a much-needed financial fillip; filling the company coffers and allowing employees to take home nice fat bonuses.

At the bankers' offices the following afternoon, Anand once again wore his jacket but with no tie. Mrs Padmavati sat next to him, besilked and earnest. He spoke of their work with conviction, needing no reference to the papers in front of him to recall figures and details. Occasionally Mrs Padmavati provided concise answers to certain questions. Their nervousness seemed unfounded. They were received with a smile; the bankers were receptive and, gratifyingly, seemed to see Anand as a man of promise and reliability; they finally said, with an ease that left Anand feeling light-headed, that they would back Cauvery Auto to the extent required, no problem at all; they were very pleased with the company's performance – words he wished to record just for the pleasure of replaying them later to himself and to everyone at work.

But the bankers were regrettably firm on one point: any loan they provided would have to be backed by Anand's personal guarantee. If his company defaulted, the bank would seize his personal assets. Anand agreed, his mind going to his house, already mortgaged, and the other asset he owned: a small flat in Mysore that his parents lived in. If Cauvery Auto ever defaulted on its loan repayments, he stood to lose everything. He could see that the seriousness of such a guarantee was not lost on Mrs Padmavati.

'We will succeed, sir,' she told him as they stepped outside the bank doors, with a queer gravitas that touched him deeply. 'We will not fail.'

Orchestrating the other requirement was less straightforward.

Land.

He called the Landbroker, who picked up the phone after five interminable rings.

'Yenu ri,' Anand said, forcing himself to sound casual. 'What, any progress?'

'What, saar?' said the Landbroker, sounding vague and distracted. 'Aanh, yes. Yes, saar?'

'Are you ready to show me something?'

'Ila, saar, not yet. You be patient . . .'

Anand thought about the long red fingernail of the Landbroker and frowned. His promises seemed like passing shadows in a dream, things of no substance whatsoever. As was his wont at moments of strain, Anand cursed multilingually: fuck, thikka munchko, behenchuth. 'Not to worry, saar,' said the Landbroker, with il-legitimate confidence, the fucker. 'One day, two days, not more.'

Anand telephoned Vinayak. 'Listen,' Anand said, 'that Land-broker . . .'

'Arrey, give him time,' said Vinayak. 'Putting together these land deals is really complicated; it needs a good guy – and takes time. If you hurry, you'll end up with some fucked-up piece of land that six other people also think they own and you'll get tied up in the courts for years. You give him time . . .'

Time, like money, was something Anand could not afford to be generous about. Over the past few weeks, he had busily investigated other land-buying options: the businesswoman, for instance, who used her contacts in political circles to put together vast swaths of land for software companies was reputedly reasonable and efficient in her approach, but, alas, seemed to work exclusively in the Whitefield area, at the opposite end of a vast city; or, another option, the government-developed properties, also too far from his current factory and not always reliable in their deliverability. What he would have appreciated was an industrial land website: simple, logical, and transparent. Instead what he faced was very different: however much he might not like to, he was going to have to speak to Harry Chinappa.

In doing so, he was going to have to violate his own precept of never combining work with his personal life, and do so, more-over, with someone with whom mutual dislike was tempered only by familial association.

He quietened his distaste: surely Cauvery Auto was worth it?

He had missed a call from him the previous night and received two messages via his wife.

'Ah,' said Harry Chinappa, when Anand returned the phone call. 'Anand. How nice to finally hear from you. I thought, from the lack of response, that you had perhaps lost interest.'

'No, no, of course not,' said Anand. He forced his voice to sound cheerful. 'How are you?'

Harry Chinappa did not waste time in pleasantries. 'So, did you get my message? I told Vidya. I have arranged the meeting for tomorrow afternoon. Come over this evening to my house. I will brief you. Don't be late,' he said, and disconnected.

Vidya, predictably, was aware of all the details about his planned meeting with her father. To this day, he knew, she talked with her parents several times a day, discussing family matters with her mother and matters of social importance with her father – unquestionably a better child to her parents than he was to his.

Now she said, 'Daddy wants you to wear a white shirt for tomorrow's meeting. With a jacket and no tie. And a nice shirt for tonight as well.'

'Why tonight?' Anand asked, puzzled. She was pouring tea: served as she liked it, English-style, with hot tea in a tea-cozy-covered pot, milk, and a bowl of sugar lumps. 'Pingu! Sweetie, no,' she said, stopping her son from grabbing a second sugar lump. 'All your teeth will fall out . . . Because,' she said to Anand, handing him a cup, 'they are having a few guests over. But Daddy says to come over anyway; he wants to finish the discussion with you. Ey, it's so nice of him, no? To help you like this. He's so busy . . .'

Yes, said Anand. It is very nice of him.

The Chinappa house was at the end of a warren of lanes off Richmond Road. It had been built in the seventies, along with a few other houses in a plot subdivided from the remains of a large colonial bungalow and – as though to apologize for the lack of taste and heritage inherent in such a proceeding – the cement-roofed, mosaic-floored house was relentlessly stuffed with memorabilia of times past.

Years before, Anand, beguiled and lulled by his college sweetheart's modesty in describing her home as small and cramped, 'nothing compared to the old bungalow,' had accompanied her to her home and stared in amazement at the chintz-covered sofas, the heavy rosewood furniture, the windows swathed in heavy curtains, the lavish precision of the manicured lawn. Anand, awed, had thought it looked like something out of a magazine. He had wondered, abashed, what she would say when she saw his own childhood home in Mysore.

He had grown up in Lakshmipuram, not in one of the lovely

old bungalows of that neighborhood but in the alleyways behind, in a tiny two-room house that was in its entirety smaller than his current living room. His parents had subsisted on the modest salary that his father made as a senior government clerk, refusing to augment it either by bribery or by better wages in the private sector. They seemed to think that the security provided by a nondismissible government job and a clear conscience were entirely sufficient to live upon – a state of contentment that provided Anand with little consolation, especially when watching classmates scatter after school to their own large homes.

Vidya's Mysore connections were of a very different nature. Harry Chinappa's family had been dignitaries in the old Mysore maharaja's court; the walls of their home were littered with fading sepia photographs of dead Chinappas with visiting members of the Nehru family, old hunting guns, and eviscerated, plaque-mounted skulls of animals killed in erstwhile times when such pleasures were legal.

The house had not changed much since his first visit. He could hear a piano being played; he did not recognize the song. He had his cellphone pressed against his ear, trying to complete a conversation with a rascally supplier, and walked straight into a chorus of singing voices that drowned the conversation on the phone. 'What? Hello?' he shouted and drew the suddenly silent attention of many astonished eyes.

Ruby Chinappa levered herself out of an overstuffed armchair and came surging toward him, breaking like a sturdy, determined wave about his ankles. He was short; she was shorter still and terrifyingly wide. 'Anand!' she said. 'Put away that silly phone; so busy all the time . . . Come and enjoy the music! We are having such a nice sing-song.'

He hesitated and was lost, swept in her wake into the paralyzing throng; he would complete his phone call later. He recognized in some of the guests the fixtures of his in-laws' social life: fossils from the club and relics of the city's old homes; as far as he knew, the patrons of the newer apartment buildings were never welcome in his father-in-law's house unless he knew their parents and approved of their antecedents – or unless their successes earned for themselves a mention in the newspapers.

Harry Chinappa was as tall as his wife was short, towering over Anand; the hospitable smile on his face tightened as he beheld his son-in-law. 'Ah, Anand, come in, come in . . . You're late,' he said, bringing his voice down.

Anand felt himself flush. 'I had some meetings with the bank,' he said.

'Anand's work is going very well,' announced Ruby Chinappa in some haste, and Anand felt the chill of polite attention settle upon him.

'Oh, yes!' said Colonel Krishnaiah. 'Vidya was telling me the other day. Factory full of orders, is it? How nice. Well done.'

'Vidya seems so proud of your successes,' he heard someone else say.

'Yes, yes,' said Ruby Chinappa. 'We all are.'

'Ruby! The chip bowls appear empty,' said Harry Chinappa. 'I have to keep reminding you. Really,' he announced, 'if one wants anything done well in this household, one is almost forced to do it oneself . . . Now, if you will all excuse me for a few minutes.' He waited until a flushed Ruby Chinappa hurried in with freshly topped chip bowls before sweeping Anand before him into a little side alcove lined with books, a desk, and uncomfortable wooden chairs that could never be criticized because they were older than all the humans in the house.

Anand settled himself into a chair, feeling the knots of wood press into his back. If the object of highest veneration in the Chinappa household was the piano, the books in this alcove came a close second. Anand had not closely encountered the first before his marriage and had never displayed any affinity for his father-in-law's library of books by dead English writers with names like P. G. Wodehouse and H. H. Munro; all this apparently served to put him even further beyond the pale of Harry Chinappa's approval.

Harish 'Harry' Chinappa was a proud man – who had made one incalculable mistake in his life – selling most of his vast Coorg coffee plantation when land prices, and coffee prices, were at their lowest. He sold and, having sold, was destined to spend the remainder of his existence watching land prices rise and recalculating his putative net worth had-he-but-not-sold. His son-in-law's small successes might be a source of comfort to his wife; he himself appeared to reserve judgment.

Harry Chinappa sat down at the table. 'The meeting tomorrow,' he said, 'is with Mr Sankleshwar.' In the brief silence that followed, he seemed to sense Anand's surprise and hesitation and said: 'Are you having any success in sourcing the land?'

'Yes,' said Anand. 'That is to say, I have spoken to a landbroker of Vinayak's. My friend, Vinayak Agarwal? But nothing has yet come through. They said these things take time.'

'Vinayak Agarwal?' said Harry Chinappa. 'That young fellow? He has no concept of these things . . . Why should it take time? What utter nonsense. No, don't bother with him. My boy, when someone says something will "take time," it either means that they don't have the resources to do the job or that there is some other unknown complication.' Harry Chinappa seemed to gain confidence as he assessed the effects of his words on Anand. 'Now, about Sankleshwar. It is a big opportunity. I think I do not need to spell that out for you. Really, you are very lucky to be invited to his office. I know people who wait weeks and months just to see him, in fact, just the other day, who was saying? . . . I forget who, someone was saying that they have waited now to meet him for two and a half months . . . You are very lucky. Very lucky indeed. But, as you know, I begrudge no effort if it will benefit you youngsters.'

'Okay,' said Anand.

Harry Chinappa waited for him to say more and then sighed. 'It might be best,' he said, 'if you were to allow me to handle it. At least initially. It would not do to say the wrong thing at the wrong time. I'm sure I needn't remind you to be anything less than respectful to Mr Sankleshwar. Such an important man. Really, you are quite lucky. But follow my lead in tomorrow's meeting and we should be okay. Let me see, we need about twenty acres for the factory . . .'

'Ten,' said Anand. 'Ten acres.'

'Yes. That is what I thought. Ten would be about right. Or perhaps twenty . . . Very good! . . . And of course I will absolutely ask for no special favors from Mr Sankleshwar. In fact, I will insist that we pay a fair and reasonable price for the land. Not only must one be fair in one's business dealings, one must also appear to be fair. At least, I like to think so.' Harry Chinappa moved a few objects absent-mindedly about his desk; his gaze encountered Anand; he continued with some effort: 'Very good! . . . Two o' clock, tomorrow afternoon; you can pick me up and we can drive out to his office together. Excellent! . . . Oh, and I hear,' he said, with that slight softened change of tone that came about whenever he spoke of his grand-children, 'that Valmika is doing well in her studies. That's wonderful! Vidya should see that the children spend more time out-of-doors. In fact, we should consider banning them from using things like computers . . . I have said the same thing to Vivek in an email,' he said, as though Vidya's brother in America were not alcoholic, divorced, and immeasurably distant from both his parents and his children.

'They should exercise,' said Anand. 'But I don't think banning computers is the answer.'

'I am not surprised to hear you say so. Vidya tells me,' said his father-in-law, 'that you are rather addicted to your gadgets . . . I am thinking of taking the children with me to Coorg next weekend. They can jump about in the fresh air . . .'

'Yes, they'd like that,' said Anand.

'Well, time for me to rejoin my guests. Come, come. Don't just sit here, come and have a drink.'

Harry Chinappa swept out of the alcove, leaving Anand mulling over the conversation, several aspects of it slowly falling into place. For weeks now, his father-in-law had enlivened family gatherings with his planned foray into the world of real estate development: an old family property that he had decided to develop into a shopping mall in collaboration with this Sankleshwar, Harry Chinappa's contribution to the venture consisting of the property itself and, no doubt, a supply of unsolicited advice. His interest in Anand was not entirely altruistic; orchestrating the purchase of several acres would add to his business credentials – which, as far as Anand knew, were otherwise nonexistent. Harry Chinappa had kept occupied his entire life by busying himself in other people's business.

But Sankleshwar was a well-known name in real estate; if he had a reputation for slightly dubious deals (which Harry Chinappa liked to gloss over), he was also a property developer of stratospheric proportions; it was very probable that he would be able to help Anand find the land he needed – that was the rice in the midst of all the husk of Harry Chinappa's words, and Anand forced himself to concentrate on that.

He trailed out of the alcove to find his father-in-law installed behind the carved rosewood bar, where he was once again dispensing drinks in his best plantation manner. 'Ah, Anand! I thought we'd lost you to the lure of fine literature . . .' Harry Chinappa laughed at his own joke. 'What will you have to drink, my boy? A beer to wash away the factory soot?'

'A beer will be fine,' Anand said. 'Or a whiskey.'

'Ruby!' said his father-in-law. 'Ask the boy to get another beer from the kitchen. And more ice, Ruby, for goodness' sake! Quickly, please. Mrs Nayantara?' he said. 'Another sherry for you?'

Mrs Nayantara Iyer shook her head, but the Colonel at the piano raised his glass for another whiskey.

'Ah,' said Harry Chinappa, in a pleased way. 'I have here a single malt that I think you will enjoy. One of my collection,' he said, 'that I save for special guests.' Anand knew that single malt; he had bought it himself (on his wife's suggestion) the last time he'd passed through the Singapore duty-free as a ritual sacrifice on the altar of family relations.

'Actually,' said Anand, 'I think I'll have a whiskey too.'

To be honest, he was not that fond of whiskey; the strength of it tested his tongue and blurred the edges of his resistance after a single sip. He saw an empty chair next to Mrs Nayantara Iyer and, on an impulse, made his way over. He sat down and wondered what to say, feeling foolish. He could not ask after her daughter; he did not know how to phrase the question in a casual way. Instead, he said: 'Aunty, I saw your granddaughter in the park when I was out running with my daughter. Very sweet child.'

He saw by the smile on her face that he had said the right thing. She reciprocated by asking after his own children; this was a topic he could converse on easily.

Kavika's mother lived next door in an old stone bungalow set in a large property; she had been a prominent High Court judge in her day. Years before, on the occasion of their wedding, Ruby Chinappa had introduced her: 'And this is our great and famous judge, Nayantara Iyer, our next-door neighbor and our dear friend.' Anand, newly married, virgin shy, awkward, had barely touched her extended hand and said: 'Oh, yes, madam. I have read your articles in the newspaper.'

The judge had smiled kindly at Anand and the nervousness within him had quieted, but Ruby Chinappa had quickly swept him away, to introduce him, in appalled fashion, to the people she thought of as her most important connections, not so much to propagate his interests as to impress upon him the heights into which he had married. She had had no intention of letting him talk to anyone, hurrying him from guest to guest before depositing him next to his parents in the far corner of the room, where they were sitting in their own distressed fashion, staring at the other guests across a wide chasm: they were provincial, traditional; caste still mattered and Chinappa social connections did not; they, as much as the Chinappas, could not approve of their son's ill-considered liaison. The Chinappas had proceeded to ignore Anand and his parents while they fussed over the rest of their guests; Anand and Vidya sat silent under the weight of general disgrace.

Now Ruby was tugging at his arm. 'Come and sing,' she said. 'You must sing. Colonel Krishnaiah is at the piano, as usual, and he can play anything you want.'

No, no, said Anand, embarrassed.

The piano started up again; everyone else seemed to know the songs and the mysterious source from which they sprang; they added their voices to the chorus, weighing it down and letting the music sink around the soft, encroaching chintz sofas. Mrs Mascarenhas, another neighbor, now opened her mouth: 'I could have danced all night,' she sang. And still have begged for more.

It was a ludicrous assumption; she was fatter than his mother-in-law; she couldn't have danced for two minutes at a stretch. Was he the only person here to catch the fucking irony of this? Apparently so. Mrs Mascarenhas's efforts were greeted with applause.

Harry Chinappa maneuvered his way to the front of the piano. 'Elvis!' said Mrs Mascarenhas. '"Blue Suede Shoes"! Or "Hello, Dolly!"'

Harry Chinappa smiled. 'I will, later,' he said. 'But you have inspired me . . .' He signaled for silence from the piano and, instead of singing, began to recite what sounded like dialogue from a play or movie: 'Look at her,' he said, 'a pris'ner of the gutters.' His gaze seemed directed at Anand, who felt himself flush.

A few years before, the old buzzard took the freedom of speech offered by his fourth glass of whiskey to lean across the dining table one evening and say confidentially: 'My dear fellow, of course you may have some, but – you won't mind me saying this – one doesn't quite pronounce the word in that way. No table in it, you know.' And when Anand had looked bewildered, his father-in-law had been happy to oblige: 'It's "*veg*-t-bil,"' he said, with a kind smile. 'Not "vegie-table." Oh, and one other thing: it's "there," not "they-are." And your daughter likes to play with "*Don*-ild" Duck, not "Don-*ald*" Duck.' In the face of his father-in-law's happiness, Anand had sat still and silent. Vidya had quickly passed him a roti, Ruby Chinappa had quickly chattered about curtains, and the moment had passed – straight into his stomach, where it lay for quite a while, leaking acid.

Now, once again, his father-in-law's finger seemed to be pointing at Anand; Look at him, he seemed to say, that creature of the gutters, Harry Chinappa's words flying, spittle-flecked, vomitous, straight at his son-in-law: 'He should be taken out and hung, for the cold-blooded murder of the English tongue.'

Loud, shattering applause greeted his words; the piano struck up again; voices rose in song; Anand looked around, bewildered.

'They have demolished the old Pinto house, those developer chappies,' said Colonel Krishnaiah, refilling his whiskey glass. 'Rascals. Really, forgive me, but that was a beautiful old home. Much like yours, Mrs Nayantara,' he said, raising a glass to Mrs Nayantara Iyer.

'So awful,' sighed Ruby Chinappa, 'to think of having another apartment building going up close by.'

'In our time,' said Colonel Krishnaiah, 'we preferred gardens and fresh air to the smell of concrete. But that was Old Bangalore . . . nowadays, money is more important.'

Anand could not understand what the fuss was all about. Yes, gardens were lovely – but a city that did not build was a city that had stopped growing and the idea of such stasis was appalling, abhorrent to his very being. He voiced none of these thoughts, noting that his father-in-law too was relatively reticent on a normally favorite topic. 'A garden,' said Harry Chinappa in some abstraction, 'is a lovesome thing, God wot!' A mall built with Sankleshwar presumably even more so.

'They spoke to me as well,' said Mrs Nayantara Iyer. 'Those construction people. Twice.'

'Dear, dear,' said Harry Chinappa. 'If they should turn trouble-some, please let me speak to them on your behalf, Mrs Nayantara. I know just what to say to them. One needs to take a firm hand. In fact, I will give them a call tomorrow.'

'No, that's all right. Thank you. I'll attend to it myself.'

Anand wished he could refuse Harry Chinappa's offer of involvement with the same ease that Mrs Nayantara displayed. It behooved him to be grateful: he did so by wishing that with any luck the construction company in question would approach the development of the Pinto property as a cost-cutting, tightfisted venture and put up a vast apartment complex of tiny-tiny apartments, all of them with their service balconies built facing his father-in-law's home, so that each morning Harry Chinappa could wake up to the sight of a hundred drying bras and chuddies, fluttering like banners in the early morning breeze.

Furthermore, Anand would, in future, take to emphasizing, particularly, the *table* in *vegetable*. And why not? He had recently read an article about how English had become a true Indian language; that from being the language of the colonizers, it was now colonized in turn; Indianized; used in ways new and original and made in India, mixing and settling with the 550 other Indian languages; that, far from languishing amid its imported Victorian roots, it (like the ancient country it now inhabited) had turned inexplicably young and vigorous. Anand would play his role. He was part of the loyal, proud, nationalistic mainstream; the language would serve him, rather than he serving the language.

His mother-in-law called her guests in to dinner, doubtless the same menu of pork and chicken and baked cauliflower that Ruby Chinappa had served with due veneration, like prasadam after a pooja, at every dinner he could ever remember, and Anand treated this as his signal to exit.

He could hear the television in the upstairs living room, tuned to a show favored by his wife and daughter. They would be settled next to each other on the couch, Vidya and Valmika, giggling and gasping over the unreal, unpleasant drama about rich teenagers and their parents in New York; Pingu dozing with his head on his mother's lap. Anand walked slowly up the stairs, the exhaustion of the day settling on him with every step. He did not join them as he normally might; Vidya would subject him to a detailed catechism that he could not yet face.

His bedroom was gifted with a momentary peace, rich in solitude, gilded in silence, the silk of lamplight captured against the warm colors of the bedspread. He locked the bathroom door and stripped, glancing at himself in the full-length mirror. He was lean, which was good, and short, which was not; his height a victim, he had always felt, of the spartan vegetarian diet he'd had growing up.

The session with Harry Chinappa had created unnatural bands of tension in his neck muscles, which welcomed the soothing fall of hot water in the shower. His right hand reached for his penis; he tugged at it briskly, catching the eventual release of semen in his cupped left hand and depositing it tidily in the drain, watching it flush away with the shower water. He was always fastidious about this, ensuring no glutinous streak left accidentally on walls or floor to be discovered later by a disconcerted wife or maid.

What is a wife?

In the simplest sense, the mother of your children.

In the grand Indian sense: the purveyor of domestic comfort; the chief priestess of patriarchy; the legislator of harmony and peace; the weaver who knots the extended family together; the Diwali firecracker who creates a sense of celebration in the home; the keeper of spirituality and a reminder of earthly goodness; the creator of future life and the guardian of the ancient ways; a partner in earthly pleasure; the feet-presser and old-age comforter to his parents; the role model for his sisters, and the object of secretive devotion of his brothers and friends.

In a more modern sense, as per the women's magazines Vidya left around in the bathroom: all of the above, but let's add to that, girls, the secrets of looking hip and sexy; of working a job that sounds glamorous (but that doesn't take time away from the home and hearth); of adding that touch of panache to your hostessing and home interiors; and the art, for god's sake, of giving your husband a decent blow job.

Anand had seen Vidya on the second day of college at St Peter's Academy. He watched her walk across the campus to her classroom; later, he watched her leave through the college gates.

If, at that stage, he had paused to examine the qualities he looked for in a wife, the list would have been short and very simple: someone with whom to share sex, some laughs, some music, some dreams. Instead, he found himself fascinated by Vidya and charmed by her evident reciprocal interest in him. There she was, beautiful, vivacious, with her precise convent accent, westernized, her father a member of the best clubs – and she had leaned toward Anand as a sunflower to the morning sun. This had completely captivated him.

If the list of Anand's transgressions against his father's wishes was long, Vidya's solitary moment of rebellion had occurred in her marrying Anand, an act of filial disobedience that was quickly buried beneath the birth of the children, two intervening miscarriages and Harry Chinappa's defiant public face of scandal-averting acceptance.

Eventually, the origins of such an association became lost in the mists of time and youthful passions. In fifteen years of marriage Anand had still not summoned up the courage to request a blow job and indeed, at this late stage of things, could not imagine ever doing so. As for the rest, he had never thought to quarrel with Vidya's choices or the pressured influences of her parents, quelling his moments of marital rebellion in the interests of domestic peace. Now they were just who they were, destined, it seemed, to continue as such until the end of time, when they would merge into one peculiar and badly-constructed unit, as his parents had done and hers. What remained vivid between them were the children; Vidya was a good mother, and whatever their own incompatibility, Anand never let himself forget that.

Ten

Like some grand official in a government bank, Thangam carefully counted the money that Kamala's slatternly neighbor handed over. Kamala, seated next to her on the courtyard stoop, was mesmerized; she washed her evening rice absentmindedly, swirling the grains repeatedly through the water, all her attention on the two women.

Thangam tucked the money into a handbag that had once belonged to Vidya-ma (cast away when the strap broke, rescued and repaired by Thangam), opened her accounts book, and entered a number neatly. The names were written in English, the numbers next to them stretching across the page.

'Okay,' said Thangam, 'that is settled. Next month, don't be late.'

'I won't, sister,' said Kamala's neighbor before vanishing into her room, her normal impudence quite subdued by Thangam's efficiency.

'So by next month this chit fund will be finished.' Thangam put her book aside, relaxing her official manner. 'And I will have made ten thousand rupees profit.' She caught Kamala's stare. 'You should come in for the next one, akka.'

'Oh, you are going to run one more?'

'Of course. I am very good at this.' This was no idle boast; respectable people in the neighborhood trusted their money to

Thangam, for, unlike Kamala, she was a ninth-class-pass with all the accompanying skills of being literate and able to do mathematical problems and, though a full eight years younger than Kamala herself, apparently privy to expertise in complicated financial matters. This was the third chit fund that Thangam had started and brought to a successful conclusion.

'I have never participated in one . . .' Kamala understood the mechanics of a chit fund: a small group of people agreed to pay a certain amount each month into a common pool maintained by the person running the chit. Every month, one member of the chit fund got a chance to collect the entire pool. It was all well in theory; it forced a savings habit, and the ability to have a large lump sum available for emergencies was useful – but Kamala could not bring herself to trust anyone else with her hard-saved money. Her preferred method of savings was to collect money in an old envelope at the bottom of a locked steel trunk.

'It is very useful. You should join. And this time,' said Thangam, 'I plan to expand it. Thirty people, two thousand rupees from each of them. A total monthly chit of sixty thousand rupees. Imagine that, Kamala-akka!'

'You also pay this monthly amount? Two thousand rupees?'

Thangam smiled in satisfaction. 'No, I do not. Because I am taking the responsibility of running it, I have to pay only half of what everyone else pays each month. That is where my profit comes from. For a chit of sixty thousand, my end profit is thirty thousand. Imagine that!'

Kamala could not. For all her savings over the years, she had barely managed to accumulate ten thousand rupees.

'And you know something else I do? Sometimes people don't withdraw the full amount. Then I put what remains in a bank account – and the bank pays me interest. Five percent! And so I make even more.'

Kamala knew that banks were fabled to dispense such charity, but she could not conceive of actually daring to enter one.

'Thange, people don't mind that you have to pay only half?'

'Of course not!' said Thangam. 'After all, if someone defaults on their monthly payment, I have to make good to the fund on their behalf, do I not? It is a great responsibility. But people have confidence in me – and quite rightly. I do a good job! You must join,' she said.

For a fleeting moment, Kamala contemplated the joy of having sixty thousand rupees to draw upon, before reality intruded. 'I cannot afford the monthly payment, Thangam,' she said. 'After all my expenses, very little is left. Perhaps if in the future you run a smaller chit, I can join.'

She ran her fingers through the water and the rice, quite forgetting to strain it out. 'Will these two join your new chit fund, do you think?' She signaled her neighbors' room with a jerk of her chin.

'Yes, of course,' said Thangam. 'He is working as a machine tool operator, a good, steady income. That little she-goat does nothing, of course . . .'

'Does Shanta join?' Kamala asked.

Thangam slapped her forehead with her fingers. 'Ayo! She did once or twice. But this last time, she has never had any money to put into it . . . You know her situation . . .'

In the contemplative silence that fell between them, Thangam said: 'Even last time he beat her . . . but not so bad . . .'

Kamala clicked her tongue. However much one might dislike Shanta, this was not a fate to be wished on any woman. For how can one break away from husbands, unless they die? And who outside the family could help? Inconceivable to parade one's family affairs – the whole world would laugh at such shameful behavior.

'Do not worry,' she told Thangam consolingly, 'not all husbands are like that . . .'

'I am not worried, akka. I am not sure I wish to get married.' Thangam extended her foot and gazed at her toes, painted a bright, shiny pink. 'I like to keep control of my money – and answer to no man.'

'What do your parents say?' Kamala was unable to hide her shock.

'What are they to say? I pay all their bills, do I not? I tell you, they may scold, but they are truly happier if I do not ask to get married . . . Tell me, sister, was your marriage such a great pleasure?'

'Of course, I was happy,' said Kamala automatically, but this was a routine, polite response. She watched Thangam search in her handbag, pulling out a small bottle of cream salve and rubbing it into a patch of dry skin at her wrist. Kamala squinted; surely this was the same bottle she had seen on Vidya-ma's dressing table? Thangam saw her glance and smiled, not without a certain pride. 'See?' she said. 'This is mine. I am able to buy it. You think I could if I were married? No, I would be working and he would be spending my earnings . . . Here,' she said, reaching for Kamala's arm and rubbing a bit of the lotion into the skin. 'How soft it makes the skin. Feel it, akka! Feel how soft . . .'

Thangam put her lotion bottle and accounts book away in her bag and stood up. 'I had better go back quickly before Vidya-ma misses me and starts shouting . . . No, no coffee, thanks, akka. I will depart and return,' she said in farewell, leaving Kamala to rinse out her long-soaking rice, the starch having leached the rice water to a paleness, using her fingers as a loose strain to prevent the escape of rice grains before refilling the steel utensil with clean water for a quick second rinse.

She might not wish to participate, but there was no denying that Thangam's chit fund business was indirectly responsible for Kamala's job. That was how they had met. Kamala had been seated, just as she was now, on her stoop after a long, unsuccessful day of seeking a suitable employment. She had been without work for a few difficult weeks, and though she had managed to fund herself and her son, the resultant dip in her precious savings had awakened an old fear that lingered, weeks later. Her previous employer had decided to move to Hyderabad and had omitted to tell Kamala so until the very last day. 'No, not for a holiday,' she had been told. 'We are moving. The furniture and so on will be moved later, but the house will be locked up, so goodbye.' Kamala's subsequent comments had been addressed to a closed door and though she knew her hot-tempered mutterings were pointless, there had been little else to turn to for comfort.

Thangam had been visiting the courtyard to collect a payment. They had fallen into the casual conversation of new acquaintances, and Thangam had looked thoughtful when Kamala asked her if she knew of a job.

'Yes, I might,' Thangam said. 'In the house where I work . . . Look,' she said, 'give me a day or two to work it out and I will come back.'

Kamala had paid her no real attention; it sounded like the vague sort of thing that people say when they wish to be comforting.

But sure enough, two days later, Thangam reappeared. 'Come with me,' she said urgently. 'Right now. Make haste!'

Kamala had been waiting for Narayan to return from school, and he was already late. 'Can we not do this later? Or tomorrow morning?'

'Not if you want this job,' Thangam said, and Kamala, leaving word for her son, immediately followed her.

At Vidya-ma's house, Thangam slipped in through the back door with the stealth and secrecy of a mouse, taking Kamala with her. 'Wait here,' she said softly and went inside a room that Kamala later identified as Anand-saar's study.

Kamala edged closer to the door to listen to what was being said inside.

Thangam was saying: 'Saar, I have brought this woman. For the cleaning job.'

'Thangam,' said a man's voice. 'I think Vidya-ma has clearly said no.'

'Saar,' said Thangam. 'The work is really too much for one person. And I know this woman. She is a really good worker. I have known her since I was a child. And everyone likes her very much. Good-tempered and hardworking.'

There was a silence, and then the man spoke again. 'You really feel that the work here is too much for one maid?'

'Yes, saar,' said Thangam. 'Every night I am so tired I feel like I am falling sick, saar. Not able to eat also.'

Kamala, summoned into the room, stood quietly, trying to appear suitable, the ideal maidservant, under Anand-saar's silent inspection. But he simply said, 'Thangam, I must first speak to Vidya-ma.'

'Yes, saar,' said Thangam.

One day later, she poked her head through the courtyard door, bright-eyed with success, and said: 'As I promised, sister, as I promised! He has agreed. Come tomorrow morning by nine o'clock, and assuredly, do not be late!'

The following day, Kamala was subjected to an unhappy inspection by Vidya-ma. Her future employer was dressed in jeans and a pretty blouse, her long hair flowing, her lips and fingertips tinted pink, beautiful like a woman in a movie or magazine. Vidya-ma did not seem equally impressed by Kamala, glancing at her and saying to Anand-saar in what was apparently an ongoing discussion: 'I really don't know why we need her . . . that Thangam is really lazy . . . I don't want to become a charity house. Oh, okay, fine,' and addressing Kamala, 'You must do a really good job if you wish to retain this job.'

I will, amma, said Kamala.

'And you must be punctual. The other two stay here, but I don't want you to come late . . . What does your husband do?'

I have none, amma, said Kamala. I am a widow. I have just one son.

'How old? Twelve, is it? That is not so bad . . . Old enough . . . It will not matter so much if you have to stay late now and then.'

And though Kamala had begged to differ, she did not do so. Not then, and not later. She and Narayan needed this job.

If Narayan was surprised, the evening after Thangam's recent visit, by the odd quality of the oversoaked rice during dinner, Kamala brushed his comments aside to discuss matters of far greater moment. 'Tomorrow we are going to make that visit,' she said, answering the question on his face with a rising exasperation. 'Who do you suppose! How many people do you know who have won scholarships and work in Pune in fancy offices?'

The apples, four of them in a thin plastic bag, looked disappointing, yellow-streaked, red-spotted, and not, in balance, worthy of the money that had been spent on them. Kamala had hesitated a long while at the fruit store – for this purchase, she had avoided the cheaper fruit carts – eyes flitting between the boxes in the front, their pink paper covers peeled back to reveal the jeweled treasures within. These were the most expensive, many from foreign lands, the apples, in particular, of a matched glowing hue like manufactured plastic balls, reds, yellows, greens, extravagantly priced, a mere kilo of fruit costing an entire week's worth of vegetables.

Kamala had examined them with her eyes but made her final selection from the cheaper-but-still-expensive North Indian apples piled to one side in little pyramids, and now, back home, she inspected them dubiously.

'Supposing he does not like apples?' asked Narayan. Dodging

his mother's reflexive smack, he repeated: 'Supposing? Supposing he hates apples?'

'He will not hate them,' said Kamala. They were simply too expensive for anyone to dislike. 'Now, get ready.'

'Mother. I am ready,' Narayan said but with a certain futility. His mother grabbed him by the shoulder and proceeded to inspect him as she had not in years, sniffing at his breath, looking at his teeth, which, like hers, were strong and white and straight. She moistened her thumbs in her mouth and ran them quickly over his eyebrows before combing his hair herself, slicing a side part with military precision and slicking the oiled hair down on either side of it until it gleamed with a solid, metallic sheen, daring him with her stern gaze to touch it, even if his scalp itched.

She inspected him again when she was done and felt pleased. Unlike the apples, he made a very good impression. The dark blue polyester pants (slightly loose at the waist, true) and the full-sleeved, light blue cotton shirt with red patchwork looked very smart. She was glad that she had overridden Narayan's foolish desire to wear a T-shirt. 'I've seen Vyasa wear them, even Anand-saar,' he'd argued, appealing to his mother's weakness. But she had been firm. 'When you are as rich as them, then you can also afford to be negligent in your dress.' Which her employers were, indisputably: she was continually amazed by the careless dress of those children, wearing their favorite T-shirts until they developed holes and, last week, Valmika leaving the house in jeans ripped and torn through, fit for dustcloths and not the movie she was headed to.

Kamala glanced quickly at her own image in the mirror: she was dressed with neatness and propriety. She was going to ask for help, it was true, but did not at all wish to appear needy.

As they neared the bright pink building, its windows and sloping concrete roof highlighted in red trim, Kamala felt her breath catch. The shiny car was still parked outside, but there were ominous signs that it was being prepared for imminent departure: a suitcase, tied tight with tape, had been placed in the backseat. Kamala debated within herself and then decided that it was all right; if he was indeed on the verge of leaving, then she could claim that they had come to say goodbye, to wish him well on his long journey to distant Pune.

'Come, come, don't delay,' she said impatiently to Narayan as they climbed the stairs, even though he was following close behind. 'Here, you hold the apples. No,' she said, 'perhaps I had better carry them. Yes, that is better. Remember, be respectful now.'

The front entrance of the house had a string of gold foil swastikas interspersed with red om symbols strung over it, as if to say, yes, this is indeed a house blessed, a people blessed. The door swung open at her quiet knock, and Kamala was instantly comforted by her reception. She needn't have been so worried, so shy; she could have made this visit a long time ago.

'Kamala-akka! Come in, come in, sister,' said the engineer's mother.

The engineer's father said: 'You have brought your son; how big he has grown.'

They received the apples with a gratifying pleasure, and Kamala soon found herself seated, with a glass tumbler full of Coca-Cola in her hand, Narayan unusually quiet by her side, sipping from his own glass.

She stared about herself in wonder. In the course of her work she had been in homes far more lavish, but none that had affected her so personally – this home, with its mosaic floor and well-constructed aluminum windows with glass shutters and walls resplendent with paint and not whitewash. Furthermore, she was seated on an actual sofa, the back and sides protected by plastic lace antimacassars. There was a fat television on a stand against the wall. The windows, beautiful in themselves, with their glass and horizontal metal bars, were further dressed in curtains. There was a separate bedroom, the door to which was kept firmly closed. Through the kitchen door, she spied a fridge.

The engineers' parents did not seem to mind her intent staring. Perhaps they were used to it from their curious, awestruck visitors. Perhaps they even liked it; after all, the joy of good fortune surely increases with the admiration of others.

'Would you like to see the bathroom?' the engineer's mother said. 'There is a geyser for hot water.' Kamala followed her and praised all she saw.

'Your good son,' she finally said, after she and Narayan had returned to the sofa and their Coca-Cola. 'You must be very proud.'

The bedroom door opened and the engineer appeared, as though, like some eager-to-please, quick-gun-murugan of a deity, the very mention of his name was sufficient to produce a manifestation, though – if truth be told – he looked neither happy to see the visitors nor all that eager to please.

He was fresh from his bath, filling the air with the scent of hot soap and talcum powder and wearing, as Narayan was quick to note and lecture his mother on at length afterward, a T-shirt and jeans. He glanced at the visitors, glanced at his watch, and then glanced helplessly at his mother. 'If I do not leave soon,' he said, 'I will not even reach Mysore by nightfall.'

Next to her, Kamala felt Narayan stand up quickly and tug at her hand, treating this as a signal to leave immediately. Kamala too felt abashed at the engineer's words but held her place. She had not wasted money on four expensive apples just to see their new hot-water geyser.

The engineer's mother, prescient, and perhaps not immune to the maternal plea in Kamala's heart, stepped in to save the day: 'Yes, you must leave,' she said, 'but at least please thank Kamala-ma for the apples she has so kindly brought to sustain you on the long drive.'

The engineer looked ashamed and sat down on the edge of the chair opposite.

'I once went to Mysore,' said the engineer's father, agreeably. 'By bus. It was a long time ago.'

'Yes, and last week, we went to Tirupathi,' said his wife. 'To give thanks to Lord Venkateshwara.'

'We drove in the car,' said the engineer's father. 'After we came back, we went to the cinema to see that new multi-starrer. It was very good,' he said. 'Have you seen it?'

No, said Kamala.

Yes, said Narayan. Ignoring his mother's sidelong, questioning glance and belated annoyed comprehension – that he had seen it on his own time with that rascal Raghavan – he continued: 'It was very good.'

Kamala finished her cola to the last drop and decided to intervene. Such general talk about travels and cinema was no doubt important to fostering good relations, but she could see the engineer sipping his way impatiently through the tumbler of coffee his mother had placed in his hands. In a moment he would be done, and then he would be gone. She interrupted, cutting short the engineer's father's description, listened to raptly by Narayan, of the multiplex cinema hall they had seen the movie in, situated in one of those new, shiny shopping malls that Kamala had seen from the outside but had never entered.

'You have been very successful,' she said, directly to the engineer. 'We have all been so proud of you . . . I have been telling my son that he too must succeed as you have . . .' She glanced at Narayan and then at the engineer. 'He is too shy to ask you, but I promised him I would do it . . . What advice can you give for a young boy to become successful like you?' She skittered nervously to a halt, suddenly appalled at her own question. It was one thing to admire someone's achievement, another to reach greedily for it, with an unseemly covetous desire to possess it for oneself.

But the engineer did not seem offended. He drank his coffee and said, 'Aunty, I can say that three things are important to achieve what you are so kind as to call my success.

'Firstly, he must be smart and work very, very hard.'

'Oh,' said the engineer's mother, 'Kamala-ma's son looks very smart indeed. I can see it.'

'And he works hard,' said Kamala, ignoring her son's surprise.

'Good,' said the engineer. 'Then, in that case, aunty, you must create the right opportunity for him. That is the second thing.'

'What do you mean?' said Kamala.

'Is he attending a government school or a paid school?'

In the silence that settled, Kamala knew that the answer was visible to all. 'Government,' she said.

The engineer shook his head. 'That is no use, aunty. You have to change that. I went for a few years to that government school.' He glanced at his parents; they were nodding at the collective memory. 'There were no teachers half the time, . . . and the other half, the teachers would not teach us anything worthwhile . . . One teacher used to send his son to sit there instead of him . . .'

'Then you won that scholarship and could go to paid school,' said his mother. 'Some company gave it. For five children.'

'We were lucky,' said his father. 'Lucky to have heard of the scholarship and lucky that the headmaster of Sri Hindu Seva Private School liked this boy and decided to enroll him and help him with his studies to catch up.'

'And that is the third important thing, aunty,' said the engineer. 'Luck. Since our good government will not bother to look after us, we need some luck. And God's blessings.'

He placed his coffee tumbler on the side table and stood up. Kamala made haste to stand up herself. At the door, she turned to ask him: 'Son, you are happy now? All is well? I can see it is so with your parents, but with you?'

'As well as can be, aunty,' said the engineer. 'The work is hard. But I am happy to have it.'

'And,' his mother lowered her voice conspiratorially, 'he has given us permission to start looking . . .'

'Oh, that is indeed good news!' said Kamala. 'I have no doubt a great match will be found for your son. You will be blessed with a beautiful bride!'

On the way down, Narayan emerged from a thoughtful silence to say, with an unusual severity, 'I do not think he was happy to see us, Mother. He was eager for us to be gone. He thinks too much of himself.'

'Nonsense,' said Kamala. 'He was in a hurry, that is all. And he was so kind with his advice . . . I want you to write to him,' she said. 'A letter. I will get his address from his parents. Just to say thank you for his advice.' She did not mean to say more, but her desire escaped in spite of herself: 'Perhaps he can help you get a scholarship also. Maybe from that same company that gave his.'

Narayan nodded but without, she was forced to note, the awe, humility, and eagerness that she would have liked to see. 'Okay, Amma,' he said agreeably, for all the world as though he were doing her a favor instead of tempting her into rapping her knuckles on his head, before slipping into his usual flimflammery. 'But don't worry, if I do not get a scholarship, then I will go work in Dubai as a driver, or go work there in construction.'

Construction, said his mother.

Yes, said Narayan, 'you do not know of these things, Amma, but there is a lot of money to be made in construction . . . Raghavan was telling me that there are people who for a fee will get you jobs anywhere in the world . . .' Kamala listened with half an ear, her mind busy with her own thoughts. She was used to his rattling nonsense, absurd, fantastical tales of untold wealth in foreign countries like America, where even cleaning women like herself had microwaves and cars; garbage stories that so filled his brain with air until it seemed that his very feet floated three feet above the earth on which they stood.

In truth, the engineer's words had only served to deepen her unhappiness. The annual fees for a paid, privately run school were at least ten thousand rupees a year. Three months' salary. How could she afford that? It would deplete her nest egg in a year. And how would she pay the fees for the years that followed?

She spied the tiny Hanuman temple in the corner. 'Come,' she said and led her son to it. At least she could pray for luck, for divine interference.

Eleven

Mr Sankleshwar's offices were at the top of a tall glass building that swooped to the sky, an aerie overlooking the rumbling city and approached through a series of portals. His private reception room was brilliant with carved white marble. When they were ushered in, Anand expected Harry Chinappa to make an acerbic comment, but his father-in-law's demeanor seemed to have altered materially. He projected a broad, appreciative friendliness that embraced the entire room and its contents with warm approval; he appeared to have forgotten his usual strictures on the unabashed exhibition of new money.

Anand's discomforts were manifold. He had done some research into Sankleshwar; his real estate empire was undeniably respected, with glorious buildings and a raft of foreign investors, but difficult to ignore were the sly rumors: of legal chicanery and bribery and corrupt political collusion. Heated whispers about Sankleshwar's side interests in the liquor and film industries, and links thereby to the underworld, prostitution, and political thuggery. The gossip was probably exaggerated, but it was enough to make Anand nervous.

Additionally, this was the first time Anand had walked into a business negotiation with his father-in-law, and, already, it seemed like a bad idea.

Harry Chinappa glanced at the reception coffee table. 'Ah,' he said, 'the favored reading of the commercially minded. Would you prefer *Fortune* or *Forbes*? No? Perhaps the comic section of the newspaper? No, thank you,' he said to the receptionist, 'no coffee or tea for us.' Anand would have liked a glass of water but said nothing. When they were summoned into Mr Sankleshwar's office, Harry Chinappa signaled Anand to stay behind.

'It might be better if you wait outside for a bit while I have a quick word with him.'

'No,' said Anand. This was the sort of thing he had been afraid of. He was not going to let Harry Chinappa discuss Cauvery Auto without monitoring the conversation very closely.

Harry Chinappa seemed slightly nonplussed. 'I do have some other matters to discuss with him, you know.'

'That's okay,' said Anand. 'I don't mind.'

He followed closely on the older man's heels, as though Harry Chinappa might slip in and slam the door in his face.

The inner office was even larger than the waiting room. Mr Sankleshwar was a round, squat man remarkable only for his long sideburns, like a seventies movie actor unmindful of the passage of time and beauty.

'Anand, you know who this is, of course,' said Harry Chinappa. 'Mr Sankleshwar, as I explained, my son-in-law here is running a small factory.' He placed a fatherly hand on Anand's shoulder, adding, in careless, happy mendacity, 'which I helped him set up . . . One must do what one can for the younger generation, isn't it?'

'Yes, yes,' said Mr Sankleshwar. 'Very true, Harry.' Except he called him Hairy. 'I too am helping my sons and sons-in-law.'

'Anand wanted some land and came to me for advice – all the children do – and a good thing it is too . . . I wouldn't want him to get caught in any of the shady dealings that can happen in this industry. Inexperience is an easy victim, isn't it? Life has taught us certain things, Mr Sankleshwar, but Anand – well, I thought it best to bring him to see you.'

Anand let Harry Chinappa's words grate and slide over him. He was here for a reason and would not lose sight of it.

Mr Sankleshwar asked: 'How much do you want? Where?'

'Twenty acres,' said Harry Chinappa.

'Ten to fifteen,' said Anand.

'So fifteen acres,' said Mr Sankleshwar. 'In that area. So much of it already bought up and landmarked for projects – but I can manage something. If it is slightly larger? Smaller?'

'At least ten acres,' said Anand. 'Ten will do.'

'Are you speaking to anyone else in this matter?' said Sankleshwar.

'Oh, no,' said Harry Chinappa, before Anand could answer. 'I mean, Anand has talked to some other people and received, I must say, some extremely odd advice – I was forced to tell him that it just won't do. Much better if he deals directly with you.'

Mr Sankleshwar's gaze flicked between Anand and Harry Chinappa. 'Let me see what I can do. I will put my men on this. Payments,' he said, 'will have to be entirely by check. I do not believe in handling cash or unaccounted-money.'

'Oh, yes,' said Harry Chinappa. 'Of course. Of course. Absolutely.'

Once again Mr Sankleshwar's eyes darted to Anand's face and back. 'I will organize this for you, Hairy. If you are serious about it, that is. I would not wish to waste my time.'

'Oh, yes,' said Harry Chinappa. 'Oh, yes indeed.'

'Well, I will first have to see the details of the land before deciding,' said Anand.

Harry Chinappa smiled. 'Anand,' he said, 'I think Mr Sankleshwar would be aware of that.'

The Landbroker called him early on Saturday morning, and Anand immediately felt better about having met with Sankleshwar.

'Saar,' said the fool. 'There is this nice site, close to you. Seven acres. We'll go and see?'

'No,' said Anand, exercising extreme patience. 'Ten to fifteen acres is what I need. Ten to fifteen.'

'Okay, saar,' said the Landbroker, 'you don't worry, tension maad beda, I will organize.'

Anand disconnected without replying. 'While we are waiting to hear from the Landbroker,' he told Mr Ananthamurthy, 'I am also speaking to Mr Sankleshwar. Yes, I know. It is very good. My father-in-law is helping me with this. There is some personal contacts there.'

'Oh, very good, that is a good backup, sir,' said Mrs Padmavati when he spoke to her in turn. 'Mr Sankleshwar may be a little more expensive, but that Landbroker fellow looks not very reliable, sir.'

His wife was going to be busy with some friend's art gallery opening; Anand planned to spend the day with his children. He pushed thoughts of work aside and drove to MTR to pick up a parcel of masala dosas, dripping with ghee and spices; the children adored them.

'So, what?' he asked them, after breakfast was done.

'Cricket!' said his son, as he usually did. 'Oh, god,' said Valmika. She had given in to her father's pleading; she would spend the morning at home and join her own friends for a movie in the afternoon. 'Let's have a picnic instead?' she said now.

'Both,' Anand said. 'Why not both?'

The rectangular lawn was small and smooth and surrounded by flower beds, not ideal for weekend games of cricket, but Anand and Vyasa never let that discourage them.

'I want to be on your team, Appa,' said Pingu.

'And what about Valmika? She can't be on a team by herself.'

An argument was averted when the side gate creaked and a small figure slipped through. Pingu saw him first. 'Yay! He's here! Narayan, come! I'll be on your team.'

The game was geared to the enjoyment of his son; yet Anand relished the heft of the ball and bat in his hands. He had been an all-rounder in school; he still followed the national team with due fervor and opinion. He would never say it out loud, but the true pleasure of these weekend matches for him was to play against Narayan. Kamala's son had a real understanding of the game and was old enough to play well, placing his ball with accuracy whether bowling or batting. The boy seemed to appreciate this as well; he was gentle and amused when playing with Vyasa, but there was a spark in his eyes waiting to bat against Anand's bowling that wasn't there otherwise.

'Get it, Narayan!' Vyasa said.

'Good catch!' said Anand, pleased in spite of himself. The boy had lifted himself into the air and caught the ball off Valmika's bat very neatly.

'Hah! Nice game!' When they had played for an hour and a half, and the game had descended into sweat and arguments, Anand flung the bat down and collapsed with the children onto the grass. 'Here,' he said, handing a glass to Narayan, 'have something to drink.' He himself drank thirstily from the glass of Pepsi that Kamala had brought out on a tray and wiped the moisture from his forehead. The children were already holding out their glasses for more. Narayan quickly drank his Pepsi, refused a refill, gathered the bat, wickets, and ball, and carried them to the back of the house, where his mother would put them away and set him to some cleaning job in the backyard.

Valmika took charge and turned her father and brother in to the house for a half hour, with strict instructions for them to stay put until she called them out. When she did, Anand was charmed to see that, with a mysterious efficiency, his daughter had organized their lunch into an alfresco picnic under the shade of the neighbor's rain tree. She had spread a coir mat and laid out dishes and plates and cold drinks.

'Arrey,' said Anand, 'why are we eating out on the grass when there is such a nice dining room inside?'

'Appa, please,' said Valmika. 'How can it be a picnic otherwise?'

He smiled at her. 'And does it have to be a picnic?'

'It does,' both children clamored. 'You know it does.'

'You're right,' he said and settled himself on the grass, the children ranged about him, opening another can of a cold, aerated drink, feeling the sugar swell the sense of well-being within him. As they ate, he competed with them in telling silly jokes. Two peanuts were walking down the street and one was a salted. What did the fish say to the greedy prawn? You're so shellfish. And their favorite: about the man who had an abscess in his bottom and whose breaking wind sounded like a Japanese car manufacturer, for an abscess makes the fart go Honda.

After a while his daughter asked, with a casual air, 'So, do you think I could go to that party tonight? All my friends are going . . .'

'Hasn't Mama already said no?' Anand shook his head. 'Then don't ask again, kutty, I don't like it.'

'All my friends are going,' she said again but stopped when she saw his expression. When next she spoke, it was on a different topic. 'Appa, what happened at the factory that day? The export thing?'

'Oh,' he said, surprised that she even remembered. 'Yes, I think it went well.'

'That's good,' she said. 'You're going to export now?'

'No,' he laughed. 'Not yet. It's not that simple. There will be more meetings and so on, it may take them months to decide, so we will have to see.'

'Eat some of the chicken,' she said now, her tone motherly. 'It's delicious, try some.' He let her fill his plate. 'Come on,' he said, 'you eat too, before Pingu eats up the entire picnic.'

There was a time when she would reach eagerly for her food, ignoring the admonishments of her mother to go slow, but she was suddenly at an age where she seemed to weigh every mouthful she ate, computing its worth in terms of calories and god-knows-what-all other fashionable parameters of nutrition offered by the women's magazines that his wife flooded the house with. Anand watched her assess the picnic, choose small spoonfuls of chicken and vegetables, and eat slowly, bite by careful bite, and he worried: was it enough?

So much of his daughter was snared in inexplicable female mystery, and even though he seized gladly on the fact that she continued to chatter away to him as much as she ever did, there were still lines between them, newly formed, that neither could cross. When she argued with her mother, for instance. The topics seemed to him very silly and trivial, certainly not worth the tears or angry faces, but he never dared point that out to either of them. Or when, once a month, he saw her prostrated upon her bed, a cushion clutched to her belly to ease the pain that attacked her abdomen. He never knew what to do. Should he step up as he naturally would if she had scraped her knee and sit by the side of the bed offering comfort and concern and busy himself with pills and prescriptions and worried phone calls to the doctor, or would it embarrass her if he did?

His concern stretched to other things too. There were times when he overheard conversations or read articles on how Indian teenagers – especially well-to-do urban ones – were changing, worryingly, into facsimiles of their Western counterparts.

'Are you talking to her?' he asked his wife. 'About drugs and sex and alcohol and so on?'

'Of course not,' she said. 'What's wrong with you?'

'I mean,' he explained, 'about whether these things are happening in her school. Her friends.'

Vidya looked troubled.

'Anand,' she said. 'Valmika is just fourteen. And she's a good girl. She is not going to go near things like that. Neither are her friends, I think. We know all their families.'

But wasn't that what all parents thought, he'd asked – and yesterday Vidya had said, 'Oh, yes, I talked to her. Or actually, Kavika talked to her for me, and it is the same thing.'

Anand did not know whether to feel relieved or awkward.

The garden doors opened; his wife had returned home. She said: 'What on earth are you guys doing?'

And behind her, another voice, amused: 'Ah. Déjeuner sur l'herbe. What fun!'

'Appa gave me permission, Mama. Hi, Kavika-aunty,' said Valmika. 'That's French, isn't it?'

'It is,' said Kavika. 'The name of a painting, actually. Hi, Anand.' He looked up from where he had been staring blindly – at his wife hugging Pingu; he smiled; he tried to think of something to say.

'Hi,' he managed. If he could remember the French phrase she'd used, he would look up the painting on the Internet; impossible; he would not be able to identify it. What else did he know about paintings? Or indeed of any art? Babble-onion art-wuk. That's what.

Vidya said: 'Oh, Kavika, can you drop something off at my mother's? It's just a shawl; she left it in my car when we went for her medical checkup yesterday. Yeah, she's fine, blood pressure's a little high, that's it. No, don't get up, I'll bring it.'

Kavika sat down on the mat, the sun catching the speckled gray in her hair and turning it silver. He wondered how to inaugurate any of the topics of conversation he had with her when she was not around. He need not have worried; it happened most naturally.

She said, just as he had imagined she would: 'Amrita tells me that they've roped you in as well . . .'

'For next Tuesday?' He grinned. 'Yeah. I don't think I was given a choice of refusing.'

Unhappy with the rampant corruption of the major political parties, Amir and Amrita and some like-minded people were organizing an event to raise awareness on the issue.

'It's a great idea,' said Kavika. 'I just hope it's effective. Amir feels that we are capable of reform, but I have my doubts. What do you think?'

'I don't know,' said Anand. 'The fact is, even if individual politicians are clean, elections cost money . . . A lot of money . . .'

'So, that's why there's no chance of someone outside of the major parties ever winning an election?'

Anand shrugged. 'Not impossible – but tough. They'd be competing against huge party machinery. It's a simple question of economics, no? It costs a lot of money to win a state election, and multiples of that to win a parliamentary seat. Which regular, middle-class professional can fight that? Even with all the goodwill and qualifications in the world?'

His son's head was resting on his lap; Vyasa had dozed off, lulled by the sun, the cricket, and the food. Valmika, he noticed, was listening intently to their conversation.

Kavika rested her head on her folded knees. 'Amrita was telling me that they're trying to see if they can get Vijayan to be the chief guest . . . I have mixed feelings about that . . .' she said.

'It will certainly raise the profile of the event,' said Anand. 'Lots of publicity.'

If Vijayan had initials or a last name, it was proof of his already iconic status that people simply referred to him by his first name alone, like the emperor Akbar-the-great or the singer Madonna. In newspaper photographs and television interviews and on posters, he appeared completely unlike the standard-issue politician: a clean-looking, pleasant-faced young man; someone one might actually be glad to invite home without first locking up the young girls and the silver. He did not wear rings or oversize, sinister dark glasses; he did not sport a neta cap to show his cultural loyalties to Mahatma Gandhi. People vied to get close to him; his wife was pleasant; they were incorruptible; he was inviolate.

Vijayan was foreign-educated and private-sector-trained but despite these attributes of elitism had nevertheless proved himself to be a genial man of the people. This was one of his better abilities: to relate just as easily to the highest and lowest of the land. Mahatma Gandhi, they said, had this quality. He was a gifted orator, they said, his mellifluous speeches invariably striking the right chord, whether he was addressing an illiterate gathering of farmers or the modern maharajas of international finance. He never spoke about the wonders of his own party or even about himself. He claimed no credit – that was the astonishing thing about him: in a democracy, where even the shiest public servant was forced to advertise his achievements to a careless voting public, Vijayan never spoke of himself. Instead, he had the knack of speaking of the problems facing them, as a people, as a country, as a village, a family, a community, a company. And he spoke of these matters with such thought and concern, with such an air of balance and morality, that one felt compelled to agree with him, and then, by degrees, that this young man was the very one to solve these problems. That was his political genius. He made even the most qualified and experienced of politicians look like greedy, self-serving grabbers. Best of all, for all his foreign-training and high education, he was born of a previously untouchable caste, a dalit family. The media framed excited headlines around him in ever-inventive and foolish ways: DALIT DAYLIGHT was one. DALIT DELIGHT, said another in thrilled one-upmanship. VIJAYAN BY NAME AND VICTORY BY NATURE, said a third.

Once before, Anand had seen him in the flesh, at a function at a five-star hotel. Vijayan had been one of the speakers and afterward, under the gleaming lights, had casually stood in the center of a shy, adoring crowd. This was not the street; the audience's extreme interest in Vijayan was tempered by their upbringing: they did not know how to mob him. Harry Chinappa had suffered no such shyness. He managed to get himself introduced to Vijayan and made Ruby take a picture of them together, asking the other people standing around to move out of the way. He then sent the photo to the newspaper offices, so that they might publish it on their party pages, and the next day, he wrote a follow-up letter to Vijayan himself, enclosing with it a copy of the photograph. So nice to meet you, he wrote. So rare to have politicians of such caliber in this great nation of ours. He sent it off, forwarding a copy to his son-in-law for his edification.

Anand asked Kavika: 'Why do you have mixed feelings about Vijayan?'

She plucked restlessly at the tufts of grass next to the coir mat. 'I don't know,' she said. 'He seems like a good guy. Clean. Qualified. But, on the other hand, he represents a traditional, established party – with all its corruption and fierce internal politics – so how clean can he truly be . . . ?' Was that sudden mischief in her glance? 'Your father-in-law,' she said, 'certainly thinks he is a wonderful candidate . . .' He could not help himself; his eyes revealed his opinion of his father-in-law, gratifyingly reflected in the merry comprehension of hers. He glanced at his daughter and forced himself to compose his face.

He could hear Vidya bustling up. 'Here it is! Thanks so much!'

Kavika got up to leave; she said, smiling directly at him: 'So I will see – both of you? – next Tuesday evening.'

'How come?' asked Vidya.

'I told you,' said Anand. 'Amir's event.'

'Oh,' said Vidya. 'Right. Amrita asked me too. So interesting, no? It really is about time that we make some effort to change the system.' Later she looked at him in some surprise. 'I wonder why Amir called you? You don't do anything that is not work-related. He really must have twisted your arm.'

That night, Anand ensconced himself in his study. His wife was out, the children were spending the night at their maternal grand-parents', for all practical purposes he was alone. He plugged his phone into the iPod dock, flipping through until he found the album he wanted. Pink Floyd, *The Dark Side of the Moon*. He adjusted the volume and reached into the steel Godrej bureau, his fingers searching past the files for the bag of hash he kept hidden in the back.

He locked the study door and drew the curtains before rolling his joint, emptying a cigarette tube of its contents, crumbling the black hash into the tobacco leaves, quickly hoovering it all back into the cigarette tube placed between his lips with an old exper-tise that, like so many things, was gained in college. He opened the curtains and the window screen as well. He switched off the lights and smoked the joint slowly, standing by the window and carefully blowing the smoke out into the night air. His son would not notice, he was too young, but Anand did not want either his wife or his daughter walking into the room hours later and asking awkward questions.

In the darkened room behind him, the music sang of money, time, and lunatics upon the grass.

Over the years, this Pink Floyd album had receded to the back of his mental musical shelf, but he had heard a couple of songs from it the previous weekend and now it leapt back quickly, engrossing him, the cadences so familiar, his body poised in ancient recognition, anticipating the next musical phrase in perfect, unfaltering sequence. It brought back memories: of the previous weekend, of college, and of the more recent, few-years-ago excitement of attending a Roger Waters concert in Bangalore.

He had bought his tickets as one might for a long-awaited pilgrimage. He arrived at the grounds an hour early, accompanied by Vidya. She was excited too, but for different reasons. She had never really listened to Pink Floyd, beyond dancing to the song 'Another Brick in the Wall (Part 2)' at the discotheques of her youth, where it was packaged among the sugar-pop, soda-pop songs of that era. She seemed oblivious to the sacredness of the moment, her head whirling, dervishlike, as she registered who else was present, which friends she could wave to and what their plans were post-concert; friends, like her, who were there not for the music but simply because it was a concert, that hitherto rare thing, a place therefore to see and be seen. But the powerful magic charms of the evening soon overcame Anand's momentary irritations: the contained energies of the crowd, the air of suppressed reverence, the pulsating excitement that swung sharply up to a boil when the first musicians walked onto the stage, the heat from the lights and the audience tussling with the cool winds of the night, and the dust that rose from the large concert grounds, so improbably situated in the Bangalore Palace compound.

'Oh, look,' said his wife, 'there's so-and-so and such-and-such . . .'

The music exploded from the speakers; Anand felt a surge of something that could only be happiness; on the face of the man standing next to him, shoulder to shoulder, there was an echo of that same demented smile he wore, and moisture on his cheeks, either sweat or tears, an old aching sweetness in him, an homage to the musical passions of a much younger, collegiate self, who had listened to this music all night long, stoned and sober, and had wondered what it would be like to listen to it live, to breathe the same air as these gods, knowing also that, for the likes of him and the world he lived in, these were not choices they would ever have. But a miracle of time and they were here: a gift from a city that had changed beneath him. Deities of music, singing just for him, taking the money and the adulation the worshipful city placed at their feet. Roger Waters, long-faced, long-nosed, long-toothed, small-eyed; a thoroughly alien physiognomy that was never quite how Anand had imagined the face of god to be.

'Standing for so long was so tiring,' Vidya later said, 'they should have provided some seats. But the concert was quite nice,' she said, glancing at his face. 'It was so fantastic! What music! I loved it!' she said to Amir, Amrita, and the other friends they met later for dinner.

The previous weekend, a new band had been playing a mixture of electronica and funk at his favorite music club. They were very good, but Anand wondered if he was on the edge of being too old to enjoy it, whether his classic-rock-trained ears could ever truly adapt. Luckily, and he had checked with the bar manager, the follow-up band would be playing some old rock covers.

He liked this place; it was not glossy but dedicated to good music and to the small indie bands that toured the country searching for listeners. Vidya occasionally agreed to come with him; she was not musically inclined, but several of her friends were; that night she was circulating about the room. He finished his beer and looked around for the waiter – and then saw Kavika at the far end of the bar, deep in conversation. Anand squinted his eyes; he knew who her companion was. Kabir, Amir's younger brother.

Kabir worked as a videogame designer, seemingly dividing his time between long days working and nights of partying, forever knee-deep in the most glamorous girls in the shortest skirts. There were, as usual, three of them clustered around him; Anand contemplated him with some awe. When he had mentioned Kabir's girl-friends to Vidya, she had looked at him scornfully and said: Don't be absurd. He's gay.

And: Of course, she said, his parents don't know.

It did not seem logical. Right now, Kabir was ignoring the girls and had his arm around Kavika, whispering in her ear, tugging at the scarf around her neck. She was laughing back.

The second band took to the stage and launched into a cover of Pink Floyd.

When Vidya wandered back to sip at the glass of vodka-tonic at their table, Anand could not help saying to her: I thought you said he was gay.

She glanced at Kabir and grinned. 'All Kavika's closest male friends are gay. She's a total fag hag. You can't be so critical of people,' she said. 'Nothing wrong if he's gay.'

'I didn't say there was,' said Anand. 'If he is gay.'

He tried to concentrate on the music. If the woman laughing at the distant bar saw him, she gave no indication of it. She seemed entirely absorbed with that idiot Kabir.

Now, in the safe embrace of his study, the music lifted his mind from that bar to the sunlight of his garden and to the entirely different creature who had discussed politics with him on the lawn; that arching connection between them, one that surely didn't exist in his imagination alone?

His mind moved fleetingly to Amir's political meeting. He entered a note on his iPhone calendar, making sure nothing else conflicted with that time.

Twelve

A letter was such an infrequent occurrence in her life that Kamala did not at first recognize that the pale blue inland cover was meant for her. She squinted at it, until her neighbor's voice demanded: 'Well, are you going to take it or not?' Kamala received it gingerly from the young bride. 'The old lady got it with the other mail and asked me to give it to you.'

'Thank you,' said Kamala, but she found the bride squatting down and, for a moment, leaving off her usual insolent manner. 'Akka,' she whispered, 'she is raising our rent again. So quickly! Is she asking more from you as well?'

Kamala was startled but did not show it. 'Not yet,' she said.

'If she does, will you pay?' asked the bride.

Kamala was troubled by the young bride's words but had no desire to discuss the matter with her, so she took refuge in rudeness. 'What business is it of yours?' she said and was gratified to see the girl sniff and bang her way into her own room.

The thin, pale blue-green paper, written upon and folded possessively three times over its mysterious contents, was decorated on top with what Kamala knew to be her name and address and the sender's identity. She studied the fat, curved squiggles marching across the paper like looped jelebis and tried to decipher their meaning like an astrologer attempting to predict the future course of life from the stars. From her sister-in-law perhaps? Possibly. But her sister-in-law was as illiterate as she was and usually preferred to communicate her news over the telephone.

She could, if she wished, knock on the young bride's door or cross the courtyard to where the landlord's mother lived and ask either of them to decipher the squiggles; both of them had that literary capability, but that would make them instantly privy to the contents of the letter. Instead, after studying it for a few minutes more, Kamala placed it away on a shelf and started her cooking preparations, fretting at the slow passage of time.

'There you are,' she said impatiently when she heard his footsteps. 'I have been waiting.'

'Why?' Narayan asked and then, as she thrust the blue cover at him, 'For us? Who is it from?'

'We will know all these things,' said his mother severely, 'if you would but hurry.'

He slit the edge of the folded letter and spread it open. Its contents covered only two of the three sides; the sender did not seem compelled to get their money's worth from the two-rupee cost of the inland letter.

'It is from Maama,' he said. 'He is coming for a visit.'

'What?' she said. 'My brother? Here? You lie! Now, Narayan, don't play the fool or I will beat you. I really will. With that broom, I will beat you.'

'I'm not playing the fool,' he said. 'Mother. What a thing to say. He is coming here . . . For somebody's wedding . . . Listen! I will read it to you . . . "Dear little sister,"' he read, '"My prayers that this letter finds you in good health. You will be pleased to hear that . . ."'

Kamala made him read it through twice. The formal written tone could not disguise the reality: for the first time in all these years, her brother would be visiting her in Bangalore. She sat still, processing this unprecedented event, until she heard Narayan ask her: 'Amma? Are you not happy? This bothers you?'

'I am happy,' she said. 'It is a good thing he is coming. Does he say when?'

'Next week. I told you. For one night.'

She nodded and, with effort, turned the conversation to other channels, distracting Narayan with some gossip about Shanta's latest crosspatchery.

Later, when he had abandoned his evening studies to play cricket in the gully, she looked around her house with something akin to panic. In an instant, that letter had snatched away her sense of peace, her casual pride, her deep comfort in her home.

When Kamala had first started work as a domestic servant, she had lived with her baby son in the homes she worked in as a full-time, stay-in maid. If she was lucky, she was given a separate, tiny room (usually off the kitchen and just large enough to sleep herself and her son). If she was not so lucky, then under the stairs, or on the kitchen floor, her belongings stored in some unused cupboard.

But things changed as her son grew older. He was in every way a beautifully blossoming little boy: noisy, curious, and his feet began to wander. He was still too young to understand that the large residence they lived in was not their home; he was not free to run about at will, touching the things that caught his fancy, reaching his hand up for the fruit that gleamed on the table; it was not there for him. And though Kamala furiously, desperately corrected and hushed him, it was not long before she was being gently asked whether she could not make some other arrangement for her son. Could he not stay with grandparents in the village? Her employers were not bad people; Kamala realized that she would face the same questions wherever she worked.

It was time then to get a home of her own. But perhaps she

was a very demanding type of person, for no matter how many places she saw, she could not be satisfied: a succession of single rooms, tiny and dingy from misuse – none of which she minded, for it was no more than she expected – but, all of them carrying with them the stench of other discomforts: potential landlords who inspected her body with disrespectful eyes; rooms that opened onto crowded, busy streets with doors that were lightweight and insecure, the surroundings so noisy that a voice raised in alarm would be swallowed up by the sounds of the street; or rooms that were so far removed from humanity that she could shout for help and go unheard. And so, like a nesting doe, Kamala had kept searching restlessly.

She had known instantly that this room was made for her. She could see her future in it: the gate at the entrance to the courtyard would keep her doubly secure; the families who lived in the dwellings within would provide her with community and security; the landlord seemed like a respectable man, and he and his family would doubtless be there for advice and assistance should she ever choose to seek it. Quickly, before the landlord could change his mind or before someone else could leap in and grab the room, she paid the advance requested (not too high, because of the unseemly location so far from the city) and arranged to move in the very next day.

If Kamala had had one wish, in those early years, it was for a shorter commute to her work, which still took her an hour and a half each day. But, perhaps because she accepted the routine without complaint, the gods took pity upon her and, with their palms raised in benediction and gentle smiles upon their faces, they addressed themselves to the blisters on her feet and moved the city closer.

She had lived here for eight years.

He would come, her brother, and he would not see the nest

that had kept her safe and cherished all these years; he would notice the peeling paint on the walls and the small size of the room and disparage her and all that she held dear, for that was what he had always done – and why should the intervening years have changed his character?

He was to attend the wedding of his wife's connection, a cousin; Kamala wished that it was his wife attending instead of him. They, at least, had maintained a steady, affectionate communication over the years, with brief phone calls, first made from the STD phone booth at the corner and, later, from her newly acquired cellphone, which was cheaper.

She wondered, all of a fidget, whether she should buy a can of paint and put Narayan to work. Should she buy new clothes for both of them? The relentless profusion of such thoughts eventually annoyed her. What nonsense, she thought. Why should she do any of these things? Let him come. Let him say what he will. Let him poke his nose in the air and click his tongue and shake his head and make his hurtful comments. Let him.

Nevertheless, she found herself approaching the visit with an air of going into battle. Her brother would actually be spending less than a day with her: he would arrive on the night bus and proceed directly to the wedding location, finding his way to Kamala's house only after the morning's festivities and lunch were completed. He would eat his evening meal with them, spend the night, and be off the following morning on the seven-hour bus ride back home to the village.

On the day of the visit, Narayan, noting the militant air with which she cooked the evening meal, opened his mouth and wisely shut it without comment, washing dishes and meekly changing into the shirt his mother gave him (his second best) and not arguing when she told him not to wander off with his friends but to stay put in the courtyard until his uncle should arrive.

Her brother arrived in the early hours of Sunday afternoon in the smart polyester shirt and pants he had donned for the wedding, a slight smattering of gray in his hair the only visible marker of the years that had passed since their last meeting. His first comment was positive: he exclaimed over how tall Narayan had become: 'Taller than me soon, I think.' He then looked Kamala up and down. 'You look well,' he pronounced, as though making an important diagnosis. Kamala felt herself relax slightly. She showed him about her room and the courtyard; he made no comment.

Her years in Bangalore had immeasurably changed her view of her brother; he was no longer the vicious, terrorizing force of her girlhood. He looked tired and uncertain, removed from the comfort of his village and quietened by the overwhelming rhythm and thrum of the big city. She set aside her fears of battle and engaged instead to look after her guest. He changed into a cotton shirt and lungi folded to his knees and accepted her offer of coffee.

He had placed his formal wear in a large jute bag; from this he pulled out gifts from his wife: a blouse piece for Kamala and a plastic comb for Narayan. Kamala received the gifts with pleasure and felt relaxed enough to make a joke: 'Perhaps now,' she said, 'Narayan will actually comb his hair,' and was gratified to see her brother and son laugh along. She too had a gift to give: a box of North Indian–style sweets for him to take home; his wife would find them novel and enjoy sharing them with her children and neighbors.

The evening passed swiftly enough on wheels of punctilious civility. Narayan, thankfully, talked sensibly with his uncle, recounting none of his wilder stories. Her brother spoke briefly of his wife's uncertain health and of their three children; he told Kamala little pieces of village gossip; he praised the food she had cooked. She in turn felt a degree of charity toward him that she had little expected. Who knew her brother could be so harmless? If this was the character-altering game the gods were playing, then – who knew? – perhaps tomorrow she would go to work and find Shanta flinging her arms about her with a smile and Thangam beavering away and Vidya-ma dispensing loans cheerfully.

Her brother seemed to be doing well; he talked about having purchased a share in a new village shop. 'Soon, Sister,' he said, 'I will bring my wife and children to visit you.'

Kamala nodded, her words preempted by Narayan's excited 'I can show them around! Everything!'

Despite the cordiality of their conversation, Kamala did not let her guard down. She told him briefly about her job, ready to deflect any question about her salary – but none came. Instead, her brother reserved his quizzing for Narayan. Here too Kamala refused to show weakness: Narayan, she told him, was doing well in school – and gods willing, would soon be shifting to a paid school with a fine future ahead of him.

'These are good prospects. Work hard,' her brother said, nodding and addressing his nephew, 'and do well.'

The conversation slipped safely back to village news.

The landlord's mother joined them as soon as their evening meal was done; Kamala was wryly surprised at how long the old lady had waited, exercising, no doubt, the utmost tact and patience. She, like the others who lived in the courtyard, was brimming with curiosity at this unprecedented visitor from Kamala's family – hitherto missing in action. For Kamala, so free with news of her present, tended to be frugal when discussing her past.

Kamala went to wash their dinner plates and throw away the little food that remained, for it would spoil overnight. She had overestimated the quantities they would eat, or, to be precise, she had not wanted to appear parsimonious. Squatting at the tap, she could hear the old lady questioning her brother like an unsparing schoolteacher.

Kamala's landlord was a simple man, fundamentally unsuited to the business of landlording, treating his tenants with a courtesy usually reserved for guests. He was unable to deny any request made to him, especially if it was phrased in polite terms and after due inquiries about his health and the well-being of his family. Since his wife suffered, like him, from an excess of sensibility, any difficult decision that needed to be conveyed to his tenants was delivered by his mother, who did not.

The landlord's mother was always ready to concede her son's superior knowledge of the ways of the world and, certainly, his right to manage his own affairs. If she voiced her opinion in his hearing, it was only to provide him with an alternate point of view (humble and fault-ridden though it may be). And if by the magic of osmosis, her opinions somehow managed to become his, that was the will of the gods. It was a process she handled deftly, bringing to it an expertise garnered through years of managing the landlord's late father; in short, the old lady was the unofficial regent of the courtyard.

Please, she prayed, she is very important to me. Please let my brother not be provoked into being rude to her. I could not bear the shame. I could not repair the damage.

Kamala had misplaced her worry.

Her brother appeared keen to make a good impression. She returned with plates clean and dripping wet to hear him holding forth to an interested audience. The landlord's mother had been joined within minutes by her daughter-in-law and by the young bride. '. . . many guntas of land,' he was saying. 'Yes, we are lucky to be living so comfortably . . .

'And yes, the shop is also doing well. The second one also.'

In a frozen, startled silence, Kamala listened to descriptions of the acres of land her brother owned, his thriving shops. And then, not content with talking so freely about himself, he proceeded determinedly to establish the worth of Kamala's late husband's family as well: '. . . even more land,' he said. 'Cows producing the finest milk. Very nice house.'

Kamala saw the open mouths, the heated rise in speculation; even Narayan listening to this in astonishment. She had no idea how to stem the flow of her brother's sudden loquacity. She could feel eyes sliding speculatively from him to her and back again. It was the bride, naturally presumptuous, who chose to ask the big unanswered question:

'Aiyo, uncle,' she said, 'if Kamala-aunty can stay like such a queen at home, why is she living and working like this?'

'Hush, child,' said the landlord's mother. 'What a question to ask.'

Her brother did not seem offended by the bride's impertinence. 'It is a good question,' he said, with a kindly solicitude that made Kamala want to bang her wet plates on his head, 'but you good ladies know Kamala . . . she can be very obstinate. How many times we have all told her to come and live with us – but she will not listen.'

'Yes, Kamala-aunty can be quite obstinate,' agreed the bride, with an unbecoming haste.

'Amma' – her brother addressed the landlord's mother – 'it is good that you have looked after her so well; she is very lucky. But why should she clean houses here when she can live in comfort at home? Her husband's family too would welcome her – our family is held in such respect in the village.'

'We are happy to have her with us,' said the old lady, 'and I thank you for your words. We have cherished her like a daughter. But she is luckier still to have a brother like you, of strong character and so caring. Lucky for her and so good for Narayan – he needs a man's hand to control his mischief.'

Narayan's protest was quelled by his mother's stern glare; she herself said nothing.

Her brother, encouraged by the old lady's words, caught Narayan by the ear and twisted it until the boy winced. 'Mischief, is it?' he said, genially. 'I see that next time, I shall have to bring my cane with me.'

When all was quiet and everyone asleep, Kamala lay awake, irritated and baffled by her brother's conduct, the careless stories that she could not, in good grace, contradict. In the space of half a day, he had spoiled her hard-won reputation of eight years. She could see it in the landlord's mother's eyes: from being regarded as a hard-working woman worthy of support and pity to being seen as a willful, obstinate fool.

The landlord's mother had been present when Kamala first met the landlord, and if Kamala had not realized, then, the significance of the little gray-haired woman in the corner with a grandchild on her lap, she soon did and never failed to pay her respects. Perhaps it was this, or perhaps the old woman just liked Kamala's company, for though Kamala led a morally impeccable life (apart from an occasional loss of temper), she was not too proud to sit in the moonlight of an evening and engage in a gentle gossip about others, listening with pleasure and interested commentary. Whatever the reason, for a long time now, Kamala had been shielded from the old lady's business instincts and from the knocks on doors, every now and then, around the courtyard, with requests for increased rent.

But now, thanks to her brother, Kamala worried that her status as the old lady's pet tenant might soon cease. The bride's words of the previous week rang louder in the night. If the rent increased – biting into a larger chunk of her monthly income – how would she be able to save for Narayan's schooling?

Thirteen

The cessation of the machines signaled the end of the second shift on the factory floor, but the sounds of debate and disagreement swirled unabated around Anand's office.

'It is the correct thing,' said the HR man obstinately. 'The workers are happy. It gives us a good reputation with the unions.'

'It is too much,' said Ananthamurthy. 'What is the need? Mrs Padmavati, do you not agree with me? Such a big increment this time – they will expect the same next time. Too much! We cannot afford this.'

'As to that,' said Mrs Padmavati with her usual precision, 'it is financially viable in the current scenario.'

Anand listened and did not interrupt. He was quite clear in his own mind: the wage increase was a good thing, especially when the company stood on the verge of gaining international contracts. It represented a vote of confidence in the workers. If he'd had any doubt, the meeting with the union leader that morning had settled it. For the union leader – face beaming, brimming over with goodwill and fervent promises of continued keenness – it was a political coup; he could take personal credit for it. Anand had always tried to maintain good relations with the workers, but he could see, in the union leader's pleasure, that their relationship had shifted to a new level of mutual commitment.

The Japanese deal had moved ahead remarkably well. The short list had now narrowed to just two companies: theirs and one other from Delhi. That was it. He and Ananthamurthy had researched all they could about their competitors and cautiously come to the opinion that they did not have that much to fear. The Delhi company was owned by a prominent businessman with a flair for getting his name in the papers. That did not necessarily make them better. In fact, according to Ananthamurthy, who had methods of unearthing strange bits of gossip from unlikely sources, they were disliked by their suppliers for their delays in payment and their habit of rewarding themselves with expensive cars before paying anyone else. Surely the Japanese would be able to sense such bad practices? Surely the very rectitude of Cauvery Auto, with its quiet offices and efficient shop floor, would speak for them?

Anand drove home, pondering if there was anything else they could do to tip things in their favor.

'Oh, thank you so much. That's lovely! Yes, see you tomorrow. Okay, then. Bye!' Vidya arrived home a few minutes after he did, her face still flushed and animated from her phone conversation, narrow, orange-rimmed dark glasses resting like a hair band on her head. She looked up at Anand, and the animation faded.

There was no question about it. His wife was molting again. Shedding her old feathers and growing ones anew. He had seen this happen before – a vivid reengineering of her entire being after time spent on the drawing board and in vacuum-sealed labora- tories, the birth of a new avatar complete with new dress, new hairstyle, new speech, new concerns.

It was usually triggered by her current friends and obsessions; over the years, Anand had witnessed the birth of the outdoorsy, sporty wife, who trekked determinedly in the nature she loved, eventually killed and re-interpreted as the Bollywood princess decked in long, salon-straightened hair and sequins, shaking her hips to persistent Hindi film music, who, in turn, gave way to the artsy interior-decorating aesthete who wore bright green glasses and patronized art shows and plays that questioned the meaning of life in modern India.

It had never bothered him until now – now, it bothered him intensely. The previous week, she had returned home with a haircut. The hair that had swung down to her waist and been straightened religiously each week at the beauty parlor was cut short to her ears. He had gazed at her, startled.

'Well?' she said, and there had been a challenge in the question.

It's different, he said. When he hastily added, 'It's nice,' she said with a particular satisfaction, 'I *knew* you wouldn't like it.'

Now she was wearing a Fabindia kurta, the block-printed tunic reminding him, appallingly, of another woman: his wife had chosen, this time, to turn herself into a horrifying, inadequate facsimile of Kavika.

He wanted to weep.

That Vidya was experiencing her own difficulties with this partic-ular transmogrification was evident when she came to the study to discuss the annual Diwali party with him. This itself was unusual.

She settled herself on the sofa, placing an ankle over her oppo-site knee, a masculine pose that he at once recognized as belonging to another woman.

'I would so much prefer to keep the whole thing simple,' she said. 'A return to simple values. A simple, quiet affair.'

He refused to help her. 'Why don't you?' he said.

'Yes,' she said. 'Yes, of course . . . The thing is, my father . . .'

Anand knew precisely what the thing was. Harry Chinappa was

not a subscriber to his daughter's current transformation. Especially now, in the face of Diwali. Over the years, what had commenced as a gentle, mocking advisory to his daughter's annual Diwali party, received by Vidya as a happy counterpoint to Anand's own perennial indifference to such matters, had escalated into a complete takeover, with Harry Chinappa orchestrating both the party arrangements and the guest list, filling it, much to his daughter's starstruck gratitude, with many of his own acquaintances. Anand, with a certain resignation, had confined his own involvement to matters of budget alone, a tail meekly attached to a kite as his wife swirled along on myriad social winds, the string that held her aloft amidst her buffeting firmly guided by the authoritarian hands of her father. The previous year, a hundred people had infested the house for the Diwali party; Anand had thought that about ninety people too many – a view apparently shared by no one else, least of all his wife, until a few days previously, when Kavika had leaned her elbows against the table in a restaurant and started talking animatedly about the Diwalis of her childhood.

They were at a Lebanese restaurant, Anand and Vidya, Amir, and Kavika. Amrita had stayed away, pleading work, and Anand had planned to do so as well – until he learned who else would be there.

'You know, it used to be this really simple affair . . .' she said and proceeded to describe customs that Anand recognized, in an instant moment of joyous enchantment, as identical to Deepavalis from his own childhood: a small family affair that started well before sunrise, with children setting off fireworks on the street in the chill early morning air until they were chased down by their mothers for the ritual predawn oil bath and donning of new clothes. Readings from the Ramayana followed by a breakfast of hot idlis and a spicy spoonful of ground herbs in a leghyam that his sister hated, finding it too strong and peppery, but that he rather enjoyed, before a day of visiting relatives and eating homemade sweetmeats and an evening of more fireworks.

He had never expected this, this gift of a shared communal past: to discover the shadings of simple brahmin austerity behind Kavika's current international sophistication.

Her words triggered within him a fund of memories of his childhood life in Mysore. He wanted to tell her these things as he had never told anyone else. She would listen in her sympathetic, intelligent way – and she would understand. She would not judge him. And she would help him make sense of these things, of the passage of his life, help him bridge the frozen, awkward moments of the past with the speed of the present.

Usually, when she was around, he found himself tongue-tied, sneaking occasional darting glances at her, fiercely concealing the dreadful exhilaration and the plunging depression that chased each other within him like mischievous children on a playground.

Vidya said: 'Oh, how lovely that sounds . . .' – as though she had not spent several years enjoying a tide of newly flashy-splashy celebrations, parties, late nights, card games, gifts, decorations, and delirious spending; the festal name itself shortened to Diwali in some weird Bollywoodized fashion – and Anand forced himself to speak up – 'We used to have really simple Deepavalis when I was a child' – and felt Kavika's eyes focus on him.

'In Mysore?' she asked. 'Ah! Beautiful city.' She frowned in thought. 'What are you, a Hebbar Iyengar?'

No, he said, 'Smartha Brahmin.'

'Oh,' she said, 'like us Iyers!'

'Well, similar, though with some differences.' Tongue-in-cheek and reveling in his own daring, he said, 'My uncle used to say: "For a restful, headache-free life, never marry an Iyer woman – too aggressive!"'

Her shout of laughter was drowned by Vidya's shocked 'Anand! . . .

How rude!'Vidya firmly returned to the original topic. 'We should really go back to that, shouldn't we? I mean, the simpler things of life. In the craziness of our lives we sometimes forget the joy of those simple traditions.'

Now, how was Vidya to reconcile this with the lavish party that Harry Chinappa liked to throw at his daughter's house at his son-in-law's unhappy expense?

In the study, she plucked nervously at her toes like an out-generaled Mughal ruler who, flanked by the Portuguese, accepted the help of the British and rather lived to regret that decision, saying of her father: 'Ey, you know how he likes to help us with these things. And I know he has already gone ahead with many of the arrangements.'

Anand refused to slip into the old, established mechanics of their marriage and rush to her rescue. Provoked by a burgeoning new obstinacy, he said: 'You like his help, no? You are always saying.'

'Oh, yes,' she said, refusing to be disloyal. 'Of course I do.'

'You should tell him, yaar,' he said. 'Tell him you want to keep it simple this year.'

'Yes. That's a good idea,' she said, getting up. 'I will.' He watched her leave, trailing indecision and strategy behind her.

He promptly forgot about the matter, his own mind utterly distracted by the prospect of the following day.

Kavika was to visit the factory, to collect another contribution to the children's education fund that she was working on with Amir and Amrita. 'If you don't mind,' she'd said over the telephone. 'I have to swing by that side anyway to fund-raise at a garment factory. The owner promised me a check a long time ago and I'm going to squeeze it out of him.'

'Please come,' Anand had said, formally, hiding his extreme delight.

She was to arrive at 11:00 A.M., and he had planned to clear his desk before that and possibly run a comb through his hair. Instead, immersed in work, he was on the telephone, wrestling in prayer and remonstrance with his steel supplier, when he saw her at his door.

'Anand! Thank you so much for this,' she said when he had finished his phone call. Her eyes swiveled to the picture window. 'Oh, wow.' She stood riveted by the sight of the factory floor. 'You know what? I've been in a thousand offices – but I've never actually visited an industrial factory before . . . This is amazing.'

He joined her at the window, heat rushing to his face at her evident, unexpected interest.

'Would you like a tour?' he asked, surprise making him cautious, delight making him shy.

'Really? Now?' she said. 'Wow. Are you sure? You don't mind? That would be very cool.'

'No problem, yaar,' said Anand, with a sense of masterly understatement.

He led her downstairs. She walked by his side along the yellow lines that marked pathways separating the rows and columns of machinery. He had made her wear a hard hat, like he did, and he paused at every turning to make sure there was no wayward forklift operator or worker with a trolley of raw materials heading toward her. He would not risk her safety.

'We don't make a very complicated product,' he said, self-deprecatingly. She stood very close to him; she had to in order to hear his words over the noise of the machinery. A gap of mere inches. He took her through the process, his explanation growing with enthusiasm when he saw that she was really interested; she was not just being polite, her breath feathering his cheek when she leaned in to ask questions, her hand occasionally touching his arm to make a point.

They wandered together through the sunlit factory to where

sheets of steel were pressed by the dyes within the stamping machines into a variety of shapes, then to where they were further welded together into new shapes by the workers at the welding machines, and finally to the loading bay, where they were stacked in bright orange crates, ready to be forklifted onto pallets that would make their way in container trucks to the various automotive companies Cauvery Auto supplied.

'It's like pieces of a three-D puzzle, isn't it?' she said, inspecting a box of stampings that waited in the loading bay. 'All of them eventually assembled into the body of a car, or a truck, or something . . .'

'I suppose so . . . It's not a very complicated product,' he said, 'but we focus very hard on finish and quality. That's what we have to achieve. A world-class finish, consistently, quickly.'

'That's what the Germans and the Japanese have mastered, isn't it? Is it difficult,' she asked, 'to get Indian workers to do high-quality work?'

'It all depends on the training,' he said. He realized, with some surprise, that he had never discussed these matters with anyone other than Ananthamurthy and a few others in the factory. He had never dreamed she would be engaged by such matters, so curious, warm appreciation in her eyes. 'We have to de-skill and multi-skill them . . . We retrain them from scratch. Even if they come to us with experience. Then we train them to work across a range of equipment.' He took her to the charts that showed how they managed quality throughout the factory and their efforts to introduce elements of Japanese production systems through the factory. 'The most difficult thing is to get our workers to follow preset processes in a disciplined way. They want to get creative, find shortcuts. Also, they don't want to cause offense to their colleagues, so if one of their friends makes a mistake, they don't like to bring it up . . . But if we are to compete globally in manufacturing, we have to address these issues . . . Plus, of course, quality inspection at every stage of the process . . .'

At the end of the tour, she glanced up at the tall yellow cranes that ran along the factory ceiling. 'So, tell me, Anand,' she said, mischievously, 'do you ever go joyriding on those cranes after-hours?'

'Kavika!' he said, laughing. 'Do not even think of suggesting such a thing to Pingu . . . He'll give me no peace . . .'

Somewhere during the tour, he had forgotten to be awkward with her.

Back in his office, he had just pulled out his checkbook when the phone rang. Absorbed in their conversation, he did not look at the identity of the caller before answering; this was his mistake.

'I find your attitude utterly unreasonable. Hello, hello, can you hear me?' Harry Chinappa's voice was sharp and loud.

'Sorry?' said Anand. 'What?' He could feel his face flush; he could tell from Kavika's face that she had identified the voice on the telephone.

'It is utterly ridiculous on your part. How can we even think of altering all these arrangements on the eve of the party? All the invites have already been sent out; everything has been finalized for weeks. I must say, I find this utterly irresponsible on your part. Utterly.'

'Sorry?' said Anand again, his voice cautious. Perhaps Harry Chinappa had raised one too many whiskeys to his mouth and blown a crucial blood vessel. 'Please, what is this?'

'If you wanted a simpler, smaller affair, why on earth couldn't you have mentioned it earlier? Any effort I put into these little matters is only to help you, m'boy. To help you and Vidya. Far be it for me to impose my point of view on others. I am simply not made that way. But to bring it up now, when it is too late . . .

ridiculous! All the invitations have gone out; we cannot possibly call people up and disinvite them just so you can have reduced numbers. Never heard of such a thing! And when I have put so much effort into planning the guest list – we cannot think of serving our guests substandard fare. Simple, vegetarian food, indeed! What, I ask you, is wrong with prawns?'

'Nothing is wrong with prawns,' said Anand, flushing in embarrassment. He wanted his father-in-law off the phone quickly. 'Sorry? No, Vidya hasn't discussed anything with me about the party . . . No, no problem . . . Well, if you think it is important, go ahead. No, I have no problem with it.'

'That's excellent, m'boy.' Harry Chinappa sounded entirely mollified. 'Vidya must have misunderstood. Good, I'm so glad . . . Such a shock to my system . . . And what do you think about lobster patties? The caterers recommend them highly – they do them with a sort of coastal masala and serve them on a small banana leaf strip.'

'Sure,' Anand said, desperately. 'Go ahead. Whatever you like.'

He disconnected and saw that Kavika was laughing. Hard. He began to laugh too – and in an instant, years of handling Harry Chinappa fell away from his shoulders. 'Uncle Harry,' she said, chuckling, 'must always do things his way and no other . . .'

'He doesn't approve of my work,' said Anand.

'Oh, of course not,' said Kavika, lightly. 'He doesn't approve of Amir and Amrita's work either. And absolutely not of mine . . . And as for my personal life, forget it! He lectures my mother whenever he can, poor thing . . .'

'How are you settling down?' Anand said. 'Let me know if there is anything I can do to help, okay?'

She reached over and placed her hand on his, warm, gentle, his skin coming to life under hers.

'Anand,' she said. 'That is so sweet. But you guys are already helping so much . . . You have no idea . . .'

He wrote out the check.

'This is fantastic,' she said. 'Thank you. I'll drop off the receipt with Vidya. I'm meeting her tomorrow. And, Anand? Thanks for the tour. It was brilliant!'

Vidya was waiting for him when he got home, her voice as loud and as sharp as Harry Chinappa's. 'Ey, why did you do that? You made me look like a total fool with my father!' she said. 'You know, I'm trying to simplify things and you are just not being supportive! I can't believe this!'

'You should have told him directly, no?' Anand said. 'You wanted to make it simple. Why drag my name into it?'

'What do you mean, drag your name into it? As though you're a bloody guest in this house and not the host of the party . . . Then? . . . Why didn't you support me?'

He would not be cowed. 'Okay,' he said. 'Sorry. Shall I call him back and tell him *both* of us have changed our minds? Both of us want to keep it simple?'

He saw the shift in her face, emotion slipping behind nervous strategy. 'No,' she said. '*Now* it's too late. Let it be.'

In a matter of a day or two, Vidya seemed to accept the inevitability of the party and very quickly get caught up in her usual excitement over such things. She said, over dinner one day, in a welter of pleasure: 'Daddy says he is going to bring a special guest to our party. I wonder who it is.' She looked at him in sudden suspicion. 'Do you know?'

'Me?' said Anand. 'No. How would I know?'

'Oh. Mummy thought he might have told you. Even she doesn't know. But I can't believe you're not curious . . . !'

As an unforeseen, if slightly amusing consequence of his having given Harry Chinappa carte blanche on the party, this was, perversely, a moment when Anand's stock with his father-in-law had never been higher. This was made clear to him when he received a phone call from his mother-in-law: 'Harry is very satisfied,' she said. 'He is very happy with you, Anand. He was saying that the party arrangements are going to be first-class. You know how difficult he is to please. He still shouts at me, after all these years, if things are not just as he likes. Everything must be of the best!'

That Anand did know, having received the catering bills. He was shocked to note that Harry Chinappa had taken his acquiescence on the prawns to heart – proceeding to order lobster and a dozen other things that had Anand gaping. He wondered whether to call him and ask him to cancel some of the more exorbitant items on the list; imagined the conversation; and decided that, after all, it was just a stupid party catering matter, expensive but simply not worth the trouble. He would put his foot down next year. He wished he could share his father-in-law's extravagance with Kavika. She would be very amused.

But that was not a privilege reserved for him. He overheard Vidya on her cellphone at a moment when she thought he was having a bath. 'You know, Kavika,' she was saying, 'I really wanted to keep it simple – but Anand, he likes these large parties and he is siding with my father on this. I know, I know, I'm absolutely dreading it . . .'

Later, she looked at him, hurt. 'Why are you so angry with me?' she said. 'What have I done to you?'

Fourteen

By late evening, the frantic, happy din, the demonic lights, seemed to have been infesting his house for years. Presumably they all had places to live in, why couldn't they just go home, motherfuckers. Vidya had positioned Anand near the garden bar with strict instructions on his responsibilities. As he dutifully propitiated guests with alcoholic libation, he restlessly scanned the gathering crowd.

Vidya was an electric force weaving through the garden, the verandah, and the adjacent drawing room; receiving guests, feeding, introducing, sparkling, laughing, her elegant dress seemingly visible at different corners of the party at the same time. She had applied a great deal of makeup on her eyes; with the newly shortened hair, her eyes looked enormous. 'Vidya,' he heard friends say, 'how chic!' In a matter of moments, it seemed, all the other women present were contemplating chopping off their hair and dressing their bodies as Vidya had; where *did* she buy her clothes? He had seen her have this impact before – there was something about hosting a party that brought out a glowing performance from her – a sparkiness, a vivacity that was entirely charming – deflecting compliments that came her way with ease, turning her large eyes and conversation to the other person, blessing him or her with the warm glow of her attention.

He too had been charmed by this, all those years ago. When had she last turned that charm, those sympathetic eyes on him? He could not remember. He hadn't registered the slow fade of her interest till, around him, she had become the person she was today: irritable, impatient, unimpressed.

His mind, with a flush of gratitude, went back to Kavika's factory visit: to her evident interest, her questions, the laughter. Her engagement, her open appreciation of his achievement. He had not thought her particularly good-looking when he first met her; now he could imagine no one more attractive.

'Isn't she just beautiful?' said a voice in his ear. 'Mama?' He turned to his daughter; she was standing behind him and following the direction of his gaze.

'Yes,' he said. 'She certainly is. But you know who I think the *most* beautiful girl at the party is?' he said, with a teasing smile.

'Appa!' she said, flattered and self-conscious. 'You're just saying that. All parents think their kids look the best . . . Do you think we could have some soft drinks?'

'I'll send some over,' he promised and watched Valmika rejoin her friends. From a distance, they stood transformed into women, shedding their girlhoods, all glowing faces and sweet-bosomed curves, newly ripened, luscious, bedecked with glitter and silk and stone, endearingly shy and uncertain of their charms. Valmika, he thought, was easily the prettiest of them all. She had evidently inherited more than beauty from her mother; he watched with sudden pride as she moved between her own friends and her parents' guests gracefully, with no hint of teenage awkwardness.

Her little brother was a fixture at the fireworks display that had started a few minutes earlier on the street. Anand had positioned him carefully, knowing Pingu's enthusiasms and worrying about him hurting himself or others inadvertently. He was on the nervous verge of banning his son from the proceedings entirely or, at any rate, condemning him to watching the display from the safety of the garden, when Narayan had appeared to help. 'I'll be here, sir, and take care,' the boy had said, and Anand had immediately relaxed. He rushed back to the bar before Vidya could notice, his eyes beginning their restless scanning of the crowd once more.

He saw Kavika's mother first, before he noticed her; the sudden marked similarity between the two women: their lean height, the varying shades of gray, the simple Kanjeevaram silk sarees, and the matching traditional flat ruby collars. This time, Anand didn't wait for a gesture from his wife; he carried a glass of sherry to Mrs Nayantara Iyer, but Kavika had already moved on, disappearing into the colored waters of the crowd.

The guests pressed around the bar; in the drowning waves of noise, Anand glanced upward to the only uncrowded space, the air that stretched and ballooned to the sky, interrupted by clouds and the fluttering leaves of trees. Someone – his wife, his father-in-law – had strung the bottlebrush tree with little fairy lights and, in a semblance of festive fun, hung elongated village dancing puppets from the branches; in the noise and the wind, the long-skirted, blank-faced puppets slowly rotated, looking like dead bodies hanging by their necks, their ghosts animating the crowds below.

Considerably later, when guests were quite comfortably finding their own way to the bar and the hired bartender, Anand was finally free to leave his post. He made his way automatically over to where Amir and Amrita stood with a group of others, Kavika among them.

'Ah, there you are! Released from your bonded labor duties, I see . . .' Amir hailed him with a grin. 'Cheer up, bastard . . . I'm guessing from your tragic expression that full credit for this party goes to Vidya?'

'Yeah . . . Oh, absolutely,' said Anand, gratefully seizing the opportunity to clarify the matter in front of Kavika. 'You know me, yaar. I'm not into these large parties . . . prefer quiet evenings . . .'

He heard Kabir say: 'You're such a bore, yaar. Thank God for your beautiful wife . . . throws the best parties around.'

'Thanks also, I think, to our good and benevolent Harry Chinappa. I detect his subtle hand behind the arrangements . . .' said Amir, raising his glass. 'A toast to him.'

In the distance, Harry Chinappa worked his way around the room as only he could, with a calm tenacity and a bluff smile that apparently hid the darker shades of his personality from the people he encountered. He had the habit of placing one hand lightly on the arm of the person he was talking to, or enclosing their hands in both of his, of staring intently into their eyes as they spoke; by the time the conversation was over, they found themselves committed to a lifelong friendship with Harry Chinappa without quite being aware of how it came about.

Anand had forgotten to ask who his father-in-law's very important guests were going to be. At the height of the party, Vinayak, standing next to him said, 'Oh my god,' and the rest of the party went silent. And there was Harry Chinappa threading his way through the guests, Harry Chinappa not alone but gilded in his hour of triumph by the man who was following in his footsteps, stopping every now and then to smile at people, to shake hands, to modestly and lightly wear the tingling cloak of celebrity that swept over the room, Vijayan.

He was not alone; accompanying him was a film actor who had a huge following in the state but even so could not detract attention from the politician he was trailing. Even Amir and Amrita, Anand saw, appeared starstruck.

Harry Chinappa looked around. Their eyes met; Anand's first instinct was to pretend that he hadn't seen him, but he could not avoid his fate indefinitely. He duly made his way over and was introduced to Vijayan. A few words, closely monitored by his father-in-law, and the audience was over. Harry Chinappa placed one hand on Vijayan's shoulder and turned away, dismissing Anand, swallowed instantly by the thronging crowd.

The politician and his actor friend were, under his father-in-law's stewardship, soon seated at a card table, where Vinayak, with unerring calculation, also quickly planted himself.

Amir began to talk politics – and if Diwali wishes came true, Anand would have guided the four of them – Amir, Amrita, Kavika, and himself – into his study, where they could sit at their ease in the peace and enjoy the luxury of their conversation. And perhaps, after a few minutes, Amir and Amrita would excuse themselves and wander back to the party, leaving him alone with Kavika. He glanced at the woman standing next to him; surely this magical creature would infinitely prefer that to the noise of this rank and fevered crowd? She was nodding now as she listened to Amir, but whatever she was about to say was rudely interrupted.

'Good point, very good point . . . now, Amir, bhai-jaan, can you quit being so fucking serious for one evening?' Kabir had reappeared with a tray with tequila in shot glasses, salt, and lime, Vidya laughing by his side.

Amir shook his head austerely. 'No, no. Shots, ugh. What are you guys, college kids?' he asked, as he sniffed reverently at his glass of single malt whiskey. Anand refused the tequila; Kavika, Vidya, and Amrita downed the shots with Kabir.

The party seemed to shift into a higher gear. The music switched from soothing sarod to muscular, drum-thumping Bollywood, and Kabir immediately swung Kavika out to dance.

Anand noticed two things: Kavika was a graceful dancer, with all the right moves. And Kabir, in his well-tailored black sherwani, looked like a movie star.

Anand himself, as a concession to the occasion, was wearing a cotton kurta, rejecting the silk one that Vidya had laid out for him.

He had looked at himself in the mirror before the party; he'd appeared normal. He hadn't been able to tell if that was good or bad. Next to his wife, he had looked plain. Now, he suddenly wondered: was everything Vidya routinely implied about him in fact true? He felt it might be; he felt awkward, boring, dull.

The heat rose within him, he was enveloped in hot glue. The tide and tug of the crowd pushed him this way and that; he smiled perfunctorily at random faces. He had an overwhelming desire to leave immediately, to go home, instantly followed by the despair of knowing he was home; he could not leave. He went to the bartender and collected a glass of beer, watching the foam slip down the sides of the glass, settle, and slowly disappear into the pale yellow liquid. The puppets danced above his head in the wind, laughing at him.

Late that night, Harry Chinappa, flushed with the success of the evening, placed his arm around Anand's shoulders. 'Good job, my boy,' he said generously, as though the party was entirely Anand's doing. 'Those tiger prawns . . . Excellent idea, if I say so myself . . . Vidya, did you see how happy Vijayan was? Excellent evening . . .'

Vidya, stretched out in exhaustion on the sofa, with her feet up and her hand wrapped around a glass of water, looked at the strange tableau of Anand and her father in silent astonishment. 'My father seems happy with you,' she said later, and there was as much doubt as surprise in her voice.

Fifteen

The landlord's mother was unrelenting. She waved a gleaming sewing needle threateningly in the noonday sun. 'Well, boy,' she said to Narayan, 'are you going to tell me, or do I have to beat it out of you? You little rascal, keeping me twitching with impatience, like a mustard seed dancing in hot oil!'

'Amma should be here shortly,' said Narayan, grinning and sidling out of the courtyard. 'She will tell you everything.'

But it was a good hour more before Kamala entered the court-yard; she barely had time to remove her slippers and splash cold water over her feet and face before she was seized by the landlord's mother.

'Come and sit,' the old lady said. 'You must be very tired. Your son is a monkey and wants a beating. His speech is like this year's rain – ceaseless when you least require it and a drought of silence when you do. No, he has said nothing, nothing! But what little he saw fit to drop before me, thrown like crumbs to a passing crow, almost made me faint. So we have been waiting for you! Sit, sit. You must be tired, have some coffee.'

But grimy fatigue chased Kamala first to the bathroom for a cold bath, and it was a good half hour more before she settled down in the courtyard with a sigh of relief, a clean saree draped about her and her washed hair loosed from its customary knot at the base of her neck and spread open and wet across her back. She felt pleasantly light-headed and loose-bodied – like a wet rag squeezed dry and left to hang in the sun. She could relax into speech, knowing that the afternoon held nothing more than the indulgence of a delicious sleep.

The landlord's mother and wife fluttered about until they settled down beside her (having pressed a glass of hot coffee into her hand), with their hands full of work, mending, dinner preparations, baby.

'So,' said Kamala.

'So, sister, what was he like?' said the landlord's wife eagerly, her knee gently rocking the baby on her lap to sleep.

'Oh, oh,' said her mother-in-law, her hands busy peeling potatoes. 'Slow down, Daughter! Let her tell the story as she pleases . . . But Kamala-child, before this impatient one explodes . . . what was he like?'

Kamala could not help laughing. 'Very handsome,' she said. 'Even more so than he is on the screen. And also very polite.'

The landlord's mother and wife sighed in appreciation.

Vidya-ma's father had inspected the Diwali party preparations and had duly chastised the household servants and Vidya-ma – but he had also, unwittingly, given them an unexpected reward. His special guest of the evening was some politician full of trumpeting newspaper pride and noise. But, traveling in the politician's uninspiring wake – like the glowing evening star to his dull new moon – was the truly famous film star.

'Yes,' said Kamala. 'When I served him a snack, he did not just take it, as the other guests might. He made it a point to smile and say thank you.'

'He spoke to you!' said the landlord's wife, in an agony of happiness. Her eyes lapsed into the middle distance, savoring the vision in her mind.

'You are very lucky,' said her mother-in-law. 'What was he wearing? And did he speak to you again?'

'He was wearing a dark blue silk kurta, with gold embroidery around the collar, a gold chain, and gold rings – very smart, very handsome,' said Kamala. 'And no – I did not speak to him again. But Narayan did.'

'Narayan? Our Narayan! What did he do? He did not shame us all by misbehaving, did he?'

'No, no,' said Kamala, her pride evident. 'Quite the contrary.'

And as she spoke, her mind still echoed with her amazement of the night before – the sights and sounds of the party pasted bright and clear, and in the midst of that, wonder at her son's daring.

Anand-saar's house looked like a white, glowing pearl floating on the dark earth. Light was everywhere, fighting the night: small bulbs in wired lines limning the outlines of the building and the garden walls; clay-mud lamp holders patterned with peepholes; kuthivellaku lamps – tall brass ones, with strong, firm stems that held the five petals aloft, each with a burning wick at its tip. The lights were interspersed with the flowers that Kamala and Thangam had spent the morning arranging: saffron-white-and-green garlands of marigold, jasmine, and mango leaves. And of course, like thunderous rainfall over it all, the brilliance and dazzle of fireworks, rending the night sky with noise, smoke, and color.

The thronging guests may have enjoyed the extravagance of it all, but the lights and flowers and beauty of the house held no mysteries for Kamala; she had worked at them all day. She, instead, found herself fascinated by the guests themselves – creatures of rare glamour, the lights of the house captured and glistening about their gilded persons. She had once, in a fit of profligacy, spent money on a pair of tickets for the Capricorn Circus when it came to the city. She had chastened herself for this indulgence, knowing that the images on the posters that appeared on the backs of buses all over the city were nothing but false drama, invention, to act as deceptive lures for the circus – the actual show was bound to be a disappointment and waste of money. No such thing; she and Narayan had sat mesmerized through the show, at the clowns, the animals, and those remarkable flying ladies, who shocked Kamala first by appearing in sequined clothes of extreme indecency – little more than a bra and panty set – and then, when she was wondering indignantly if she should cover Narayan's young and innocent eyes, they proceeded to swarm up those ladders and fly through the air in a fashion that made her forget her son, their clothes, and everything else.

That same sense of unreality pervaded Kamala as the party unfolded. She gawked, amazed, as she once had at the ladies in golden chuddies who had tumbled from ring to ring and who had danced playfully around their pet tigers and bears like goddesses immune to the laws of the natural world.

Every now and then, Kamala and Thangam were required to carry a tray of hot snacks into the crowd. Kamala held the heavy silver tray gingerly, like an alien thing, nervous lest she bump into one of the silk-encrusted guests, gorgeous and gregarious, laughing and chattering, and splatter them with chutney. She (as per her instructions) was to invade each cluster of guests, smile, and proffer the tray, but she could not bring herself to do that. Instead, she carried the tray stiffly and walked steadily around the drawing room and the garden, avoiding all the large clusters and definitely going nowhere near the men clinging boisterously to the bar. Her goal was to return to the safety of the kitchen as quickly as possible, all the snacks on her tray preserved intact if need be.

She kept a wary eye out for Vidya-ma but did not spot her in the crowds. In the distance, she could see Thangam in a colorful

dress, holding out her tray of snacks quite nonchalantly and smiling
at the visitors, in an act of daring that left Kamala awed and
wondering.

If she was content to stand at the kitchen door with Shanta,
who seemed to have lost her acrid bite and gazed, subdued, into
the crowd, Thangam, next to them, compensated with a stream of
excited commentary. 'Look at that one!' she would say. 'Does she
not look like a queen?' That hair. That dress. 'And see that one
dance?' she said, gesturing toward a woman moving enthusiastically
on the verandah. 'She is doing the dance steps from that disco-
dancing movie.' And Thangam's own feet would move in rhythmic
imitation, in steps she apparently knew quite well.

'Do you know,' she asked Kamala, 'how much money they are
gambling for on that table?'

The card tables had been placed in a relatively quiet corner of
the drawing room, away from the bar and the dancing and the
noise of the fireworks, to enable the players to concentrate on their
game and to hear one another's bids. The tables were draped in
white cloth, each with a large silver bowl placed in the center. All
the action took place around this bowl: money flung in, cards dealt
and displayed; the women, their gold-littered robes of silk and gauze
sweeping to the floor, reaching for their cards with eager bejeweled
hands; the men, balancing glasses of whiskey and cigarettes and
cards; the rising tides of excitement that swept through them all as
the silver bowls rapidly filled and then overflowed with money.

'At that table,' said Thangam, 'each game is for hundreds of
rupees.' Really? said Kamala. That much? 'And there, that table,'
said Thangam, 'they play for thousands.' Ignoring Kamala's ignorant
gasp, she pointed her to the table in the far corner, where the film
star sat with his politician friend, Vidya-ma's father standing by in
close attendance, his daughter at his side, laughing and talking. 'And
in that table,' said Thangam, 'they play each hand for a lakh.'

And thus it was that Kamala overcame her shyness and nervousness and made her way to that table with the next tray of snacks, to serve the film star and politician and others. She wanted to see what one lakh of rupees – two years' salary – would look like all at one time.

Before the party started, Kamala had given her son some words of instruction:

'Keep yourself to the shadows. Do not show your face where it is not required. Stay in the kitchen with Shanta or, if you so wish, engage in conversation with the tandoori-oven man. Do not think to thrust yourself into the glare of Anand-saar's party. Be not tempted by the snacks they will serve; I am sure our turn will come later – or so it is to be hoped. Step not on passing toes; speak respectfully to the catering company people; and, in general, keep yourself to the shadows.'

He had meekly agreed, and she was pleased.

But, at some point shortly thereafter, he slipped away from the kitchen. She saw him befriending the barman, assisting him by pulling out soft drink bottles from the ice basin where they lay submerged. Eventually the lure of the fireworks was too strong and he darted away, and when Anand-saar summoned her out to the fireworks, Kamala instantly suspected trouble. She rehearsed worried answers and scolds in her mind – she should have locked that mischievous boy in the storeroom. But instead, she was sent to fetch a shirt, a brand-new shirt, worth hundreds of rupees, for her son to wear.

He reappeared a whole hour later, his face bearing a satisfied grin and his hands the blackened evidence of much lighting of rockets and crackers. Vidya-ma's father had instructed that they were to be burnt without cessation.

Kamala met him in the kitchen on her way out with a tray of snacks and paused long enough to say, 'Where have you been?

Have you filled yourself to the brim with fireworks? Your very body bears the trace. Go drink some water, but wash your hands well before you do.' He dutifully washed his hands but vanished before she could say more.

She was amused at his eagerness to return to the fireworks and thought no more of it, happy that he was getting such a fine reward for all his obedient work of the day – for Narayan had toiled fully as hard as a grown woman and earned a warm, fine reputation in the process. 'He must have inherited his nature from his father,' said Shanta. No one begrudged him his joy at setting off the fireworks. Just as no one would begrudge him later when it came time for all of them to eat.

Her next sighting of him, therefore, almost caused her to drop the tray of snacks. She froze into position, hardly noticing the guests' fingers that hovered greedily above the tray, like bees nursing at a nectar-filled flower.

She had a clear view of the card tables; she stared at the film star – memorizing his various aspects, the manner of his sitting and the angle at which he held his head (so familiar, and yet so startling to see it in the flesh). Her eyes (having drunk their temporary fill) wandered indifferently past the others at the table – the women, the men, the politician dividing his scattered attention between the cards and the conversation, Vidya-ma's father standing by in benign hospitality – when she saw him.

Mr Little Boy in Big Shirt.

He stood not three feet away from the film star, so close, staring at that great man with such a fixed intensity of purpose that Kamala became truly frightened. What ailed the boy? Had he lost all his senses? Had he sent his brains up into the sky on one of those rockets?

The landlord's mother leaned forward. 'Rama-rama!' she said. 'He must have wanted to get close to him . . . That is understandable, I myself would be tempted, but he should have concealed himself behind something. Foolish child! You must have been very angry.'

No, not then, said Kamala. I was simply scared.

No one paid him any attention – but Kamala knew that was a short-lived state of affairs. At any moment, Vidya-ma, or her father, or Anand-saar would spot Narayan, and there would be the reckoning. Shoutings. Shame. Perhaps an instant firing of his mother. Sure enough, Vidya-ma's father said something to the politician – and started to turn around. Run, thought Kamala. Move. Go hide yourself. A great anger began in her, that Narayan should ruin all that day's effort over a piece of foolishness.

But she was once again surprised. Vidya-ma's father glanced at Narayan, who, as though waiting for a signal, stepped forward alertly. Vidya-ma's father gave him some instruction, and Narayan hurried to the bar and returned bearing a drink on a tray. Vidya-ma's father handed the drink to the politician. Narayan returned to his watchful post, three feet away.

'Ah, so Vidya-ma must have placed him there,' said the landlord's mother approvingly. 'That is good. Very good. He surely would not have been given such a magnificent responsibility if he had not behaved with the utmost credit to us all.'

'Yes,' said Kamala. 'Vidya-ma asked him to be there.'

And in so saying, she knew she was not articulating the entire truth of the story. This business of waiting on the film star; of being positioned exclusively where none but he would have the pleasure of serving him; of having the film star wink at him and smile and call him by name, Narayan, as though they were childhood friends; of being treated to jocular exclamations of 'good boy!' – was, in fact, a situation that Narayan had brought about himself, with a temerity that none of the older employees – no, not even Thangam – would have dared to muster.

Narayan had hung around his friend the barman until he saw the film star raise his head, as though seeking a waiter. Vidya-ma and her father had stepped away to look after some other guests, and Narayan, sensing opportunity, had wasted no time. He had simply precipitated himself in front of the film star.

'Sir,' he said, a little shyly, 'what is your pleasure? How may I serve you?'

The film star, if a little amused by his underaged servitor, had not hesitated in asking for a glass of beer. After Narayan (ignoring the amused jibes of the barman) carried it to him, he did not return to his former place next to the soft drink bottles. He simply waited, three feet away from the film star, who, in no time at all it seemed, needed other things – a napkin, an ashtray, matches – and Narayan quickly provided all of these to him and to the politician and to the other players at that table.

And so, Vidya-ma returned from her hostessing rounds to find her most important guests being well looked after by the temporary-and-most-junior member of her staff. If she was startled by this, she did not show it. It had not occurred to her to provide a personal attendant to these guests, but the idea had merit. The film star was pleased. The politician was pleased. Her father was pleased. That was all that mattered.

'He is a good lad,' said the landlord's mother. 'So smart! Our Narayan.'

Her praise made it easier for Kamala to speak her burning desire. 'He is smart, mother, and I would so much like him to go and study in a paid school . . . he would do so well . . . but the money they charge is so high!'

'Child,' said the landlord's mother, after a moment of silence. 'You fully well know what the answer is to your problem.'

'What is it?' asked Kamala, surprised.

'Speak to Narayan's father's family. Speak to your brother,' said the landlord's mother. 'They will help you.'

Mother, said Kamala, and fell silent.

The landlord's mother shook her head. 'There is such a thing as too much pride, Kamala-daughter. There is such a thing as being too obstinate. And you should not let your son suffer for it.'

Kamala kept silent, not knowing what further to say.

She slept deeply in the afternoon and so found herself awake late at night, the memories of the party returning, reconfigured as worries, blowing through her mind, rising and falling to the rhythm of Narayan's sleeping breath. So bright, her child. So determined. How was she to provide him with a suitable education? With proper guidance for his life?

The landlord's mother's advice intruded, abrasive, grating like rough concrete against skin. If one had a duty to one's family to be loyal, then surely family too had a reverse duty to make the task an easy one.

Let her brother help, indeed. As though he were full of the caring, charitable impulses he pretended to. There was no prosperity waiting for her in the village. There never had been. Her brother knew that as well as she did.

She picked up an onion from a basket. It was a little past its prime, with skin lying pale and dry and brittle on the pink flesh beneath, slipping and tearing easily under the pressure of her fingers. The taste of it, strong and pungent, would be quieted only by fire, which soothed its acrid bite and allowed the mellow inner sweet-ness to emerge. An onion had a special magic; unbidden, it could take her back to her village and childhood, where her mother supplemented their variable income with a few onions and chiles grown in the dirt behind their hut.

Twelve years earlier, when the course of her young life had left her widowed and alone, expelled from her husband's modest family hut by his parents, the starving mother of a baby boy, she had turned to her brother for help.

He was living with his wife in what had been their late mother's hut, where her sister-in-law now tended to the onions and looked after her own children. Far from being the proud owner of many acres, he too struggled to make ends meet, and his response to his sister's predicament was unhappy; the far greater misfortune, he seemed to feel, was his; the tragic tide of events that had made her his responsibility.

His frustration and anger were nightly expressed in shouts – as though Kamala herself had been responsible for the accident that had relieved her husband of his life – and finally, when he returned home one day to find her lining her eyes with kajal, in a cruel, intemperate beating for behaving in a manner unsuited to a young widow. Especially one who was such a monstrous burden on her family.

With no resources apart from the sinewed strength of her body, Kamala knew quite clearly what she was going to do – get away from her brother and the village, travel to the big city and get a job that would flood her body with nourishment, and, through her, enter the eager sucking mouth of her son, who, unlike his predecessors, had not perished in the womb and miscarried but had fought his way out of that hostile tomb and now lay drinking greedily at her breasts, which, as if to compensate for those previously lost chances of succor, swelled gratefully with milk every time they were sucked dry, draining her body and filling her with pride at the same time.

'Please stay with us, Thange,' her sister-in-law said again, when Kamala whispered these plans to her. 'Your brother does not mean all he says. He often acts in a temper. You know that. He is very proud.'

He is a fool, said Kamala. You are too good for him, Akka.

'How will you live? Thange, how will you survive?'

'I'll manage, Sister. You'll see.' She did not tell her sister-in-law about her secret resource, given to her by a friend's mother – the name and telephone number of a job broker in the city.

The phone call to Bangalore was short and expensive, but very productive.

'Can you speak Hindi?' the job broker asked her in a business-like fashion.

No, said Kamala.

'Can you speak English?'

No.

'Do you know how to clean houses?'

Kamala paused in surprise before replying, wondering if this was one of those trick questions whose answers were cunningly other than the obvious. For who did not know how to keep a house clean?

Yes? she answered cautiously.

'Good. Are you honest, and a good, hard worker? . . . Are you of decent morals? . . . My good ladies are very particular, and I have never disappointed them . . . And, most important: Do you know how to keep a respectful tongue in your head?'

Certainly, said Kamala, for there was no one standing by to click their tongues and contradict her.

'And can you look after babies?'

Oh yes, said Kamala, hugging the tiny sleeping bundle held in a sling around her neck fiercely to herself. 'That is what I am best at.'

It had been a foolish plan from the start, but it had taken hindsight for her to realize why. It was a foolish plan for one very obvious reason, which was made immediately clear to her.

The job broker lived in a government compound, in a dirty two-story building painted blue that housed several families, for her husband worked in some capacity for the city corporation.

Kamala had spent half an hour staring at the building from the opposite side of the road, wondering how she was ever to reach it.

She had traveled from the village overnight on the bus, covering the four miles that remained within the city on foot, asking directions as she went, sticking nervously to the broken footpaths to avoid the rush of the traffic that skimmed past her on wings of steel. She stopped once to buy a banana, almost shrieking at the price she was asked and waiting suspiciously to see if the banana seller charged others differently before handing over her money. For all its extravagant city price, it tasted overripe and soggy, but its sweet flesh insensibly lifted her spirits.

And so she had arrived at her destination. Or almost arrived, separated from the government compound by a road of a nature she had never before encountered, even in her walk through the city – as wide as the broadest river, with screaming lines of traffic: buses, lorries, cars, vans, auto-rickshaws, motorbikes, scooters, all rushing back and forth without break and without pause, pouring onto a bridge that soared high. Kamala, clutching her baby against her with one hand and a jute bag with all her worldly possessions with the other, finally decided to ask for help. 'Anne, brother,' she asked, of a man walking by. 'How is one to get to the other side?'

'By crossing the road, sister,' he replied without breaking stride, 'like everybody else.' Kamala sat down and weighed the truth of his words. She discovered it was indeed true: people were walking across the road all the time, each time, it seemed, placing their lives in peril, leaping and dancing as they moved, jerking this way and that to avoid the oncoming traffic. They would start on their perilous journey, and she would hold her breath and almost close her eyes, opening them to see the people safely crossed to the other side.

It took her half an hour to decide to try it herself. Her strategy was to cross along with someone who looked sensible: not like the young boys who seemed to take pleasure in the daring crossing; and not someone so old that they might decide, halfway through, that they had seen enough of life after all and simply stop to meet their fate. She finally threw in her lot with two respectable looking women; they did not seem to mind the addition to their party; perhaps there was a greater strength in numbers. Kamala held her baby tight against her chest and kept close to the two women, moving in concert; dancing forward when they did, stepping back, freezing, running a quick yard or two, freezing again, moving forward, moving back, feeling the gusts of air from passing vehicles, in front of her, behind her, so close that she had almost felt the touch of their metal upon her skin, until they finally reached the other side. A deep gasp released the breath in her chest. Kamala turned to thank the other women and perhaps to share a laugh at the narrowness of their escape, but they had already moved on.

The job broker's husband's government job was possibly a post of some prestige, for their building had electricity and running water. The job broker herself worked part-time as a cook and made her money, really, from the people she placed − collecting from them a full two months' salary, payable (if she knew them to be reliable) in installments of up to six months.

All this had been explained to Kamala over the telephone, and Kamala was entirely agreeable. For a good job, even a payment of three months' salary seemed a small price. But now, as she waited for the job broker to appear, she steeled herself for the discussion about to come. What if the job broker, having coaxed her this far, now demanded four months' salary as her pay? Should Kamala demur or pay up without argument? Or perhaps argue a bit to save face, and then concede? Wasn't, in fact, even five months' salary, an indenture of almost half a year, worth it ultimately? To have good food in her belly and the promise of more?

The woman appeared on her landing, and Kamala looked down at the ground in relief. The job broker had the generous girth of someone who stretched her employers' budget to feed both them and her own family on ample scale. She had the calm demeanor of a woman who did not break her promises lightly. Kamala felt her fears quieten.

'Namaste, aunty,' she said respectfully to the massive and competent figure who stood a few steps above her. Her laden arms prevented her from joining her palms in greeting, but the job broker did not seem to take offense. She nodded back, looking over Kamala in a considering manner. Her eyes rested first on Kamala's face, and something in it brought a hint of a softening smile to her own; then they swept downward, dismissively, over Kamala's body and dress, before coming to a sudden, freezing halt halfway down.

'What is the meaning of that?' she said, pointing to the sleeping bundle tucked under Kamala's arm. 'That's not a baby, is it?'

'Yes,' said Kamala, smiling proudly. 'That's my baby. My little one, my son.'

'You are to be congratulated,' the job broker said. 'And do you have somewhere to leave it while you work? Someone who can look after it for you, this baby?'

No, said Kamala. I am alone.

The job broker stared at her before turning away to spit on the ground, the bubbles of her saliva resting on the earth before sinking and converting a small circle of dry sand into mud. 'You stupid, stupid girl,' she said. 'Have you no sense at all? Should you not have told me about this earlier? Who will hire you with a babe in arms?'

I can do the work with him, Kamala said. Really. Please believe me, aunty.

He is a good baby. No, he will not cry and disturb the masters, she said.

No, aunty, how can you say such a thing, yes, of course I was married and widowed – I did not lie about that.

No, he is not a mistake.

I can do the work with him. I promise.

But the job broker, as job brokers will, kept her eye on her own internal quality standards and could not be swayed. 'Come back when he is older, or when you have made other arrangements for him,' was all she would say, before turning away with a censuring shake of her head and disbelief at the naïveté of village girls.

And, as with all foolish, ill-considered plans, it had come to naught, as simply as that.

Sixteen

If someone were to ask her today how, as a young, widowed mother of one, with no experience and (in the light of this fiasco) very little of either judgment or brains, how then had she managed? – Kamala would rely upon the full serious weight of her dignity to reply, 'Well, sir, I contrived. Somehow, I contrived,' and she would clack her thin gold bangles together to indicate that, by some measures, she had done even better than that.

Returning to her brother's house was not an option she was willing to consider, come what may. When she went back to her village, she would go in strength and self-respect, or not go at all.

There was only one alternative open to her.

She became a coolie, a day laborer. A life immeasurably distant, it seemed to her, from the respectability of those who earned their wages monthly, or who toiled on the farmland that they and their ancestors before them had owned. A coolie worked through the day, took his money, and was free to drink it or spend it or lose it. A coolie had no fixed job, or job title. He went where the work went, one day to work on a construction site, another day to clear out a dirty gutter. And with the influx of village people pulled daily into the city, a coolie missing today, for whatever reason, was a coolie replaced with ease tomorrow.

Kamala joined construction work. Not, of course, on those large city sites that grew quickly into tall buildings of steel and glass – those were built by men in hard yellow hats using large, fantastical pieces of machinery – but on the smaller constructions: houses, small offices, which were built, brick by brick, entirely on the muscular strength of workers, male and female, just like her.

The supervising building contractor looked her up and down, and signed her up on the spot. She learned quickly, training herself to walk upon the narrow planks of wood that bridged one half-built wall to another with rounded trays of cement and stones and bricks balanced upon her head; sure-footed, so she would not slip and fall into the open foundations below and break her head. She learned to form part of the winding lines of workers who lifted, carried, passed, and dropped mechanically, as they were instructed, in work that used the skills of a monkey and the brains of a child and the strength of every muscle in her body for ten hours a day.

For her work she was paid only half what the menfolk earned. This was natural, she was told; it was a job that relied on muscle power, and the men had much more of that to offer. The money she earned was not enough to feed, clothe, and house her in any respectable manner, but the job had one saving grace: she could take her baby with her to the job site and fashion a sling for him on the branch of a tree, and let him sleep there while she worked. And, if he should wake hungry, nobody minded if he cried loudly until his mother could attend to him. In the clang and clamor of a building construction site, a baby's voice disturbed no one.

She lived with an acquaintance she met on the very first day, someone who swayed under a loaded head on the narrow plank bridge before her and whom Kamala instinctively steadied with her free hand. The white-haired woman thanked her in a voice rich with the stink of alcohol. She was fifty years old and as gnarled and dried as an old piece of firewood; she dealt with the circumstances of her life in the simplest of ways: each evening, she converted the day's wages into arrack and drank herself to sleep.

Their home was a makeshift tent constructed from debris rescued from job sites. There were a whole row of these slum tents along the edge of a road, close enough for the residents to walk to their jobs on the construction sites nearby, then dismantle them and move on in a year or two, when they were chased away by municipal authorities or when the jobs ran dry. Like the other tents, hers was waist-high, with a triangular frame of low, crossed wooden poles covered with old rags and bits of asbestos sheeting, and draped over with a blue plastic sheet held down by stones placed along the edges. Inside, another sheet of blue plastic was spread on the floor, sufficient for the summer but none of it very effective against the wet of the monsoon, which sank, dense and cold, through all the layers – the plastic, the asbestos, everything – to embrace them to its poisonous bosom. At those times, Kamala would let the baby sleep on top of her, the chill and damp of the ground below rising through her body and making her tremble, but the blood flowing within her strong enough to keep her child warm, especially if she covered them both with rags and more plastic.

As payment for the use of her tent and stove, Old Gowriamma asked for nothing more than a mouthful of the food that Kamala cooked at the entrance to the tent. Kamala fed her baby on her breast, supplemented with a thin gruel of boiled rice kanji. She fed herself and the old woman on the same kanji, adding to it, for their adult delectation, a bit of salt and a few red chiles. Water they kept in a small pot at the rear of the tent. Once a week, Kamala queued up with her neighbors at the roadside tap and attempted to wash off the accumulated dirt on her body while the others shouted at her to hurry up, for god's sake, for the tap was government-supplied and whimsical, running dry often and without notice. Under their gaze and shouts, she washed her arms and feet and face as best she could, wiping off the rest with a wet cloth, doing the same hurriedly for her child, and after a while, just letting much of it be. It was too much bother for a life that, every single day, led her straight back into the dirt.

Her peers on the construction sites were as hard as the concrete blocks they worked with: the harsh nature of life never allowed them to be otherwise. They handled their work without complaint and expressed their opinions with a forthright ease in voices strong enough to generate a headache and be heard three roads away and with endurance enough to maintain a point of view for hours. In such an environment, Kamala, with her head-tossing pride and sharp-edged tongue, might have been held by those who had known her well to be a candidate for a fight within the first week. But bewilderment had rendered her mute and, for the first time in her life, without argument.

Her companions formed their own notions of her character: she was a quiet one, keeping to the shadows of the world in a watchful way, never staring at others or challenging their gaze with her own, no matter what the provocation; volunteering no facts about herself, so tightfisted with her words, it was annoying for those who liked to enliven their work with casual conversation. In mitigation, however, it was also acknowledged that she worked hard; she learned quickly; she picked arguments with no one and gave no trouble; she raised her head from her work only, it seemed, to listen intently to the sound of her baby's cry.

After a few attempts to draw her out, most of the women left her alone in some sort of acceptance. Of the Kamala who had left her brother's home in anger and eagerness for the excitement of a new life, they knew nothing. And Kamala's silence grew and grew, blanketing her mind, her skin, thickening her sense of taste and the sensitivity of her fingertips, rendering them, like the rest of her, hard and dead.

The months slowly turned into one year, and then two, and then moved into a third. It looked very much as though this state of affairs might continue endlessly, until her hair whitened and her teeth fell out and she learned to take comfort like her tent mate in a bottle every evening. Except, of course, the gods had made her of a certain temperament and finally decided, one fine day, to put it to some use.

The day started out much like any other. The house they were working on had been in progress for six months now, and Kamala had seen it change from a weed- and wild-bush-encrusted plot of land that had taken them a week to clear to a three-story edifice, the layered slabs of concrete rooted deep into the earth with steel-spined cement pillars. This morning, she formed part of a line of women who passed heavy concrete bricks along, hand to hand, from the pile on the roadside where the supplying lorry had deposited them, up two temporary wooden ramps to the second floor, where they were stacked once more, this time behind the stonemason, the maisthri, who was layering them with cement into the wall that when completed would face the road.

Kamala did the job automatically, her body well used to the mechanics of hefting and passing. She stood second in the line, next to the woman who hoisted the bricks from the roadside pile, and from her position she had an unobstructed view of the construction site, the bricks that left her hand reappearing eventually in the hand of the maisthri perched like a large squatting frog, two floors above.

Her wandering eyes came to rest on her son. He was two and a half years old. Small, dark, and dust-covered, he played, as he did every day, with the young children of other on-site mothers, in the heaped piles of sand and chipped granite stones that fronted the site and spilled onto the road. His legs and arms were sturdy, his belly was round – and that thin protective layer of flesh was, for Kamala, her single greatest achievement. She still breast-fed him at night, just before he slept. Was it milk that flowed into his eager suckling lips, or her blood itself? Whatever it was, it drained her as it filled him, taking with it the last vestiges of her youth and leaving her body scrawny and roped with muscles, but that precious nighttime feed had filled and coated his body, shielding him and keeping him alive and strong.

He, her baby, had grown up on the construction sites; this was his natural world. He had learned to walk among the heaped mounds of sand and stones, staggering on little bare feet past rusty nails and sawed-off, treacherous pieces of wood, their shards reaching out greedily for his soft baby flesh. Kamala had fed him his first foods in such surroundings, had watched him holding unsteadily on to the sweet biscuit she might buy him for a treat from the corner bakery shop, watched him drop it in the sand and stuff it back into his mouth before anyone could run to him and stop him.

He never lacked for peers; there were always at least two or three other young children playing around. They appeared at work, on the hips and heels of their mothers, to the loudly exclaimed irritation of the contractor. What, was he running a nursery school or a badly paying construction site? But the contractor's irritation became the pearl in the shell of Kamala's life.

Even now, her son was following the leader of the pack, a little girl of six, who supervised the other children with an air of authority undiminished by her ragged, dusty locks and oversize dress, which slipped off one shoulder and hung forlornly to her ankles. She bounced a large baby on her hip and scolded the other toddlers if they dared to act obdurate, smacking them if they strayed past the area demarcated for their on-site existence – a great comfort to the mothers, for the road to the east was frequented by fast-moving cars, and the sand piles to the west guarded their children from the deep foundation pits and the risk of a careless slide into great injury.

Sometimes, when the work was going smoothly and the money flowed in without argument, or perhaps simply when his wife and his mother had between them allowed him a good night's sleep, the contractor would watch the little girl commanding her brood and joke, 'Perhaps, little one, you should supervise the full site for me, uh? Work will happen superfast then, no?' and give her a one-rupee coin, being careful not to let his fingers touch hers, for she was filthy and he was a fastidious man.

But this was not destined to be one of those days.

There was a tension in the air this day, but the workers kept unusually quiet since the site was being toured by the property owner and the architect. The contractor, who treated the workers either with civility (if things were going well) or (if things were not) with high cursing and shouting, now assumed a third, coy aspect: nervous as the owner and the architect inspected the house, ingratiating and seeking, as soon as possible, to plead for more money. In this mission, he was hampered by his own actions: he had not planned for the sudden rise in cement costs and for the delay in raw materials caused by the overwhelming building demand in the city. In such a climate, when voices had been raised, dissatisfactions expressed, and the money had not been forthcoming in satisfying quantities, the late and drunken arrival of the mason had been the thunder that presaged the storm.

The maisthri was a man whom Kamala had never liked, for he partnered his undoubted skill in masonry with a roving eye and foul mouth and a manner that implied that the women who worked on the site without the protective eyes of their menfolk were there for his personal delectation. Today he arrived two hours after everyone else, right when the owner was making his tour of inspection. The contractor opened his mouth to shout and then, realizing his audience, subsided until the owner should leave. The maisthri sullenly fell to work; the women were organized into a line to feed him the bricks he needed.

As quiet as she appeared, Kamala was not indifferent to the atmosphere on the construction site. It was rich with anger and tempers held in check. The voices kept suppressed while the owner toured the property emerged rested, refreshed, and stronger as soon as he left. And in the beating of the voices around her – the maisthri surly, demanding; the contractor angry in turn; the spreading excitement of angry comments rippling through the rest of the workers – Kamala could feel, in soothing counterpoint, the rhythm of her breath within her, the strong pull of air in her nostrils fueling her labors; the weight of the stone placed in her hands; the strength and play in her muscles as she hefted it from one side of her to the other; the welcome give in her body when she released the weight into the hands of the woman next in line.

You drunken, misbegotten rascal, she heard the contractor shout from his position next to the sand heaps where the children played, his rage magnified by the two floors that separated him from the mason. You come to work late, drunk, and then you ask me for more money? You rascal.

What, sir? said the maisthri, putting his tools down and staring at the contractor in a manner most disrespectful. You want good work, but you are not willing to pay. Why should I work for you? Other sites pay much better.

A few of the workers, sensing opportunity, agreed in loud mutters. Others, like Kamala, did not want disruption in their lives and kept quiet. She kept her eyes lowered, not wanting, even by accident, to offer anyone the direct gaze of confrontation. The bricks continued to pass through her hands, from left to right.

'You rascal,' said the contractor. Who will hire you? Only a trusting fool like myself. Go from here, you little rascals. Almost causing me to trip! Go that side!

Kamala looked up hastily; the last few phrases were addressed to the clot of little children. Her eyes searched urgently for the little six-year-old girl – she would surely lead the children smartly out of the way of adult noise and trouble. But the girl had stepped away, busily escorting a smaller child to the corner tap for a drink of water. The four other children, toddlers all, moved uncertainly in her absence.

'Did you not hear what I said?' the contractor shouted, his choler welling further at their lack of comprehension. He cast a look of dislike at the women working in the line, the sins of their babies visited upon their heads. 'Go that side! Cluttering up my site!'

After some hesitation, the children began to move away. All, Kamala noted, except her son.

He sat halfway up a sand pile, scooping the fine grain with his hands and letting it trickle through his fingers atop a growing miniature hillock. He was absorbed and pleased with the results, oblivious to the adult cacophony around. Kamala felt her breath speeding up and breaking time with the rhythm of her muscles. Was there a way for her to run to her child and move him out of wrath's path, without bringing the entire brick-passing line to a halt?

But the contractor's attention had already shifted away from the children, and her anxiety receded. The contractor now worked to restore his dominance, turning his furious attention to the other workers.

'Why are you all standing around? Is this a street dance, being played out for your entertainment? Get back to work!' Sullenly, everyone, including the maisthri, did.

Perhaps the contractor should have left it there. He had achieved obedience. He controlled the purse strings. The sullenness, if given a day to fade, would be replaced by industry. Everyone present knew that the contractor, in fact, did the best he could. He was far from being as bad as some others in his position, and if he had difficulty in managing rising costs, well, then, he was not alone in that.

But the contractor, today, would not let himself be soothed. A semblance of peace returning to the site was broken once more by his voice, loud, embittered, querulous, weighed down by the injustices he labored under.

'Why I need to be burdened with you,' he said, 'the gods only know.' His words were addressed generally but directed, everyone knew, at the maisthri. 'What have I done,' the contractor said, 'to deserve it?'

The maisthri perched above them all and continued to layer the concrete blocks, his work slowing down as his own voice began to rise, once again, in audible counterpoint to the contractor's. That this was heading toward a bigger fight was in no doubt.

The tension began to infect Kamala. The maisthri was aggressive by nature; it was not likely that he would be content with words. Kamala kept her body poised and her eyes on her son. In a few moments, she was sure, the maisthri would abandon his bricklaying and storm down. And when that happened, she herself would swoop out and pick up her baby, still sitting peacefully with his hands in the sand, not one foot away from the contractor.

The bricks were not the usual red-brown ones made out of kiln-baked mud; these were of gray concrete, with a rough, grainy texture that could sear the flesh off your knuckles if you were careless. They were hollow, which rendered them, oddly enough, all the stronger. They were much bigger than the traditional mud bricks – and much heavier as well. Old Gowriamma had gotten careless one day and dropped one on the edge of her toenail – within a day, it had blackened and died. Their weight was sufficient that they had to be passed one at a time, hand to steady hand, instead of being loaded onto trays and balanced up the steps on the heads of the women. The maisthri too was careful with them; he had worked with them for years, his movements in his job as precise and restrained as his mouth was not.

So did the hollow concrete brick tumble out of the second floor by accident, the mason's hands getting careless as his temper rose, or did he engineer its fall on purpose? In all fairness, his cry of warning indicated the former, a shout that caught everyone's attention and echoed through the spectators in gasps and cries. The block tumbled heavily downward, striking a protruding steel rod on its descent, and getting gently deflected on a path that arced, with horrifying accuracy, toward the contractor and the little two-year-old playing in the sand at his feet.

The contractor saw the brick descend and hit the steel rod; he shied in fright and glanced at the child. There was just time for him to pick up or push the child out of the way – if he was the type to move quickly and in a well-coordinated manner. Perhaps he was not that type, or perhaps, with the child so dirty, he could not bring himself to touch him with his hands. Some would later remember him making a weak, ineffective motion, as though to push the toddler out of harm's way with his foot.

And then the brick landed safely upon the sand.

The maisthri, shocked out of his own temper, came hurrying down. The contractor, shocked in turn, could only stare blindly at him, searching within himself for words to deal with the situation. The silence was broken by neither of them. 'You dog,' she said. 'You street-filth-eating dog.'

Kamala had dropped the brick that was in her hands, careless of where it landed. She ran to her startled child and settled him tightly astride her hip. And thus bolstered and fortified, she turned to the speechless men confronting each other and seemingly unaware of her diminutive presence until she opened her mouth.

'You could have killed him,' she said. You rascal. You careless dog. He could have died. What did he do to you, my poor child, that you should want to kill him?

And then, with all the force of her well-developed muscles, she slapped the maisthri across his face. Next to him, the contractor flinched, as though he had received the slap on his own face.

Sister! she heard someone say. Don't do this. Come away. Your child is safe.

She saw the stunned look on the maisthri's face succeeded by growing outrage. 'You whore,' he said, stepping toward her. 'Who do you think you are? I'll teach you a lesson.'

He was prevented from doing so by the contractor, who restrained him with a warning hand on his shoulder. 'It was an accident,' the contractor said, as though more for his own comfort than for hers. 'It was an accident.'

But Kamala would not be comforted. Two and a half years of dammed anger broke through, sweeping everything – judgment, economics, her future – before it. Her child was, after all, not harmed. But her anger seemed to have nothing to do with that. 'You rascal,' she said. 'Scoundrel. Despoiler of your sisters and mother.'

Sister, sister, the voices around her said. The contractor said, 'Come, come. You cannot behave like this. What is this.'

She swung her hand again toward the maisthri; he stepped back and avoided it. So she collected her breath in her lungs and spat into his face. Hands tried to grab her and restrain her.

Do not touch me! she said.

And it was undoubtedly the force of her temper, radiating

powerfully from every inch of her, that kept everyone at bay, silent and watchful, as she went to the corner of the site, picked up her plastic woven lunch basket, and, holding her baby tightly against her, walked away from them all.

Her temper kept her company through the day, as she fed her son some food and scowled at the road that ran in front of her tent. Her only continuing regret was that she had missed striking the mason's face on her second attempt.

But by sunset she had calmed to the point of taking decisions. The anger that flooded through her lent a great clarity to her thoughts.

The next day, she rose before dawn. She quietly collected everything she would need that morning into a large jute bag. Then she woke her sleeping child, quieting his protests with the comfort of her breast. He did not wake fully, and so she maneuvered herself out of the tent with him sleeping on her shoulder, the bag clutched awkwardly in her hand. She quietly crossed the road, leaving behind her other possessions and Old Gowriamma, who slumbered on undisturbed with soft alcoholic snores.

The previous evening, she had reached up her saree skirts in the privacy of her tent and untied the strip of cloth that she always kept mid-thigh. The papers that crackled within were her talisman. She had told no one about it, even if it occasionally constrained her movements, feeling it fatten over the months with the same satisfaction with which she had witnessed the flesh collecting on her son.

She had counted them all out, the paper notes old and worn and sometimes dirty, but with their value undiminished. From the bundle she extracted a few rupees and proceeded briskly to make certain purchases that she would have considered very frivolous even half a day earlier.

And now, in the predawn chill, she planned to make a business-like use of them.

A lane led off the main road that housed the slum tents, and Kamala walked toward it. Down the lane, right at the end, in this quiet corner of Koramangala, was a large two-story bungalow, clean and new. Kamala knew it well; she had worked on it for much of the previous two years, moving to the new site only when the construction work on this was completed. The house was still unoccupied, its windows bare of curtains, the front door firmly locked. Some fellow came every now and then to attend to the garden; the only person who remained daily was an old watchman who spent his day hours squatting by the gate, smoking beedis and communing with the wall opposite. At night, he engaged in a flurry of activity – drinking a tot of arrack (purchased alongside Old Gowriamma), trying his luck and limited economics with the prostitute who opened for business at night in one of the slum tents after concluding her daytime labors as a construction worker, and finally, rolling himself into a tight, blanket-covered ball at a sheltered corner of the house's pristine verandah and sleeping the whole night through, waking a little after sunrise.

That was usual. Once a week, he vanished for a day and a half, attending to business god knows where. And that absence was perfectly timed for Kamala's needs this morning.

In the predawn darkness, Kamala paused outside the gate of the bungalow, hushed and abandoned. She opened the latch of the gate and slipped through, shadowlike, on the path that led to the rear. There, surrounded by high walls that would assure her of privacy, stood the object she sought: a cold-water tap that was used to water the back garden. The rooftop tank that fed it was kept full by the watchman, and now, when she turned it on experimentally, the water gushed out, cold and clear and priceless.

Her son, well fed on her breast, was content to sit sleepily while his mother grimly made her preparations. Then, when her fell intent became clear, he burst into tears, but to no avail. A quick smack reduced his wails to a continuous, grizzly whimper, and Kamala tucked her saree up at her waist and proceeded to give her son the first full bath of his life.

She stripped him of his nightshirt and rubbed him down with expensive sesame-seed oil, working it deep into the skin to soften it and dislodge the dirt, in a cleansing ritual she had almost forgotten. Then, when his body and head and hair were so well oiled he almost slipped from her grasp, she doused him with cold water from the tap and proceeded to use the soap that she had purchased along with the oil the previous day. She used it once to get rid of the oil and dirt, washing it away, and then, without mercy, used it once more until it bubbled and frothed under her fingers, rejoicing in the sweet smell that rose from his skin. When he was washed clean, she unraveled the top half of her saree and used it to dry him. The bath, or rather its earnestly awaited conclusion, revived him, and clad in nothing he capered about the lawn while Kamala attended to herself.

The sky was still dark, but the blue bloom of predawn was upon them. She had to hurry. She kept her underskirt on but removed everything else, unmindful of the depravity of the act in her desperate desire to feel the rush of water on her body. The oil gleamed against the darkness of her skin, burnishing it, and the cold water cascading through her hair seemed to wash away two and a half years of construction site dust. She raised her skirts to wash between her thighs and down the oiled length of her legs, and then, finally, she was clean.

As with her son, she dried herself with the saree she had just removed, and then reached inside the jute bag for a change of clothes, pulling out a clean cotton saree that she had carried with her for two years and rarely worn, saving it blindly for just such an occasion. For her son too, she dressed him in a new shirt and combed his locks. The kajal stick for both of them, to line their eyes. And for herself, as a finishing touch, a dot of kajal as a bindi on her forehead. Her hair ran wet and loose down her back; when it dried, she would tie it into a braid, and decorate it with a bunch of jasmine flowers behind her neck.

She wore no jewelry around her neck, wrists, or on her ears except for a black amulet thread that she wore like a necklace, but that did not matter. She was dressed and prepared as a bride might be, ready for a momentous change in her life. In the early morning light that began to glisten off the house windows, she caught sight of their reflection and rejoiced. The baby at her hip was clean and glowing and well dressed; if the contractor were to see him now, he would not hesitate to pick him up and hold him tight. And the calm, respectable woman in the plate of glass showed no sign of the desperate life she had led for over two years. True, her face was thin and dry and her body a little scrawny, but that could not be helped. And perhaps, if she handled the day with due attention, she might eventually have a chance to reverse some of that damage.

And thus, washed and attired, she turned her attention to the next step.

When the job broker emerged from her house, she was met by Kamala, who had arrived an hour earlier and squatted down on the dry earth in front of the building, waiting for her quarry to appear. She had moved only once in that hour, to peel and feed her son a banana. Now she rose and folded her hands respectfully.

'Namaste, aunty,' she said.

The job broker returned her greeting with some reservation. She was good at quickly sizing up people; there was an air of implacable determination about this girl that might signal trouble.

'You asked me to come and see you, aunty,' said Kamala.

'Oh,' said the job broker. 'It is you. Yes, yes. Finally . . .' she said. 'You must be Saroja, and you, wretched girl, are a whole two days late.'

I am not Saroja, said Kamala. And I am right on time.

Seeing the job broker's confusion grow, she explained. 'You asked me to come and see you when my baby was older,' she said. 'He is now two and a half years old, and I can perform any household job you want me to.'

The job broker stared at her in some astonishment and curiosity, as though hoping to penetrate this shroud of confusing statement. She seemed to notice everything, the job broker, from the happy toddler, clinging to his mother's saree and smiling up at her with a full-fed, sunny chubbiness in odd and telling contrast to the hollowness of his mother's cheeks, to the awe-inspiring aura of cleanliness that clung to Kamala, the washing and bathing and donning of scrupulously clean clothing. And, in the serious intensity of her face, the job broker finally registered a fleeting contrasting memory of the same face: younger, fresher, sparkling with a look of eager anticipation. 'Why, I remember you,' she said, her face incredulous. 'You came from that village, I remember, and with the baby.'

Yes, said Kamala. And now, as promised, I would like that job.

The job broker opened her mouth to indignantly repudiate this claim of old promises – for surely such statements were implicitly accompanied by expiry-dates and a time-bar? – but instead she said nothing and stood pondering.

Perhaps she was troubled by the weight of professional demands caused by the errant Saroja and her urgent need for a hirable maid. Or perhaps it was simply that Kamala's sudden and desperate appearance triggered some latent sympathy within the job broker, jostling her, for a minute, by the recollection of chances she had received in her own life that had allowed her to prosper. For, in spite of her brusque, businesslike exterior and her capacity for holding the hearts and dreams of others in her hand, the job broker was not, by nature, a bad woman.

'Fine,' she said. 'I will keep my promise.'

And so it was that Kamala had at last slipped upward into the ranks of the domestically employed, where she had remained for the past decade, working hard to raise her son respectably. She was proud of what she had achieved, alone, unaided. Prouder, perhaps, than her brother was of anything he had done.

But it was the unacknowledged truth of her life, celebrated by no one but herself. She had kept those years of her past secret, when she lived in a roadside tent and toiled amidst cement and stone; speaking about that time to no one, not even her son, for everyone she knew would find it shameful and degrading, not recognizing the strength she had discovered within herself because of it, or the fears of destitution that haunted her even today of waking up to find herself living by the side of the road in a tent, white-haired, drunk.

and, of course . . .

satyameva jayate
truth conquers all

Seventeen

Mr Ananthamurthy was fond of discoursing on the auspicious nature of Deepavali – and as though to prove him right, Anand received a surprising phone call.

'Happy Deepavali, saar,' said the Landbroker. 'I have good news for you . . . I have arranged some land for you to see.'

'Really?' He had not believed that the Landbroker would ever deliver on his vague promises. 'That's great.'

Early the next morning, Anand passed the biscuit factory and parked his car next to the bicycle repair shop opposite the Mariamma temple. The Landbroker was waiting for him, emerging from his nondescript car into the brilliant sunshine, wearing his oversize, gold-rimmed dark glasses and a tight pink polyester shirt.

'Namaskara, saar,' he said as he clambered into the passenger seat next to Anand and pulled a large satellite photograph out of a file. 'Gugalarth,' he said, and Anand blinked uncomprehendingly for a moment before he realized he was looking at an image downloaded from Google Earth. On this, the Landbroker had drawn the outline of a spread of land that enclosed several contiguous farms, his stained finger stabbing at the paper while he spoke at length and with some intimacy about the land, twelve acres, saar, and the price per acre. On paper, the land looked small and somehow false, as the earth does when seen from a plane, a piece of a strange planet that cannot possibly translate into human concerns.

In a manner that invested the proceedings with a pleasing frisson of secrecy, they left Anand's car tucked into a side road and drove across to the farmland in the broker's nondescript car, inconspicuous and incapable of alerting anyone to their presence or their interest in the property, fluffing the golden dust of the sandy road about them.

The Landbroker explained that acquiring this land was not going to be a straightforward process. The land was owned by different farming families. But no problem, he could and he would bring them to the table — that was his job, after all — and he was very good at it. 'I know them, saar,' he said. 'And they know me. Most importantly, they trust me. They know I will not cheat them; promise them one thing, give them another. Trust is very important, saar.'

They stopped down a narrow, bumpy road. Night rains had washed the countryside; in the morning sun, the burnished earth glowed an ancient emerald green. Anand was instantly captivated. The crop cultivation had stopped; quick-growing eucalyptus formed a young grove in one field; others were bare, dotted with wildflower bushes and solitary trees. He was reminded of growing up in Mysore; of gardens and endless trees, of cycling past open spaces; he went tumbling hastily into a future where he would buy this land and he would bring the children and they would tumble through the fresh air in turn, enjoying picnics and racing through the wild grass with the wind on their cheeks.

The arrivistes of the city were in the near distance; the newly built warehouse walls, the distant buzz of chain saws cutting trees and drills boring their way through stone, the gentle mist of cement dust, settling like perfume on the leaves of the eucalyptus trees.

The land was pure, so beautiful. So suitable for his factory. He wrenched his mind away from fantasy. He turned to the Landbroker, waiting quietly to one side.

'Listen,' he said, 'I do not like to deal with underhand fellows. No rogues. No political parties or goons. No criminals. Nothing like that.'

'Me neither, saar,' said the Landbroker. 'Hai-yo. They are all rascals. I do my work and like to live a peaceful life. But some bribe,' he said, 'will have to be paid to the registrar clerk. For registering the sale deeds.'

'Why?' asked Anand.

'Come, saar. What are you saying? How else will it get done?'

'Right,' said Anand.

'So, shall I proceed with this?' asked the Landbroker. He outlined the rates and terms in greater detail. 'Some portion will have to be in cash – that you organize. I will do as quickly as possible, saar. It all depends. Some families will agree quickly; others may take more time. Some will have brothers who are living somewhere else and so on. It is complicated and it will take some time and effort, but I can do it for you, if you are sure . . . So, saar, I can proceed freely?'

Anand did not allow his anticipation to show. 'Let me see the land papers first,' he said, frowning slightly. 'Before I give final okay.'

'Yes, saar, of course. You will need to show your lawyer.'

The Landbroker gave his sudden smile. He scooped up a handful of the red earth between his fingers, crumbling the soil before looking up at Anand. 'Very good, saar. It is a lovely land, you will enjoy. You can grow things in one corner, even if you are building factory on one side. That will give you some flowers or some fruit trees. You can take home for your family.' He whacked at a wild-flower bush with a dry twig, beheading a few buds, as iridescent in his pink shirt as a large butterfly against the brown and green of the earth.

Anand would not let himself get excited about the land he had seen. There were two vital, monsoon-engorged Ganga-Yamunas that must be crossed before they could proceed. First, the Land-broker had to collect all the land papers from the various sellers. And then, a lawyer would need to vet those papers for signs of fraud or wrongful ownership.

But without any fanfare, the Landbroker arrived at Anand's office a few days later carrying an outsize plastic bag. From this, he pulled file after file, piling them on the table in front of Anand's astonished eyes. 'The title papers, saar, for the land . . . These are all copies, saar. You can leave with the lawyer. But no need to worry, saar. They are all good.'

The real estate lawyer's waiting room was filled with urgent, busy people on cellphones carrying oversize documents and trying to assess, out of the corners of their eyes and in between their phone conversations, who the other people in the room were, new money sitting uneasily amidst a pervasive atmosphere of old legal mustiness.

Anand was currently working with three separate lawyers: one for the factory work, reviewing contracts. One, an internationalist maven, who charged exorbitant rates for his advice on the Japanese contracts and who always seemed to be traveling to exotic loca-tions whenever Anand needed to speak to him; traveling, Anand speculated darkly, on the very fees that he had paid him for his time. And now this real estate specialist, to review the land papers that the Landbroker had given him. At this rate, he would soon know sufficient law to hang up his own board: ANAND K. MURTHY, LSL (LAWYER, SCHOOL OF LIFE).

Anand was given to impatience, but he sat quietly. Today he would hear his fate. He had left copies of the Landbroker's papers with the lawyers. Rural land records were notorious for their dubious provenance. If the papers were dubious; if the titles were not clear; if there could be multiple confusing ownership histories; if the deal smelled even the slightest like fraud, Anand would learn of it today.

At some point in the past, someone in the law firm had made a redecorating effort with heavy wood and potted plants, but like the junior lawyers and clerks bustling by, the plants looked tired and gray, as though they too were fed on half-emptied, cold cups of tea. At last, a clerk summoned him into the air-conditioned inner office.

The senior lawyer, despite his reputation for real estate prowess, was dressed in a badly fitted suit and glasses that slipped down his nose and framed an overgrowth of nostril hair. He sat behind his desk, imprisoned by stacks of files. 'Come, come, sir, sit,' he said to Anand, while simultaneously dictating to a clerk in a corner. 'Vere-to-four – and he-yur-under – the ven-daar – shall be – required . . . Please sit, sir . . . Required! Fool!'

Anand sat.

The Landbroker was waiting by his car. 'Well, saar?' he said and smiled, seeing Anand's expression. He removed the gold-edged glasses and flung them on the car seat beside him.

Anand laughed in response. 'Go ahead,' he said. 'I'll organize the money as you require.'

He gripped the Landbroker's hand. When he turned away, the scent of soil, of that rich, magnificent piece of land seemed to linger on his skin.

★   ★   ★

His relief was enormous; in the car, flush from the Landbroker's success, he telephoned Harry Chinappa.

'Ah, Anand,' said his father-in-law. 'So glad you called. Now, about Sankleshwar . . . I have been in touch, things were a little slow because of the Diwali holidays but should get moving now. I don't want you worrying.'

'No. That's okay,' said Anand. 'Actually there is something else that has worked out, so there is no need for me to proceed with Sankleshwar. Thank you,' he added as an afterthought.

'Something else?' said Harry Chinappa. 'What do you mean, something else?'

'Twelve acres,' said Anand. 'Remember that Landbroker I was telling you about?'

'What? That Vinayak Agarwal's fellow? I thought we had decided that he was entirely unsuitable, most unreliable . . .'

'He seems reliable. I have just received the lawyer's opinion on the title papers.'

Harry Chinappa was silent. 'I see,' he said, finally. 'One rather wishes' – and Anand could hear the wind that presaged the storm – 'that you could have told me a little earlier that you were dealing with that fellow.'

'I did,' said Anand, and he was surprised when Harry Chinappa said no more.

Anand asked: 'Shall I speak to Mr Sankleshwar? About this?'

'Good lord, no,' said Harry Chinappa. 'I'll tell him myself. I'm meeting him next week for my own development work. I don't want you saying something to mess that up.'

'Okay,' said Anand. 'Excellent. Please tell him thank you.' He felt a ridiculous sense of freedom, like a schoolchild who learns that dreaded exams have been canceled. Around him, the traffic seemed to toot and whistle in happy celebration.

★   ★   ★

His mother telephoned on a Sunday morning as Anand and his daughter grappled with geometry, Anand applying a varied and pungent vocabulary to a cylinder that defied the normal rules of existence and presented a new surface area with every calculation. Anand turned to the phone thankfully – his mother's plumbing problems were surely easier to solve.

His mother was not calling about plumbing. He listened to her, sat in silent thought, and then went in search of Vidya, finally running her down in the bathroom where she was applying hot oil to her hair.

He tried to keep the momentousness of his announcement out of his voice; the doubt that had flooded his system when he listened to his mother, the sense of awkwardness that still would not fade, even half an hour afterward.

'My father,' he said, 'is coming on a visit.'

Vidya's eyes widened in the mirror; she continued to massage her scalp. 'Oh.' Hot oil in the spoon, onto her palm, into her hair. 'After all these years? Wow.'

Fingers on the scalp, running down her hair. 'When's he coming?' she asked. 'God, yaar, what will he eat? He's very strict veg, no? Remember that fuss he made at that hotel? We'll have to not cook any meat in the house. Is he just dropping in, or will he actually spend a night?'

Actually, said Anand, I think he is coming to stay for a while. A few weeks.

'What!' she said, finally stopping the hair massage. 'How come? What happened? My god!'

His mother had maintained a studied carelessness over the phone, as though this arrangement was standard operating practice between them: she was to go nurse her mother, who was teetering, aged ninety-three, on her deathbed in Anand's maternal uncle's house. In the interim, could Anand please take care of his father. 'Come to Mysore,' she said, 'this very week and pick him up and take him back. I will keep everything he needs packed. Good, very good. And don't forget that he has to take his blood pressure pills. He does not like to and he pretends to forget.'

I won't forget, said Anand.

He recounted his mother's conversation to Vidya very briefly, and something about his demeanor altered the multiple hasty comments that rose to her lips.

'I'll get the guest bedroom ready,' she said.

'Will he be here very long?' she couldn't help asking.

Anand did not answer.

His father spent the drive from Mysore to Bangalore with his eyes closed, sleeping or otherwise. He emerged from the car and confronted the bulk of his son's house, representing as it did the fruits of a path he had always opposed. Anand kept silent, embarrassment warring with the pride within him. Would his father see his house as an affront? As a repudiation of his own strictly austere, lower-middle-class brahmin lifestyle? Why couldn't Vidya have agreed to a smaller house? Happily, the house did not suffer its supersize alone: every home in this neighborhood seemed to suffer from architectural avoirdupois. And, at least, thank god, it wasn't showily encased in sculptured white marble like the house opposite. The garden flowers were nice. And the house, though overly large and gleaming, was considered, by their friends, to be in good taste. Would his father recognize that?

His father turned to him. 'Where is my bed? I hope,' he said, 'it is not too soft.'

Years before, when Anand had told his father about his choice of profession, the conversation had not proceeded successfully. 'A factory? But you are talking of becoming a businessman!' his father had said. 'That is no sort of profession for us.' A businessman. A profit maker. Someone who spends the day counting money and then holding out his hand for more. That is who you wish to be? There is no respectability in such a work. What learning does it require? Tchi-tchi. Anand's family had agreed.

'Child, you do not come from such a tradition,' said an uncle. 'Leave it to those who do.'

'One cannot maintain sound moral and spiritual outlook in the face of the temptations that such a choice of work will bring,' said a grandfather, before passing away.

His father, of course, knew where he had erred: in letting Anand go, at the age of eighteen, to Bangalore to study; and in compounding that mistake by not forcing him to choose between the serious-minded Venkata Iyer Engineering College and the Sri Guru Sevak Engineering Institute, both with excellent academic reputations and very suitable, but allowing him to opt for the Jesuit-run St Peter's Academy of Arts, Sciences, Commerce, and Engineering.

Like Mysore, Bangalore might be in South Karnataka but, alarmingly, it prided itself on being 'cosmopolitan.' Anand's parents had had no illusions as to the meaning of this word: an influx of people from the farthest reaches of the state, well beyond the influence of Old Mysore. Worse: people from North India, as bad as foreigners in their habits. The very brahmins of Kashmir were rumored to eat meat – and when you said that, you had said everything. His father had inspected the two-page cyclostyled college prospectus dubiously. 'Studying engineering? In this place? They are also teaching science, and your marks are good enough to register for either. One may say that science is a good subject, one can obtain a Ph.D. and become a professor, good, good, but,' his father said, forcing himself to practicalities, 'an engineer has more scope.' Medicine or law would have done just as well; Anand's father had a classical respect for all three. Later, when

Anand's mother was absent, he had given his son advice that embraced the nonacademic as well. 'They drink,' he said, with a vague notion of Christian mores derived entirely from the cinema. 'In church. They drink wine to show that they are good Christians. Please don't drink.'

Very quickly, Anand's father settled into a daily regimen indistinguishable from his routine in Mysore – establishing himself on the sitting room verandah mid-morning, cross-legged on a divan, a stack of newspapers at his side. His spine was invariably upright, his feet neatly submerged beneath his thighs; the vibhooti-ash markings on his forehead indicating that he had finished with both his bath and his morning pooja. His clothing was free of the shirt-pant-belt-shoes he had worn to work for forty years as a minor bureaucrat; instead, he dressed in a faded banian vest and a white cotton dhoti, freshly laundered and crisp. As the weather cooled through the day, various other items settled like sediment over this basic outfit: a half-sleeved shirt, a sweater, socks, and, finally, the sign of true winter: a long woolen muffler wrapped under the chin and over the head.

Vidya, in some consternation, suggested to her father-in-law that on unseasonably warm days he might, in his son's house, consider donning a shirt and (if he so wished) turning on the air conditioner, but Anand's father dismissed such artificial measures with scorn. 'I am quite comfortable,' he said austerely, returning to his daily solution of the sudoku puzzle printed in the newspaper, which exercise, in its wake, left the paper littered with pencil markings and creases where it had been folded down to a small square, the size of the puzzle. Anand was in the habit of reading his newspapers with his morning coffee; his father rose betimes and got to them first, subsequently regaling anyone who passed with a précis of the daily news that he considered important. 'The blighters,' he would say, 'have increased the price of the rail tickets again. Is this how they practice socialism? Will this help the poor?'

His conversation with his son revolved around the news. He evinced no interest in visiting Cauvery Auto, evidently not hearing the question when it was asked.

Vidya brought Anand a message from her father, sandwiched between the stress his father's orthodox lifestyle was placing on the house. 'Shanta is really grumbling; she is having to cook two separate meals: one veg, one nonveg – using separate dishes. By the way, my father called. For you.'

'Why?'

'Because your father won't eat from any dish that has been previously touched by meat. You know that. And now she may quit.'

'I'll speak to Shanta,' said Anand. 'Why did your father call for me?'

'Call him back, no?' she said.

But he did not need to. Harry Chinappa, after waiting impatiently for his message via his daughter to take effect, called him directly, the phone buzzing relentlessly at Anand like a highly strung mosquito. 'My dear boy,' Harry Chinappa said, 'I believe your father is in town. Excellent! Must plan a visit. Or perhaps you can bring him by one day with you after work? We can have a whiskey and catch up.' This was his father-in-law's number two method of dealing with him: orchestrated cordiality when he needed something done. 'By the way, I've had a word with Sankleshwar. It's a good idea if you come and meet him with me anyway.'

'Why?' said Anand. 'You've told him, no? That I am not interested.'

'It doesn't pay to be shortsighted about this, m'boy. I am not at all convinced about this Landbroker of yours.'

'Why?' said Anand. 'He's okay. I think. I am moving ahead with that.'

'Well, come for this meeting anyway. Mr Sankleshwar is an important, successful man, and it behooves you to at least say thank you to him personally.'

'Fine,' said Anand. 'Fine. Fine. I'll come.'

Eighteen

If her opinion were solicited, Kamala might have said otherwise – instead, it was generally accepted that an old man of particular habits placed fully as much burden upon the household as a demanding new baby.

Shanta, naturally, was the first to complain. 'Separate vessels,' she said. 'Separate menu. Who is to cook? Who is to clean all those extra vessels?' But this was Shanta's normal mien, usually ignored by everyone else. Except this time, when she won an unusual sponsor: Vidya-ma herself, who, instead of rebutting each of Shanta's complaints with one of her own, only said: 'You are right. It is too much. You are right.'

Shanta was unused to such easy victory and received it with open-mouthed befuddlement, but it quickly spurred on Thangam, who, nose twitching, complained to Vidya-ma dolefully about her own workload. 'Extra clothes to wash, ma,' and Vidya-ma listened again, though perhaps not with the same sympathy she had displayed to Shanta (for everyone knew that it was technically impossible to increase Thangam's workload: work added in one area yielded an instant scrimping in another).

Thangam and Kamala were summoned to Anand-saar's study

that evening. It was immediately evident that he was angry, a state that was rarely directed at them.

'The work in this house is too much for you, it seems,' he said, addressing Thangam.

'Saar, no . . . that is . . .'

'If so,' said Anand-saar, 'perhaps I need to look for someone new, Thangam.'

'Oh, no, saar,' said Thangam, hastily and with undue fervency. 'I can manage quite well.'

'Good,' said Anand-saar. 'I am happy to hear it. What are your responsibilities?' he asked Kamala and listened, frowning, as she enumerated her daily tasks. 'Well, Thangam,' he said. 'You will be happy to hear that you no longer have to wash my father's clothes or clean his room. Instead you will manage the upstairs by yourself, for Kamala can no longer help you with that; she will attend to his room and his clothes before her other duties.'

Thangam dared not complain. 'Okay, saar,' she said meekly enough and was dismissed, shutting the door behind her. Kamala waited alone. Anand-saar said: 'Vidya-ma tells me that Shanta has plenty to do with her regular work . . . Can you cook?'

Kamala said, in some alarm: 'Very simple food, saar,' but Anand-saar did not seem concerned. 'That will suit him well. A little anna-soru, without garlic or too much spice. Some curd rice. Dosa in the afternoon for his tiffin . . . You can manage?' Kamala nodded. Such dishes were well within her capability.

Anand-saar had more to say: 'Vidya-ma is also very busy, so if there is any problem or anything else, will you please come directly to me? Do not bother her.' He smiled. 'I rely on you to keep my father comfortable.'

Kamala nodded dutifully, though she was far from comprehending.

Beyond the paying of their monthly salaries, Anand-saar had

never directed household activities before. Certainly, beyond his occasional interactions with Narayan, Anand-saar did not intrude into Kamala's daily consciousness beyond the detritus of his existence, the socks and underwear she washed, the clothes she ironed, matters that did not bring her into any direct contact with him. Occasionally, he returned from the office before she left for her house; in such a case, she might bring him a glass of water or the tea that Shanta made, spilling not more than a few drops in the process.

Mostly, what she knew of him was derived from the truisms that Thangam offered with her superior knowledge of the workings of the household. 'One must never approach Vidya-ma for money. Speak to Anand-saar. He is the one who fixes and pays our salaries.' Kamala would listen to such statements with half an ear, for how did it matter who fixed the salary as long as it was paid regularly?

And now here he was, asking her to report directly to him, in a manner most unprecedented.

The duties were simple enough, easily accomplished but for the complications thrown in her path by the rest of the household. It started that very day, when Kamala entered the kitchen and approached the storeroom.

Ey, said Shanta. What do you think you are doing?

'Anand-saar's bidding,' said Kamala, facing her foe and not attempting to hide a slight smugness. 'Since you are too busy to cook for the grandfather, he has asked me to. If you have a problem with that, my dear sister, please go tell him yourself.'

It was a temporary victory. Shanta did not dare complain to Anand-saar, but Kamala quickly discovered that her daily task of entering the kitchen and emerging with meals for the grandfather was not to be a straightforward process. She had recently seen a movie with Narayan where the hero, armed (like all heroes) with little more than good looks and excellent musculature, had to penetrate a chamber of villains and extract a precious jewel, dodging (in the process) flying bullets, well-aimed knives, and a villainess who kicked in high-heeled shoes. Her task, Kamala considered, was no easier than his.

She could reach for no knife without Shanta grabbing it first, the cutting board was always busy, all four burners on the stove occupied and Shanta not above pushing her rudely out of the way. Every half hour's job doubled in time. Worst, when Kamala's cooking was done, Shanta would make a great show of smelling the food and gagging. 'Poor old man,' she would say, addressing Thangam if she happened to be around, or the refrigerator otherwise, 'his aging digestion is sure to suffer. I hear,' she would say, 'that you were raised like a royal princess in your village. Perhaps that is why no one taught you how to cook.'

'If it is so terrible,' said Kamala, 'do it yourself then.'

'I most certainly cannot,' said Shanta. 'Vidya-ma has forbidden me. Poor old man!'

Kamala managed with quiet grumbles – until Vidya-ma summoned her irritably one day. 'Kamala, what is this nonsense? Shanta says that all our food is getting delayed because of the time you take over some simple dishes. Why is this?' Vidya-ma was seated at the computer, her fingers clicking on the keys in time to her speech. 'And you must clean the utensils as soon as you are done. She has to reuse them, doesn't she? You cannot behave as though the kitchen is only for your use. You must learn to adjust with others . . .'

Yes, Vidya-ma, said Kamala and went in search of Thangam. This was intolerable.

But Thangam was full of her own woes and was not of a mind to listen patiently to Kamala's bitter grumbles. 'At least you don't have to clean the full upstairs, as I have to,' she said. 'I tell you, sister, by the time I get through my day, I am so exhausted, my very bones hurt. By the way,' she said, her face full of a recent worry, 'what has happened to your neighbor?'

'Neighbor?' said Kamala. 'Which one? That drunken Chikka-gangamma? Such a sad story! Her children are still working and sleeping in that canteen.'

Thangam interrupted. 'No, no. That young girl! Married to the machine tool operator. Your direct neighbor!'

'Oh, that one. So disrespectful! Yes, she was saying something,' said Kamala, trying to recall. 'Aanh. Yes. Her husband has lost his job. Perhaps now she will learn some humility. Why do you ask?'

Thangam was looking horrified. 'Lost his job? And you could not tell me this? You keep silent!'

Kamala eyed her in genuine confusion. 'Thange? Why does it matter to you?'

Thangam flung her duster down. 'Because she has missed her last two payments for the chit fund, that's why! If she cannot pay, I have to pay! How can you ask this! I tell you, Kamala-sister, not all of us are propertied as you are. No, do not deny it. That girl told me – she heard it directly from your brother himself. You have all the luck – so do not come here and complain. How on earth am I to find the money she owes for the chit fund? And what about the months that remain? Tell me that!'

'Do you not have savings, Thange?' Kamala asked tentatively. She knew that Thangam liked to spend and also supported her family every month, but still . . .

'Whatever I have will be wiped out in a couple of months if she doesn't pay, akka,' said Thangam, wretchedly. 'All of it will go . . . This chit fund is so large . . . Cursed thing!'

Kamala put her arm around the crying Thangam. 'I am sure she will pay, sister,' she said. 'Do not worry. Do not cry. Come now!

And,' she said, when Thangam eventually wiped her eyes on the edge of her khameez, 'I do not know what you have heard, but I am not propertied. That is not true. I have to work for every paisa just like every other human on this earth.'

Thangam sighed and involuntarily ran her hand over the glittering silk dupatta lying tossed on the bed. 'Except Vidya-ma,' she said. 'She does not have to work for her paisa.'

Apart from the skirmishes with Shanta, Kamala very quickly settled into her new duties. Anand-saar's father was very different from his son. Old-school in his manner and behavior, his needs simple, disciplined, and meticulous, reminding Kamala of the schoolteacher in the village, who had combined an interest in furthering the education of the village children with a strict brahminical aversion to letting them within two feet of him. When he asked something of Kamala, his voice was peremptory: 'Girl!' he would call, and Kamala would go running, to fetch the flowers for his pooja that she procured each morning on her way to work; to ready his bath, placing the stool in front of a steaming bucket of water and the mug in readiness; to fetch his food, freshly cooked and piping hot. After this flurry of morning activity, she cleaned his room and washed his clothes, and only when that was done could she turn her attention to all her other chores: the cleaning of the downstairs, which Thangam, on principle, now refused to help her with, and the myriad other duties that Vidya-ma – who seemed unaware of Anand-saar's strictures to the contrary – kept adding, daily, to her list.

Kamala returned home later and later each evening, until Narayan's face started appearing worriedly at the gate, waiting patiently for her until he was discovered there one day by Vyasa and dragged in to meet the grandfather.

The first Kamala learned of this was when she entered the

grandfather's bedroom, carrying his evening palaharam meal of fruit and hot, unsweetened milk and saw her son there. Valmika was on the bed, engrossed in her grandfather's stories about his own childhood in Mysore, so different from hers. Vyasa, having quickly lost interest in what was to him a bland and unheroic narrative, was absorbed instead in the activities of Narayan, who was carefully mending a bedside light.

Kamala did not know what to say, but she was saved from the effort by Anand-saar himself, who had entered the room behind her.

'Ah, very good, you have fixed it,' he said. 'Clever boy. I was planning to call an electrician for that.'

Narayan grinned shyly. 'It was just a loose wire, sir,' he said and proceeded to screw the fixture firmly back in place.

The grandfather seemed pleased as well. 'He has done a good job,' he pronounced. 'Yes. Is he studying hard in school? That is very important.' Kamala did not know if she was expected to answer this question, but once again, Anand-saar spoke: 'Yes, it is very important . . . Pingu, I hope you are listening to your grandfather?'

Kamala was thrilled at Anand-saar's praise of her son and hugged her pride to herself. She was careful not to mention it to anyone, but nevertheless, that simple moment of excessive pride was enough to invite jealous mischance – for the very next evening, she proceeded to burn Anand-saar's shirt.

She was busy ironing, but her attention was focused on ignoring the steady, poisonous drip of Shanta's grumbles. Kamala concentrated so hard and with such a sense of victory that when she finally looked down, the shirt was burnt. Shanta had her back to her; she hadn't seen. Quickly, Kamala folded the shirt and thrust it to the bottom of the pile of ironed clothes.

Upstairs she scurried, before anyone could notice, and buried the burnt shirt right at the back of Anand-saar's clothes cupboard, praying it would not be discovered until weeks later, when everyone had forgotten who had done the ironing on that particular day.

But when she heard Vidya-ma's voice raised in anger, Kamala knew her plan had failed. The three of them in the kitchen eyed one another.

'Go,' said Shanta to Thangam.

'No,' said Thangam. 'What does she want this time? You go,' she said to Kamala, who vigorously shook her head. Thangam sighed. 'Coming, amma!' she called, but she had barely hidden her accounts books away when Vidya-ma burst into the kitchen. 'Have I lost my voice, or have you all lost your hearing?' she cried. 'I've been shouting and shouting! What is wrong with you all?'

Kamala expected to see the burnt shirt flying like a wartime military banner, but no, fortunately Vidya-ma's hands were empty; she was upset about something else. Kamala lowered her eyes prudently to the curd rice she was mixing for the grandfather.

'I simply cannot find my dupatta,' Vidya-ma said. 'I have looked and looked. Where is it? Peacock blue with gold weave. Where is it?'

Kamala did not open her mouth. She had seen that dupatta just the previous day, in the ironing pile. Shanta had pulled it out and could not resist fingering it, her harsh face softened by an unusual yearning. 'So pretty. This must be very expensive, no? Very expensive.' By rights, that dupatta should have gone upstairs with the other ironed clothes. It was not in the current pile of laundry either; its glorious colors were too bright to miss. Could Shanta have been tempted? She too seemed frozen where she stood, next to the stove.

'Don't worry, amma,' said Thangam. 'We will find it.'

'You'd better,' said Vidya-ma. 'I'm not having my things missing, on top of everything. Find it right away!'

Kamala put the curd rice, lime pickle, and a plate on a tray and left the room; by the time she returned with the empty dishes, Thangam had smoothly produced the dupatta. 'Where did you find it?' Kamala whispered, but Thangam, instead of implicating Shanta, merely said: 'Under that pile of laundry, where else?' and would say no more.

Kamala knew it was useless to pursue the question. Her mind traveled, unbidden, to the Diwali party, to the end of that strange and glorious night.

It was close to the dawn. The lights were out in much of the house; Anand-saar and Vidya-ma had retired for the night. The messy aftermath of the party had been tidied. The kitchen was the only area that was still brightly lit. Kamala was spending the night and was to sleep alongside Shanta and Thangam on a bedroll. Their work was finally done; Narayan lay fast asleep in the darkened storeroom; in a couple of hours, Kamala would rouse him and send him home. She herself would follow as soon as she could.

Kamala felt her face fold downward with fatigue, her ears buzzing, a rush of relief through her body. Thangam was inspecting the almost empty bottles of soft drinks and alcohol that lay on the kitchen table.

'Did you see him, sisters?' Thangam asked, referring to the film star. 'Did you see how splendid he looked? What do you fancy, sister?' She glanced at Kamala.

'Is it permitted?' Kamala asked, eyeing the bottles on the table.

'Why not?' Thangam shrugged carelessly. 'We were asked to throw these away, were we not? What difference does it make if we dispose of them in our stomachs or in the dustbin outside?'

Kamala made her way over to the table and, after some hesitation, chose the dark brown cola that was usually advertised by a pretty actress who always seemed to be enjoying herself when she drank it. She poured herself a glass and, on impulse, added two ice cubes to it from the bag that lay melting in the sink. She sipped it gratefully; her budget rarely left room for such luxuries.

'Are you not having any yourself, sister?' she asked Thangam.

'I will,' said Thangam. She poured a little of the soft drink into a glass. Then she picked up a bottle of whiskey and poured the leavings into the same glass. 'Ah,' she said. 'What a man he was.'

Kamala glanced uncertainly at Shanta. But the cook was leaning against a counter and did not meet her gaze. Thangam filled a second tumbler with a similar concoction and handed it to Shanta.

Kamala hastily took a sip of her own drink in an effort to hide her shock. To drink alcohol as a female meant that you were very rich or very poor – in either case beyond the confines of ordinary respectability and dignity.

Thangam swallowed her whiskey and cola, and switched on the kitchen television. The screen was very small and the remote control had long since stopped working, but none of them cared. By a strange coincidence, their own personal film star, the hero of the party just finished, appeared on the screen, in a song and dance they had seen him perform a hundred times before. Thangam watched mesmerized, her empty glass in her hand. She set it down and began to move along with the actor, her steps in perfect timing, her arms raised, her breasts and hips thrusting forward in a manner that grew increasingly provocative.

'Come, sister.' Thangam waved a hand, but Shanta merely emptied her own glass and walked over to the drinks, collecting Thangam's glass en route. This time, she filled them both with only alcohol.

After finishing a third drink, Shanta joined in Thangam's dancing, her face transformed, their bodies moving in full enjoyment, oblivious to their audience. 'Will you not join us, sister?' Thangam asked Kamala at one point.

'Nay, I thank you,' said Kamala, scrupulously polite, careful to display neither bemusement or disgust. 'My back hurts too much.'

Shanta turned to Kamala – but with none of her usual hostility. 'He is a good lad, your son,' she said, smiling, leaning close, her words smelling of the sour-sharp whiff of alcohol. 'Yes,' said Kamala, not knowing if she should feel repelled or happy. She would have said more, but Thangam was already making a lewd comment about the film star that caused Shanta to double up in laughter. When they had finally lain down, the three of them, to sleep, Kamala realized that this was not the first time they had done this, these two. None of this was new to either. Not the late-night drinking, not Thangam's lewd dancing and comments, and not the manner in which Shanta too began to unravel before her very eyes, giggling foolishly, her hair unwinding, her laughter turning coarse and free.

And on the heels of that awareness came another – that this, then, was the inexplicable liaison that existed between these two women, which Kamala had sensed but never before understood. This was what kept them united despite all the daytime bickering, this unseemly core of secretive understanding that was absent in her own relationships with either. It was nothing she would ever discuss with anyone else; it still raised odd feelings of discomfort within her when she thought of it. She had, for the most part, pushed it out of her mind.

The following morning, Anand-saar summoned her to his study.

'Me?' said Kamala. 'Why does he wish to see me? Why do you suppose?'

'I do not know,' said Thangam. 'You might find out if you deign to go meet him.'

Kamala made her way to the study, a dozen guilty thoughts flying like scared crows through her mind. That shirt? Could he have found it already and known through some mysterious investigative process that it was her hand that had done the scorching? Or, worse, did he wish to speak to her about the computer?

If Thangam obsessed about Vidya-ma's wardrobe and liked to play with her lotions and cosmetics when their mistress was away, Kamala had her own, very different set of fascinations about the house. Occasionally she might linger in Vyasa's room, examining his things, wishing them for her son. But the true object of her secret fantasies was in the upstairs living room, on the table next to the window. This computer was used by the children and Vidya-ma, and here, every single day, Kamala felt herself grow greedy with desire.

This complicated gadget, with its little alphabet keys and shiny screen, the big box that rested under the desk and hummed – this was magic. Somehow, she would see to it that Narayan's education would lead him to this, to mastery over the computer and the tapped incantations that allowed the screen to glow to life and hum under the fingertips. To master that knowledge would make his future soar. Sometimes when the family went out and in the hallowed silence of their absence, while Thangam drank tea in the kitchen and listened to Shanta's diatribes, Kamala would give in to her urges and press down on the keys, in imitation of the movements she had seen the children make. Most of the time nothing happened; the screen lay black and blank. Only once had she gotten a response; she pressed a key, the screen sprang to cheerful life, and in the shock of it Kamala realized that the computer had not been switched off and kept ready for her play; it had been left on; the black screen had been deceptive. With trembling hasty fingers, she had turned the main power switch off and watched in agony as the screen pinged back into darkness like something killed.

Four hours passed on that dreary day before the family returned from their outing. She waited tensely for the first scream of discovery, for them to notice the meddling that had destroyed the computer, but nothing happened. When she ventured upstairs after a few minutes, Valmika was at the computer, typing. Her tampering had not been noted; the machine had somehow, like a compliant lover in a secret affair, managed to keep Kamala's flirting concealed.

Now, she fretted. Had Anand-saar learned of her computer-meddling?

'Come in,' said Anand-saar. 'Kamala, I am very happy with the care you are taking of my father. You are responsible and reliable.' He hesitated. 'Are you facing any problems?'

'No, saar,' said Kamala. She did not say: Actually, sir, Vidya-ma is so angry and she directs all her anger big and small at whoever stands around at that moment; Shanta is Ravana's progeny, a veritable she-demon; Thangam is consumed by her own problems right now; and I would indeed appreciate it if I could manage to leave work at the time I am supposed to each day. 'No problems, saar,' she said.

'Good, good,' said Anand-saar. 'But, I wanted to talk to you about Narayan.'

Kamala rushed into nervous speech. 'I'm so sorry, saar. Pingu was the one that called him in . . . I will tell him, saar, tell him to wait outside.'

'Kamala.' Anand-saar spoke patiently. 'That is no problem. He is very smart. How old is he?'

'Twelve running, sir.'

'And is he working hard at school?'

Kamala told him truthfully that Narayan was the most clever boy imaginable and, mendaciously, that he was very diligent at his studies.

'Good,' said Anand-saar. 'I am pleased to hear that. Education is the only way he will progress in life. Which school is he attending?'

'The government school, saar,' said Kamala and was not at all surprised when Anand-saar frowned.

'That is not good. He will learn nothing there,' he said. 'Now, I feel that education is very important. It is the only way our children can progress in life . . . I work with a small trust that helps to educate young boys and girls. Would you like me to sponsor Narayan's education?'

In an instant, transformational moment, Kamala's opinion of her employer shifted from tolerant indifference to passionate, astonished devotion.

'We can place him in an English-medium school close by – and tutor him in English so he can catch up,' said Anand-saar. 'But he must work hard and prove himself worthy.'

'He dreams of working on the computer, saar,' Kamala said.

'Oh, wonderful,' said Anand-saar. 'That is good. If he is keen, I can see to his training. But, Kamala, you in turn must see that Vidya-ma is happy with your work . . .'

'I will, saar,' said Kamala. And the fierceness of that promise, a resolution made on the altar of Narayan's future, hardened within her like tempered steel.

Later, in the kitchen, she said quietly to Thangam, 'It was good news!'

'Really.' Thangam looked at her with sharp, assessing eyes. 'Has he increased your salary?'

'No, no, nothing like that,' said Kamala. 'But he is going to sponsor Narayan's education.'

Thangam nodded, already losing interest.

Kamala walked home, thinking about how she would advertise such good news: especially making sure to tell that complacent mother of the stolid, hard-studying Ganesha across the way about the prospective brilliance of Narayan's academic future. And that, thought Kamala, was the miracle of the young. They could fulfill your deepest wishes in a manner that you could not predict.

Nineteen

It seemed he was expected, but where was his father-in-law? The profusion of marble Italian nymphs in Mr Sankleshwar's reception room remained silently unhelpful on the subject. The receptionist had asked him to wait and then retreated into some inner sanctuary. Anand ignored the magazines on the glass table; he checked his watch. It wasn't like Harry Chinappa to be late. He would give him five minutes more and then call.

The door to the inner office opened; Harry Chinappa stood framed in the doorway, a file in his hands, a smile of great cordiality upon his face.

'My dear boy,' said Harry Chinappa. 'There you are.'

'I have been here for a while,' said Anand.

'Excellent. I thought to myself,' said Harry Chinappa, 'that it is not like Anand to be late. Now, to more important matters . . . Anand, you know me, I'm not one to interfere, but I do not want to see you making a grievous mistake . . . Mr Sankleshwar has arranged a very beautiful property for you – I think it is extremely suitable.'

'What?' said Anand. 'No, that's okay.' He was instantly annoyed; he perceived that he had been enticed here on false pretenses – Harry Chinappa had not given up on making him buy something from Sankleshwar. 'I told you. I have no need. I have already proceeded with that Landbroker.'

'Oh, *that* fellow,' said Harry Chinappa. 'Don't worry about him. Agreements of that nature can easily be put aside . . . We can't be foolish, m'boy. That fellow sounds like trouble. Now, I want you to look at these . . . I'm so pleased; the land is an absolute treasure . . .'

He opened the file and pointed to a map, in full spate, seemingly oblivious to Anand's growing irritation. 'I imagine we can head out for a viewing after this morning's meeting. It sounds simply perfect for our needs. Sankleshwar has really been magnificent. Beyond my expectations, really . . . It's all here,' he tapped the folder again, 'the land specifications, the term sheet, everything. I reviewed them in some detail, and even managed to tweak them in our favor. And,' he lowered his voice, 'not everyone can say that in their dealings with Sankleshwar. He is famous for being extremely shrewd, you know.'

'No. Thank you. But no.' Anand spoke wearily, feeling as though he were speaking chaste Kannada to an uncomprehending foreigner. 'I am not interested.'

'Don't be silly. We haven't seen the land, true, but Sankleshwar wouldn't recommend something that wasn't completely appropriate. Not to me, I fancy. I think we can trust him completely. And the terms are extremely reasonable. All that remains is to draw up the papers, and we can proceed with that right away. This meeting, I told Sankleshwar, is a mere formality, after all.'

'A mere formality? What do you mean? What? You haven't actually agreed to buy something from these people?' Anand stared at his father-in-law in shock.

'Anand. One can't delay in matters like this. One could lose the property to a faster mover,' said Harry Chinappa, the fucker, as though this were a matter of no greater import or consequence than choosing bloody prawns from some chuthiya catering menu.

'What? I told you. This will not work. I am buying something else.'

'My boy, what are you saying? You're backing out completely? Don't be foolish. You cannot seriously be thinking of doing business with that other fellow? Mark my words – you'll get into trouble with him. What do you even know of him? Don't be stupid now. This is ridiculous! We've got an excellent deal here. Besides, we can't back out now. I've spent hours with Sankleshwar on this. I've agreed to all this. I've given him my word. We can't back out. That's impossible.'

'Excuse me,' Anand said. 'But I have not agreed to anything. I have not given my word. And you had no business doing so. On what basis did you agree? I told you no. This is not,' he said, 'some matter of some stupid prawns for some fucking party. This is a matter of my company, and here you will not interfere . . . I will talk how I like! I will use what words I like! . . . Yes, I know very well who I am talking to . . . You please do what you like with the family but you please keep your distance from my work.'

And with the weight of his words pressing down like death in the silence of that marble-encased room, Sankleshwar's comely secretary spoke, with a cheerful, astounding normalcy: 'Sir? Will you both go in? Thank you.'

Anand did not even glance at her. He glared at his father-in-law – and turned and walked out of that room. Harry Chinappa could shovel his own shit. Anand was not going to be a part of his explanations.

He drove straight home. His father was seated on the verandah with his newspapers.

'Have you eaten, Appa?' Anand asked, forcing himself to a dutiful courtesy. His father usually consumed his main meal of the day at

9:30 in the morning, in a strict schedule that followed his morning walk, bath, and worship.

'No,' said his father. 'Your wife is cooking pig flesh in the kitchen; the smell is upsetting my stomach – so I have decided to go on fast. A banana and one glass of milk – later, when the smell has died down – will be sufficient. A fast,' he said, 'is good for the digestion, very cleansing, though the subsequent bowel movements take a day or so to settle down. Are you not going for your bath?'

'Later,' said Anand. 'I have to finish some work in the study.'

'When I used to return home from outside, I would first head straight for the bath before saying even one word to anybody. But those are the old ways, is it not?'

'Is Vidya upstairs?' asked Anand.

'I believe not. I believe not. The servant,' his father said, 'told me she has gone out.'

Anand headed to the study, his father's voice following him: '. . . and by raising rail prices, the blighters will raise the prices of onions also. This country,' his father said, resorting to the expression he had employed as long as Anand could remember, 'is going to the dogs.'

He heard Vidya enter the house and walked out of the study. He could see from her grim face that she had heard from her father. Thankfully, the children were at school. She addressed her father-in-law: 'So I have bought some bananas for you. Will you eat them right away?'

'A little later,' Anand's father said. 'After the smell has died down. No, no, nothing else. A glass of milk and a banana will be more than sufficient.'

She followed Anand into the study and shut the door. He said, still seething: 'Listen. I don't want you discussing my work ever again with your father. Okay? After what happened today, I don't want him involved. At all. Understand?'

'Understand? Do you think,' she said, 'he would want to be involved after what you did?'

'What *I* did? What the hell are you talking about?'

'Ey, my father told me everything. Okay?' she said. 'You ask him for help – he runs around for weeks organizing things for you, and then you coolly just turn and walk away. He told me. You shouted at him and abused him and used all kinds of foul language. He is really shocked, Anand. So am I. He has never been spoken to like that in his life. I was so shocked, I began to cry. How could you do this to him?' She sat down on the sofa.

'He had no goddamned business doing what he did. He had no business agreeing to anything.'

Vidya spoke through his words. 'And that's the other thing. Because of you, his reputation will get affected. He said that Sankleshwar actually accused him of double dealing – my father! – but thankfully, he put him right . . . Otherwise, Daddy's good name would be in tatters! Even so, he says, because of you, his own real estate development scheme could get messed up . . . Anand, how could you!'

'What? What the fuck did he tell Sankleshwar?'

'Don't use that language with me now!' said Vidya. 'He told Sankleshwar the truth: that you were the one who did the double-deal, agreeing to Sankleshwar and agreeing to someone else at the same time . . . Anand, don't look like that! Daddy's reputation is important to him.'

'And mine isn't?' Anand asked, so furious he could barely speak. 'Vidya, listen. I didn't do a "double deal." I only agreed to work with that other Landbroker person. Your father had no right agreeing to anything with Sankleshwar. What he did was wrong! Are you listening to me?'

'He risked his entire reputation for you. He's bending over

backwards and you bloody go and do something that he says no self-respecting businessman would do.'

'Vidya, are you even listening? He had no business agreeing to anything. He had no right.'

'Yes, only you can do whatever you want. No one else has any right! That is just how you want your world, isn't it? No need to show respect to anybody else. He put his integrity on the line for you. He's a man of his word – and you are not. You are not! That is the person you've become.'

'Well, you and your father are the only two people who think so.'

'And, of course, we are the only two people,' said Vidya, 'whose opinion doesn't matter to you . . . I can't believe you would treat my father so badly, while expecting me to cater to every whim and fancy of yours. It's driving me crazy.'

'Fine,' he said. 'Don't do it. I'll take care of my father – and you please take care of yours.'

'He'll never forgive you, Anand,' she said, bursting into tears. 'And neither will I.'

Great, he said. Don't.

Later he heard her on the phone. 'Kavika,' she said.

Fuck, he thought. Not that.

Twenty

The courtyard was quiet these days, for more than half the rooms that surrounded it lay empty. The landlord had sent tenants on their way as their leases had come to an end, without renewing them or replacing the tenants with fresh ones. But early this morning, the silence was rent by noise that showed no signs of diminishing.

Kamala opened her door and quickly shut it again in shock, before sitting inside the darkness of her room, listening hard. Narayan sat cross-legged next to her, barely discernible in the dark, offering the mute comfort of his hands, which Kamala clasped tight, as much to soothe as to be soothed.

Loud wails, shouts of anger, the drag and thump of heavy household objects.

'But where are we to go? Mother, please!' The young bride wailing. 'Brothers. Please. You are like family to us. We have no one else.'

If you throw us out like this, where do we go?

If we have nowhere to live, how can he find employment?

Please give us another month. We will find the rent. Mother, please. Brothers!

But the landlord's two oldest sons, normally so polite, would not relent. They dragged the belongings of the reluctant young couple out onto the street, under the unyielding supervision of their grandmother. The landlord himself was nowhere to be seen. It was well known that he could not bear to witness scenes of sorrow among his tenants.

At some point, Kamala and Narayan crept out of their room and, unnoticed, past the shouting figures outside the courtyard, he to school, she to her work. Today, Kamala was sure, the landlord's mother would ask for increased rent. And how was she to handle that? She recalculated, again and again, the figures in her mind. Would Vidya-ma agree to a small raise in her salary? Would Anand-saar? Who else could she turn to for a little extra money?

The landlord's mother was indeed waiting for her that evening. But she did not ask for increased rent. Dumbly, Kamala listened – and finally much of what she had seen over the past few months became clear to her. Things she had stupidly ignored, small, telltale signs, were suddenly connected to one another in a hateful pattern. The reason the courtyard lay silent and empty. The reason the bride and her husband had been so rudely evicted. The growing sorrow of the landlord's face, where unhappiness multiplied every time he glanced at her. And right there, on the corner where the main street touched her gully, stood the reason why.

For a thousand or more years, this little neighborhood had slumbered as a village. Then, the distant city rumbled closer and closer until, one day, it was entirely swallowed up: a village no more. The farmers sold their fields and turned shopkeepers; erstwhile village homes were offered up for rent to any passing stranger; trucks and buses and bicycles flooded through without courtesy and with easy right-of-way. Opinions were generally divided as to the desirability of all this. There were those who bemoaned the loss of the fields and the cool, clean greenery of the village – they were usually old or idle. The others were too busy trying to create employment from their altered circumstances. Overnight, the villagers' character changed: from farmers protective of their own to businessmen eager to engage with the strangers in their midst.

And thus it might have remained: a malodorous, low-grade urban neighborhood, teeming with life and refuse, if a fundamental shift had not happened in the newly developed rich neighborhoods that lay alongside: the land prices there began to rise rapidly. Rumors flooded down the linking road to the slum: over there, earth that had once existed as ragi fields was now turning valuable, earning per square foot, the rumors said, sums that a provision-store keeper might be hard-pressed to earn in a month. What madness was that?

Whatever the nature of such insanity, it began to seep into the village-slum. And the first proof, that it was not just idle talk and the stuff of male fantasy around the tea shop, was right there on the corner of the main road.

The little provision store had vanished, along with the butcher next door, who had always kept a cage of long-suffering chickens at the entrance to his shop. In their place stood a brand-new building, three stories high, glossy, gleaming, girded with fresh paint and steel. Inside, people had already set up shop: a lawyer, two doctors (one for general sickness and the other with a piles and fistula clinic), and an Internet café. The basement bore a sign that proclaimed the future location of a language training center for English. The erstwhile butcher and store proprietor now danced about like vastly superior beings, buying clothes, televisions, scooters, and sending their children to English-medium schools.

And this was what Kamala learned from the landlord's mother: how could any rent she paid – even if it were doubled – compare to the sums the landlord might earn if he sold his property to the real estate touts sniffing around daily like eager dogs scenting the tracks of a bitch in heat?

★   ★   ★

When Narayan returned in the evening, he discovered his mother seated on her haunches in a darkened room and staring at the wall. She had not lit the lamp. She had not prepared any food.

'Amma,' he said, her very silence alarming him. 'What is it? What is it?'

She hesitated briefly, but the story quickly spilled out of her. He would bear the consequences of it soon enough; he may as well hear of their fate right away.

They were going to lose their home. Mindful of their eight-year friendship, the landlord's mother had approached the subject adroitly, describing the deep financial difficulty her son found himself in, the claims of others upon him. Poor man, she'd said, the troubles multiply about him and age him before my eyes. To meet these claims, he was forced to put this courtyard up for sale. What choice did he have? She felt terrible, she'd said. But Kamala had the bounty of her brother to rely upon, a prosperous life waiting for her in the village if she so wished, so she did not worry.

Kamala had known, instantly, that it was time for her to plead. She could not think of leaving her job for another: the salary was decent, the gift of Narayan's education a pearl beyond price. She needed to safeguard that at all cost. She also could not afford to move anywhere else. New rentals in this area had become recently unaffordable; the day she moved out, this neighborhood would be closed to her. The nearest affordable places were far away in the distant tendrils of the city, in strange new neighborhoods among unforgiving strangers. To reach her workplace, Kamala would have to begin her commute before dawn – and what would happen on the nights when she was required to stay late? Buses late at night were difficult beasts to catch, slippery with their schedules, murky with nameless predators who feasted on lone female travelers. Narayan too would have an equally long commute to his new Anand-saar-sponsored school. She would never see him; he would be entirely out of her control and management, prey to his own inventiveness.

So Kamala had pleaded. Please increase my rent, Kamala said. Just for a little bit. Or allow me to make a large lump-sum payment that will help your son. Something to delay the sale of this court-yard by a year or two. Please. Amma, please.

The old lady had listened, and something in her implacable face had yielded to Kamala's tears. She'd placed her hand upon Kama-la's head. 'You have been like a daughter to me. I cannot promise anything, but let me speak to my son.' She'd nodded. 'And you in turn speak to your brother and see how much you can raise.'

I will, Kamala had said. I will.

Now she gazed hopelessly at the wall in front of her. It was one thing to make such an offer, but how was she to raise a sufficiently large sum of money? Her mind spooled forward into ever-widening aspects of misery.

'How large, Amma?' asked Narayan. 'How large a sum?'

'Why?' cried his exasperated mother. 'What difference does that make to us, the size? It is so large that it doesn't bear speaking of. When one cannot put two-pie together, what use is it to speak of whether lakhs or crores are required?'

'They would want so much?' Narayan asked, startled.

'No,' she said grudgingly. 'But they may as well. It would be a sum as much out of our reach.' Then, in response to the persistent question in his eyes, she said: 'I don't know, perhaps as much as fifty thousand rupees?'

This sounded to her like a substantial offer of money. Would it be sufficient? Would the landlady expect much more? Fifty thousand rupees was forty thousand more than she had saved in the little cover at the bottom of her trunk. That ten thousand had been accumulated over ten years, painfully, squeezed out like blood from a bone when all the flesh has withered away and the bloom of life long vanished.

'Oh, Narayan,' she said. 'We will be forced to roll up our beds and sleep on the streets. Where will we go?'

She glanced at him helplessly. She had been so proud of him; so proud of the ease with which he had settled into the new school, so smart in his new uniform and proud of his book bag. His English tuition master had reported that he was learning the language quickly; good news, so pleasing to his mother – and now this. Why did the gods envy the little she had? And immediately temper the good with bad?

They ate their night meal in silence; Kamala could not cook in her distraction, and the meal of dry chapattis and pickles would not settle in her mouth. She tore at half a roti before giving it up. Narayan too ate absentmindedly, his young brow furrowed in thought. 'Can we not raise the money, Amma? Somehow?'

'Forty thousand? How is it possible, Narayan?'

'My uncle,' he said. 'He said we have wealth waiting for us in the village. From my father's family.' His mother's silence was eloquent. 'Amma, do we really have cows and fields waiting for us in the village?'

'You and I do not. That is certain,' said Kamala. 'But do not be spreading that around the courtyard. It would be disrespectful to your uncle.'

'Can you ask him for the money?'

'I have not asked your uncle for a paisa since you were a baby. I should be ashamed to start now.'

'Can we start a chit fund like Thangam? She has made a lot of money with it.'

'Us? A chit fund? Are you crazy? Who will run it? You? It is not so easy. And besides, I think it is one of those things that gives trouble more than it helps.'

Narayan did not look convinced by his mother's lack of enterprise. 'In that case, do you suppose Thangam might be able to give us a loan?'

'Aiyo! Ask! Ask for money!' She slapped her hand on the ground next to her, feeling the pain radiate powerfully through her palm. 'I, who have never asked anyone else for a paisa, not for a glass of water that I have not earned, now you want me to lower myself, abase myself, abase the entire work of my blood and body, and go, like a beggar, and ask for money? Did you not hear what I said? That chit fund of hers is in trouble. More than you know. People are defaulting. So eager to join, greedy for the big payout, but now they find they cannot keep up with the monthly payments. She has to be ready to pay on their behalf, but she also cannot afford to, this chit fund is so big. In fact, she is so frightened, she has been asking *me* for money.'

'Anand-saar,' he said, after some further moments of silence.

But Kamala was already shaking her head. 'Anand-saar is already giving us so much. I will not go ask for more.'

'Yes, my education, I know,' said Narayan. 'But, the truth is, it is easy for them. This is not so big from their side. They can easily afford it.'

'That does not change the generosity of this gift, Narayan,' said his mother. 'Or lessen its rarity.'

'They spent twenty thousand rupees just for the fireworks at the Diwali party. I heard her say so.'

'Yes, and the corner shop man spent thirty thousand on a new scooter,' said Kamala. 'How does any of that affect us?'

Dissatisfaction was easy to feel and could twist the mind into unprofitable thoughts. Narayan would have to learn that lesson for himself. If he ever did. Or he would spend his entire life unhappily chasing after the shadows left by the lives of other people as though they were real.

She said: 'Your education. I did not ask. He offered . . . To ask for money . . . I have seen that, with others. It is not good. There is no self-respect in it.'

Narayan said nothing more, but the question that shone from his eyes echoed loudly around the little room: was there any self-respect in being thrown out of their home?

Twenty-One

This was one of those mornings when he rose well before the alarm. On the balcony in the cold dawn, he watched the lightening of the sky and listened to the neighborhood muezzins. They had acquired competing loudspeakers, the mosques; one maulvi's voice had a magical, haunting quality, the other squawked self-importantly. Behind them, like so many echoes, the sounds of prayer ebbed and flowed over the awakening city, the suprabathams from the temples and, when the sun strengthened, distant bells from the Catholic church.

There was nothing left for him to do. He had fussed over the paperwork for a week. The demand drafts were ready and waiting in the safe.

He went downstairs to fetch another cup of coffee and joined his father on the verandah, where the older man was working his way through a sudoku puzzle. 'I am a little surprised,' said his father, on Anand's appearance, for this had evidently been bothering him, 'that he has still not come to visit me. Or invited me to their home. It is disrespectful, is it not?'

Anand kept silent. He could not explain to his father why Harry Chinappa was maintaining an unusual distance from his daughter's house. And why he, Anand, could not care less. Instead, he listened to his father on the subject of Ruby Chinappa, who had visited the previous day, seeking, by her nervous presence, to diffuse her daughter's anger and atone for her husband's distance.

'Your father is looking so well,' she had said to Anand. 'So good to see him in such health. Harry is very busy right now, so many things, you know, but we really must have your father over for a meal, we really must, I will speak to Vidya about it . . . Anand, are you keeping well? Is everything okay?'

'I'm fine,' Anand said, but that did not appear to reassure her. The worry in her face was tangible as she went slowly up the stairs to see her daughter, and deepened when she eventually scuttled back to her car.

Anand drank the last of his coffee. On an impulse, he told his father, 'Today, I am going to register the purchase of some land . . . twelve acres of farmland . . .'

'Is it? Good, good,' said his father. 'You are planning to become a farmer now?'

'Not exactly,' said Anand, wryly recognizing the real anxiety that lay behind his father's jest. 'I am buying this for the company – to expand our facilities.'

'Oh, is that so?' said his father. 'In that case, be sure to avoid signing the agreements during the rahu-kaal times.'

'Rahu-kaal?' said Anand. He had never worried about scriptural notions of auspicious and inauspicious times; he could not see the sense of such superstitious behavior, though he was aware that no one else, including Ananthamurthy, seemed to share his view. 'What would happen if I did sign in rahu-kaal?'

His father shook his head. 'Do not joke about this. It is important. Suppose something went wrong just because you signed in an inauspicious time?'

'Nonsense, Appa,' said Anand, but minutes later, as though on cue, he received a phone call from Ananthamurthy. 'Sir, I hope,' said the operations manager, 'that you are avoiding the rahu-kaal.'

Anand called the Landbroker. 'Are we avoiding the rahu-kaal for signing today?'

The Landbroker said: 'Yes, sir, not to worry. Today's rahu-kaal is finished six-thirty to seven-thirty in the morning.'

'Right. It doesn't matter anyway,' said Anand. 'How much time will the registration take? The full day, is it?'

Much had happened in the two weeks since he had last seen Harry Chinappa.

Anand and Mrs Padmavati had signed the agreements to purchase the land, below the company seal and next to the fingerprints and the signatures of the farmers who were selling. They had handed over large sums in both check and cash to the Landbroker. They had paid more than Anand would have liked to at this preliminary stage, but the Landbroker had echoed what Vinayak had told him at the very start: such large payments were needed just to convince the farmers to sell. The concluding payments would be correspondingly less, of course, but the risk was unquestionably higher. If something went wrong with the registration, they would find it difficult to recover the money. Their financing in the factory was so tight, it was not a loss they could bear easily.

'Sir, do you think he is trustworthy?' Mrs Padmavati asked.

Anand smiled wryly. 'I hope so, Mrs Padmavati.' He devoutly prayed he was not making a mistake. As much as he tried to ignore them, Harry Chinappa's words of warning preyed on his mind, louder and louder as the registration date appeared. Mrs Padmavati and Mr Ananthamurthy had started vociferous discussions with the earnest architect, newly hired for the project, not too expensive but competent. Anand kept himself aloof from the process; he would not feel truly confident until the sale was complete. The agreements may have been signed, but until the final sale deeds were executed, until the land ownership papers were handed over, until the land was safely registered in the name of Cauvery Auto – the deal was not done. The Landbroker had laughed at Anand's caution. 'Not to worry, saar,' he said. 'The land is yours. We will register immediately. You please start your planning. We can start building a compound wall right away. And leveling the land for your future construction. Shall I have all the trees removed?'

'After we register,' said Anand.

The Sankleshwar fiasco continued to sit in his mind. Mr Sankleshwar was a powerful businessman – with a formidable network of political contacts and a history of ruthlessness. Anand would have liked to maintain a good relationship with him – and certainly not have his own reputation spoiled with such a man. He deeply regretted, again and again, the loss of temper that had made him walk out of that second meeting with Sankleshwar. If it had involved anyone else, he would have immediately written to clarify the matter. But to write and accuse his own father-in-law of lying would be to create an extraordinary scandal – and probably do nothing to restore Anand's reputation.

He debated the matter in his mind for a half a day before leaving it unhappily alone. There was nothing he could do about it. Harry Chinappa might be willing to sacrifice Anand's reputation to save his own. Anand could not bring himself to reciprocate. He wished he could talk this through with someone; he searched his mind for possibilities and failed; the very notion felt awkward, the situation too personal, too much of a family matter to make public.

The subregistrar's office lay an hour's drive away; to reach it he had to pass the farmland. He didn't slow down, just glanced quickly at the land lying lush in the sunlight, as a groom, full of future avarice, might sneak a peek at his bride's breasts and bottom. The iPod was plugged into the car's speakers, and he sang along softly to 'Sugar Magnolia' by the Grateful Dead. In the bright morning light, it did something to ease the tension within him.

The rural land registrar's office was far removed from urban congestion, housed in a sprawling, yellowing colonial-era government office building that abutted a village school. The building was a warren of rooms organized around a central courtyard, the dust-encrusted architecture in slumberous contrast to the busy buzz and press of humans who entered its portals. Anand knew better than to go wandering through the warren. He parked his car and called the Landbroker.

'Yes, saar, I am already here,' said the Landbroker. 'I will find you; you please wait in the car. Namaskara, saar,' he said, magically appearing at the car window before he'd finished speaking.

The Landbroker, a curious mixture of eagerness and pride, sitting next to Anand and telling of his achievements: Sakkath difficult, sir, to get everyone to agree. This was his moment of success: the bringing together of different farming families, entire disputing clans whose members had frequently left the land years before for the urban welter; to convince them to sell their land and divide the money, to negotiate across grievous family divides and old accusations of greed and sorcery on the unborn child and the division of dead goats, to cajole them into signing the documents of agreement a few weeks earlier, and again, today, to sign over the title deeds to their property and accept in return the money that Anand carried in his briefcase as a series of bank drafts.

In the distance, through the cacophony and crowd, the other parties to the deal clustered under the spread of a tamarind tree. They had about them an air of festivity, as though this were a picnic of no uncommon interest. Entire families: aging uncles and grandfathers, dressed in shirts donned specially for the occasion over their usual singlet vests and dhotis, towels placed around their shoulders like shawls; young mothers, neatly groomed with well-oiled and flower-bedecked hair; gossiping grannies with thinning gray hair twisted and knotted at the nape and red-stained teeth revealed in ancient laughter; squealing babies handed around to love and kissed foreheads and pinched cheeks. The middle-aged males of the family, clad in shirts and pants, stood together, talking, parrying, thrusting, taking one another's measure and, according to the Landbroker, trying to evaluate the relative terms of the deal each was getting, hoping to learn more than each revealed, for the Landbroker had done his work well, sowing money and secrecy through the group, leaving each person convinced that he was possessed of a better deal than the others.

'Everyone has arrived?' asked Anand.

The Landbroker looked at the group under the trees. 'Almost, sir. Almost. Eighty percent. Not to worry,' he added, 'everyone will come.' He left the car, first providing Anand with strict instructions. Anand was to stay in his car, keeping a low profile; it might take a while to put through the initial paperwork, and the Landbroker did not want any seller chatting with Anand and impulsively deciding to increase the asking price. That could jeopardize the entire deal . . . Did Anand understand this? He would wait in the car and not take it amiss?

'No problem,' said Anand, tapping his laptop bag. 'I have brought work.'

'And the money?' said the Landbroker.

'Here,' said Anand, this time tapping the briefcase. The money payable was divided into three categories: the demand drafts, the unaccounted cash in neat packets, and a third bundle destined for the registrar to ensure the smooth registration of the property.

The Landbroker took the bribe money and vanished. They had argued about this earlier: that essential services had to be double-paid for, once with taxes, again with the bribe. The Landbroker had looked at Anand as an elder might at a particularly foolish child. 'Saar, how can you complain that this is unfair? These people who work here have in turn paid bribes to acquire such high-bribe government positions, isn't it? How can they repay everyone they have borrowed from and support their own families if they don't take bribes? Have they not worked very hard to get to this position?' This baffling argument left Anand bereft of speech and argument. Greedy fuckers, he now said to himself, resigned to the headache that inevitably set in when dealing with any government service. Whoring bastards.

The sound of trouble did not at first attract his attention; he was immersed in his work, his music, and the air-conditioned cool of his car.

When he finally looked up, suddenly alert, he couldn't make sense of what was happening. The crowds had increased and seemed uneasy, but there didn't appear to be evidence of any altercation. And was that a procession in the center? And who was that with the film cameras? He quickly put away his files, got out of the car, and locked it.

'What is going on?' he inquired of someone standing by. He received a muttered laugh in response. 'It is the Lok Ayukta.' The anti-corruption cell had received information on bribes being paid and was raiding the land registrar's office. To ensure their vigilance received due credit, they were being trailed by some media people.

The procession entered the building, and Anand returned to his car, frantically wondering what to do. He had spent his adult life grumbling about government corruption – but today was not the day he wanted the Lok Ayukta involved. Where was the Landbroker? Should he call him? What had happened to the bribe money? Was he to be implicated in any manner? All the documents had Cauvery Auto's name on them. What the fuck should he do?

As though in answer to his panicked questions, the passenger door opened and the Landbroker jumped in. 'Here,' he said, handing the bribe money back to Anand. 'You hide this.' He was exuding the thick sweat of fear and, without permission, reached for Anand's bottle of water and drank it down.

'You got caught?' asked Anand foolishly, for the answer was evident. If the Landbroker had been caught handing over a bribe, he would currently be parading in front of the television cameras, his career as a deal broker effectively over. 'What happened?'

Somebody, it seemed, had phoned in a tip to the Lok Ayukta. But thankfully, said the Landbroker, the ill luck had befallen the briber just ahead of him in the queue. He, and the official he had paid the bribe to, were both under arrest. The Landbroker pulled out the image of Goddess Lakshmi, who swung on a pendant at the end of the thick gold chain around his neck, and pressed it to his forehead, offering prayers and thanks for his safe deliverance. A few moments later, and it would have been him in the dock: the Landbroker, the official – and Anand as well.

'Not to worry. It's okay, saar,' the Landbroker said after a while, his brow cooling. 'It happens sometimes. But now, see, they are leaving, and we can continue our work.' And sure enough, the Lok Ayukta people, the arrested villains, and the media cameras trickled away and life in the subregistrar's office, the exchange of property and bribery, could resume as normal. 'Okay, saar,' the Landbroker said, energetic once more, vanishing back into the fray. 'Very soon now.'

An hour later Anand was accepting the transfer of the first piece of farmland into his company's name. The people selling to him, getting their photographs taken, affixing their signatures to various documents, were a family of four: a mother and three sons, all grown. The widowed mother bore the evidence of a hardworking rural life: red betel-leaf-stained lips and gums over strong white teeth, skin darkened and wrinkled by sun and wind, wispy hair, and an eager, interested vigor in her eyes. She would not meet his gaze directly, but when he looked away he could sense her quick inspection. The sons looked like minor city clerks; they were no longer working the land; their hands were soft. When the time came for Anand to hand over the check, he smiled at them respectfully and was pleased at their cordial response. Three more plots of land were registered. Cauvery Auto was the proud owner of five acres of land. Four hours had passed. Another five registrations to go.

'So how much longer?' Anand asked.

'Not long,' said the Landbroker, leading Anand back to his car. 'Sir, you please wait here. I will send the boy to bring you some coffee and tiffin.'

'Why? Where are you going?' said Anand.

'I am taking the sellers out for lunch, sir. It will keep them in a good mood,' said the Landbroker. It seemed another unorthodox procedure in an unorthodox day, but Anand did not doubt anymore that the Landbroker knew his business well, that his particular mixture of treats and cajolery and curses was what had brought all these people to the dealing table. He spotted the family he had bought the first small half acre of farmland from in the distance; they bore large smiles and no signs of ill usage.

An hour passed. Anand drank some coffee brought to him by a little urchin and began to fret. He finished his emails. He read all he could of the documents in his briefcase. He finished several phone calls. Twice, he walked about the grounds. He even relieved himself against the far wall, along with a row of men similarly engaged.

And then the shadow of the Landbroker appeared at the car window and Anand knew, immediately, that something had gone wrong.

'There is a problem,' the Landbroker said. 'One of them is suddenly refusing to sign.'

'Why?'

Little, hot gusts of wind tugged at the Landbroker's red shirt, which puffed ineffectively in the breeze before sinking back, dispiritedly, plastered against the skin. 'I don't know, sir.'

'Is it a question of more money?'

'I asked, sir. He is not saying yes or no. He is just suddenly saying he will not sign. Perhaps it is more money. I have to find out.'

'Which one is it? Which plot of land?' asked Anand. If it was a side plot, perhaps they could go ahead and complete the purchase without it; it would mean a couple of acres less, but they could manage. The Landbroker shook his head as if he had anticipated Anand's question.

'It is that one right in the center, saar,' he said, 'that eucalyptus grove. Right in the center. We cannot proceed without it. You would get a piece of land like a vada — with a round hole in the center. It belongs to an old man. He is willing to sign, but his son is suddenly saying no . . .'

'Why?' Anand asked again.

'I don't know, saar. But, not to worry. Let me talk to them and I will solve it. He is being very stupid.' The Landbroker leaned a hand against the hood of Anand's car. He seemed to have great difficulty with his next words. 'Saar, this will take a day or two for me to sort out. I am so sorry, saar.'

There was nothing to say. Anand could feel the Landbroker's tension, a physical, palpable thing that coursed through Anand as well. They were finished here for the day. There was no point in completing the purchase of the other pieces of land without the central eucalyptus grove.

The remaining farmers waited — watchful, turned wary by the flood of speculative rumor; the Landbroker walked back to them with a desperately manufactured confidence that insisted nothing was wrong, nothing that could not be easily handled, a small matter, easily resolved, and surely the balance of the registration would proceed apace at the very earliest.

Anand drove straight to the factory in the late afternoon. He had told no one he was coming, but nevertheless it seemed that he was expected.

'I knew,' said Mrs Padmavati when he walked in. 'I knew you would come here first and tell us the good news. I was saying so to Mr Ananthamurthy, and he also agreed. Is it not so, sir? Just to be prepared, we have kept ready a box of sweets to celebrate. Where is that box, Mr Kamath? Oh, sir, what?' she said. 'What has happened?'

Anand attempted to make sense of things even as he described the events of the day: the registrations that first went smoothly – and then the sudden appearance of the Lok Ayukta, followed by the previously eager farmer who mysteriously refused to sell.

'But why should he rethink? Can it be for more money?'

'I don't know,' said Anand.

The Lok Ayukta appearance could have been just a coincidence – an unfortunate matter of timing. But the farmer? Was this just a last-minute ploy orchestrated by the Landbroker to get more money? Anand had felt sure that he was trustworthy; had he been mistaken? He recalled the Landbroker's shame at the end . . . was he just incompetent?

Cauvery Auto was now the proud possessor of an additional five acres, expensive and utterly insufficient for their needs. Anand handed over the property documents to Mrs Padmavati to lock away and went to his car. There was work waiting for him at his desk, but he had not the heart for it after the disappointments of the day. He could hear Harry Chinappa's laughter. I told you so, his father-in-law said. What else did you expect to happen?

At home, he searched blindly for his children and found them with his father. 'Appa! You're home early,' said Valmika.

His father chose this day of all days to inquire about his son's work. 'Your land registration went well?'

Anand hesitated, taken aback. 'There was some complication.'

His father nodded with a certain sorrowful satisfaction. 'Matters of real estate should be left to those who understand such businesses, is it not? They are not for us.'

Anand swallowed the words in his throat and turned to his children. 'Do either of you want to come swimming with me?' He wanted to immerse himself in water, wash away the stink of disappointment and something that felt like pollution.

'Right now? Yes!' said Pingu.

'Okay,' said his daughter.

'I will come too,' said his father, to everyone's surprise. 'A dip in cold water in such weather is extremely beneficial.'

'Yay!' said Pingu, who, with the innocence of extreme youth, retained a staunch belief that any expansion to the party only added to the fun. 'I know how to do handstands in the water, Thatha. I'll teach you.'

Surprise touched by horror held Anand mute. His father was not used to the conventions of a swimming pool. Distantly, Anand remembered him bathing in the ocean decades ago; he had visions of his father appearing at the pool dressed as he had been then: in the loose cotton undershorts he wore beneath his pants, ungainly, mended in two or three places, the string hanging brown and dirty. He could not let that happen, but did not know how to prevent it without causing great offense.

'Oh, great, Thatha,' Valmika said, adding, 'I have a present for you that you must promise to use, or I won't give it to you.' Her tone was playful; it won a smile from her stern grandfather.

'What is it, child?' he asked. 'The child has a present for me,' he said.

Valmika slipped away and returned with a package that Anand instantly recognized: it had lain unopened in the back of his drawer, a spare swimsuit that bore the logo of a well-known sports brand. His father opened it and exclaimed over it with pleasure. Anand grinned at Valmika in secret relief; he could have hugged her. 'Let's go?' he said.

Valmika hesitated. 'Shall I ask Mama if she would like to come?' She ran upstairs, only to return disappointed. 'She's heading out to meet Kavika-aunty.'

Later that night, in the study, he felt the disappointments of the day gather once more inside him. He could not attend to his email. Instead, he clicked on Google, typing Kavika's name into the search engine and trawling through the listings to see if there was anything he'd missed. There were the glancing references to her work with the United Nations; she had presented a paper at some conference; there she was, on some panel discussion; there again, a photo in some humanitarian aid situation. There was no mention of a marriage, no glimpse of her personal life, but for that Anand switched to Facebook.

He would never confess to anyone, even to himself, how much time he'd spent on the social network, gazing at every link, comment, and photo she posted. It was like waving a magic wand and opening a graphic window into her personal life, receiving answers to questions he could not ask her directly, answers that served only to raise more questions in their wake.

She had sent him a friendship request a couple of weeks after befriending his wife. Anand, not an active user himself, had discovered

it to be otherwise with Kavika. Her friends were numerous, of widely
varying nationalities, and frequently male. They left cheery messages
on her page and seemingly endless photographs of her, alone and in
company, appended with admiring comments. Anand knew all the
photographs. He had studied each of them in depth, like a jungle
anthropologist positing furiously and analytically on the nature of the
relationships contained therein. This man, for instance, appeared with
her in a formal, work-style setting, but reappeared in some other
photograph holding a beer and laughing. Was he a friend? Or just a
former colleague? Could he be the mysterious father of Kavika's little
daughter? If someone wrote 'Love ya!' on her page, was it casual or
was there some deeper significance?

There was just one photograph with the two of them, Anand and
Kavika as part of a larger group photo, posted by his wife. Anand
did not like himself in the picture; he looked as he always did: ordinary. But he had downloaded the image onto his laptop, deleted it
– and downloaded it again: it was the only evidence he possessed
of the two of them inhabiting the same physical space. He pictured
himself as a part of her other photographs, as a part of the rest of
her life: his arm around her, casually, as though it had a right to be
there, his face alive, captured in a moment of happiness.

Her visit to the factory replayed through his late night mind in
an undying loop, as though she made a habit of visiting, coming
there to listen to him, to laugh, to flirt, her casual touches meaning
so much more, reserved only for him, her fingers sliding their way
across his impatient skin until everyone else in the factory magically vanished and he possessed her body as thoroughly as she did
his mind. His intense fantasizing in front of the computer never
sustained itself in the bathroom; he found himself overwhelmed,
crippled, frustrated, his wayward penis, usually so easily aroused by
the slightest passing image, turning flaccid despite fervent tugs, his
ineffective hand rising to wipe his eyes in the cooling shower.

Twenty-Two

The first person Kamala encountered when she stepped out of her room the next morning was the landlord's mother. What the old woman saw on her face had her hurrying forward. 'Oh, daughter,' she said. 'Such misery! What a wretch I am to have caused you such anguish. Don't distress yourself, do not. If only I could spare you this, I would. I will convince my son to agree to your offer, you do not worry. The gods will help you. Or your brother will. I know this. I wish I could spare you this.'

'Thank you, mother,' said Kamala. 'That is kindness. I will raise what money I can.'

The fight in the kitchen was different. Kamala could sense that in an instant, even through her own worries. Shanta washed dishes in a sullen silence, while Thangam muttered in anger. 'You promised,' she kept saying. 'You promised. And I was a fool to believe you.'

Vidya-ma had yelled at Thangam the previous evening – not for her work, which was getting more careless as her financial troubles increased – but for the ruckus that had taken place at the front gate, where a member of the chit fund had arrived, along with her family and friends, to demand the payout that was her

due. Two other chit fund members had joined in, calling for
Thangam, panicked about rumors of the failure of the fund and
the possible loss of all their savings. Thangam, with growing numbers
of defaulters and unable to compensate all of them, had cowered
within. Vidya-ma had suffered a profound shock to find her house
besieged by the denizens of the adjacent slum, barely repulsed by
the feeble efforts of the watchman, much to the good-natured
amusement of neighboring watchmen, drivers, itinerant laborers,
and ragamuffins. Thangam's angry creditors had refused to be
dislodged by Vidya-ma's threats and scoldings; she had finally retired
to her bed with a screaming headache and a bad temper, none of
it improved by Thangam's abject apologies.

Kamala was surprised that Thangam wasn't fired for this, but
beyond shouting at her through the day, Vidya-ma did nothing
further. Thangam's face this morning was swollen with tears. She
had asked Shanta to return the money Thangam had loaned her
in happier, easier times. You keep saying you will, she said, unmindful
of Shanta's shame and unhappiness. You promised, sister. Now do
it.

Kamala kept well out of their way. After days of praying ineffectively, she was finally resolved to do the one thing she had
promised herself she would not. She would approach Anand-saar
for a loan. She was frightened by the potential consequences of
this: suppose he was annoyed by her request and canceled Narayan's education sponsorship? Suppose Thangam's ruckus of the
previous day had adversely affected his attitude toward all the staff?
Vidya-ma must surely have complained.

She rehearsed her speech; she would start by thanking him for
all he had given her; she would praise him – and Vidya-ma, and
the children, and his father – for their benevolence; she would beg
leave to ask him for a further favor. Her words sounded stilted and
awkward in her mind; she knew, with a gathering sense of doom,

that they would sound still worse when spoken aloud. She wished
fervently for her son's eloquence and ease of manner. When the
day's work was done and Thangam had resumed her quarrel with
Shanta in the kitchen, Kamala gathered her resolution, said her
prayers, and made her way to the study.

The door was partially open; a quiet light burned within. She
thought that she would knock and poke her head through the
door, that Anand-saar might see her and summon her, but instead
she paused and sniffed. Sniffed again. She dithered in the shadows
of the stairwell, not knowing what to do. Anand-saar alone at his
table and drinking alcohol was not normal. His chair scraped back.
The light clicked off. He emerged, his posture straight and his
movements brisk, but so unapproachable, his eyes, sorrowful, tear-
reddened. Kamala remained in the shadows, feeling like she had
intruded upon a moment not meant for her to witness.

Kamala walked home slowly, her mood tinged with failure. The
bright streets of her employment yielded, at the corner tea shop,
to the dull lighting of her own neighborhood. Without warning,
the whole area was plunged into darkness from an unscheduled
power cut.

Kamala stood still, waiting for her eyes to adjust; stepping inside
the gutter would not aid matters. Behind her, in the distance, she
could hear the sounds of private generators gunning and starting,
harnessed to the electrical systems of large bungalows. Ahead, the
tea shop owner lit a kerosene lamp; the light guided her forward.

A group of males, an undifferentiated, dark mass barely illumined
by the kerosene lamp, were gathered near the tea shop. Something
about them made her watchful. Even in the dark, it was easy to
distinguish between men relaxing after a long day of honorable
work and the malignant attitudes of those who spent their hours
in less constructive ways. They were smoking, for one, a habit she

despised. The intermittent glow of a puffed cigarette was succeeded by a golden arc as it was thrown into the gutter.

A woman walking alone past such a group was an invitation for trouble. Kamala slowed her steps. She could feel them watching her. One of the group disengaged and moved toward her. She tensed as he approached.

He seemed smaller than the rest. In a flash, she realized: the disquieting group by the tea shop was Raghavan and his friends; the slender figure approaching was her son.

'Amma,' he said happily, taking her small bag. She accompanied him silently, her mind burning. When had he started seeing that good-for-nothing Raghavan again? One of the benefits of the new school was that, in its strict attention to matters of attendance and homework, many of Narayan's old, worrying ways and companions, including these loafers, seemed to have fallen away. When had he started seeing them again? Narayan spoke before she could. 'Mother, listen . . . I have been thinking about our troubles, and, well, I have spoken with that Raghavan – you remember him? – and from the things he said . . .' he rushed his words past his mother's defenses, 'there might be other methods of earning money. Quickly. Enough money.'

The bile rose sharply in Kamala's mouth; she spat into the drain that ran alongside, her spittle landing sharply on the dark earth below. 'No.' As though he might not have heard, she repeated: 'No.'

Never. For her son to throw away all his chances, his future, to engage in whatever lawbreaking ventures that Raghavan amused himself with. No. A secondary fear arose: that Narayan, with his independent mind, would not listen to her, would be tempted by notions of quick, easy money earned through disreputable means. She forced herself to smile reassuringly, as though she were a film star with an innate ability for lying drama, and patted his back. 'I have a plan myself,' she said. 'You don't worry.'

'Really?' he said, doubtfully.

'Really,' she said. 'You do not worry. Just concentrate on your work and make sure Anand-saar gets good reports about you from the school. That is the only thing for you to think about. Have you done your homework?'

The question distracted him. She observed the lightening of worry in his eyes, his guileless trust in her words.

At home, she prepared a meal, supervised and scolded him through his homework, and when finally he lay asleep, hunted through her belongings for a recent letter from her sister-in-law in the village.

The landlord's mother could be right: perhaps there was such a thing as too much pride.

Twenty-Three

Two months of monsoon rain and the approach of winter had tempered the blazing heat of summer. RAINFALL LOW, the headlines had screamed in June, DROUGHT A POSSIBILITY, before abandoning that viewpoint a few weeks later and rushing to other extremes. FLOODS, they shrieked. But despite the coolness of the day, despite the air-conditioning that further cooled Anand's office, the Landbroker seemed to be feeling the heat.

'It has never happened before to me, saar,' he said.

Anand absorbed the misery on the Landbroker's face and knew that, whatever was going on, the Landbroker was not complicit in it. 'Tell me again,' he said. 'Tell me again.' He calmed his own breathing and kept his voice soft, his eyes on the agitated rise and fall of the Landbroker's shirt and the nervous vibration of his fingers on his knees. It seemed that any sudden gestures might set him to fleeing, startled light-foot, like a gazelle in the jungle.

'It has never happened to me before, saar,' said the Landbroker. 'Usually, when such a phone call comes – and it happens, I'm not saying it does not happen – it is a simple affair. Some political fellows will call, they will ask for some money, I will pay, the deal will proceed. Normally, I would not even mention it to you. Just like I do not mention the number of times I might have visited this farmer, or drunk coffee with that one, or even helped that other one organize his daughter's wedding.'

Anand knew all this, the laborious process of relationship building that underlay the Landbroker's deals, part of his efforts to join a patchwork of independently owned fields into a single, consolidated sale of land. 'Yes, yes,' he said encouragingly.

'All that is normal. I am doing every day. This is my work. And if a particular political party can benefit by such a sale, they will try. After all, they have to raise funds for elections, isn't it? As I said, that too is normal. So when I received the call yesterday, at first I was not worried. I thought, okay, it will be some routine haggling with a cup of coffee. They will say a price. I will say something lower. Then we settle. As simple as that. And then that farmer will be instructed by them to sell. But this time . . .'

'Yes,' said Anand. 'Tell me again.'

'This time, they are not fixing a price. They don't want to meet me. They want to meet you. They say that, otherwise, they will not allow the deal to happen. They will not allow that farmer to sell.'

'Can they do that?'

'Yes, they have the power,' said the Landbroker. 'This particular party is very strong in this area, many supporters. If they decide that this one sale should not happen, the farmers will listen to them. And for those who protest, they will be threatened by the party goondas.'

'If we have no choice,' said Anand, cautiously, 'then I suppose I will have to meet them.'

The Landbroker nodded, so unnerved that he did not seem to be able to utter his usual comforting mantra of 'not to worry, saar.'

Anand briefed his colleagues about this new development. Mrs Padmavati listened to him in a wise silence, but Ananthamurthy turned voluble, in his agitation asking the same question that had first troubled Anand. 'Why Cauvery Auto?'

Anand wagged his head, but Mr Ananthamurthy's question was apparently rhetorical; he had launched into a diatribe, triggered by god-knows-what memories and years of democratic injustice. 'See,' Ananthamurthy said, 'this is how it is. This is the very truth of the matter. We can work. We can create. We can work very hard – and the minute we can say, yes, we are having a little success, there they are, hands outstretched like beggars. Rubbish political parties! As though this country will not run better without any of them. They dare to speak of returning to Ram Rajya, but instead of setting up a kingdom of the gods, a land of honor and justice, they create a Ravana Rajya instead, unleashing a hundred demons across the land. I tell you, sir, there is no hope. With government like this, there is no hope. I tell you, sir,' he said, 'I have been expecting this. The minute we gave that last wage increase – you remember? – three months ago? – I said, now they will smell money, and they will come. Rascals! Scavengers! Feeding like hyenas off the work of others. Hyenas – and as stupid as owls, no doubt.'

'Yes,' said Anand, aiming for soothing acquiescence rather than actual concurrence.

'But, sir,' said Mrs Padmavati, taking his words with a certain particularity, 'that wage increase was a very good thing, is it not? Our workers are happy.'

'Yes,' said Anand.

'It is a good thing,' said Ananthamurthy, with decision. 'But see? It has attracted these rascals.'

Anand felt a matching exhaustion; it seemed he was infected by Ananthamurthy's sudden pessimism. Perhaps it was never going to be possible to outrun the system. It reminded him of the story in his son's book about the girl Alice who ran and ran in a night-marish way and, when she stopped, found herself in exactly the same checkered square where she had started.

★   ★   ★

His father was cross-legged on the sofa in the drawing room. He was not alone, Anand saw; he was entertaining a friend.

'Ah, Anand,' he said, including his son in the conversation, 'we were just discussing . . . Those government blighters seem to be making no progress on the power situation. What do you feel?'

'Your father tells me,' said the visitor, 'that you are in business now. But that you are very successful! Very good, very good.'

'It is now the fashion,' said his father. 'Changing times! These brahmin boys are no longer interested in academics or medicine or law, they all want to make money. And they are succeeding! You know why? I will tell you. It is because of their heritage: strong academics, especially science and mathematics, strong discipline, clean personal habits. It is the mantra of success in this new software world! . . . With our traditions, it is only natural that our children will succeed. It is a question,' he said, 'of cultural habits. Like the Gujarati, the Marwadi, and the Jew, who all have the culture of understanding money, and so they rule the financial world, is it not?'

'Yes,' said his father's friend. 'Very true. Of course, my son is a lawyer and my daughter is a cardiologist, but I have heard. Your software company,' he suggested, 'must be doing a lot of work with America to be so successful.'

Anand glanced at his glass of water. Empty. 'I am not in the software industry,' he said. 'Manufacturing,' he said. 'Engineering.'

'Technology,' his father clarified. 'It is all technology.'

'Of course,' said the friend. 'So good that you are doing well.'

The dosa restaurant was next to the golf course and one street away from the state ministries of Vidhana Soudha. When he first moved to Bangalore, Anand had learned to love the dosas here along with his college friends, partly for the taste, and partly because they added a strong dose of garlic to the potato palya, a rabid unorthodoxy his parents naturally frowned upon. Shortly thereafter, his comfort levels with garlic had risen and he had upgraded the breaking of parental strictures to cigarettes, alcohol, and sex. Garlic, in effect, had been his gateway drug to defiance, the potato palya in this hotel an early pusher.

Anand was visiting the restaurant after a gap of several years, the slight apprehension within him echoing the excited defiance that had marked his early visits. The small hotel attached to the restaurant was rumored to rely, for profit margins, on hidden operations as a whoretel, but the restaurant itself sported an air of vegetarian innocence, serving a standard South Indian breakfast in the mornings and switching to large thaali-meals and gobi-manchurian for lunch and dinner. But true renown was saved for the dosas, which, on a Sunday morning, attracted herds of families, clustered at long tables of eight or more: complaining grandfathers, mothers-in-law in best sarees flashing ruthless smiles, aging uncles with special dietary requirements, budding girls with beribboned braids sweetly looped upward and tied under their ears, teenage boys in desperately bright polyester shirts, mothers-outside-kitchens at their ease, and harassed fathers collating the menu selections for them all. And among them, scattered and clumped like so much driftwood in the tides, lured by golden dosas and proximity, gatherings of golfers, college students, and legislative assembly members.

This was not a Sunday, yet there was a fair crowd of people from the surrounding law courts and ministry offices. Anand pushed his glasses up his nose and glanced around the Formica-topped tables in the central hall. There was another dining hall upstairs, air-conditioned, quieter, more suitable for families, but not so good for a private conversation. Here, human chatter competed with the clatter of plates and the barely hidden noise of the kitchen; one could discuss anything and not be overheard. Somewhere in here was the Landbroker and the man he was bringing with him. A man who referred to himself as Mr Gowda and by others as Gowdaru-saar.

Before coming to this meeting, Anand had made a few phone calls and had learned, from Vinayak, that, if he wanted to see either his money returned or the land deal completed, he would have to meet this man and pay, and, from Amir, that Gowdaru-saar was a well-known political functionary, whose job it was to strong-arm financial support for his party from that particular taluk. Anand was not dealing with a two-bit criminal he could threaten in turn; he was dealing with someone far more consequential.

He quickly spotted Gowdaru-saar against a far wall. If the Land-broker was a cinematic hero, then Gowdaru-saar looked indistin-guishable from a Kannada movie villain: large to the point of obese; his pockmarked face sporting a mustache of magnificent propor-tions; frizzy, unruly hair that haloed out around a receding hairline. But where was the Landbroker? Surely he had not left Anand to meet with this political thug on his own?

Anand's gaze cleared. He had been staring at the wrong table. The Landbroker was with someone quite different at a window seat against the far wall. Anand made his way over, feeling like he was attracting stares, even if he knew he wasn't.

'Namaskara,' he said. In contrast to the flamboyance of the Landbroker, his companion was quietitude itself, in a simple cream shirt with signs of great piety about him, the turmeric and vibhooti dotted post-prayer in the center of his forehead, a red thread tied around his right wrist to ward off evil. In other circumstances, Anand might have identified him as a small-time merchant in Chickpet, selling bangles or hosiery or vessels, or an accountant in someone else's firm. He did not make the mistake of treating him as either.

Gowdaru-saar returned Anand's greeting with calm, smiling eyes, urged him to sit down, and summoned the waiter to order breakfast, his air of placid goodwill in shocking opposition to both the Landbroker's nervous energy and Anand's overwired tension. He seemed in no hurry to broach the matter they were there to discuss, as though this were nothing other than a cheerful, whimsical gathering of friends out to enjoy a lazy midweek breakfast.

'The traffic was very bad this morning,' he said, in typical Bangalore small talk; the traffic: auto-rickshaw drivers with their freewheeling style and panicked foreigners shrieking in the passenger seats; trucks and people-fattened buses that held their breaths and inched their way through improbable, ever-narrowing lanes; the fumes, mingling with the rising heat and rising fury, tamped eventually by rain and resignation; and the spasmodic beat of a passing Bollywood film song – ah baby, oh baby, sexy sexy baby baby.

A passing waiter quick-slammed three steel plates onto the table – fluffy rice idlis and a crisp brown vada, the sambar and chutney slopping over onto the plates from their steel cups. Gowdaru-saar's food vanished quickly, mashed idlis moving along the conveyor belt of his tongue. Anand broke off a piece of vada and dipped it into the pale green, watery chutney before placing it in his mouth; it stuck in his throat and took forever going down. Cups of coffee arrived, and he sipped gratefully on the hot, sweet liquid.

The Landbroker was vibrating like a bee, unable to touch the food in front of him. Anand wanted to place a hand over his, to calm him, but with Gowdaru-saar's sharp, observant eyes on him, he did not even venture a sympathetic smile at the Landbroker.

'Saar,' said Gowdaru-saar, 'I am so happy to meet you. We have heard wonderful things about you and the work you are doing. So many jobs you are creating. It is very good, very good, saar.'

'Thank you,' said Anand. 'You are too kind.'

'And it seems that you are expanding your factory. That means more jobs for our people. That is so good, saar.'

Anand tired of this. 'Not so good,' he said. 'There will be no new factory if I am prevented from buying the land that is required.'

'Ila, sir. No one is preventing you. Why do you say like this?' said Gowdaru-saar. 'Yes, I heard. There was some confusion with the Lok Ayukta. Someone has mistakenly informed them. That is all. And it is really unfortunate that some fool is unwilling to deal with you. But we will take care of that. Not to worry, that land is as good as yours. Your friendship is important to us, saar.'

Through the grease- and dust-darkened window Anand could see the endless passing traffic, metal glinting in the sharp, white light of November and framed by the political posters and bunting that decorated the far side of the street. An enormous poster held Vijayan's head over the streams of traffic that went past, painted in gorgeous tones of pink and white, the shadows on his face picked out in green. THE NEW HOPE FOR DEMOCRATIC INDIA, the sign said, next to an Ashoka Chakra, the blue spokes of a great forward-moving nation.

Harry Chinappa had received a very nice letter from him, personally signed, thanking him for his hospitality. Vidya had shown it to Anand, so excited he was surprised she didn't frame it and hang it on the wall alongside the brightly painted oil canvases of turbaned men and bejeweled women that she paid significant sums of money for. They called it the best of Indian art, she and her friends, but to Anand it was hardly Indian; the romantic rural images depicted had nothing to do with the life any of them lived or indeed would want to live; it was all fantasy, like one might see in a film.

Gowdaru-saar noticed the direction of his gaze. 'That,' he said, 'is a great man. Very great, very great.'

Anand said nothing.

'It is an honor,' said Gowdaru-saar, 'to be a member of his party. Like you, I too have a duty, Anand-saar. Is it not our duty, Anand-saar, to elect the best? For years, we have suffered with bad leaders.

Now, finally, we have someone who we can respect. Who we can trust. An educated man. A good man. If we do not, right now, do everything we can to see him elected, would we not have failed in our duty? What use is it for me to talk of my love of my people and my village, if I do not guide them properly . . .

'So, Anand-saar, I know you can help us. You are such an important man, so much wealth in your factory.'

'No, no,' said Anand. 'There is no wealth. We are a small company. We are struggling. You have been misinformed.'

'No, saar. You are doing well. After all, you are buying this large piece of land and even more,' said Gowdaru-saar, smiling, 'you are buying even more, is it not?'

'What do you mean?' said Anand, puzzled.

'I mean you are buying some land with our good Landbroker here,' said Gowdaru-saar, 'and we have heard that you have also met with Mr Sankleshwar to buy land from him. Such an important man you are.'

'No,' said Anand, 'I am not.'

Who else had Harry Chinappa told? And why? Ah, yes, Anand puzzled it out. Not Harry Chinappa at all.

Mr Sankleshwar.

Anand at last had a gasp of insight: could this be why things had started going wrong with the registration? Somebody had instigated the Lok Ayukta – and somebody had brought him to this political thug's attention. Who else but Mr Sankleshwar, who was powerful, ruthless, politically connected, and – thanks to Harry Chinappa – convinced that Anand had wasted his time and, in scheming duplicity, reneged on their agreement and signed this land deal with the Landbroker behind his back?

The realization made him catch his breath in dismay.

If he was being maliciously targeted, then he was possibly headed toward bigger trouble than he imagined. Fucking hell. He glanced at the Landbroker, who was also looking taken aback at Gowdaru-saar's words; Anand had made no mention of buying land from Sankleshwar.

Anand tried to appear calm, saying firmly: 'No, I am not dealing with Mr Sankleshwar. I am only buying land from our Landbroker here. And really, we are a small company. You have misheard.' He could see the Landbroker trying to assess his truthfulness, nervous, unsure.

'Is that so?' Gowdaru-saar looked tranquil. 'But we have heard otherwise from a close friend, saar. It does not matter. But you are not a small company, you are a great success. We have heard. From a very reliable source. We are sure you can help us.

'You see, Anand-saar, I am not asking for money for myself. Myself, I am content to live in a simple way, in the village where I was born, now part of this great city, with my family and my people. But I am asking for money for the party. Because without money, we cannot win the election. And this country needs people like that, is it not?'

Both their gazes shifted to the poster of Vijayan, smiling through the traffic at them in gentle benediction.

Twenty-Four

The possibility of Narayan being influenced by Raghavan so troubled Kamala, it pushed her into making a plan. She would speak to Vidya-ma as soon as she could. No, not for money, for that was futile. Instead, she would ask for leave. For a day or two. That should be sufficient. Since she had not taken even a half day's leave so far, not for sickness or festival, hopefully Vidya-ma would not think badly of the request.

Her sister-in-law's letter went through her mind. It was cheerful; scribed by her sister-in-law's neighbor and read aloud by Narayan, but the important part had stayed clear in Kamala's memory: that the small store in which her brother had acquired a share seemed to be prospering.

Over the years, she had received numerous offers of help from her sister-in-law, and had been steadfast in refusing it all. Now was the time to relax her pride on this. Narayan, in a smart pant and shirt uniform, a bag of books hoisted like a proud banner upon his shoulder, was enjoying school for the first time.

After all, what had she asked of her brother since she had left his house twelve years ago? Nothing. And he had repaid that favor with his foolish, proud words to the landlord's mother. Perhaps he did indeed, after all these years, feel a brother's duty to her. She would ask him for help.

That this was not a fortuitous day for requests was evident the minute she entered the kitchen; Vidya-ma was in full spate, not discouraged by Thangam's sulky silence or Shanta's grimness. 'You do nothing but ask me for things! And in return you are so careless with your work! It's ridiculous! I ask for a cup of tea, it comes cold. My clothes are not ironed. And when they are, they are burned!' She brandished Anand-saar's shirt in one hand. 'Who did this! Tell me that! No, utter silence from you lot. And then, on top of that, you come running to me for loans. No, no more! I will not give another loan to anyone. You seem to think . . . Kamala, you are late!' Kamala glanced at the clock; she had stopped to buy the grandfather's pooja flowers, but the sight of them in her hand seemed to aggravate Vidya-ma all the more. 'You're wasting your time on all kinds of useless jobs, and when I need you, you are not available!' She marched out of the kitchen; they heard the front door slam.

They were working these days in a house strangely divided: the grandfather stayed downstairs on the drawing room verandah in the day hours, returning to his bedroom in the late evening, his retreat almost acting as a signal for Vidya-ma's own descent for her dinner. Otherwise, when she was home, she stayed upstairs, watching television or on the computer.

Vidya-ma had lost her happiness.

Thangam was unsympathetic when Kamala tried discussing this with her. 'Aiyo, who has time to worry about her. She is constantly crying over problems that do not exist.'

When the doorbell rang hours later, Kamala ran to open the door; she still had her request to make and hoped to catch Vidya-ma in a better temper. Kamala collected the various shopping bags from the car and followed her mistress to the bedroom.

'I know,' Vidya-ma said into the phone, 'I swear I wake up exhausted. I don't know what to do anymore. I've tried talking to him, but seriously, it's just not worth the fucking effort.' She dropped the shopping bags carelessly on the bed, the contents sliding out. Blouses, pants, a handbag whose price tag rippled seductively over the bedspread: Rs 10,000/ – 'Kamala, a glass of water please,' she said, and by the time Kamala returned, her conversation had shifted. '. . . I was thinking of wearing an embroidered chiffon saree, but I'm planning a traditional maanga necklace with it.' She pulled a jewelry case out of her handbag and removed a necklace from it, her fingers playing over the ripe gold and pomegranate beauty of the ruby paisley pendants strung along its roped length. 'It's my mother's. Belonged to my great-grandmother, actually. A gift from the Mysore maharaja.'

All day long, Kamala waited to ask for permission – and by late afternoon, she knew she would not get it. Vidya-ma remained closeted in her room. Having made up her mind to ask her brother for help, Kamala wanted to do it before her resolve faltered. She would have to absent herself without leave and claim that she had been sick, meekly swallowing the scolding that would follow.

In preparation, she said to the other servants while they were seated at lunch, 'Oh, I am not feeling very well.'

No one seemed particularly inclined to comment or sympathize. Thangam was brooding, and Shanta just stared at her sharply.

'My head,' said Kamala, 'it hurts. My legs also.'

That she was not very successful at dissimulation was clear; Shanta snorted and said, 'You look well enough.'

Kamala's temper unfortunately chose this moment to flare. 'Are you saying that I lie?'

'I'm saying,' said Shanta, with an annoying acuity, 'that you are pretending to be sick just to take some leave.'

'Have I ever done that?' said Kamala, outraged by the accusation (which her past behavior had certainly not merited) and by the truth of it in the present instance.

'How am I to know what you have done or not done? Why should I care about such a topic? Of what slightest interest is it to me?'

'Oh, for the sake of the gods!' said Thangam, entering the fray. 'Is it not possible to eat a meal here in silence and peace? And, if I were you,' she told Kamala, 'I would worry less about my health and more about my son's companions.'

'What do you mean?' asked Kamala.

'I saw him yesterday. Hanging around with that lout Raghavan and his friends. I went to collect a payment, and he was loitering with them. I am surprised to see him in such company. They are not good men, Kamala,' said Thangam. 'You should tell him that. I am surprised you have not already done so. You take such pride in him.'

Kamala put away her plate in silence, upset to hear her own thoughts echoed by Thangam. Was this what everyone thought? That because Narayan hung about with Raghavan and his crowd, he was like them in character?

When her son arrived at the kitchen door that evening, Kamala was happy to see that Thangam's attitude to him remained cordial. She welcomed him, and when Vyasa discovered him and wanted to take him upstairs to his bedroom to show him something, she was the first to encourage him.

'Let him go up,' she said, when Kamala hesitated. Narayan had never been allowed upstairs in the house. 'Pingu cannot bring that huge train set down.'

Kamala followed her son and Pingu up the stairs with a pile of ironed clothes but could not help feeling uncomfortable at the expression in Vidya-ma's eyes when they encountered Narayan on the landing. Her mistress did not look at all pleased at the intrusion.

Twenty-Five

The meeting with Gowdaru-saar and the realization of what Harry Chinappa's careless, self-serving lies had thrown his way unleashed an unprecedented anger that propelled Anand through his home in a great, all-consuming silence. The fat house, overbuilt, overspent; the mechanisms by which it had been created, the human infrastructure of his entire life; all existed, it seemed, to oppress him. He lived mute within it, his silence punctuated by the angry mutterings of his wife and watched in gathering bewilderment by his daughter.

Valmika saw something in his face that she had never seen before, and worked up the courage one morning to ask, 'Appa, what's wrong?'

They were headed into Cubbon Park. 'Nothing,' he said. 'Nothing, kutty. Come on.' They stretched perfunctorily before starting to run. His legs stretched farther today, moving lightly over the ground, feeling an old, forgotten power for the first time in years. At the corner, he glanced back, but Valmika had been keeping pace with him.

There she was. Kavika. In the distance, holding the leash of her mother's aging dog. He felt like running right up to her, shouting at her for her obliviousness, grabbing her arm, pulling her to the car, and driving away with her. Somewhere.

He accelerated, leaving Valmika behind, and came to a despairing halt in front of her. Kavika's cheerful hello seemed unaffected both by his fevered fantasies and by whatever stories his wife was feeding her. 'This guy,' she said, bending and fondling the dog's long ears, 'would lose a race with a turtle.'

Her eyes roamed his face; her voice was friendly, kind. 'Anand,' she said. 'Amir told me something in confidence. About your company. It really worried me . . .'

He couldn't speak. Valmika had reached them and was sucking in shuddering gasps of breath. She fell to her knees, and Anand suddenly felt ashamed. He tried to speak to her cheerfully: 'You ran really well, kutty. Great job!'

Kavika waited until Valmika had recovered her breath. She said: 'Sweetie, do you think you could just ramble about with this fellow for a few minutes while I talk to your father? Thank you! And don't go too far, stay within our sight all the time.' She turned back to Anand. 'Amir told me that you were being pursued by some political goon for money . . . Is that true? Are you okay?'

Anand sat on the grass and started talking, telling her, freely, easily, of everything that had happened. He was no raconteur; the narrative was bald and shorn of decorative detail, but she listened with an attentive sympathy that pulled the words out of him. He started with the land investment; he was soon speaking about Harry Chinappa with an honesty that he had never before managed with anyone. He knew that he could trust her, that she would not go running with these tales to either his wife or their friends.

She offered no conventional platitudes. Instead, she asked directly: 'So do you think he is behind this political party coming after you? Harry Chinappa? Would he actually go that far?'

Anand sighed. He had been debating the same point himself. 'No. I don't think so. Actually, I doubt if he is even aware of it. Family is too important to him – believe it or not – even though he lied about me . . .' This was something Anand knew, he would never forget and never forgive. But even so, Harry Chinappa wasn't behind the political parties. 'I think Sankleshwar is the man behind it.'

'Fuck,' she said, digesting this, slowly, implications feeding through.

'That's bad, right?' she said. 'So . . . what is he after? Is it money? Is this Gowda person collecting the money for Sankleshwar?'

Anand did not need to think it through. 'Sankleshwar doesn't need my money. Fuck — it's peanuts for him. He's a vicious son-of-a-bitch who is pissed off at me. Thanks to Harry Chinappa. He's pissed off at me — and wants to teach me a lesson.'

'So he put those political guys onto you?'

Anand looked up at the sky, fighting the tears of anger and fright welling up within him. He hadn't cried since he was a teenager. 'Yeah.'

'He has that kind of political muscle?'

'Yeah. He's really connected. Apparently, in his early days, there were some very shady deals where he got his political buddies to convert large tracts of greenbelt land into far more valuable industrial through some rezoning — and in return the fucker helped them launder black money into land. And, according to Vinayak, some business of violence in his early years. He got rid of some guy who didn't want to sell to him . . .'

'Boy, Vinayak and his stories. Sometimes you just don't know what to believe . . . I discount half the things he says.'

'Well,' said Anand, picking up a stone and flinging it against a tree, 'that's what I did too, right? What a fucking mistake. I should never have gotten involved with either Harry Chinappa or Sankleshwar.'

'Anand.' She placed the warmth of her hand on his shoulder. 'Don't be too hard on yourself. You couldn't have known. But this is a really crappy situation to be in. You know, it's one thing to hear of the routine daily corruption we all deal with — but I had no idea that this sort of thing happened with companies. How do you function with this sort of political arm-twisting?'

'Jesus, Kavika, this isn't normal,' Anand said. 'I mean, you do hear of politicians and their goons sniffing around certain industries . . . real estate, for instance. Or liquor. Or mining.'

'Ah. Places that tend to need a helping, corrupt hand . . .'

'Exactly. Or getting kickbacks from companies who are chasing government orders. But normally they leave us manufacturing or software companies alone. At least if we keep our heads down . . . Of course, we still have to deal with what you said: the routine, daily corruption – which is fucking bad enough. But this . . . thanks to Sankleshwar, they have their claws into us, and they're not going to back off. It's scary.'

He could see his emotions reflected on her face. She was appalled. And angry.

'Oh, Anand. That is such bullshit. Bastards! . . . You know, I remember reading about the company that refused to support one party and, as revenge, the party members planted porn on the company premises and then got the police to raid them and arrest the CEO . . .'

Anand looked grim. 'Yeah, I remember that too. Poor bugger.'

'Sorry, that wasn't the most comforting thing to say . . . So if Sankleshwar can set these guys on you, then presumably he can get them to back off. He's the guy you must talk to.'

'He's not returning my phone calls,' said Anand.

The jacaranda and rain trees made a high canopy of green over their heads, filtering the early morning sun. In the distance, they could see the cocker spaniel snuffling along, smelling the long grass, Valmika having released him from his leash.

'Someday,' Kavika said, 'I will tell you my own story. Difficult choices there too – and I am not always sure I have made the right ones. It's not always easy to see, is it?'

Someone had spread birdseed, and a large flock of birds had settled in the spaniel's path. As he approached, nose and ears to the ground, they rose, the pigeons, in a single gray cloud of fright. The startled dog backed hastily away, almost tumbling over his rear legs, and peered in astonishment at the flying bird-carpet from behind the safety of a bush.

Kavika's laughter bubbled up; she was sprawled on the grass, her giggles shaking her stomach. Anand found himself laughing too, for the first time in days – and he was still laughing when his daughter rejoined them, the dog back on the leash.

'Did you see that?' Valmika asked. 'It was the funniest sight.'

Kavika stood up and gave Valmika a hug. 'Thank you! I hope this fool did not trouble you too much? I'm glad!'

As they headed back to their car, Valmika said: 'Appa. You're smiling.'

'Yes,' said Anand. 'I think I feel better after my run.' He remembered his earlier mood. 'I'm glad you came running with me, kutty. And I'm sorry if I made you run too hard.'

Valmika snorted. 'Hard? Appa, next time, I'll beat you!'

He put his arm around her and hugged her hard.

He waited until 10:00 A.M. and called Sankleshwar's office again. The great man was traveling, they told him. In meetings. Busy elsewhere.

Ananthamurthy and Mrs Padmavati worried over the financial end of the matter with him. Gowdaru-saar had sent word through the Landbroker: the sale price of the remaining land had gone up by 20 percent. This additional amount would have to be paid in cash. If they didn't pay, the land purchase would not happen.

'We will have to pay,' said Mrs Padmavati. 'We have no choice. We must pay and hope that they do not once again ask us for more.'

'Mrs Padmavati – how do we pay the full amount? We cannot pay more than ten percent; they want twenty. Even ten percent will stretch our budget to the maximum. The banks will not lend us more.'

'Sir, can you tell them this?' said Mrs Padmavati. 'Tell them we can only afford so much and no more.'

'It is worth a try,' said Anand. 'But it will probably not work. I'll speak to the Landbroker about this.'

He met with the Landbroker at the Swamy Miltry Hotel, just off the highway. Dark, low-ceilinged, tiny, walls stained with cooking grease and clumps of decaying cobwebs; the rancid odor of burnt sambar; what the place lacked in comfort, it made up for in anonymity. The Landbroker fetched two coffees from the serving counter, the tumbler inverted into a steel cup. They stood at one of the tall, Formica-topped tables that dotted the premises.

'Listen, not to worry.' Anand knew he first had to soothe the Landbroker, to return to him a sense of confidence that the meeting with Gowdaru-saar had undermined.

'What, saar,' said the Landbroker. 'This is the first time this is happening to me. The first time I am having to face such political pressure and the first time' – the Landbroker was upset, barely meeting Anand's eye – 'where I am not sure if a client is buying from me or from someone else.'

'No, no. I am buying only from you. Not to worry. That Sankleshwar is a friend of my father-in-law's; that is why there was some conversation. But that is all. Not to worry. Nothing has been signed; no money has been exchanged with him. I am only working with you. Where this Gowdaru-saar has got this information from I don't know. And I do not know why he has approached me like this. But no matter,' said Anand, gliding lightly over his father-in-law's dealings. 'We have to now deal with this, and we will. You please tell him that we will pay, but you must make it clear – we can only afford ten percent more.'

The Landbroker looked doubtful and worried. 'They will not like to bargain this way, saar.'

'Tell him this is all we can afford. You please tell him this. We are not as big as he thinks.'

'I will try, saar,' said the Landbroker, unconvinced.

An email pinged across his phone. It was a cheerful, encouraging letter from the Japanese company, looking forward to their next meeting. In Copenhagen, this time. Anand had planned to take Mr Ananthamurthy and Mrs Padmavati with him. For both of them, it would have been their first trip abroad. 'We are very much looking forward to doing business in India,' the email said, 'to participating in the growth of your great nation and, if all goes well, of your company.'

The first time Anand had traveled abroad, years before, to meet a potential client in Germany, he had not been able to stop staring: at the roads, the bridges, the tunnels, the cars, the trains, at the organized reliability of it all, so startled by such careless munificence he almost wept. When asked later to describe his trip, he was typically laconic: 'Everything works,' he said. He had not been successful with the client; they had doubted Indian manufacturing capability.

That same trip, on a flight, he had met a German engineer who had complained bitterly about the proposed extension in Germany of a thirty-five-hour workweek. 'So terrible!' the German had said. Anand, working a seventy-hour week with Ananthamurthy, had agreed politely, but inside, he had doubted. Within that conversation, he knew, lay the seeds of Western downfall, the stoic industry of their ancestors deteriorating into whining, waffling plaint, as full of fidgets as a spoiled child. It was the mirror image of his own existence.

★   ★   ★

The phone call came when he was stepping into the shower that evening. The voice was uneducated and slightly unctuous: 'Mr Anand, saar?' The voice went on, starting in English and continuing in Kannada: 'Ah, wun min-nut. Woru nimisha. If it is convenient, Gowdaru-saar would like to speak with you.'

Anand sat on the edge of the bathtub, the granite cool against his buttocks, a towel quickly pulled across his naked shoulders. 'Namaskara.'

'Ah, Mr Anand-saar,' said the quiet voice at the other end. 'You seem to be very upset with me.'

Chuth. Behenchuth. 'No, no,' Anand said. 'Why do you say that?'

'Saar. Yes. Otherwise why else would you bargain like this? You are such a big man. You are not a small shopkeeper to bargain like this. Our party can thrive with your assistance only . . . You please help us. What we have suggested,' said Gowdaru-saar, 'is a very small sum for a man such as yourself.'

'It is very kind of you to think so highly of my company,' said Anand. Fucker. 'But please understand. Ten percent is all that we can afford, Gowdaru-saar.'

'You can afford more, saar,' said Gowdaru-saar. 'Twenty percent more, you can easily afford. We have heard. It is a small thing for you. Why you must say no? You please support us – and we will be like your brother, saar. We will support you for everything. Your land purchase, everything. Not to worry.'

As Anand stayed silent, the texture of Gowdaru-saar's speech changed. 'You please reconsider, saar,' he said. 'We will definitely attend to this matter for you. One way or another, saar. One way or another.'

The threat was explicit. Anand felt fear rise from his stomach, from his heart, from the very center of his being, and collect in his mouth.

'We will speak again this weekend. Goodbye, saar.'

Anand stared uncomprehendingly at his surroundings: at the steam emerging from the still-running shower, at the vapor that clung to the mirror above the basin.

How was he to raise the money? Even if he could, wouldn't Gowdaru-saar simply assume that Cauvery Auto could indeed afford it – and keep asking for more? What then?

His study supplied no solace that night. The passing hours only increased his foreboding, his sense of impending loss; waking night-mares populated by political goons and bank managers, multiplied like many-headed, fang-mouthed rakshasas until they passed the realm of the practical and danced fancifully about him, Kathakali dancers gone wild. His desk sat solidly before him, providing no answers.

Vidya appeared at the study door in an old T-shirt and pajama bottoms; her hair was unbrushed, her face flushed. She did not seem to be able to sleep either.

'Ey.' She looked stormy, spoiling for a fight – and for a brief moment he wondered if Kavika had spoken to her on the matters he'd discussed in the park. 'Enough is enough. I want you to apol-ogize to my father. I can't live like this. You better apologize to him.'

'No, I won't.' Anand discovered a new domestic implacability. 'I won't. Dammit. He owes *me* an apology.'

'I don't know what's gotten into you these days. It's like nothing matters to you!'

'I know what matters to me.'

'Then, it's like *I* don't matter to you!' she cried. 'My family doesn't matter to you. What I want doesn't matter. My father . . .'

'Your father,' he shouted, 'has bloody ruined my life, okay? . . . You happy about that? What, aren't you going to run to Kavika to complain about this too . . . ? Your father . . .' He found the courage to say the words. 'I wish I had never met him.'

And then he said, unplanned, but the truth, blunt, recognizable as soon as it was uttered: 'I wish I had never met you.'

He watched her jerk backward as though she had been punched. A part of him wanted to move quickly to her rescue, as he had always done, routinely, to shield her, to smooth her way, to make the patterns of life easier for her – buying tickets, paying bills, staff salaries, fixing cars, plumbing, the bubble of support he had built so she could play within. But another part of his brain – victorious, battle-scarred, finally at liberty, heady from speaking the truth – held him back, and he watched her stumble, look to the sofa, look to the door, look at him, and bewildered, lost, retreat unsteadily from the room.

Twenty-Six

Kamala's plan was quite simple. She would telephone her sister-in-law in the morning. She would explain her difficulties and ask her to intercede with her husband and arrange a loan on Kamala's behalf. That would be better than pleading with her brother directly. Then Kamala and Narayan would catch a bus to the village and return with the money.

The consequences of such an action would be inevitable and mortifying to contemplate: a loan of such magnitude would leave her beholden for years; for the duration of that period she would have to endure her brother's taunts and insults, as she had when she was dependent on him in the first year of her widowhood. Endure them – and perhaps never be free from them, for who knew how long it would take her to repay him?

The landlady had indicated that fifty thousand rupees, coupled with a slight increase in rent, could buy Kamala an additional year in the courtyard. The following year, Kamala would need to pay another lump sum. That was the best the landlord's mother could do. Two additional years of schooling for Narayan – and Kamala, used to planning their lives a few months at a time, was content to trust the rest to the gods. Surely she could suffer her brother for such a cause? Dealing with Shanta these few months, she thought with a sudden deepening of amusement, had certainly been good training for what was to come.

She had forgotten to recharge her prepaid mobile phone card, so she made her call from the corner STD-ISD phone booth. It was mid-morning; her sister-in-law would have finished all her morning chores and be in a position to listen.

'Akke,' said Kamala, 'I have something to ask you.' She glanced around; the door to the booth was firmly shut; Narayan, who had accompanied her, was chattering to the ISD booth man. Kamala hesitated no longer, comforted by her sister-in-law's evident tongue-clucking sympathy. When at last her tale was done, she plucked up her courage. 'Akke, I was so pleased to read of my brother's success with the shop. I was wondering . . . is it possible for you to ask him for a loan?'

'Oh, little sister,' said her sister-in-law. 'Thange. It is good that you have come to us for help. For years I have asked you to do so, but you have always refused and I have felt so terrible. I am glad you have asked. The thing is . . .' she said, and at Kamala's soft comprehending groan, 'No! Do not worry. We will contrive some-thing. What a fate this is! What a karma. That I should urge help upon you unavailingly for years and finally, when you do ask – I am in no position to help. This is a cruel fate, indeed!'

'It is a large amount,' said Kamala. 'I was a fool to think of asking.'

'Who else would you ask? You have done the right thing. The problem is that stupid shop.'

'Is it not prosperous?' asked Kamala.

'Prosperous?' Her sister-in-law began to cry. 'That shop is like a hungry python, swallowing-swallowing every paisa that was ever saved in this house.'

Far from being a prosperous businessman, Kamala's brother had growing debts and was essentially serving an indenture in the shop that would allow him to pay off all the monies he owed. 'Do not tell him I told you,' said her sister-in-law. 'He would be very angry with me.'

I will not, said Kamala.

'In fact, he was speaking of someday coming to Bangalore to look for some alternate employment. Do not tell him I told you.'

I will not, said Kamala.

She talked a minute more and settled the bill. She answered the impatient question in Narayan's eyes. 'Your uncle is in great debt,' she told him. 'Helping us is beyond his current powers.'

They made their way slowly back to the courtyard. The landlord's wife saw them enter and called, 'Kamala-akka! Your employer's watchman was here.'

'Is it?' said Kamala, barely listening, still digesting the phone call. 'Narayan, do not wander far away. What did he want?'

'I do not know,' said the landlord's wife. 'He did not stay long. He saw the lock on your door and left.'

Kamala nodded. Telling her son to sit on the stoop, she went into her room and locked the door. There was one last thing left to do. She unlocked the steel trunk and, from the very bottom, took out a little cloth pouch and examined the contents: a small pair of gold earrings, a chain. She took off her thin gold bangles. She removed the slender gold chain from around her neck. She unscrewed the gold earrings from her earlobes. She put the jewelry she had removed into the pouch and tucked it safely in her woven plastic bag.

She examined herself in the mirror: bare of adornment, except for a black thread around her neck, and one more around her wrist to ward off evil. In the space of a minute, she was returned to the young girl who twelve years previously had stolen a bath for herself and her baby from a garden tap.

She felt bare and vulnerable, but preferred not to dwell on it. She called to Narayan and locked the room door.

'Where are we going?' He scanned her bare ears and neck and wrists.

'Hush! So many questions!' Walking down the road, she relented. 'I have the name of a reliable pawnbroker, who will give us a good rate and not cheat us. We have to go to Chickpet.' The pawn-broker's shop was in the depths of the old mercantile quarters of the city, an hour's journey by bus.

Kamala was not used to Chickpet; the pawnbroker was hard to locate, and when at last they did find the shop, it was closed for the afternoon. Establishments in Chickpet, it transpired, kept old-fashioned timings: open from 10:00 to 1:00 P.M., and again from 4:00 to 8:00 in the evening. Kamala crossed to the opposite side of the road, where there was shade, and squatted on her haunches. It seemed likely, from the look of the pawnbroker's establishment, that he lived above his shop. She doubted if he would welcome being interrupted during his lunch. She would have to wait. Any hopes she'd had of quickly finishing her work with him and salvaging a half day of work were quickly extinguished. The watch-man's visit meant that Vidya-ma was upset; perhaps there were guests for dinner that evening; perhaps Thangam was acting up and refusing to work. It could not be helped; she would not worry about it right now. Kamala gave Narayan some money to buy lunch at a nearby canteen; she herself was too anxious to eat.

The trip home in the evening seemed interminable. She felt naked without the comfort of her jewelry; the negotiation had not proceeded to her satisfaction; the amount she had received from the pawnbroker entirely inadequate. She sat silently next to Narayan on the bus, the fatigue and despair sinking so deep within her that tears slipped softly to the edges of her eyes.

At home, she crept into a corner of the room and fell into a deep sleep. When she awoke, it was the early hours of the morning;

Narayan had covered her with a sheet and placed a pillow under her head in the course of the night. She looked around the room and saw his plate, newly rinsed and to one side; he had obviously managed to feed himself some dinner. Even in the repose of sleep, his face was no longer that of a small child. The gathering shadows of adulthood about him, in the gentle feathering above his lip, and in the changing smells that rose from his body.

Twenty-Seven

He spent the remainder of the night in the study, worrying and dozing on the small sofa. In the early morning he slipped into his bedroom. Vidya did not acknowledge his presence, then or later, when he crept out of the shower. He could tell she was awake, his statement of the previous night still raw and trembling in the silence between them.

He escaped from the house, Gowdaru-saar's threats urging him to the factory. The drive to work was agonizingly slow; some government VIP had flown in from Delhi; vehicles on all roads were stopped so that he or she or it might travel in speedy comfort to its very important destination; policemen, in their white-and-brown uniforms and squinting in the sharp early morning winter sun, fighting to hold back the steaming, frothing traffic.

At the factory, he parked the car and sat behind the wheel for a few minutes, fighting his fear. The path that led from the parking lot to his office was paved with hard-packed mud; at the last meeting with the architect, Ananthamurthy had suggested that, for the new factory, they might consider paving the paths with stone. Expensive, but smarter, he had said, Ananthamurthy, his enthusiasm making Anand smile. Paved roads that gleamed in the distance, like a mirage, now seemed to be vanishing into the mud beneath his feet.

Occasionally, Anand had daydreamed of a future where Cauvery Auto flourished to the brink of a public stock offering, where the large gifts of stock he would give to Mr Ananthamurthy, Mrs Padmavati, and others would secure their futures along with his. Should he tell them about the threatening phone call with Gowdaru-saar? He wasn't sure. He worried about what it would do to their morale.

At his desk, once again, he called Sankleshwar's office. Once again, he could not get through. He polished his glasses on the edge of his shirt and placed them on his nose. They slipped a little; he would have to get them tightened. He removed and polished them again. He tried, unsuccessfully, to immerse himself in routine matters.

His fears of the night before returned. He felt overwhelmed, powerless; these were forces outside Anand's normal world, functioning by different rules that he barely comprehended. He needed help; he wondered who to turn to for advice.

Vinayak, in whose endless contacts might lie the answer. Anand stood at his window, watching his beloved factory floor, mastering his breath before picking up the telephone. 'Hey, buddy, listen, I need your advice.'

'Oh, shit,' said Vinayak several times as Anand talked about Gowdaru-saar's escalating demands. 'Fuck, bugger, how did you get caught in this? Did you do something to piss someone off?'

Anand carefully avoided any mention of Sankleshwar.

'Or maybe someone else wants that land you are buying? See, this is why it's damn important, yaar' – Vinayak switched to political philosophy – 'to have a good relationship with politicians. Those buggers control everything; they can make or break your life. You have to build your network. And the simplest, best way to do it is by paying them off. Before every city, state election, you know what I do? I go and meet the key guys from each party personally – and promise them a certain amount. You have to do that. You have to show your support.'

'Isn't that why we pay taxes? And vote.'

Vinayak laughed with the heartiness of someone hearing a first-rate joke. 'Too funny, yaar! So, how much are you going to pay these guys? You are paying them, right?'

Anand said, reluctantly, 'I can pay a certain amount if I have to – but I don't want to bleed.'

At the end of a twenty-minute conversation, Vinayak's advice was, ultimately, brief. 'You have to talk directly to Vijayan. If you can. This fellow is his party man.'

Anand immediately knew that Vinayak was right. Sankleshwar was powerful – therefore Anand needed the help of someone even more powerful to put a stop to this.

Vinayak said: 'Your father-in-law knows him, no? Vijayan? You should ask him to help, yaar, your father-in-law. That's the best.'

You're right, said Anand. Thanks. Good talking to you.

The Landbroker sitting in the shadows of Anand's office, nervy, looking for solace. 'That Gowdaru-saar . . . He is not leaving me alone, saar,' he said. 'I am not able to speak to the farmers or, in fact, to anyone else. They are following me. Even now, there are two fellows waiting outside the factory.' Anand went to the window and peered out at the distant factory gate. Sure enough, two men stood there, indistinguishable in the distance, deep in conversation with the watchman. He felt an irrational anger toward the Land-broker.

'Why did you bring them here,' he shouted. 'Why to the factory?'

'I am sorry, saar,' said the Landbroker. 'I was not thinking very well. I am so sorry.'

Anand instantly felt ashamed. The Landbroker was not responsible for the mess they were in; Anand was miserably aware of the irony of having worried that the Landbroker would bring in political goons when in fact they became involved through the doings of his own family.

'No, no,' he said. 'Sorry for shouting. They would know where I work anyway.'

The Landbroker leaned back against the chair, his shame a palpable thing, a man with reputation and livelihood entirely at stake. If he couldn't fight off the political forces, the five acres Anand had bought would be shockingly useless, a wasted purchase. If he couldn't complete the deal, he would lose face with the farmers; the news that he had made promises he could not deliver on would spread through the district, the city, the state; the laughter and humiliation would chase him out. If the deal didn't close, he would, honor-bound, be expected to pay back the sums that Anand had already paid out for the land that they could not now buy. But such sums would not be even remotely recoverable from the farmers, not immediately, not in one generation; they would have long ago vanished down the greedy gullet of farming family expenses. He would have to find the money himself, the Land-broker. That would wipe out his entire stock of fragile capital – he would be returned, in one lifetime, to a life of penury.

Anand's 'don't worry, we'll do something, we'll do something' was said more to buoy the departing Landbroker's spirits than with any real hope.

The first sign of trouble occurred later that morning.

Anand, immersed in financial spreadsheets, was suddenly roused by a strange sound, which, he realized after a bemused moment, was actually the cessation of noise.

The machines were quiet.

The thrumming that drove his work life, like a mother's heart-beat echoing through a womb, had fallen silent.

He went to the production window and stared, shocked, as rows of workers left their spots and filed toward the exit. His mind played for a desperate, foolish instant with various far-fetched hypotheses — could it be a fire drill? Had his watch stopped and he'd missed hearing the lunch siren? — before accepting that it was something far more serious. His workers were downing tools, unauthorized. This was a strike. Cauvery Auto had never experienced one before.

At that moment, Mr Kamath burst in, closely followed by the HR man and Mrs Padmavati.

They have stopped work, said Mr Kamath.

It is crazy, said Mrs Padmavati.

I have no idea why, confessed the HR man.

Mr Ananthamurthy has gone to speak to the union leader, said Mrs Padmavati.

But the union leader is waiting outside your office. He has come to see you, said Mr Kamath.

I have no idea why, confessed the HR man.

Let me speak to him, said Anand. Is everything calm?

Yes, they said. So far anyway.

I don't understand, said the HR man. We have just increased their wages and all the workers seemed so happy.

The union leader who entered Anand's office was very different from the energetic young leader Anand was used to dealing with. He looked scared and unhappy, evidently under considerable strain.

'What is it, Nagesh, what's going on?' asked Anand, but he already knew. The labor unions had their political affiliations; the union leader Nagesh was operating under pressure from a higher domain than his particular fiefdom.

Now he would not meet Anand's eye. 'We are instructed to start work after two hours, sir,' was all he would say, but with so much misery in his face and voice that Anand could not chastise him.

This was a message to him not from the unions but from Gowdaru-saar: that he had control over Cauvery Auto's workers. A two-hour stoppage of work today could become a full-blown strike tomorrow. And there was nothing that Anand or the union leader Nagesh or Ananthamurthy or anyone else in the factory could do to stop him.

Nothing, that is, except pay Gowdaru-saar the amount he had asked for.

Two hours later, the machines started again, as though by remote control.

It was late evening; the workers were completing their last shift, in a semblance of normalcy. Anand leaned his head against the production floor window. Were they in any greater control of their fate than he was? He glanced around his office before leaving, with a feeling of doing so for the last time.

The parking lot was in a distant corner of the compound. It was slowly emptying of the cycles and scooters that filled it during the day. Buses to ferry the last-shift workers home waited at the factory gates. His car stood alone, illumined by a tall lamppost. The light seemed to bounce off the bonnet in an unusual way; as Anand approached the car he realized why.

Someone had carved a deep, vicious gash into the hood.

When questioned, the watchman was predictably blank about it. 'No, saar,' he said. He had absolutely no idea how it had happened.

Anand felt people collecting behind him. 'Oh my god,' said Mrs Padmavati.

'Who can have done this? Who?' In the glassy lantern light, Ananthamurthy looked old and frail and distraught.

Anand touched the scar lightly; the surface had been cut through, leaving the metal below violated and exposed. This was meant to scare him. No doubt.

Instead, he felt something shift inside, his fear lift, a welcome anger warming him deep within.

He moved quickly; he did not want to advertise this to whoever remained on campus. He reversed and parked his car on the other side of the parking lot, the gash concealed.

When the last shift ended, he personally saw all the workers off the premises. Over their protests, he sent Mrs Padmavati and Ananthamurthy and Kamath home. He did not want them exposed to violence – or to whatever those political goons might have planned for the long night ahead.

He was going to stay behind. He would not abandon his factory. Perhaps all would be quiet. It didn't matter. In case of violence, he was not sure what he could do anyway, but he could not just leave. He called up the security company and asked them to send two more watchmen for the night shift.

He wondered whether to call Vidya or not but had no idea what he would say to her. They had not spoken since the previous night. Instead, he compromised, sending a text message to his daughter: *Some problem here. Spending night at factory. C u tomorrow.* She would let her mother know.

The factory settled into a profound silence. Anand kept the lights on and walked endlessly around the production floor and the offices.

And as for Harry Chinappa, what had he done, really, to earn anyone's respect? He belonged to the generation that had achieved nothing – suffocated, they claimed, by the government's restrictive socialist policies, but, in a democracy, was that really any excuse? Theirs was the generation that had refused to look forward, gazing instead for inspiration to the British, whom their own parents and grandparents had kicked out of the country, aping their mannerisms and talking, like sighing damsels in unrequited love, of the wonder of times gone by and the marvelous organization of the British empire. Which one of them had stepped forward to embrace the freedom so hard-won, which of them had dared to contemplate empires of their own? No, much easier to mope and romanticize the past – as though the British, when in India, had invited these people to tea, torn down those signs in front of their stupid, beloved ex-colonial clubs that said: INDIANS AND DOGS NOT ALLOWED. Did he remember any of that, Harry Chinappa? Did he, in his own life, demonstrate what it took to be a man?

At about 11:00 P.M., Anand heard a small disturbance at the front gate. He went out to the steps of the admin building. The lights blazed behind him; he knew he would be seen.

One of the security guards approached, the union leader Nagesh following. 'He wanted to see you, saar,' said the guard. 'He insisted.'

The union leader was alone. Anand wondered whether he was bringing a message from Gowdaru-saar. Anand let him approach, eyes restlessly scanning the darkness beyond the gate. There didn't seem to be anyone else there, lurking in the shadows; no crowds, no goons.

'Sir, I heard you were staying here,' Nagesh said, abrupt, uncomfortable, not to be thwarted.

'I just heard about your car, sir. I wanted to say: we had nothing to do with that. We would not do that to you, sir. I came to say that.' The union leader's concern and worry were palpable. 'They are some goondas who did this. We have nothing to do with them.'

Anand nodded, concealing a huge sense of relief. The possibility of his own workers turning against him had worried him more than anything.

The union leader seemed reluctant to leave. He blurted out: 'Sir, are you planning to spend the night?'

'Yes,' said Anand. 'I am.' He frowned. 'Why, have you heard anything? Are they going to do something?'

'No, sir, I have not heard,' said the union leader. 'They would not tell me even if they were planning something. But, sir,' he said, 'you should not wait here alone.'

'I am not alone,' Anand spoke firmly. The three security guards waited at the entrance. 'If anyone comes, rest assured, I will call the police.'

He turned to go in and found the union leader hard at his heels. 'I will wait here with you, sir,' said the young man.

They set up two chairs on the factory shop floor. The union leader organized some coffee, and Anand unearthed the glucose biscuits from Kamath's stockpile. 'Hopefully there will be no trouble,' Anand said. 'But I am glad you are staying, Nagesh. Thank you.'

'No need to thank me, sir,' the union leader said, with a great seriousness of purpose. 'I was thinking about today. I did not like that. Having to stop work because it suits some political party. I was thinking: how does this benefit us working on the floor? If we lose our jobs, will the politicians give us another? No. They will not. That is why I am here, sir. If the company suffers, we all suffer. We can't let that happen.'

Conversation came naturally between them, the odd circumstances of the night breaking through barriers. Nagesh eagerly shared his life story: he was the oldest son and great hope of his family, the first to complete schooling, the first to finish his technical training, now bent on ensuring good marriages for his sisters; himself the father of two young children whose cellphone pictures Anand duly admired.

Anand, in turn, talked of his early years – and went from there to discussing his ideas for the new plant. He described the shop floor of his dreams, one drawn from a real-life visit that he and

Ananthamurthy had made to a stampings plant that supplied a rigorous Japanese car company. They had followed the famous Toyota Production System, and Anand described in detail to the union leader what he'd seen: just-in-time processes; the kaan–baan system; the unidirectional flow of work through the shop floor; the increased automation; and the detailed training that each worker received. 'You will not believe,' he said. 'They supply fresh batches of sheet metal pressings to the main car factory every twenty minutes. Can you imagine? Every twenty minutes, made to order!'

'This is in Japan, sir?' Nagesh said, wide-eyed at the notion of such efficiency.

'No,' said Anand. 'This is right here. In Bangalore.'

'Sir, do you think someday we might do so as well?'

'I hope so, Nagesh. I hope so. Certainly the new factory will be a step in that direction.'

The night was trouble-free, as Anand had suspected it might be. The two-hour strike and the damage to his car were Gowdaru-saar's way of indicating future possibilities. A negotiating point, nothing more.

In the late nocturnal quiet, he found himself wandering about the deserted shop floor. When he was a child, his family would make vacation trips to see the temples of South India. It was a habit he'd continued with his own children: driving out and letting them explore. The family usually followed some guide who would ramble on about the religious symbolism and cultural history of the temples, but Anand would trail after them lost in the wonder of his own contemplations. For him, to visit Pattadhakal was to witness not only the genesis of stone temple architecture but a laboratory, where cutting-edge design and engineering excellence were birthed over a thousand years before. And so he would wander, through Pattadhakal, through the cave temples at Badami, through the Meenakshi temple at Madurai, marveling at the craftsmanship and technical skills that had engineered miracles. And that, ultimately, was what spoke to the depths of his soul: a desire to belong to a people who, once again, reclaimed their ability to engineer objects of great beauty, form, and purpose. Who stood for perfection. Who knew what it was to toil, to craft, to construct things of truth and excellence that made onlookers gawk in wonder.

The machines, silent sentinels, the crates of finished metal pressings, the young union leader dozing on a chair. So much depended on his, Anand's, ability to save this place.

No matter what the cost to his pride. Vinayak was right.

He would have to call Harry Chinappa.

Harry Chinappa, who had so painstakingly cultivated Vijayan, who would be able to put a stop to Gowdaru-saar's demands. Harry Chinappa, who single-handedly had created the trouble they were in and then behaved as if Anand were to blame.

Twenty-Eight

Kamala placed breakfast before her son, her mind full of a strong determination: today, for Narayan's sake, she would set aside her pride further.

She would speak to Anand-saar; she would ask him for money. She would throw herself at his feet; she would do as she had seen others do before her and as she had never done in her life: plead, cry, hug his ankles, pledge her labor for all eternity if necessary. She would hand over her entire salary to him to repay her loan. And – in order that they might eat – she would take an additional job. The canteen up the road might hire her in the early mornings to cook and clean – they were always busy. She could work an early morning shift there before reporting to Vidya-ma's. She would seek an additional, third, late-night job somewhere else, cooking or minding a baby. Somehow she would save her son's future, and shield him from the likes of Raghavan.

Before leaving for work, she whispered her plans to Narayan: 'I am going to speak to Anand-saar. I may be home a little late.'

'I might come there in the evening,' said Narayan. 'Pingu wanted me to play with that train set.'

Kamala hesitated, remembering Vidya-ma's expression from the last time. She did not want anything to jeopardize her loan. 'Better not today,' she said. 'Wait for me here.'

To ensure her success, to give her voice strength and eloquence, Kamala stopped a moment to pray at the corner Hanuman temple: as Hanuman had transported mountains across the oceans, as he ferried the life-giving sanjeevini herb to Lakshmana, so too may he guide her steps, to move mountains, to find fresh life, to protect her son, whom she surely loved and cherished and served no less than did Hanuman, Lakshmana.

She hurried to work. She would be nice and early, a necessary atonement for the previous day's unauthorized absence. She would first apologize for her absence to Vidya-ma, meekly accepting whatever scoldings her mistress saw fit to throw at her. Then she would look after the grandfather and do all her chores to the best of her capability. And then, in the evening, no matter what, she would corner Anand-saar and launch into her petition.

Oh, Narayan. Oh, Narayan. In her mind, the sky grew dark, and once again, a cigarette butt went flying through the air, launched by a disreputable, corrupt hand that waited to clutch at her son.

When she reached the house, her unusually serious demeanor kept even the watchman from the casual remarks he was wont to make as he unlocked the gate for her. The kitchen was preternaturally quiet. Both Thangam and Shanta reacted differently to her arrival. Thangam, folding clothes, glanced at her and looked quickly away; Shanta narrowed her eyes. 'You have come back.'

'I told you,' said Kamala shortly. 'I was not feeling well.'

'I think everybody' – Shanta spoke with a curious triumphant aggression that Kamala couldn't comprehend – 'knows that is not true.'

'I do not lie, sister. Where is Vidya-ma?'

'She was asking after you,' said Shanta. 'Perhaps you should go and see her.' As Kamala left the room, she heard the cook say: 'After this, just let her try and act big with me in my own kitchen! Just let her try!'

Vidya-ma was in the bedroom. Kamala paused at the door. Her mistress lay prostrate upon the unmade bed, her eyes reddened, the room darkened, as though she might be sick. She did not look happy to see Kamala.

Of all possible receptions, this was the worst, but Kamala launched quickly into her apology. 'Vidya-ma, forgive me,' she said, 'I was unwell. I am so sorry.'

Vidya-ma eyed her contemptuously. 'Lies!' she said. 'I sent the watchman to your house to check. You were not sick. You were not there!'

Kamala had planned to say that she had gone to see a doctor when the watchman visited, but instead, on the spur of the moment, she decided to tell Vidya-ma the truth. It might awaken her sympathy. 'I'm so sorry, amma,' she said. 'The truth is I had need of a large sum of money and went to the pawnbroker in Chickpet to sell some jewelry . . . I need fifty thousand rupees, ma.'

The look of intense anger on Vidya-ma's face shocked Kamala. It was more than anger, it was rage. She sat up and flung her tissue to the floor. 'How dare you!' she said. 'You speak of it so brazenly? Sell some jewelry – as though it were yours to sell!'

All Kamala could say in her bewilderment was: 'Vidya-ma?'

'Do you think your need excuses what your son has done?' Vidya-ma's voice began to escalate to a shout. 'For him to steal? Could you not have asked me for the money? Would I not have given it to you? Am I not generous? Why should he steal? Oh, don't look so innocent! Don't think I do not know! Your son. I saw him come up the stairs that day. That very day that my neck-lace was lying on the table. Fool that I was! I assumed I could trust everyone in this house. But he was very clever. For a moment of carelessness, this is how I am repaid. Do you know how much that necklace is worth? Much, much more than fifty thousand rupees! Could you not have just asked me for that money?'

'Amma,' said Kamala, truly frightened. 'Narayan has not taken any necklace. I went to sell my own jewelry. I promise you. He is a good boy. Amma, everyone knows that!'

'Good? Rubbish! He might be able to fool Anand-sir, but I have been told about his character! He may look innocent, but he hangs about with all manner of ruffians. I was told this!

'No, do not tell me you know nothing of this. How dare you! After all my care and concern. Do not tell me this!

'Shanta tells me you often lie.

'Now, you go and you bring that necklace back to me. Get it back from the pawnbroker! And if you don't, I will tell the police and they will put your son straight in jail. Oh, god, that little thief. How freely I have allowed him in this house!

'Oh, god.' Vidya-ma began to weep again. 'Who knows what else he is planning to steal? Awful, wicked boy.'

Kamala stared at the sobbing, raving woman, and an old hidden anger emerged, like a serpent, coiled, taut, ready to attack.

Stop it! she shouted, the volume of her voice easily competing with Vidya-ma's.

Stop it. My son is not a thief and he never will be. Do you hear me?

She could hear the thudding of feet, the hasty collection of an astonished audience: Valmika, Thangam, Shanta.

Kamala, awash with a glittering, righteous anger, did not care.

Twenty-Nine

The first text message from Valmika said: *Pls call mama necklace trouble.* The second, sent minutes after the first, said: *call!!!!*

Anand checked his phone. There were no missed calls from his wife.

Around him, the noise of the factory resonated reassuringly. The machines were running; administrative staff were filing in. Kamath had arrived early, his concern evident as he surveyed his unshaved, sleep-deprived boss.

'Don't worry, Kamath,' said Anand. 'Everything will be fine. Don't worry.'

He projected a similar confidence to Ananthamurthy. He did not want his team demoralized further. He himself desperately wanted a bath, to cleanse his mind and spirit with buckets of hot water. A bath, and something to eat.

He didn't want to return home for either.

He received Valmika's messages as he walked out to the car. He called her – but he didn't have to ask why she was calling. Over his daughter's nervous, thankful 'Appa?' he could hear Vidya's voice in the background, crying, hysterical, shouting. 'I'll be there,' he told his daughter. 'Kutty, I'm leaving right away. I'll be there.'

★　★　★

Valmika met him at the entrance of the house. He placed a comforting arm about her, this beautiful girl, his daughter, already taller than he was, with Harry Chinappa's genes unfolding inside her. 'It's that necklace,' she said. 'Appa, there was a *huge* uproar this morning.'

That seemed to be an understatement. His arrival appeared to trigger a Brownian motion of people about the house. Thangam and Shanta came tumbling down the stairs and scurried into the kitchen. His father emerged from his bedroom to say, 'Something has happened . . . I don't know what . . .'

'Kutty, what is it?' He could see Valmika hesitating, not used to broaching discussions about her parents' affairs. 'It's okay,' Anand encouraged her gently. 'Tell me what happened.'

'That necklace,' she said. 'Mama has been . . . sick . . . in bed . . .' He could see the tears rising in her eyes.

'It's okay, tell me. Mama has been upset, I know . . .'

'Yes. And yesterday, the necklace went missing. Remember? From Thatha's family, really old, priceless. I'm not sure, I don't know why, maybe the other maids said something, but when Kamala came to work this morning, Mama shouted at her. Something about Narayan taking it – and, Appa! Kamala got so *angry* . . . She shouted back at Mama. She picked up an empty water glass and *threw* it against the wall. Even Shanta screamed. Then she left the house, and Mama . . .'

Ruby Chinappa appeared on the landing. They had spoken with each other on the telephone early that morning, but they had not discussed her daughter at that time. Now, she did not seem to know how to proceed. 'Oh, Anand,' she said and burst into tears. He pushed past her into the bedroom.

The shouting he had heard over the phone had died down. Vidya had subsided into silence. She was sitting in bed, still wearing the same T-shirt and pajamas he had seen her in two nights ago, surrounded by snot- and tear-filled tissues. Her features appeared dead, drowned, distended. She would not look directly at him.

Out of the corner of his eye, Anand could see his daughter and mother-in-law at the door. He asked Valmika, softly, 'Where is Pingu?'

'School,' his daughter whispered. 'I thought he should go.'

'Good girl,' he said. 'Kutty, why don't you take Avva downstairs and ask Shanta to make a cup of tea for her before she goes home. Ask Thangam to bring one for Mama as well. Also, ask her to bring a broom and sweep up this mess.'

Anand turned to Vidya. He sat down on the edge of the bed. He didn't know what to say. His insides felt like rough gravel after the events of the previous day; he wished he could turn and walk out.

'The necklace went missing?' An obvious question, tentatively uttered, in lieu of all the other unresolved quarrels that lay between them.

'Fuck the necklace,' she said. Flat-voiced. 'If she took it, let her keep it. Who gives a shit?'

He had spoken the truth two nights previously – and part of him still exulted, whooping rebelliously, in the freedom. Another part, which had supported this relationship for fifteen years, knew the hurt his words had inflicted.

'Ey,' he said. 'I'm sorry. I shouldn't have said that to you. I'm sorry.'

She met his eyes finally. 'I've done my best by you, Anand.' But the sharp doubt was in her, he could see that, razor-edged, slicing through her self-respect, the rationale for her entire adult life.

'I know. I know . . . We've built some good things together . . . And you're a good mother. Ey, don't cry.' His inarticulate words tugged the tears out of her; she cried like a woman abandoned.

He placed a hand on her back and rubbed gently, an old, comforting gesture he had not used in a long while.

His children. His daughter, so caring, so worried, and his son, a laughing ball of trust. To regret his marriage was to regret his children, and he could not do that.

Anand had never thought of his emotional needs when he was younger; now, years too late, he was seeing the gaps in his existence, but it was knowledge he could not act upon. To walk away, to reach for his own personal happiness would be at the expense of theirs. His children. His silly mother-in-law. His father, resting downstairs.

That decision descended heavily upon him; he felt the squeezing pain of it and an instant corresponding doubt – would he be strong enough to shoulder it for the rest of his life?

'Don't worry,' he said to Vidya. 'Everything will be okay. And we will find that necklace. Don't worry.'

Her sobs slowly settled into hiccups. Valmika brought a cup of tea and helped Thangam sweep up the pieces of the broken glass. Vidya drank her tea, Anand sitting on the bed next to her. After a while, she slept.

Anand joined his daughter for breakfast.

'Let Mama sleep for a while,' he said. 'She'll feel better.' He saw his daughter's relieved acceptance of his words, her attention turning hungrily to the food on the table. He watched her eat. A bite of toast. Forkfuls of scrambled egg. 'Oh, and, Appa,' she said, when she was done. 'I helped Thatha organize stuff for his pooja.'

'Oh, great, kutty,' he said. 'That's a big help . . . Now, shall I drop you to school?'

'No, I hate going late,' she said, heading up to the stairs. 'And I won't miss much; we're spending most of our days rehearsing for the school play. I'll stay here and do some maths revision for my test tomorrow.'

The day's newspaper lay folded on the dining table.

Early this morning, he had called Harry Chinappa from the factory.

Harry Chinappa had ignored the first phone call, made to his cellphone. Anand, full of a steady purpose, had dialed again. His house this time.

Ruby Chinappa had picked up the phone. 'Anand!' she said, her voice full of false cheer. 'I was just saying that we have not seen you in some time . . .'

'Is he there?' he asked. 'Can I speak to him?'

He could hear the loud whispering in the background, Ruby Chinappa saying: '. . . you must talk to him! You cannot ignore him forever . . . so awkward . . . No, I don't think it is something to do with Vidya, he would have told me.' When she came back to the phone, her voice wobbled with effort: 'Anand,' she said, 'he is in the bathroom, can't speak now . . . Yes, of course, call back . . .'

Anand waited fifteen minutes, working on his resolution.

When he called for the third time, Harry Chinappa came on the line. Anand had vaguely rehearsed a speech in his mind, calm and clear and convincing. Something about putting aside their differences and working for the good of the company and the family future.

Instead, he found himself saying, brusquely and without preamble: 'You must help me.'

'What?' said Harry Chinappa, outrage evident in his voice.

Anand blurted out his story, speaking with a dreadful urgency, almost forgetting, in his haste, the implacability of the man at the other end of the telephone. Harry Chinappa waited for Anand to stop speaking.

'No,' he said.

'You cannot say no,' said Anand. 'Did you not hear me? This is the result of your actions. You have to help.'

His insistence triggered a rush of words from Harry Chinappa: No, he said again, he bloody well would not help. Who did Anand think he was, speaking to him like that? After making a fool of him, Harry Chinappa, he now had the impudence, the temerity, to ask for help again?

'Please.' Anand belatedly shifted to pleading and hated himself for doing so. 'Please.'

No.

The phone call ended; Anand found himself trembling in revulsion. In the quelling of their hapless mutiny, in retribution for their massacre of English women and children, the Indian sipahis were made to lick the bloody floor of the massacre site before being shot alive out of British cannons. Anand could taste the blood of that floor in his mouth, feel his own impending annihilation, his body and spirit rending in the fast-speeding wind and fire, his life's work collapsing into rubble.

Anand carefully unfolded the newspaper, not really looking at it. He sipped at coffee; he could not eat anything. His hands were trembling, he noticed, quite disconnected from his brain. Everything – the night, the phone call with Harry Chinappa, the scene with his wife – pressed into him like the pleated bellows of an accordion, filling him with heavy breath and aching teeth and little else. He felt voided. Of ideas, of hope, of desire, of thought. He was nothing.

The headline ate at his eyes. VIJAYAN ADDRESSES INDUSTRY LEADERS.

The words reconfigured themselves in front of him, dancing, calling. Clapping their hands. Shouting. Dancing. He went to the little powder room and cupped his hands under a stream of cold water, running it over his wrists, touching chill, wet fingers to his eyes. Then he returned to the paper.

VIJAYAN ADDRESSES INDUSTRY LEADERS. The subheading said: INDUS-TRIAL PRODUCTION IS THE WAY FORWARD FOR THE COUNTRY, TO COMPETE WITH CHINA, TO RAISE STANDARDS OF LIVING.

He read it over and over, a great realization born within him, growing stronger by the second, spreading with the strength of a metal sheet through his body. The trembling in his fingers stopped.

There was nothing, really, to stop him getting in touch with Vijayan directly.

It would not be easy, or straightforward, or use any of the skills he had developed over a lifetime. In fact, in order to pull this off successfully – he experienced a sudden twisted moment of mirth – he would have to do that which he had avoided for his entire married life: he would have to take a page from Harry Chinappa's book.

Thirty

'Amma!' said Narayan, when he saw his mother step into the courtyard. 'Back so quickly! She has given it to you, then?'

Her demeanor alone should have told him it was not the case.
Still in a towering rage, she could barely recount what had happened.
'There is a necklace missing,' she said. 'They thought . . .' she
faltered; the branding shame of it. 'Vidya-ma thought I was absent
because I was disposing of it.'

Her anger was instantly reflected in him. 'What! How can they!
How can they think that about you, Amma!' He stood up, shaking.
'I hate her! That Vidya-ma. How could she say such a thing! It is
just as Raghavan says. Those people! I hate them all. Just see what
I will do to them. Raghavan says—' And he stopped, for his mother
slapped him hard across the face.

'Raghavan!' She slapped him again. 'You stupid boy. *I* was not
accused. *You* were. And do you know why? It is because of your
stupid friendship with that evil fellow. Because of that, they think
you are also a rogue!'

He was shocked into silence.

'I had to stand there and defend you. I told them you would
never steal. I told Vidya-ma so. I shouted. They would not believe

me. And now,' she said, 'I have no job. You have no school. She will send the police after us. We have lost everything.'

And Kamala, who never cried, sat down and wailed as though all was dead.

Her anger was at all things: at Vidya-ma, for her careless, life-destroying assumptions; at the thief who had created this mess; at herself, for losing her temper and her job in a quick, thunderous flash; and, finally, at her son, for his bad judgment in friendships.

In the corner, collapsed, Narayan sat silent.

Tears drying on his burning cheeks, his eyes flickering for a brief instant up to his mother's and instantly reverting to the ground.

The cold descended upon them that evening. Suddenly, as was its wont at this time of year. A warm morning, a brief afternoon cloudburst, and in its wake, the arrival of winter.

In a dark corner of her little house where the shadows gathered, there was a bag that held a dusty roll of clothes: a few stored, a few outgrown and destined for the old-rags man, and a few, Kamala was ashamed to admit, so full of memories that she could never bring herself to get rid of them. She dug through this bag and pulled out two sweaters. She put Narayan's sweater to one side, worrying, as a mother will, about the chill winds that must be surrounding him even as they embraced the city; knowing, as a mother should, that even if he was feeling cold there was little she could do about it until he returned home. He had left the court-yard in the middle of the morning and she had not seen him since.

With the donning of her own cardigan, her mind seemed to absorb a measure of calm. She closed her eyes in prayer, but the futility of her morning's worship at the Hanuman temple remained with her. She searched her mind for other gods; they seemed elusive, slipping away, hiding behind the branches of distant trees.

She busied herself with preparing a small meal for Narayan; there was a measure of comfort at the thought of feeding him. The anger she had seen in his eyes worried her. He was at that age when he was prey to adult emotions without the corresponding wisdom that led to their resolution. Where was he? Where could he have gone for all this time? His new school bag lay in a corner; he had not gone to school. She thought of Raghavan; her heart clenched.

It was well past dinnertime when he appeared, stepping through the shadows of the courtyard, a shape, a shadow, scarcely more defined than the shadows around him. Where have you been? she wanted to ask, but when he stepped into the circle of her Petromax lamp, she saw that the darkness still remained on his face. She silently placed his food on a plate; equally silently, he ate.

He rolled himself into a sheet and fell asleep, her son, turning as elusive as the gods hiding behind the leaves of the trees. Restless herself, Kamala could hear him shifting through the night. At one point, she thought she heard a stifled sob. Who knew what fears chased themselves through the dreams in his mind? Once, she put out her hand, placing it on his shoulder – and felt an instant easing of tension within him. She longed to be able to enclose him in her arms and soothe away his fears easily and naturally, as she could when he was younger.

Both of them were quiet the following morning, Kamala rising first and preparing rotis for breakfast; Narayan visiting the bathroom before wrapping some sugar in a roti and stuffing it quickly into his mouth. He dusted his hands and came over to her, wrapping his arms around her fiercely in a hug that almost extinguished the breath from her, a hug so stern, so full of purpose, so full of love.

He slipped out of the courtyard without saying anything.

'He is a good boy,' said the landlord's mother, materializing at the door. 'Yesterday. Did you see what he did yesterday?' Apparently, Narayan had spent the entire day outselling every other man and boy at the street corner, working at such a furious pace, even the policeman said he had seen nothing like it. 'Surely he must have handed the money to you,' the old woman said.

'No,' said Kamala, listening with a fierce, tender pride, 'not yet,' understanding all at once his seriousness of purpose, that adult intent to do what he could to help. Such a boy he was.

The courtyard gate creaked open. There was no mistaking who stood there; that precise arrangement of bells and tinkles, of bangles and anklets had accompanied her work for over a year.

'Thangam,' she said. 'Come in, my little sister. Come. What is it?'

Thangam sat down hesitantly on the stoop, her expression a mixture of sorrow, coyness, nervousness, and numerous other things, like a hungry peddler of dubious wares. She whispered, not to Kamala but to the ground in front of her: 'The necklace has been found.'

The news imprisoned Kamala; she could not move.

'The necklace was lying behind Vidya-ma's dressing table.' Thangam's words tumbled and spilled, urgently, full of a hidden pleading. 'Everyone realizes that Narayan could not have done it, sister. Everyone! He is a good boy. And Anand-saar would like to see you . . . I spoke to him about you myself, akka, and I asked him if I could run here and tell you the news, I know what it must mean to you, that is what I did, Kamala-sister.' And so saying, Thangam bent her head in abasement.

'Who found it?' Whoever had 'found' the necklace was most likely the thief who had abstracted it in the first place. And who else could it be but Shanta? Who else would allow Kamala to suffer as she had done? Who else would rejoice to see her lose her job?

'I did,' said Thangam and burst into tears.

A great, sharp anger mingled with a vast, comforting relief. Kamala found it in herself to hug the girl close and pat her gently on the back until she got up to leave.

Alone, Kamala felt her fury rise once more, against foolish, greedy Thangam and Shanta the rutting bitch, who had not hid her savage enjoyment of Kamala's plight. She knew, without having to ask, that her display of anger against Vidya-ma the previous day, however righteous, had surely cost her the job.

Anand-saar had told Thangam that he would see Kamala the following week. This would be to settle the salary she had due. She, in turn, could thank him then for supporting Narayan's education for a few short weeks.

She thought of her old hopes and stopped herself. That was foolish. She had to look for another job. She had to find another home. She had to find some other method of educating Narayan. She sat silent upon her haunches, lacking the strength to move, utterly exhausted, drained of hope and will.

Thirty-One

A call to war. The plotting of a campaign. Already the schemes were unfolding within him, spores planted, the fungus spreading through, feeding on a hot, moist bed of anger. To twist things in his favor, Anand would have to employ not only his father-in-law's manipulativeness but also a page from Vinayak's cynical approach to democratic government. If that was what it took, he would. But how to get access to Vijayan?

The following morning Vidya, unwittingly, showed him the way.

She appeared at the breakfast table, freshly showered, wrapped in a shawl, taking refuge behind a cup of tea. Like him, she seemed to focus her energies on interacting with the children. By the end of it she had relaxed a little, the very normalcy of the meal calming her. 'Ey, you know, I was supposed to go with Amir and Amrita to that fund-raiser this evening. But I can't do it. I'm too exhausted. Can't face anyone. Amir is going to be so disappointed.'

'You shouldn't go,' he said, with sterilized, routine comfort. 'Rest up.'

She said, and he snapped to attention: 'Vijayan is going to be there, you know. First time I would be meeting him since Diwali . . . But I just don't feel up to it. I can't even think of an excuse.'

'You know,' said Anand, 'why don't I go? Instead of you? I'll speak to Amir.'

'Really? You will? That's great . . . Yes,' said Vidya, her eyes moist. 'I really need my rest.'

He called Amir immediately from the study. He could not share his various schemes with him, for Amir might not understand; he would urge Anand not to pay any bribes and to stand strong and watch his company fail. 'Hey, buddy, listen, Vidya is not feeling very well and I was wondering if I could come to the fund-raiser instead of her? Yeah, should be interesting . . . Yeah, I'll swing by and pick up an invitation. Are you sure Vijayan will be there tonight? Great!'

Amir was in the small office he and Amrita used for their charitable work. It was cluttered with papers. When Anand arrived, Amrita was on her way out. 'Hey, you!' she said. 'Stranger! Don't see enough of you . . . But thanks again, for the latest check . . . Are you coming to the fund-raiser tonight?'

Anand grinned. 'Maybe,' he said, and she left in a flurry of busy-ness.

He checked at the door. Amir wasn't alone; Kavika was seated there as well.

He didn't know how to react to her presence; he wanted her gone so he could compose himself; he wanted her there; he wanted to pour his soul out to her and her alone. Instead, he held out his hand to Amir for the invitation. 'You're sure Vijayan will be there?'

Amir laughed at him. 'Yes, bugger, but why do you care all of a sudden?'

Kavika walked out with him, heading to her own car. 'So how are you doing? Any solutions?'

'I'm working on it,' he said.

'Why do I get the sense that your interest in this fund-raiser has something to do with the problems at your factory?' He said nothing, but she saw something, surely, for she said: 'Anand. Good luck. Whatever you have planned. Good luck.'

She leaned forward. He knew she was going to hug him before it happened. He felt her arms lightly about him, her breath on his ear, the fleeting touch of her lips on his cheek. Her skin had an ancient familiarity to him, a coming home. He held himself still, the moment spinning out to all eternity, loss already gathering deep within him.

She smiled and was gone.

Thirty-Two

He lay on a mattress on the floor of their courtyard room, the fever soaking through his heated skin. The room stayed cool and dim, cocooned from the sharp winter light outside by the recessed door and the window, which had stayed firmly barricaded with plastic through all these years. The green paint on the walls had faded; in between the stains Kamala could distinguish where a much younger Narayan had left his scratches and scribbles, drawing idle pictures on the walls rather than attending to his homework.

She dipped a cloth in cool water and wiped it over his forehead, registering the temporary ease it brought him. He had developed the fever from hours of trying to sell magazines in a cold winter rain.

'Did you give him the tablet?' the landlord's mother asked from the doorway.

'Yes, mother, I did,' said Kamala.

'Good,' said the landlord's mother. 'Good. That will bring the fever down . . . Do not worry, daughter,' she said. 'He will be whole again soon and delighting us once more with his mischief!'

Kamala said nothing, dipping the cloth in the water, squeezing it out and dipping once more.

Behind her, the landlord's mother kept talking, a garrulousness that would not cease, that must be replied to, even if there were no resources within Kamala to assuage her neighbor's concern beyond the mechanical use of common courtesies. 'Would you like something to eat, daughter?' the landlord's mother asked again. 'I have made some garlic saaru, hot and fresh; it will heat your vitals and give you energy.'

'No, mother, thank you,' said Kamala, again. 'I have made some food for us. Narayan is not eating much, and I do not seem to have much appetite either.'

It was a while before the light behind her brightened; the landlord's mother finally moved away from the door to attend to her own tasks. Kamala applied the cool, wet cloth to her son's forehead once more.

When the light dimmed again, Kamala thought for a moment that it was already nightfall, that the entire day had just vanished beneath her squatting feet. But the sound of ankle bells roused her. Thangam stood without; beckoning to her.

'Let's not wake him up,' she whispered. 'Let's talk outside.'

Kamala did not know what remained to be said, but Thangam was a woman determined.

'Listen,' she said. 'I have made some arrangements for you . . . You have to move, you cannot stay here anymore, is that correct? Right. So the old woman who lives next door to us? Do you know which house I am speaking of? Not that big one with the shouting Sindhi lady, but the small one on the other side. Where the old man died some months ago, those Andhra people. Well, her maid just quit. Getting married; a nice man working in the garment factory; good prospects. He seems too good for her, but such is the luck of life! So the old widow is looking for someone new, and the minute I heard, I went over and spoke to her. She first thought that I was looking for a job – and she said no, nothing doing, she did not want to hire another pretty girl who will just work for two months before running off and getting married, so I said, "No, no, this is not a pretty young girl, this is Kamala, who is most reliable." That is what I told her, sister.'

Seeing Kamala's continuing look of incomprehension, Thangam tugged at her arm. 'Don't you see? It is a live-in position. You will get your salary and your food and everything, and no rent. Haven't I saved you, Kamala-akka!'

But Kamala just stared at her, puzzled, and then turned to look into her little room, where her fevered son still slept.

'Ah,' said Thangam, following her gaze. 'Yes, that is a problem . . . I do not think she will want any family staying with you. You will have to think of some other arrangement for him.'

'Now, daughter, have no fear,' said the landlord's mother. 'He will be fine. They will feed him well . . . You have forgotten that vessel, see? Over there . . .'

Kamala reached for the cooking vessel and stuffed it into the cardboard box that contained all her worldly possessions. There was another small one full of her clothes and, the part that grieved her the most: a separate coir bag for Narayan's things, destined for a different journey.

'He will be fine,' said the landlord's mother again, with a firmness that seemed to comfort at least herself. 'We will keep an eye on him for you, you may rest easy on that. My nephew is a good man, and he will feed him well. I would not have suggested it otherwise.' It was the landlord's cousin who ran the canteen on the adjacent road, a small idli–coffee place that catered to the busy workers of the area. The landlord's mother had arranged for Narayan to stay with him, sleeping nights in the canteen while his mother worked at her new job as a live-in maid.

Kamala nodded, trying to appear grateful, as indeed she was, for this arrangement would at least keep Narayan in the neighborhood. It was not an act of charity by the landlord's cousin; he was used to employing the indigent children of the neighborhood, whose parents could not provide for them; Chikkagangamma's children had worked for him for months.

When Anand-saar had summoned her, she had debated whether to go. She did not want to face another scene with Vidya-ma. But the thought of the balance salary had decided her; she could not afford to leave it unclaimed.

She took Narayan with her, for Anand-saar had requested his presence as well. The watchman told them that Vidya-ma and the children were out of the house, and she was grateful.

Anand-saar studied Narayan, quiet, sober, and thinned by his recent illness. 'You have had some fever, I was told . . . It has settled now?'

'Yes.' Narayan was almost inaudible.

'Kamala,' said Anand-saar. 'Tell me what happened.'

With no further prompting, Kamala told her story: needing the money, the threat of losing her home, visiting the pawnbroker, Vidya-ma's false accusation, and her own grievous subsequent loss of temper. Of all people, given his past kindness and support, she wanted Anand-saar to understand. When at last she fell silent, he said: 'Kamala, you have done nothing wrong. Apart from taking leave without permission, and that is a small thing. Unfortunately,' he said, 'you cannot work here anymore. Vidya-ma will not allow it. But I understand you are to start work in the house next door?'

Yes, saar, said Kamala.

He nodded. 'That is a good thing. At least that will keep you in the neighborhood. Well, I cannot offer you employment in this house. But I think there is no reason for us to stop Narayan's education.'

Kamala felt her son's hand clutch at hers, and her eyes filled. Anand-saar continued to address Narayan. '. . . I want you to continue your studies. Do you understand? I will support you. And if you work very hard and do well – then that is the way you will repay me. And secure your own future. Do you understand me?'

It seemed that Narayan did.

'And you are not moving far away either,' continued the Landlord's mother, 'so we shall continue seeing each other, which is a great comfort to me, for you are like my own daughter, Kamala. You must visit us often in our new home . . .' The landlord's family was moving out soon themselves; the courtyard had sold quickly; they were shifting into a small, newly built apartment on an adjacent road. It had a bathroom built in and tiled floors, and they were proud and shy about their sudden newfound prosperity.

'You are too good, mother,' said Kamala. She wondered what she would do with her cooking vessels; there was no point in carrying them with her to her new job, and she had no one to leave them with. To the raddi-man they would go, sold as they had once been purchased. She put the last item into the box and stood up to stretch her legs.

I will return shortly, she said, and she picked up Narayan's bag. She hesitated; she hadn't packed his cricket bat and scuffed ball, for where would he have the opportunity to use them? But now she pushed the ball into the bag. She would keep the bat safe for him. She hefted the bag onto her shoulder and made her way out of the courtyard, down the crowded gully, and onto the main road. There, a little way up, was the canteen. She squeezed past the vegetable carts and came to a halt. She could see him. He was wearing a brown shirt and shorts, the uniform slightly ragged and stained and left behind by the boy who had worked there before him. He moved between the little tables that had people clustered around them, eating as they stood. In one hand Narayan carried a plastic basin, into which he piled the dirty plates and tumblers left behind by customers. He wiped each table down hastily with a dirty, wet rag before moving to the next one. He was concentrated upon his task and did not look up.

He would attend school in the mornings and work for his keep in the evenings. He would make much less at this job than he would selling magazines at the street corner, but he would have a place to sleep and, hopefully, hot food in his belly at night.

Be good to him, she whispered, to the cook behind the counter, to the canteen owner at the cash counter, to the gods. He is a good boy. Be good to him. As his mother would.

The watchman at Anand-saar's house nodded at her, but she did not stop to chat, walking past the familiar gates to the ones just beyond. These were smaller, as was the house that stood beyond them. A small house, neatly confined, not so difficult to clean, she judged. The peeling paint and slightly unkempt garden spoke of parsimony, or a lack of attention. She rang the bell.

Thirty-Three

For the first time in his life, Anand prepared to ambush someone
at an event. As soon as the speeches were done, he pushed through
the crowd, smiling with the same implacable tenacity he had
witnessed in Harry Chinappa at important social moments. 'How
are you?' he said, extending his hand to Vijayan.

His first level of worry – that Vijayan would have no idea who
he was and brush past him impatiently – proved baseless. Vijayan,
with a politician's mastery of names and faces, remembered him
well and spoke warmly about the Diwali party.

Anand said quickly: 'Sir, I was wondering if I could have a
photograph with you?' He'd been ready to add: 'For my wife, she
could not be here and she would be so excited,' but he did not
reckon with a politician's appetite for being photographed with
supporters. What felt awkward to him was natural and easy for
Vijayan; Anand merely had to signal Amir, who was waiting nearby
with a camera ('For Vidya,' Anand had told him. 'You know what
she's like'), and they were photographed together: Vijayan posing
with practiced ease and Anand with a grim, smiling determination.

The camera safely in his pocket, Anand took the next step. He
said: 'I am so pleased, sir, at your comments supporting industry.'
Especially when so many other politicians in India cater to the

populist, rural vote, with its focus on agriculture. We really need people in government who recognize that industries provide jobs and growth and an economic future for the country. People just like you, sir.

'That is at the heart of my campaign,' said Vijayan warmly. 'To create magnificent opportunities for industry without, of course, in any way compromising rural development. In fact, as I said in my speech, my dream is to seed industry across India's rural landscape and to do so in ways that are socially responsible, environmentally responsible, and economically viable.' He leaned in, enfolding a moment of intimacy about them. 'Mr Anand, successful businessmen like you are vital to my vision for India's future.'

'Thank you,' Anand said. 'I hope that your campaign is going well?'

Vijayan smiled. 'I am blessed,' he said, 'with tireless supporters.'

'Yes, I know,' said Anand. 'I've had the pleasure of meeting one of your party men, a Gowdaru-saar.'

In the act of turning away, Vijayan paused. There was no mistaking the change in Anand's tone: 'He has raised an interesting . . . dilemma for me. I was hoping to discuss the matter with you personally.'

'Of course.' Vijayan, alert, wary, instantly breathing concern and confidentiality. 'Of course. Certainly. Not a problem, I hope?'

Anand was not to be charmed. 'I certainly hope not.'

'We must meet.' Vijayan nodded to his assistant, hovering at his side. This man, equally alert, took Anand's phone number and promised that he would call to set up a meeting.

'Great,' said Anand. 'I'll be waiting.'

Anand left the party, camera in hand like a prize, one more job to perform. He would leave nothing to chance, or to minds changing after a distracted night. Vijayan's assistant would call him in the morning. He would ensure it.

Vijayan was famous for not employing the campaign money collected by the party for his personal use. But surely he was familiar with all the ways in which such money was raised? How could one rise to a leadership position in a major Indian political party with all its hurly-burly corruption and be entirely free from taint?

At breakfast the next morning Vidya gazed at the newspaper, refusing to hand it to him in her surprise. 'Oh my goodness. Look at this!' She reexamined the photograph of her husband with Vijayan. 'It's not bad,' she said. 'I mean, it's quite large and they have placed it in a really nice position. Goodness,' she said.

Anand drank his coffee without comment. He had orchestrated the publication of the photograph through a contact Vinayak had provided him with at a prominent newspaper well known for its propensity for combining genuine news with happy promotional pieces for anyone willing to pay for them. Vijayan's team would know that he too could access the media.

'How cool, yaar,' Vidya said, with a reluctant, growing enthusiasm. '"Prominent businessman Anand K. Murthy." Prominent! Damn cool . . . I wonder if my parents have seen this. Has your father seen it?'

Anand finished his coffee and retired to his study to wait.

The phone call from Vijayan's chief assistant came early, as Anand knew it would. Would Anand care to meet with him? Vijayan was busy, but, if necessary, he too would be happy to meet with Anand a little later. Yes, he, the assistant, could meet Anand this very morning, no problem. Happy to, sir.

Anand preferred to deal with the assistant, Mr Rudrappa. Despite the subordinate title, the man was Vijayan's gatekeeper and very powerful.

Vijayan's team worked out of an old, yellowing house in Jayanagar, converted to an election office and already, at ten in the morning, thrumming with energy and bulging crowds waiting to meet the candidate and his party members: people from the city, the hinter-lands, offices and farms. Mr Rudrappa had positioned an assistant on the pavement, waiting to receive Anand, to help him park his car, to guide him past the waiting people into the house and his own inner sanctum, next to Vijayan's office. Mr Rudrappa's office was a small, spare room, bare of all but a desk, a briefcase, an iPad, two phones, a Kannada calendar, and a poster of Vijayan, identical to the ones permeating the city, on the distempered walls.

Mr Rudrappa projected an efficient friendliness, as though Anand were nothing but a well-wisher. 'Some coffee, sir?' he offered, but Anand waved the offer aside. He was prepared to be civil but did not care about being nice. He went straight to the point.

'I am a great supporter of Vijayan,' he said. 'But I do not like to be pressured. I don't think any businessman would. And certainly, it is not the right image for a man of Vijayan's caliber. His supporters would be shocked to hear of such things.' The photograph that had so magically appeared in the morning newspaper lay heavily between them.

'Yes, yes,' said Mr Rudrappa immediately. 'No, of course not. I am so sorry. Sometimes, our party functionaries can get overen-thusiastic in their support. I will speak to Gowdaru-saar. Yes, imme-diately. Kindly accept our apologies. And, sir? Please let me know if I can help you in any other way.'

Anand did not have to follow up on that promise. A few hours later, the Landbroker arrived at the factory, flowering with relief. 'Saar,' he said, laughing. 'How did you do it?'

The recalcitrant farmer was willing and eager to complete the transaction. Gowdaru-saar himself had called the Landbroker, to confirm that he was to proceed with full haste and no impediment. 'How did you do it, saar?' The Landbroker's happiness was contagious; he prowled the office in a bright celebratory pink shirt, glancing at Anand in some wonderment. 'I saw that photo, saar. In the paper.'

Anand waved him off. 'That was nothing. Now tell me, how quickly can we complete the land registration?'

The Landbroker's gold-edged sunglasses joyfully caught the fluorescent office light. 'Immediately, saar. Immediately.'

He returned home early to find his father was waiting for him. Waiting to speak. 'My presence here,' his father said, addressing the matter directly, 'is making your wife uncomfortable?'

Anand was mortified. 'No, Appa, no,' he said. 'That was something else. She is happy to have you here.'

'She is not happy,' his father said and moved on to his next concern. 'You did not come home one night. You stayed in the factory. Everything is all right, there?'

Anand sighed. 'Yes,' he said. 'There was some problem. I have sorted it out.'

His father inclined his head. 'Good, good.'

He seemed to have more to say: 'Anand, I still do not think that you have chosen the right path for yourself. In work and other matters. But perhaps you were destined to select such a path? . . . If that is the case, then there is nothing I or anyone else could have done to thwart you, is it not? . . . I see that you work very hard. That is good. After all, if this is your karma, then you have a moral duty to give it your best, to persevere. You are doing that.' The old man nodded. 'You are doing that.'

'Why don't you come see it?' Anand said, surprising himself. 'The factory?'

His father responded as though it were the most natural

suggestion in the world. 'Next week,' he said. 'Your mother will be here by then. One of her sisters, your Meena Chikkamma, will come to sit with your grandmother and we will be able to go home. We will both come to see your factory.'

Anand's initial shock gave way to reluctant laughter, but his father did not seem to notice. He was absorbed, once more, in the day's paper, his pencil at the ready.

Anand had one more thing to do that day. Valmika had spent the past two days at a friend's house on an extended sleepover; Vidya was surprised when he'd volunteered to fetch her. 'Are you sure? It's in Koramangala. That's an hour's drive. Why don't I just send the driver?'

Valmika smiled when she saw Anand in the car. 'I didn't know you were coming to pick me up,' she said, climbing into the passenger seat beside him.

'Had a good time?' he asked. 'Had fun?'

'So-so,' said Valmika. 'We watched a movie. Mostly, we talked. Painted our nails. Look, Appa!' She waved her fingers in his line of vision; each nail was painted a different color and studded with glitter.

'Very nice,' he said. Despite the gesture, she seemed unusually sober and thoughtful.

Valmika fell silent, then: 'Appa. Why are you so angry with Mama?'

'Me? I am not, sweetie. I am not. Why do you say that?'

She didn't reply. After a silence, she said: 'My friend, Anamika? Her parents are divorcing . . .'

Anand pulled over to the side of the road, switched off the engine, and caught his daughter by her shoulders. 'Listen,' he said, 'Listen. Mama and I are not going to divorce. Understand? Okay, laddu? This is a promise. Okay?'

'But you're angry with her, Appa. I can see that.'

'Arrey. Last week when I made you study your physics, you were angry with me, no? It happens. Let it be.'

Valmika relaxed. Sighed. Anand started the car and eased into the traffic. After a while, she said: 'They say Anamika's father has a girlfriend in Brazil.'

'In *Brazil*? . . . All the way over there? . . . Not a very practical fellow, is he?' he said and was gratified to hear his daughter giggle.

Eventually his friends learned that his political troubles had lifted, but Anand never volunteered to any of them the details of how he had pulled it off – or the fact that, once the registration of the land was complete, he wrote a check to Vijayan's party, unsolicited, from his personal account, even though it irked him to do so. He wanted to ensure their continuing goodwill.

The elections drew nearer; the headlines had a photograph of Vijayan addressing a public meeting, with the caption: YES WE CAN! VIJAYAN VOWS TO FIGHT CORRUPTION.

Thirty-Four

From her vantage point on the balcony, Kamala could see party preparations in full swing next door. Vidya-ma's new maid appeared in the garden – a replacement for Thangam, who, unable to bear the pressure from her chit fund creditors, had packed her bags and vanished in the middle of one night. No one knew where. The new girl did not seem very curious about her predecessor; she was far more engaged in talking to the old, married watchman in her spare time. Shanta reigned unchallenged in the kitchen.

Kamala's current job involved housecleaning and some light cooking for her aging employer. It was a simple existence: a day of work, an evening of rest and quietude, with time enough, after the old lady went to sleep and the television they watched together was switched off, for Kamala to contemplate the accumulating losses of her life: her beloved courtyard home, or any home at all, and the one loss that grew more unbearable with time – the daily absence of her son.

Kamala saw him once a week, for a few brief hours. His days were full: in the mornings he attended school, in the evenings he still toiled as a table cleaner and dishwasher at the canteen, sleeping there at night. The canteen owner spoke of Narayan with affection, and Kamala listened but could not rejoice as she should. She yearned to cook for him and care for him.

She shared her sharp grief with no one, not even in occasional phone calls to her sister-in-law.

Indeed, the only person who stood firm in her life, surprisingly, was Anand-saar. He had kept his word. Narayan met him regularly to report on his academic progress, and it was in those repeated meetings that a small, flickering hope still lingered within Kamala, a shy hope, not to be dwelled on, not to be subjected to untoward prayers and lingering fervent desires, no, never again, no, no, but it remained.

What a good son you have, Kamala, the old lady, her new employer, often said, adding: 'What a shame I cannot ask him to stay here also. But really, I cannot afford to feed an extra mouth.'

Narayan, if he were there to hear this, always smiled politely and said, 'Thank you, aunty, but we can use the money from the canteen, my mother and I.'

What a good boy, the old lady would say. An answer to a mother's prayers.

'Yes,' Kamala would say, and through her mind would fly this thought: Yes, an answer to my prayers, but did the gods have to let it take this form?

She could see him now, in the distance, walking toward her. He had grown taller and thinner still. His mien would be serious; he seemed to have completely lost the sparkle and mischief that had so delighted and exasperated her. He would, she knew, be bringing her the weekly money he earned and telling of school, where his progress was good.

Who were his friends, these days? she wondered. What were his dreams? These were not questions she could easily ask of him; they were fraught with discomfort; if she did ask, his answers were vague. The loss of her ability to feed him daily, to put nourishment into his mouth, to care for him, to wash his clothes, to pat his cheek and tug scoldingly at his ear seemed to echo her growing inability to pull answers and conversation out of him.

She watched her son walk toward her, the tar on the newly paved road yielding slightly beneath his feet. As he approached, it seemed he retreated farther and farther away.

Thirty-Five

The women's voices soared over the gathered crowd, the Sanskrit words and Carnatic melody rising above the silent, glistening machines into the triangulated factory eaves above.

Machines had been cleaned, desks tidied, and every machine, every tool, every computer, the stapler, the Xerox machine, and even the pen that Anand used to sign checks had been pain-stakingly decorated with vermilion kumkum powder, sandalwood paste, flower petals, and garlands in readiness for this day of Tool and Implement Worship. Ayudha Pooja. Even the cars out in the parking lot awaited their turn to be worshipped: in addition to sandalwood and kumkum and flowers, their bonnets bore jaunty banana fronds, which flapped cheerfully in the passing breeze.

Anand was not a man given to ritual, resonating as it did with the annoying, restrictive platitudes of his childhood, yet he enjoyed this particular festival. There was something very apposite about a day of thanks and celebration of the people and machines that worked together, every day.

Four goddess images lined the altar that had been temporarily built in the middle of the factory floor: Lakshmi, giver of material strength and prosperity; Saraswati, for knowledge and learning; Durga, destroyer of negative tendencies; and above them, Chamundeswari, a Shakti composite of all three.

The bhajans signified the end of a long morning of worship. Mrs Padmavati led the singing with a surprising muscular vigor, accompanied by Ananthamurthy's two daughters. Behind him, Anand could hear Ananthamurthy explain to Valmika the symbolism and meanings behind the worship. 'When we perform a pooja,' said Ananthamurthy, 'we do not pray to some abstract god in the sky. That is a wrong interpretation. Instead, the prayers, the rituals, allow us to focus on evoking those divine energies within us. Thus Saraswati, so we may be ever-learning seekers of true knowledge; Lakshmi, that we may guide our fortunes well; Durga, that we may conquer our deepest fears within. For mindful work' – Ananthamurthy's voice turned stern and sonorous – 'is true spiritual grace. We worship our tools so that we may work mindfully and with correct humility, for best results.'

Valmika said, with a sudden touch of gloom: 'I should probably worship my physics book before my test tomorrow.'

'Yes,' said Ananthamurthy with a twinkle, 'but perhaps studying that is best.'

The previous day, they had inaugurated the new factory. Construction on all buildings was not complete, but the main production floor was ready, machinery being moved into place. Two executives from the Japanese parent company had flown in for the event, Ananthamurthy in assiduous attention; they had seemed pleased, the ordered beauty of the new structure validating their decision to pick Cauvery Auto. The bank manager too expressed his pleasure to Mrs Padmavati in an animated discussion that celebrated his own foresight in lending to them.

Anand had made a few phone calls before the inauguration; this time, his father had accepted his invitation. As had Harry Chinappa

– whose rigid decorum, much to Ruby's and Vidya's relief, melted to a benevolent, if startled, approval once he realized who the chief guest was going to be: on the heels of a successful election, getting Vijayan to accept, said Harry Chinappa, was a coup.

Vijayan had played his role in the inauguration, cutting ribbons, making speeches, and planting a sapling. The Landbroker wore a silk shirt for the occasion. Next to him stood Gowdaru-saar, unctuous. The word from Vijayan's office had caused Gowdaru-saar to back off, to vanish, to sink like a startled crocodile into the depths of the water, surfacing, with beady eyes greedy and glistening, just two days before the inauguration. He had arrived in Anand's office, eyeing the new factory. 'Congratulations, saar,' he had said. 'We look forward to your future success.'

I bet you do, motherfucker, thought Anand, smiling politely.

Sankleshwar had shifted his residence to Dubai, forewarned, the rumors went, about an impending tax investigation. 'It's all these new-money rascals,' said Harry Chinappa. 'It's a good thing I stopped my development deal with him. I always had my reservations, you know, m'boy. By the way, this year,' he said, 'we really should change the caterer for the Diwali party. The last fellow was terrible.'

On the drive to the factory, Anand had glanced at Vidya and had searched for something nice, something true, to say: 'You look pretty,' he said. 'That's a pretty outfit.'

'Do you like it?' she said, immediately flattered. 'I found it at a boutique that showcases ecologically conscious designers. They make things with a smaller carbon footprint. Such an important issue, I can't see why more people don't feel more strongly about it.'

Toward the end of the tree-planting ceremony, when all the chief guests and managers had had their turn, Mrs Padmavati guided Valmika and Pingu in planting theirs, aided by a gardener.

'Perhaps your daughter may one day work with us, sir,' said Mr Ananthamurthy at his ear.

'Only if she wants to,' Anand replied, absurdly pleased with the notion, watching covertly as Valmika gazed curiously about at the factory buildings.

At the end of the Ayudha Pooja, the red-stained kumkum-and-coin-stuffed pumpkin was ritually shattered, symbolizing the animals sacrificed in ancient times. The cars were driven over the good-luck-giving lemons and the aarti plate containing a single flame carried through the crowd by the priest.

Anand did not consider himself a particularly religious person. For him, worship lay in the doing, in working each day to extrude from the center of his being the very best that he could give. When the aarti plate reached him, he placed a fifty-rupee offering on it, ritually passed his palms over the flame, and raised them to his face, the warmth touching his eyes just like a blessing.

BEHIND THE SCENES
AT TINDER PRESS . . .

For more on the worlds of our books and authors
Visit us on Pinterest
🅿 TINDER PRESS

For the latest news and views from the team
Follow us on Twitter
🐦 TINDER PRESS

To meet and talk to other fans of our books
Like us on Facebook
🅵 TINDER PRESS

www.tinderpress.co.uk